The Angel
of The
Streetlamps

THE
ANGEL
OF THE
STREETLAMPS

Sean Moncrieff

NEW ISLAND

About The Author

Sean Moncrieff was born in London to an Irish mother and a Scottish father. When he was twelve, his family moved to Ballinasloe, County Galway. He has worked a journalist in Dublin and London and later became involved in broadcasting; presenting a string of hit television shows on Irish television. In the UK, he has worked for the BBC, Channel 4 and Channel 5, both as a scriptwriter and presenter.

His first novel, *Dublin*, a needle-sharp, funny and scathing thriller, was published in May 2001 by Doubleday and reached the bestseller lists in Ireland. A non-fiction book, *Stark Raving Rulers: Twenty Minor Despots of the Twenty-First Century*, was published in October 2004, followed by *God, A Users' Guide* in 2006. A second novel, *The History of Things*, was published in 2007.

Sean writes a weekly column for *The Examiner* and hosts *Moncrieff*, a multi-award winning radio show every afternoon on Newstalk in Ireland.

THE ANGEL OF THE STREETLAMPS
First published 2012
by New Island
2 Brookside
Dundrum Road
Dublin 14

www.newisland.ie

ISBN PRINT: 978-1-84840-123-5
ISBN EPUB: 978-1-84840-212-6
ISBN MOBI: 978-1-84840-213-3

Internal Design by JM InfoTech INDIA
Cover Design by Nina Lyons
Printed by TJ International Ltd, Padstow, Cornwall

New Island received financial assistance from
The Arts Council (An Comhairle Ealaíon), Dublin, Ireland

10 9 8 7 6 5 4 3 2 1

For Sencha, Keelin, Ellie and Saoirse (Wanda Wabbit)

CHAPTER ONE

The Fall

After the apparitions began, some claimed to have seen the girl go out the window: a pale pink blur of limbs and panic that landed with a rattling thump in the crusty builder's skip.

Others said they didn't see the fall, yet they had a skin-prickling sense of horror. They felt the arctic whoosh; their breathing was thickened by the massive pant of dust.

Some contended that they saw the election poster wafting down and settling upon her. But dozens, possibly hundreds, claimed to have passed the skip on the day the girl died. Not to stare, but to record their mute disapproval of all the others crowding around; their mobile phones already aimed towards the shining silk bridesmaid's dress covering her smashed and twisted body.

PATIENCE IS A VIRTUE

Socialite Patience dresses up for charity

By CAROL MURPHY

THE country might be might be gripped by recession – but that's not stopping Patience Gannon from slipping on a designer frock. This time though, it's for a good cause.

Blond bombshell Patience – wife of disgraced property developer Michael Gannon – has got together with a few of her socialite friends to organise a fashion show in aid of...

CHAPTER TWO

Carol Murphy

So I'm in the smothering newsroom waiting for Don to talk, and only now do I think about the state I'm in. This is what I look like: my hair is shining with grease; one of my shoes has a loose heel; the trousers I swore I wouldn't wear until I'd lost at least a stone – I don't trust the zip – and I've just realised that my blouse is on inside out.

I retreat to a corner where I hope I won't be noticed, and calculate if there's enough time to get to the loo and fix myself. But everyone is here now: all of them, of course, neat and shiny faced. A couple of the girls from the subs desk grin over and make *how's the head?* gestures. I grimace back. One of the Sports lads sidles up and gives me a shoulder nudge. I feel my skull wobble and catch him eyeing the label on the back of my blouse.

'Carol,' he whispers, 'is your shirt –'

'Yes. I know. Shut up.'

He sniggers and shoulders me again. I want to scream with pain.

But I made it in; which is something, I suppose. When you wake up with a bit of a head, there's a moment of optimism: as if you've come around from a long coma and have to struggle to remember who you are and how you got here. It's a wondrous second chance. And then you notice that your lips seem welded together and when you manage to prise them open, the odour curling out is of ammonia and rotting fish. This morning it felt as if my mouth had been scrubbed

9

with sandpaper and every attempt to sit upright was rewarded with the sensation of needles being jammed through my neck and head. I ended up having to slide off the bed like a bad limbo dancer, crawl to the wall and slowly ease myself into a standing position. Even then I couldn't bear to open my eyes for more than a few seconds. I got dressed mostly by feeling around for clothes. Considering all that, I've done pretty well.

I loaded up with coffee and paracetamol and my preferred hang-over cure, Coke and a Breakfast McMuffin. But I can still smell the alcohol. My internal organs feel as if they've been wrenched together. To take my mind off it, I scan the room. No sign of lanky Brian from the Features Desk who I let drag me home from the pub. Again. Harmless young guy, really. Sweet. But then he had to look down at me with those globy eyes and announce: *I'm falling for you, Carol.* God love him.

Dizzy. Wish I could sit down.

I wonder if Don has heard about last night. He'd be concerned, given my recent form. I love Don. No, not in *that* way. It's just that he's been very good to me. A father figure, of sorts; my actual father having departed for Anywhere But Here. Don wanted me to be his protégée. Let me run the news meeting once or twice, until the morning I got a pen stuck in my hair and couldn't get it out and had to spend the next twenty minutes going through the stories with a Parker swinging across my forehead.

Don starts speaking in his forty-a-day voice. He smokes out the window in a hallway upstairs. Totally illegal, but no one is going to complain. Everyone likes him too much. I already know where he'll send me: another photocall for some charity run by a load of botoxed poshees. Even with an election on, with the country gone bust, I still get nothing but crap to do.

But that's all my own fault.

What day is it?

I used to bring in cakes. Every Friday. Just to mark the end of the week; to hug ourselves for all the work. They were nice too. I'd get up early so I could stop off at this bakery on Chatham Street. Here comes Carol with the cakes.

I don't remember when I stopped going to the bakery. The people here would ask: no cakes, Carol? And then they stopped asking. They didn't want to be cruel. They didn't want to interrupt my busy schedule of career ruination. Turning up late, or a bit tipsy, or not at all. Mistakes and lies and missed deadlines and a couple of threats of libel. Why am I not fired? I don't know. Don has been far too kind. Two written warnings and one week's suspension is my tally so far. One more incident, even a small one, and I'm gone.

Jesus, I'm a mess.

I should jack it all in. But to do what? Any other paper would be the same. I wouldn't have the nerve for telly or radio. Not skinny or blonde or insincere enough for PR. I don't know. I used to love all this – not too long ago either. When? Last year? Eighteen months ago? Not *that* long. I used to bring in cake.

So what's the problem? God, if I knew that… I suppose: a lack of *joy*. I used to get that, working here. I did. I was always *on*, foraging for stories, and I was good at it too: at getting people to talk, at zinging out reliable copy.

Yet I suddenly started to feel contempt for my job; not just mine, but for the whole pointless cycle of work: of earning money to buy crappy products; of borrowing to spend a lifetime paying back. I'm choked by a mild disgust which I can't scrub away, and which seems to radiate to everything around me: the hollow-eyed people and the crumbling streets. Myself most of all. Every day Don says: how are you, kid? And every day I let him down.

He's asked me what's wrong; asked quite a few times. He wondered was it because of my mother. I said yeah, probably. But I don't know.

So he said he'd give me lighter markings for a while; you know, the fluffy stories until you get back on your feet. You tell me when you are ready. I never did.

He runs through the usual things. Where the party leaders will be campaigning today, a couple of policy document launches, a protest over education cuts, another over health cuts, the Supreme Court appeal of a jailed banker, a knife attack in Carlow, a bank robbery in Limerick, an illegal-cigarettes haul, a sex-abuse case, the visit of some Hollywood starlet…

My attention has already started to crumble, my gaze shifting to the raindrops pattering on the window. I wonder where Dad is and hope that he's safe on that yacht, and I wonder should I get my teeth whitened (and I've got to give up the ciggies), and take that red streak out of my hair. Dye all of it. Black? *Again?* Must have a chat with Brian. He's too young.

Daddy, Daddy, where are you?

Yeah, go on Doctor Freud: tell me what my problem is. I've had some sort of mentaller since my mother died; since my father ran away. Everyone says that. And I can see how it makes sense. But I just don't believe that's the reason I'm screwing up at work; I can't explain it. Yes, she died, and it's tragic, and yeah, I am sad. I'm mourning. It feels as if I always will be. For months afterwards I would wake every day and tell myself: your mother is dead. She's gone. I saw them lower the box into the black clay. I saw her face swelled with embalming fluid: a grotesque mockery of her vivid life.

It has got better with time, though it can still take you by surprise: someone calls me Carol in a certain way or I catch the scent of the sea or even when I look in the mirror. I look a lot like her. Everyone says so.

But I'm *aware* of all that. I know I have to push through it, and I'm doing OK, thanks very much. I'm not crippled. I pay my mortgage and talk about the tragic state of the country or who might win the *X Factor*. This is different.

A name snaps me back to the meeting. Manda. Manda.

Well, it's unusual, isn't it? And I know by looking at him that Don thinks it's a good story. His bushy eyebrows move towards each other like mating caterpillars; the nostrils on his slightly hooked nose flare out. He looks a bit like a bloodhound; the faithful sort that sleeps at the end of your bed.

'Hmm,' he says. 'And the Belton poster landed in the skip on top of the young one? Jesus.'

Rachel Belton is a candidate who so far has had a disastrous campaign: mostly because every time she opens her mouth, something stupid pops out of it. She's a former Miss Ireland with an MBA and is married to some squillionaire. She seems to have assumed that everyone would love and admire her for these facts alone.

'Well there goes the election for Belton,' says Don, not unkindly. 'What do the cops say?'

'Murder, deffo,' says Tim. 'Guy was seen pushing her out, then did a runner.' Tim is our crime reporter, though he's just as often on telly or radio talking about broken-hearted mothers or sinister above-the-law Mister Bigs with nicknames like Hobnail or The Kipper. I suspect Don doesn't like him much. But he brings in readers.

'That's terrible,' says Don, which means he really likes this story. Don is an old-school hack. He likes yarns with a beginning, middle and an end. We have the end already.

'Guards released the name?'

'No,' drones Tim in his private eye voice. 'Family overseas to be contacted.'

'What was it again? Amanda?'

'No, just Manda. Weird one. *Manda* Ferguson.' He says the name as if it deserves to be treated suspiciously.

'OK, so we need to find out about her. Think we could get a nice picture?'

Tim shrugs.

Nice picture is code for: was she pretty? Dead pretty girls always sell newspapers.

'She was pretty.'

Everyone is looking at me.

I'm just as surprised as they are.

'In a hippyish way,' I add, redundantly.

Tim scowls. He tried it on with me once – or he was leading up to it – but you just couldn't imagine it with someone who's an inch shorter than you and who keeps a hairdryer the size of a rifle in his desk.

'Very pretty,' I say. 'I can get a picture this afternoon. I knew Manda Ferguson quite well.'

Tim twists his face even further, but Don smiles.

'OK, Carol. Tim, you don't mind?'

Tim waves the question away. I nod dumbly. I don't say anything else because it strikes me what the entire newsroom is thinking: he's giving her *another* chance? I'm not even sure if this is the same Manda Ferguson that I know. Or knew. It must be. The name is too unusual. Manda Ferguson, by the way, was my cousin, though I'm not going to share that with anyone here.

I'm not upset. At least not now. My cousin has been murdered and all I want to do is use it to show Don and all the others that I haven't been a total waste of time.

CHAPTER THREE

Rachel Belton

Aidan Haslett flounces into the lounge of our home as if he's my oldest friend in the world. I don't know how he managed to get the code for the gate, though I suspect Renata. He never asked me for it; nor did he ask for permission to treat this house as his second office, a place where he assumes he is welcome to leave crumbs on the floor or rest his grubby shoes upon my couch. He flops into the seat on the opposite side of the large table upon which I have carefully stacked various files; the dull accoutrements of our electoral efforts.

He doesn't say anything at first. He shifts his translucent red and blue tie to cover where his stomach is straining the buttons of his pink shirt. Then he leans back, extending his left arm outwards. He folds one leg over the other. He's wearing faded chinos that could do with an iron. He's never attempted to dress smartly, to look the part. He seems to revel in his grubbiness; or perhaps he does it to antagonise me.

Like a bad actress, he emits a melodramatic sigh, then lightly drums the fingers of his left hand on the table, the polished surface reflecting his viciously bitten fingernails. I can see flecks of blood.

Finally, he looks up. I can well imagine how this routine might unsettle the red-nosed farmers and schoolteachers in Head Office. But it's not necessary for me; there is no advantage to be gained here. We both know what's coming.

I present my best sad smile.

'Well,' Aidan Haslett announces. 'I don't know what to say, Rachel. I don't. I mean, nothing like this has ever happened before.'

Now he tells me all about this girl in the bridesmaid dress and the fall out the window. The collision with my poster. I know all this already. But, being Aidan, he's saving what I don't know for the end. People took pictures of the body with their mobile phones. They have already been posted on the web.

'Fucking internet,' snips Aidan. 'No control. None. There are no relationships. These weirdos don't see the story in any *context*. Elections are all about context. It's you versus the other candidate. The only question is: who's better? An axe murder will get elected if he runs against a paedophile.

'But it doesn't exist out there.' He waves towards the sky. 'It's a huge puke of information which doesn't mean anything. There's no paradigm, other than paranoia, apart from some nutcase getting his rocks off feeding the other nutcases conspiracy theories to chew on.'

He shakes his head, then holds out his hands: like Jesus in a religious painting.

'How can we have message control with *that*? How can we control anything? I mean, you do know what they are saying?'

I shrug lightly. Of course I don't know.

'On these blogs. They're saying she had the poster on her *before* she was pushed out the window. That it's a warning against you or *by* you depending on which blog you read. One claims that she was your secret love child.'

Aidan chortles at this. He interlaces his fingers and holds his stomach while his body gently wobbles.

'Mathematically impossible, I would have thought.'

He glances at me, apparently seeking confirmation of this. I nod.

The chortling abruptly ends. Aidan stares at the floor.

'People in Head Office have been on the phone, to see can we get some of it taken down. But that disgusting picture is everywhere now. Tricky to stop all of it.'

He glances at me again, almost furtively.

'Which means the proper media will be all over it. Because the story is already out there. It's the duty of the Priests of News. All that. Fucking hypocrites.'

Aidan enjoys accusing people of hypocrisy.

He waves a hand.

'You know how serious this is.'

Of course I do. But Aidan Haslett has long since made it plain that he doubts my pedigree. Admittedly, there have been one or two problems. On the first day of the canvass, I found myself being harangued by some oddball who seemed to feel that I alone was responsible for the failure of Irish politics and the dire straits of the country. He called me a snob; a class traitor. I told him to piss off.

How was I to know that this took place within earshot of a reporter? Or that the oddball would then relate his tragic story to the press (recent unemployment; a squad of ugly children; a wife with some dubious malady), thus casting me in the role of the heartless madam?

I apologised, naturally. But the controversy hung around me like a bad smell; to be reinvigorated every time some spite-filled reporter had the chance to toss me a provocative question. I ignored them all: until a journalist who Aidan claimed to be sympathetic asked about my accent. If you're from the area, why do you sound so different to everyone else here? I mean, you sound *middle-class*. He hissed the words like it was some sort of embarrassing ailment.

Calmly, I explained that I haven't lived here for some years. Accents evolve over time. The reporter scrunched his face into an ugly, unconvinced expression: and foolishly, I rose to this: because I was born here I'm supposed to sound like some sort of skanger? Is that it?

'Ya wha' Belto? "Posh" Candidate in "Skanger" Slur' was the headline. The story featured expressions of outrage from various community stalwarts, including the oddball from the first controversy.

Yet despite this, my campaign was not destroyed. Rookie mistakes, Aidan called them (especially as the second was partially his fault); the sort of thing you could expect from any newcomer. Don't worry about it. Move on. And anyway, who is going to vote for the other mob? They destroyed the country.

No: it was not the errors that bothered Aidan, but me. He is the real snob here. Despite my accent, my nice house, my various accomplishments, he views me as a fake. Behind my carefully constructed persona, there is nothing but a sordid proletarian desire to succeed. No real intelligence. No pedigree. No *class*.

He sighs again and starts nibbling at a nail. If this had been earlier on in my short political career, rather than at its apparent end, I might have been pleased with his outburst, his display of passion and bad language. But it's not about, or even for, me. A lot of what Aidan says is not what it appears to be about. It's as if he's been delivering this speech to an invisible audience. Aidan Haslett has better things to be doing than wasting his time as my Director of Elections.

But this is what happens in politics. Events, dear boy, and all that. This was an act of God; something neither he nor I could have anticipated. It's something Aidan cannot be blamed for.

This is the key fact.

He'll make a few discreet calls to Head Office, and then be called into a meeting to be told that, really, it would be a shocking waste of resources and his talents to continue with *this* campaign. Aidan will nod sadly while they ask him: and how is Rachel?

Meaning: when is Rachel going to resign?

They know I will. It's inevitable.

In private, he will allow himself to be pleased. The Gods of Election were bound to punish my temerity. A dizzy former model presumptuous enough to think she could understand the ways of *dēmokratía*; to think that she could actually add something to it? Such hubris! Silly little girl!

I've often wondered to what degree are we the authors of our own stories; are we the heroines of our own novels. No, that's too literary and self-conscious; the kind of thing I often think but choose not to say out loud. Put it this way instead: when I was a teenager, I used to think of my life as a television serial, and when something bad or good or strange would happen, I'd say: that was a hell of an episode. Bet that had them sitting on the edges of their seats, wondering what would happen next – and this was years before reality television, before people actually turned their lives into television stories. Before I did it myself.

But being thoughtful isn't *helpful*, as Aidan might put it. Aidan isn't stupid – far from it – but would consider it a waste to apply his brain power towards anything that doesn't have a precise objective. Now his objective is to get off my campaign.

Naoise should be up by now, gobbling his breakfast, drops of milk spattered on the front of his giraffe pyjamas. He won't want to get dressed. He never does. He'll want to play spaceman. Renata will have to negotiate. Let him do it for an hour. *Pleeese Neesy.* She still can't pronounce his name. He thinks this is hilarious.

I had foolishly hoped to win Aidan over. I thought I was making some progress, until now. I suppose he is what he is, a political commando, ordered into what he considered the showbiz end of the election; when there were so many other juicy partisan battles to be involved in. I don't think he dislikes me. How could he? He hardly knows me. All he can see is the blond hair and the nice clothes.

'Is Daniel around?' he says, like a doctor who has just delivered the bad news but now needs to dump the grief-stricken housewife back on her husband.

'In town, I think.'

Daniel is in the Westbury Hotel, meeting with a group of Welsh and Irish climbers who want to make an attempt on Makalu but can't raise the finance. Daniel doesn't climb any more. But he likes helping others get a start. Well, I don't know if he likes it. That's another story.

I'm being vague with Aidan because I know it irritates him when I start to approximate the dumb blonde he assumes I really am.

Perhaps he resents me because he feels I had it too easy. I was running for the seat of a TD who had died. I was parachuted in. I avoided any inter-party nastiness, at least to my face.

'Do you want to give Daniel a call?' he says. Aidan Haslett is, I estimate, in his mid-forties, though he could be ten years older. He's one of those slightly shambolic, dotty people who probably always seemed middle-aged. He has a standard south Dublin accent, which seems wrong. Aidan should speak as if he had been educated at a minor British public school: where, of course, his nick-name would have been Paddy. He's not married, though I don't think he's gay. He's sexless. I suspect the whole business of having a partner baffles him. He regularly asks do I want to give Daniel a ring: an indication that he knows little of the protocols of spousal communication.

Daniel is useless in situations like this. I say, 'The campaign is finished, isn't it?'

I want these words to come out as cutting, even angry. But my voice remains maddeningly smooth.

'Well,' he says. 'Rachel.' He sits up, looks at me.

'I'll be honest. It's not good. There's no doubt about that. It's a blow. I mean, taken together with our other problems, there may be an element of embarrassment for the party. But all elections have ups and downs, Rachel. It's part of the challenge.

'What we need to do now is evaluate how to respond. Because, as I say, something like this is unprecedented. But I've already been on to Head Office. I'm going to head in there now to see what they think, what support they can offer us. In the meantime we should all sit tight, say nothing to the press and think about how to move this forward.'

Aidan will go into Head Office this afternoon and I'll never see him again. They'll decide that I am a liability: a candidate who is arrogant, stupid and unlucky. They won't want the papers asking why I was selected in the first place; why the judgement of the leadership was so poor.

I wonder will he ring to tell me? Or text?

'Have you told the others?' I ask.

Mary, Michael and Agnes are our full-time workers. They marshal a battalion of volunteer canvassers from a dusty office in Phibsborough, and every day present me with a list of meetings to attend, schools and sports clubs to visit. They tell me the names of the people to greet, and what details to slip into the conversation, to demonstrate my concern for the gawping proletariat. They lick stamps, make calls and try to outdo each other in their smiley devotion to the cause. I don't know that much about them, other than they are local and worked for the previous TD. They came with the election.

'No,' says Aidan, a look of brimming disgust on his face.

'I'll do it,' I say: a suggestion he seems pleased to accept. He stands. Meeting over.

'So you're OK?' he says.

'I'm fine.'

'Not disheartened?

'It's politics. It's what happens. I'm tougher than that.'

He pauses: perhaps to acknowledge that we both know what we are really talking about. Eventually he says, 'Oh.' He is trying to sound pleasantly surprised, though it just comes out as surprised.

But it's the truth. I *am* tougher than that; I just never got a chance to demonstrate it to Aidan. I am the candidate who failed before she started.

Aidan winks at me, attempting to be chummy. He promises to call later, and then leaves hurriedly. I remain alone at the table. At the other end of the room is the massive window which frames a cinemascope view of Killiney. Soggy purple clouds tumble over each other from the east, darkening the serrated waters of Dublin Bay. I see a faint reflection of myself. I wave a hand, to make sure I'm there. I look like one of the ghosts Daniel talks to.

Perhaps it's this house; using it as an office when the constituency is the other side of the city: physically, economically, in *every* way. He did once make a comment about the candidate fitting the voters. Perhaps that's what he meant. Too posh for north Dublin. I see the point. I see the contradiction – though I can hardly move my family to some Corporation dump just because that's where the party chose to plop me down, can I? I am out there all day, every day as it is. For God's sake, Rachel. Justifying yourself to a man who has just left, who rarely visited the constituency anyway. He always preferred to meet here, to sip cappuccinos from our nice machine and stick his filthy shoes on my furniture. The variables of any election are essentially the same, he said, and differ only in proportion: a dynamic system of strengths and weaknesses which sometimes attack each other head on, which sometimes coalesce or cancel each other out. You don't win. You force the others to lose.

I get in the car and head for the northside. I don't bother to change. The jeans and sweater are fine. Best to tell them in person what's happened, give a small inspirational speech. I switch on the radio. The murder of that girl is already on the news, though there's no mention of me yet. I switch off my mobile anyway.

Many months from now, I will wonder about the wisdom of making this journey: how different things would have been if I'd accepted Aidan's verdict and stayed at home. Daniel would not have been outed as some sort of superstitious simpleton. There would have been no spectres, no creaking Catholics and hippies and witches and pagans gathering under lampposts, waiting for dispatches from beyond Death. An innocent few words from my gentle husband and the Ireland of thirty years ago tries to make a comeback. And he looks at me and says: what? What did I do?

But I do not know this now. I'm irked by Aidan Haslett. I suppose I haven't let all hope die away.

I *do* fit the constituency. As well as any of the other candidates. It is where I'm from. Originally. Where my mother still lives. Myself and my parents and four brothers in a pebble-dashed, three-bed-roomed house with friendly looking gnomes in the tiny front garden. Occasionally the gnomes would disappear or be moved up the street. No, it wasn't some sordid working-class tale of incest or drug abuse. Nothing as exciting as that. Daddy worked most of the time and as a family we were largely happy. Even when they split up, it was civilised. I was twenty when it happened, and none of us were surprised. It wasn't that they argued so much as that they didn't: at the end they couldn't even provoke anger from each other. They lost interest.

It's where I'm from; though it never felt that way. I was the child who convinced herself that she must be adopted, who prayed for the day when her real parents would show up at the front door and whisk her away to the life she deserved. I was that child. I must admit, I still am. I visit my mother and listen to her dribbling inanities and I am astounded that we share the same genetic code.

When my rescue fantasies became too fragile to maintain I realised I had to engineer my own escape. I spent most of my teenage years plotting it. Even when I was still young, when three streets away seemed foreign territory, and my friends and I would boast of our territorial loyalty, our hatred of southsiders, I would be quietly thinking: this place is horrific. It's Death. I must get out. I must become someone else. And I did.

I'm trapped within her now.

So you can imagine my unease at returning here as a candidate, offering myself up to the Proles; at having to ladle praise upon a place I had fled from. But, naturally, I didn't have to: because you never say anything directly. You say the area has many challenges. Challenge is a synonym for *problem*. Many challenges is a synonym for *this place is a dump*.

I studied hard. I learned. I learned that when you are the candidate, you have to be completely devoid of ego and nothing but ego at the same time. You have to be able to step outside yourself and with others coldly assess how you speak, walk, gesticulate, smile, and dress: everything is rated for acceptability to the stupefied voter. Yet you also have to be able to walk into a room full of strangers and tell them how marvellous you are without sounding arrogant. Forget all the 'be yourself' clichés, the Proles aren't interested in that. They want a father or a mother or a champion. Someone who will say to them: I will solve all your problems because you are helpless.

I won't miss that; I won't miss the canvass. Most of them would leer at me druggily, their brains frozen by the thinning fumes of my celebrity; or one might occasionally decide to be bold and demand: *what are you going to do for me?* They get exactly what they deserve.

Even Aidan said it: people won't vote for you just because you're from the area; they'll vote for you because you're from the area but *not like them.* No one votes for people like themselves. They'll vote for you because they think you are better than them: that's what they want. Just don't injure their working-class pride by pointing it out.

Easy for me. I was the icy princess who looks a bit like Grace Kelly: beautiful and remote; serene and humourless. I was a blank page upon which they could scribble their fantasies.

Sometimes I'd get mugged by guilt. On the canvass, in the evenings when I knew Naoise would be asleep when I got home. Sometimes

I wouldn't have seen him that morning either. I'd want to give up there and then, though of course I didn't say anything.

Yet when I'm at home there's this prickly craving to get out of the house; to do anything.

I love my little boy.

As I get to Phibsborough, I start to wonder: those pictures of the dead girl, do they really destroy the campaign? I look at the grimy terraces and the smoky flats and it strikes me that a lot of people around here don't even have computers, wouldn't know how to use one. Will the papers publish? Unlikely. Aidan wanted off the campaign anyway; to hell with him. Maybe there is a way to rescue this. The girl was murdered, is there an angle there? Get together with the parents, if they're from the constituency. Lots of outrage about crime or drugs or deprivation, whatever. Don't let whatshername have died in vain. Something like that.

Yes, perhaps. To hell with the Party and Aidan Haslett. I let myself into the poster-festooned office, already composing a list of tasks for Mary, Michael and Agnes. They are seasoned campaigners. They should be put to better use anyway.

Naoise should be dressed by now. Waddling around the kitchen and chattering to his teddies. No rain forecast today; Renata should bring him to the playground. I'll ring later.

The office is empty, and this strikes me like a punch. My Director of Elections decides the campaign is over and scuttles off the ship, yet these people are still out, knocking on doors, grinning through the countless rejections. I am, for want of a better word, briefly moved by this thought.

I sit down, not sure what to do with myself. It's only then that I notice the box of Milk Tray with the card attached. The card carries a pastel drawing of two moustached, nineteenth-century men out for a stroll: an image that has no relevance to me or the campaign that I can think of. It was probably the first one that came to hand.

Rachel,
We were very sorry to hear the bad news. We're all devastated. It was a great honour to work with you. We wish you the very best for the future.
Mary, Michael and Agnes.

I almost start laughing; except it's not my habit to laugh. Only now do I notice that a portion of one of the walls is bare: where the maps used to be. Detailed depictions of the constituency, colour-coded, street by street, house by house, listing the voting intentions of most of the seventy thousand poor souls in this area. Mary, Michael and Agnes spent far too many years collating that intelligence to leave it behind for me. They are gone, along with their expertise, their power to create.

Some politician I am, not to have seen this coming. I open the chocolates. I like the orange creams. I'll just stay here for a while. For a few minutes, or hours, or days. Until something occurs to me.

CHAPTER FOUR

Michael Bourke

I might have kept walking, oblivious to the horror just landed beside me, if it wasn't for some flailing passers-by, beseeching my aid. I had no alternative then but to crawl into the disgusting skip, careful to keep my eyes from the thick, tangy gore already pooling beneath her body.

An audience quickly congealed. They stood and gawped as I clambered towards her, the dark growl of traffic masking my quick breaths. I heard myself muttering: *God, God, God*. But not as a benediction; rather, an ejaculation of disgust.

I tried a hasty Lord's Prayer, but then came her last strangulated gasp, the flicker of the eyes and the smile widening her face. For a few moments, every morsel of priestly training seemed to scamper away from me, leaving behind a trembling man in a black suit.

God, God, God.

Everyone else looked on, expecting me to know what to do.

Their eyes gorged on the girl with hungry horror. But the gazes directed at me seemed to contain a question. What do we do now? What are you going to do now? How do we make sense of this? What does it mean?

Ah, *meaning*, the spiritual heroin of our age, the added ingredient which can retrospectively transform any senseless action or event into something virtuous. Aquinas and Denys would have yodelled their derision at such ideas. Their God was unknowable, unnameable: a deity that flimsy human speech can never describe. A God with a plan? Think I'll make a few earthquakes today and arrange for little Jimmy to get that job interview. Such rot.

Naturally, I didn't say this. I never do. Instead I played my usual part: a role I have refined through decades of practise; and in which I take a certain professional pride. I removed my jacket and placed it carefully over the girl's face and shoulders: my black clothes over her light. I formed the sign of the cross while muttering nothing words.

God, God, God.

The guards arrived then, and once out of the skip I continued my work with small clumps of anguished onlookers. Forcing just the right amount of moisture to my eyes, I prayed with some and cooed religious platitudes to others. All regarded me as a hero, even some of the younger ones. I was looked upon as some marvellous freak of nature, a genius-savant able to recite pi from memory. My back was patted as the guards took my name and phone number.

I felt nothing other than an understandable disgust. I wanted to flee the place as quickly as possible, have a bath and reorder my mind with the Lutheran rigour of Bach. I didn't know who this girl was. I didn't realise that the dullards around me would demand to make her a saint.

CHAPTER FIVE

Carol Murphy

I hear the global shush of radio waves as I wait for the third time to see if Dad's phone will ring. Distant voices fade in and out. Something in Spanish. An American says '…and do you think she cares about that?' I feel myself shiver. For God's sake answer, Dad. Don't even know where he is, whether he's well or ill, whether he's alive or…

I swear under my breath, then light a cigarette. I'm in the neat park across the road from the newspaper. It's shielded by trees from the traffic swirling around; the thick grass absorbing the thump of footballs and the gentle scolds of parents. Of course it's in use now at all hours of the day; people desperately filling their time. But I try not to think about that. I like to come here to hide from the office, but I rarely look at the people.

A gash of light blue has been revealed in the sky and appears to be widening. It's stopped raining too, but, stupid cow that I am, I didn't check the bench before I sat. I can already feel the wet patch on my backside.

What do I remember about Manda? Not that much. As a kid we visited their house a bit, the way you do with relations. Yet I can't conjure up any particular images. The visits just stopped. Can't remember why. Grew out of it, I suppose.

She was a few years younger than me. Had a huge collection of dolls and a small village of dolls' houses, though her games were never the usual mammies and daddies and trips to the shops: they were always some drama involving poverty or eviction, with a wealthy family deciding, after a bit of a row, to allow the poor family to move in with them.

That never changed about her, now that I think of it. Here's a memory: there was a time in Dublin. I suppose she had started college then and I was in my first job on that freesheet. We bumped into each other – on George's Street, I think. Yes, it was close to the Arcade and even then she was dressing like a hippy. After all the squealing howareyou and howisyourfamily, I asked, 'How do you like Dublin?' Her eyes shot open as if she had just been thinking about this, or hoping someone would ask.

'Absolutely fascinating!'

She talked strangely too; like a university professor. But with lots of exclamation marks. 'It's not at all how I expected it to be! I thought it would be nothing but oppressed people, but many of them are quite optimistic, which is great! You can really sense the start of a spiritual awakening. The white phallocentric middle-class power structure is definitely starting to crumble! I'd say you sense it, yes, yes?'

Yeah, that was Manda. She had a good heart.

I hang up the phone and try Dad again. There's a brother, Conor, due to get married (presumably Manda was a bridesmaid, even though she wasn't the bridesmaid type); the mother, Hazel, a bit of a live wire; and the father, Bob, whom I can't remember ever meeting. Bob and Hazel split up years ago and now he lives in Singapore or Hong Kong or some such. There's money though – he's some sort of fancy-pants architect and the house in Loughrea is huge, if ramshackle.

Dad never spoke about Hazel much, even when we used to visit. She is his sister, yet all I can remember him saying about her is *Ah, Hazel* in a worn and amused tone; as if this was explanation enough.

After another mash of whistles and scraps of conversation, I get a slow beeping. Dad answers in a slightly breathless, slightly delighted voice, as if he's already having a fantastic time and this call makes it even better.

'Dad?'

'Carol! Darling! How are you?'

He's always like this; always has been. For close to thirty years he was a GP, hmming and smiling his way through the outflows of withered prostates and bad nerves. Yet it never seemed to put a dent in his exhaustingly sunny outlook. Most people find my father adorable, and with good reason. He's charming, funny, and handsome in a dishevelled, outdoorsy sort of way. When I was a kid, holidays would consist of hill-walking in Peru or sailing on the Mediterranean. My friends envied me for having a dad like him, and I reckon quite a few had a crush on him. But after Mum died he didn't know how to react: he couldn't metabolise the idea of long-term grief. So he chose to ignore it. Sold his practice and sailed off. Literally. She's called the *Shooting Star*, a forty-foot ketch that Dad was rebuilding for most of my childhood and which was something of a family joke until she finally took to the water. I was about fifteen at the time, and fell in love with her instantly. They've been gone for nearly two years now. I miss them both.

'I'm great,' I say.

Already I'm trying to please by chiming in with his mood.

'I was just thinking about you,' he says.

'Really?'

Since he left, not once has he rung me. I know why. It's obvious. I remind him of her. I look like her, I sound like her, my voice still carries tiny trembles of grief. But knowing this doesn't make it any easier. My father can't bear to see me; just when I need him the most.

But I never say it.

'Where are you?'

He likes this kind of question.

'Santa Margherita. You were here once, or close enough. We stayed in Camogli, up the road. Do you remember?'

He really wants me to, though all I can conjure are images of pastel blue; of trees parched after a burning summer and waiters too cranky to serve one last grappa. Which Mum was miffed by and Dad found hilarious. But this could be any one of the places the three of us sailed into along the Mediterranean coast. Even beauty can become monotonous.

'Think so,' I say.

'Just on the deck having an espresso. Absolutely gorgeous. Tourists all gone. Nice and quiet. You should come over. You'd love it.'

I smile, imagining him there.

'One day I might call your bluff and do that.'

'You'd be very welcome,' he says, quickly adding, 'how's the job?'

'Oh, great.' I lie so convincingly, I almost believe it myself. 'But Daddy, I do have a bit of bad news.'

'Oh?'

His tone is almost accusatory, as if I should have warned him this was coming.

'Manda Ferguson is dead. She was murdered.'

The line goes quiet, and for a moment I fear he has hung up.

'Daddy?'

'Yes, yes, it's terrible isn't it?'

He has adopted his official doctor voice: the one that enables him to make compassionate noises without any real involvement; as if this was some story he read in the papers about someone he'd never met.

'You already knew?'

'Hazel rang,' he says. 'I knew you'd be busy. I was going to leave it a couple of hours before I rang you.'

No he wasn't.

'She's very upset, of course. They've had to postpone the wedding. Terrible, terrible. And that was to be, when? Next week or something?'

'Yes,' I say, though I haven't a clue. An invitation did arrive for the afters, but I threw it in the bin. I don't know why.

My father sighs without conviction.

'I suppose it will be in the papers?'

'Oh, it will be huge. Because she was in the bridesmaid's dress and all that when it happened.'

'Really? Hazel didn't mention. And do they know? Do they have any idea who or why?'

'None that I know of. But I will be working on the story.'

'Will you?' he says as if I just told him I had won the egg-and-spoon race in school (which I did, by the way). 'That's good, that's good.'

It's like he's not listening now, not really taking in any of this – just the surface meaning of the words; just enough to offer stock responses.

'Will you keep me posted on the funeral arrangements?' he says finally. 'Just text me.'

I'm being dismissed.

'Getting back would be tricky for me, you know, with the boat and everything.'

I say nothing.

'She was a lovely girl,' he eventually offers. 'Terrible thing.'

I say, 'Does her father know?'

He knows that by saying nothing about the funeral, I've conceded a point; he has to indulge me a little now.

'Bob? Oh, I don't know. Hazel didn't say. I'm sure he does. A ripe chance to make him feel guilty, she wouldn't pass that up.'

'Their divorce was bitter then?'

Another pause. 'Ah, can't really remember. It was years ago. It's just Hazel, she was always over – well, you know what she's like.'

'I don't know. I was just trying to remember. We never really saw them that much.'

'Really?'

He sounds genuinely surprised.

'You did,' he says. 'You spent summers there. When you were younger.'

'Did I?'

'Yes, of course.'

I feel an odd flash of annoyance.

'What are you going to write about Manda anyway?' he says. 'Surely not about Bob and Hazel's divorce?'

'No. It's just a general background piece. It just struck me since I heard that I didn't really know her that well at all.'

'Hmm. Well, you should get yourself down to Loughrea then. Hazel would be delighted to see you. Especially now...'

His voice trails off, and behind the wash of the sea, I hear greetings being yelled. A woman saying his name.

'Carol, I'm sorry sweetie but I have to go now. I'll ring you tomorrow.' He always says that. 'Good night, princess.' He always says that too. Even though it's morning.

I take the phone from my ear and stare at it. A woman? What woman? It sounded like she knew him well. Has he got himself a woman already? Why am I saying *already*? It is two years. Why not? It's a good thing. Perfectly understandable that he might be reluctant to say it to me.

I recite all this good sense to myself, yet each word disintegrates as soon as I think it. It strikes me that I am furious with my father; that I have been for some time.

CHAPTER SIX

Rachel Belton

Why do I hate this place? Well, just look at it. When I was a teenager, and my loathing was more visceral, it was because my home was guilty of the worst crime of all: it was boring. While trapped here, I would never meet David Bowie. I felt condemned by the smoke-stained buildings and the foggy air and the slow-moving neighbours who didn't seem to notice any of this; who didn't seem to care that all the colour around them had been rinsed away. Beauty was a new gas fire or a fake-pine dining set; a floral dress from Penneys. Souvenirs from Playa Del Ingles.

What confounded me most was how I seemed to be the only one who felt this way. Even among girls my own age, it was as if some agreement had been struck which I didn't know about, where everyone was allowed to improve themselves, but only up to a certain point. To express a desire to push further was met with puzzlement. Sure, you have a job. What do you want a better job for? Everyone around me was dull, ugly and pitifully stupid.

I was young. All I knew then was that I didn't share the devotion to our quadrant of streets which everyone else seemed to carry, and it was probably best to remain quiet about it. I didn't tell anyone about my weekly pilgrimage to Grafton Street. Usually on a Saturday afternoon. I would get off at the ILAC centre, just in case anyone saw me. Then scuttle over the Ha'penny Bridge and up the quays. I suppose no one would have said anything if they had known that I went to the poshest street in Dublin every weekend. They wouldn't have *said*

34

anything. Yet I know they would have found it unaccountably odd, slightly uncomfortable. As if I had suddenly changed religion.

I didn't go there to shop – I couldn't afford anything – but to look: at the clothes and the people. They had an ease about them; they could talk and laugh out loud as if they were entitled to. Borders are porous and imprecise, but to my teenage mind O'Connell Bridge was a frontier as absolute as the Iron Curtain (which still existed back then). Westmoreland Street still felt a bit like the northside, but would flow into College Green: bordered on both sides by the soot-blackened grandeur of Trinity College and the Bank of Ireland, the former Irish parliament. Even the history seemed better here. I would stroll down to Grafton Street and do a turn around the perfumed, Christmas-lit counters of Brown Thomas, watching the people move, seeing how to change myself so I could seem to be one of them.

Looking the part was easy. Long before the term *vintage* became fashionable, I'd learned what could be found in second-hand shops. I knew a good education was my way out, though this would require some cunning: never *appear* to be swatting, to know too much. I remember once at a school play rehearsal using the word *gesticulate*. Even my teachers seemed uncomfortable. So I kept my books under my bed and pretended to have a hangover when I wanted to study. I don't think I told any of my friends what I got in the Leaving Cert; they were too busy whooping and screaming to notice. Anyone who asked, I told them I was going to do Business Studies. I'd won a scholarship to study Economics in Trinity. My parents didn't know what that was. I told them it would get me a good job in a bank.

Being the youngest in my family, and the only girl, you would expect me to have been spoiled. But the opposite was the case. By the time I arrived, my parents were exhausted from celebrating engagements, christenings, jobs in the ESB. They were relieved when I told them I had a plan of my own: even if that plan left them baffled. I suppose they assumed that my education didn't matter. I was pretty. I'd get married eventually, and that would be that.

The first bit of genuine enthusiasm they ever mustered for me was when I started winning beauty contests. I suppose this was finally something they could understand; and I was, I suppose, pleased for them in return. My pictures appeared in the *Northside News* and the *Evening Herald*: tangible evidence of achievement which could be stored away and flourished whenever an uncle or neighbours called in. My mother still has those cuttings, I'm sure.

My father died two years after my parents separated: turned out that what he had grown indifferent to was keeping him alive.

By the time I started college I had already become a stranger to my parents. They never commented on it, but they must have noticed the changes: the way I dressed and held myself, the way my accent had flattened out. The way I didn't babble like most of my peers; carefully parsing each word as it entered and left my mind. They knew nothing of all the preparation I'd done, all the dreaming about the person I wanted to be.

It was a kind of spin, I suppose. I could go home looking and sounding like a middle-class Trinity student, and let them assume that it was no more than a transitory affectation; that at heart I was still a working-class girl most interested in the news from the area: the deaths, the engagements, the babies. *Hatch, Match and Dispatch*, as my father used to say. At college, I looked and sounded like everyone else. I never lied about my background, but didn't correct them either when they assumed I was from Dalkey or Blackrock.

For a second-year Trinity student to win Miss Dublin was, of course, bizarre. Not the sort of thing Trinity students do. Some of them treated the news with polite puzzlement; others pointedly didn't mention it at all. But I didn't mind. Really, I didn't. By then I had come to the conclusion that I needed more than just a good degree. I needed to make money, and I was doing that even before I won Miss Ireland the following year. Modelling is easy. Not the clothes/catwalk sort: that's too time-consuming. But the sort for adverts or photo opportunities: a couple of hours, work not wearing very much and looking enthusiastic. Easy. I graduated from Trinity with a first-class degree, thirty-three thousand in the bank and the deposit paid on a tidy apartment on Poolbeg Street, around the corner from where the immigrants queue hopefully. In the centre of town, and on the southside.

You could put all this down to good luck, though I think you make your own luck. I've always landed on my feet, put it that way. I have a knack for planning, for studying how others succeed and learning from that. I was twenty-two and already I had to choose between two careers: what I had been studying for and what was now bringing in an income.

But that was years ago. My knack for planning has failed me this time.

Yet I can't fault my strategy. There's nothing I would have done differently. I am stuck. Stuck in this office with its sweaty plywood walls, wolfing back the Milk Tray and wondering should I cry; though I know I won't. I can't. I have the option to carry on miserably by myself or resign. I do have the right to be upset.

I stand and look out the window. I wonder should I visit my mother. I could walk there. Left up Viking Street, right at the Centra which used to be called Kellys' – once the place to stand outside if you were twelve years old.

No. Couldn't face her. *How's Naoise? Is he wearing a vest? It's chilly, you know.* I'll eventually tell her what happened with the campaign, and in that poisonously positive way mothers have, she'll tell me that Mrs Murphy and Mrs Corbett and all the Dunnes are going to vote for me: as if this is enough to get elected.

A clump of footsteps on the stairs gives me a start, and for moment makes me want to assume a posture of busyness: as if, even now, I can turn this around by having the right attitude.

The woman who walks in is stuffed into a threadbare woollen coat with a scarlet lining which probably fitted before the fifth child came along. She knows it too, but hasn't had the time to lose the weight or buy a new one. Instead she assumes an apologetic demeanour. I know I'm pathetic. I'm sorry. I've seen her before, though I don't know her name. She's one of the volunteers, devoted to Mary, Mark and Agnes. Worker ants like her would be shooed out the door whenever I arrived; a policy I appreciated as I had no desire to be fawned over by star-struck housewives. Turns out, though, that Mary, Mark and Agnes weren't being protective of me, but of their greatest asset: the names of the volunteers. As long as they controlled that list, they controlled the local party: no one would get elected without their approval. Should have done *that* differently.

Hard to imagine, but I was naive.

'Sorry,' says the woman, now lodged in the half-open door. 'Sorry, Mrs Belton. Sorry.' She talks as if this is a situation we should both be embarrassed about: as if she's interrupted me on the toilet or with a lover. I say nothing at first – I don't know what to say – but eventually I hold up the half-eaten box of Milk Tray.

'Chocolate?'

The woman looks at the box, then back at me, then back at the box again: as if this might be some sort of trap. She seems to have a quick internal debate, then reaches out a hand.

'Coffee,' she says. 'I like them.'

'I hate them,' I say.

She freezes: as if by stating her preference she has somehow insulted me.

'Which is good,' I say. 'It means they won't go to waste.'

Satisfied with this, she gulps back the chocolate. I point at a chair.

'Why don't you sit down?'

She scowls, as if I've suggested something far more transgressive than eating chocolate.

'No, I couldn't.'

'Please.'

'Ah no, I've disturbed you enough as it is.'

'No you haven't.'

'Oh, I couldn't.'

'Go on. Sit.'

She glimpses back down the stairs, to the life she had before, then in at me. She tugs on her coat lapels, then does a little dance – a literal dance – so intense are the opposing forces apparently acting upon her. Her desire to come in and sit down is palpable. Yet she seems scared.

'I insist,' I say. 'All these people are here canvassing for me, and I haven't met a lot of them. Or know their names. I mean, it's not right, is it?'

What am I up to? I have no idea.

The woman doesn't reply, though her moony eyes seem to widen even further. I guide her into the room and sit her down and set about making tea while I chatter on about the weather and the area and how it's changed, and about hanging outside Kellys' shop when we were kids, and snogging boys in the Grove in Raheny when we were teenagers, and anything else non-threatening I can think of – just to keep her here. I don't know why I want to speak to this woman; or what it is I want to say to her.

But as I lay out the tea like an offering, I know she's not going anywhere: now that I've relieved her of the responsibility, I can see she's intrigued; her face betrays a kind of hunger.

I sit down, sip my tea, have another chocolate. I force myself to be quiet for a moment, to let the silence settle around us. Eventually, I extend a hand.

'Sorry,' I say. 'How rude of me. Rachel Belton.'

We shake in that rather uncomfortable way women do. Women shouldn't have to shake hands – the entire ritual is about a display of strength and to discount any suggestion of homosexuality. Women don't need it. It's only something I started to do since I joined the Party: a physical tic to prove that really, I'm one of the lads.

'Sandra Keogh,' she says, as if the utterance of her own name is something of a novelty; as if she hasn't really needed it until now. She tries to sit neatly, her knees tightly together, her coat drawn so tightly around herself it is shaped by her rolls of belly fat. It's preposterous. Perhaps Sandra Keogh senses my thoughts. Now she stands and removes the coat, revealing a simple white blouse and a hip-hugging skirt which complements her voluptuous figure.

She is quite a magnificent-looking woman. She has deep brown hair, almost black, sea-green eyes and lips which roll like waves.

She sits down again, a girlish smile wriggling on her face. She stares at me for slightly too long, rating me – as people always do – against the pictures she has seen. I've looked at the pictures too and failed to recognise myself. Depicted beauty is a form of blankness, for others to see what they will. She nips at her tea, then says,

'You're probably asked this all the time. But I loved you on that programme. You know, the one where you had to survive in that forest?'

'That was years ago,' I say. 'I'm amazed you remember.'

I don't know why I come out with this, because I *do* get it all the time. Tediously predictable. I don't get asked about the programme itself – a dreadful piece of derivative gunk which had the sole aim of manoeuvring the contestants into situations which involved conflict or nudity – but about all the press coverage. It made me a household name, for a while.

Which was the point, I suppose. After eight or nine years on the circuit, years in which I could feel a literal pain in my face from having to smile while embracing a giant rabbit or wearing a bikini in March, the work had begun to dry up. I was facing into my thirties. The good gigs were going to younger girls far more adept than I at transforming every scrap of their life into newspaper copy. A surprisingly Victorian impulse left me loathe to do that. No one ever read about me going to nightclubs or who I was dating. Though if they had known. My God.

So to pump the deadening chest of my all-important profile, my agent, like the most sombre medical specialist, informed me that reality television was my only hope. Credit to him, though: it worked. My profile exploded back into life. And then I realised I didn't want one any more.

Ten years later, Sandra Keogh is asking about my thighs.

Danger Island – yes, even the name was dreadful – was a cheap copy of a British format, where a number of people with near-extinguished media careers spent a month together on an island in Clew Bay. We had to endure various physical trials, each more silly and mud-strewn than the last. We were subject to public eviction votes and we would all protest our enormous commitment to *charidee*. As I said, at least half the challenges involved something in water – which meant wearing a swimsuit and the titillating possibility of the odd boob making a bid for freedom. We all knew what the deal was.

But unlike all the other girls, I didn't wear a slip-off-at-any-moment bikini: a decision which seemed to work in my favour initially, as the attempts by some of them to generate public support by flashing their cleavage were so obvious *so* obvious, even the piggish tabloids felt their intelligence had been insulted. For the first few days I was depicted as 'sensible' – meaning not a slut like the others. My degree from Trinity was mentioned a lot – meaning I wasn't stupid like the others.

But as time went on, and most of the stupid sluts were voted out, the rest of us became frayed and irritable. As the producers hoped, we began to squabble. We all said things. It was television, not real life.

My intolerance for the other remaining women became increasingly difficult to disguise; and eventually, wasn't disguised at all. It wasn't because they were using their looks to regenerate their media careers – I was doing the same thing – it was because of who they had chosen to be. To a woman, they were all pitch-perfect portraits of stupidity: and this wasn't because they were born that way or didn't have a chance at education. It was a choice; it was *deliberate*. To sell their bimbo image they had to *be* the bimbo, they had to avoid contamination by any form of knowledge or anything that even approximated intelligence. I have spent years schooling myself to be unfailingly polite; even a bit bland. But even I have limits. One night, I told them what I thought. They said they didn't understand.

They got my hostility though; they got that. They loathed me and for days the cameras hoovered up their bitchfests about me or my impersonations of their squeaky-dumb voices. It all came to a wonderful crescendo during yet another water-based challenge where I, dressed in my sensible swimsuit, had to traverse between two trees while balancing on a wire. As I did this, the other two remaining female contestants had a rather detailed discussion of my body. It was generally positive until one of them noticed a small accumulation of cellulite around my thighs.

For them, it was difficult to imagine a more shocking discovery: they moaned and oohed in disgust, as if I had a swastika tattooed on my bum. Helpfully, the cameras moved in for a series of lingering close-ups.

My backside appeared on the front page of every tabloid newspaper the following morning, along with extensive coverage on the inside pages. They took one of two angles: firstly, the 'shock' revelation that a 29-year-old former beauty queen could have cellulite, or secondly, the pots of venom which my fellow contestants were prepared to spew. Luckily for me, the second angle became the dominant one over the next few days. Even the broadsheets took up the issue, with pieces about body image and the pressure on women to look good. It all came to a climax with a thirty-minute discussion on *The Late Late Show*, during which I was praised for stressing brains over looks, for my dignity. The phrase 'feminist icon' was used.

I wasn't being dignified. I was still on the island, insulated from any media. I didn't know any of this had happened.

The following week the other two girls were voted off the show. It was the largest vote of the series and generally interpreted as a show of support for me.

I didn't win in the end – I got down to the last three – and only when I emerged from the island did I realise what had been happening. My agent presented me with a brick-sized stack of clippings and said we should get to work straight away to take advantage of this. He had a strategy.

I fired him.

An idea had been dormant in my mind for some time, though I had been reluctant to act upon it: I had fretted that it might signal some sort of failure, my falling back on Plan B. Somehow, the simple act of glancing through those press cuttings freed me from such concerns. I enrolled in the MBA programme at NYU and, six weeks later, I was living there. Daniel followed me, as I knew he would.

This is what Sandra is referring to. And like many people since that time, she wishes to praise me for something I didn't do; to congratulate me for the simple choice of wearing a swimsuit.

'Them two women,' she says. 'They were awful bitches weren't they? I mean, to say that about anyone is bad. But on the telly? I'd have gone through them. I don't know how you didn't.'

'I didn't know,' I say. 'We were on an island, cut off from everything.'

'Oh yeah. But afterwards, I mean. You didn't do any interviews or go on *The Late Late* or any of that. You showed great restraint.'

'Well. Not quite. I ran away.'

Sandra does a little start.

'You ran away?'

'To New York. I went back to college.'

'Oh yeah,' she says. 'I remember that now. But were you not going to do that anyway?'

'I had been thinking about it. But all the coverage made me realise that modelling was not something I could do for the rest of my life. I realised I didn't want to be in the newspapers. It was horrible. The people, the media. All of it.'

'Really now,' is all Sandra can say. 'Really now.'

There's a more formal account of my time on *Danger Island* which I usually serve up to those who ask: one which indicates my pain without directly criticizing anyone. And I never admit to running away to New York. Now that I think of it, I can't remember describing it in those terms to anyone, including myself. Especially myself.

It was my first time to run away; the first time to fail. Yet at the time it seemed more like the failure of others; one I put right by switching careers.

Sandra nods to herself, apparently satisfied with my answers.

I had it mapped out; what would happen after the election. It would take at least a few months to learn the arcane ways of the Dáil. At least that; and I'd also have to calculate how much of my time to devote to constituency work: just enough to give the right impression. But I would make it a priority to meet with the whips as often as possible, tell them what I'm interested in, mention a few committees (Health and Children, Social and Family Affairs), throw a few statistics around. Then meet the Minister or at least a Junior and do the same. I didn't plan to *do* that much for the first year; just enough to impress the right people. Do as much media as possible; drink pints in the Dáil bar with the other TDs; avoid being seen too much with other women.

I'd done my homework: I'd read lots of political biographies. The fresh TD is a single-celled organism, whose only function is to vote in the way they are instructed. The real power flows through the bones of only a few: the inner circle of the inner circle of Cabinet; and to slither into that group requires years of cunning and monastic obedience.

Yet I estimated I could make a Select Committee within nine months, then a Standing Committee (Public Accounts, preferably) within a year and a half. I'd be a Junior Minister in two to three years, if the timing was right. Then I'd be able to do something. Three years later. Three years. Easy.

'Sorry now,' Sandra says, 'for bringing that up. But I always wondered about it. About how you coped and that.'

'I coped by not knowing about it at first, and then by running away. I avoided it.'

'And the whole country feeling sorry for you?'

This isn't judgemental. More amused.

I shrug. 'I got on with my life.'

She seems to think about this for a second; as if genuinely considering it against other options.

'Good for you,' she says.

Good for me. The other girls on the island hid their brains. I hid everything.

There is a lull in our conversation. Without doubt, there are many more questions she could ask me: about every aspect of that programme and my life before and after. But she knows that to push it further now would be crass. She seems to have a functioning brain, this woman.

'So what about you,' I say. 'Have you always lived here?'

'Yes,' she whispers, as if this is some shocking admission. 'Born up the road. Lived there, got married up the other road. Bought a house around the corner from my parents, though they're dead now.'

She leans forward.

'Can you imagine it? I'm forty-seven and I've only spent three years away from this area. And that was only when I was doing me apprenticeship in Galway. The rest of the time,' she points at the floor. 'Stuck right here.'

'And do you regret that?'

Perhaps I sound too formal, too self-consciously concerned. But now she smiles.

'No,' she says. 'That's the odd thing. I don't mind, do you know? And I could have travelled the world, when I got me apprenticeship. I could have gone to America or Bahrain. Malaysia. There was offers. And we've been all over on our holidays, but I just never wanted to be anywhere else.'

She tells me this with amused surprise; as if it's a present she hadn't expected to get.

'I love it here, I suppose. Not even sure why. It feels like…it feels like I wouldn't be myself if I was living anywhere else. Some people go away and it's the making of them. With me it's like the opposite of that, if that makes any sense.'

'Yes.'

Curiously, I think I understand.

She sips more tea, looking slightly shy now, wondering perhaps if it was wise to divest herself so much to a woman she has just met; a woman who previously she had been instructed to stay away from. Silly girl, melting before the celebrity. I ask about her family. Four kids, her husband a baker, which makes me smile.

'Everyone smiles,' she says. 'When I tell them that.'

'And what do you do?'

'You know, at home. Minding the kids.'

'But what did you used to do? You mentioned an apprenticeship?'

She smiles indulgently, and it strikes me now why I'm talking to Sandra, why I haven't told her that the campaign is over, that she wasted her time by coming here today. Because I don't want to. I don't want to give up, and I want Sandra to give me a reason why.

How ridiculous.

'Oh *that*.' She holds up her hands to me like a magician, displaying each side. Her nails are a vivid aqua, as if her fingers are moving through water. 'You wouldn't know it from my hands, but I was a bricklayer.'

Sandra giggles, and I find myself laughing too: just because of the way she says it. I don't usually laugh like this. I don't usually laugh at all. My laughter is squeaky and consumptive-sounding. The involuntary series of jerks it causes hurts my ribs. I can see a look of concern on Sandra's face as I wonder if I'll ever be able to stop.

CHAPTER SEVEN
Baz Carroll

It's easy to talk when you know nothing about it, but I know loads of fuckers deserved to get rubbed out. The cops do *nothing* most of the time; sitting around scratching their holes. It's the fucking gangsters who are making the streets safer. At least they take out the odd madman, fellas who are making it dangerous for everyone. Loads of them out there. You wouldn't believe it.

Listen to me, would you? Talking like the hard man. That's not me; not at all. I don't know any gangsters or madmen. You hear stories, see blokes on the street, but I don't *know* them. They don't know me. I'm a nobody and that's the joke of it – now *I'm* the marked man. Them blokes from Georgia are fucking headers, they don't give a shit. There's no one to help me out, have a word, offer them a few bob for their trouble. They wouldn't take it anyway. And I don't have it to give. They'll want to cut me to ribbons for ruining their business and that's that. It doesn't matter if I was able to give them a million quid to make up for it. They'll still want to kill me because that's the way them mad fuckers are.

But they were the ones that wanted to get rid of that girl. They were the ones going on about how she was a pain in the arse, standing in the doorway of her flat, talking to the punters, asking them about drugs. Obviously not a copper, but it was bound to start putting people off. Bound to. And I'm the stupid fucker that happened to be there, desperate to get me gear while they're giving out about her and looking at me like I'm the man for the job whether I like it or not.

I could have had a different life, you know. Sometimes I imagine that there's this other bloke that's me and he's wearing a nice jacket and he's got a family and a job; all that. He's happy. I don't know if I'm happy, a lot of the time. Everyone says: Baz, he's a happy guy, a bit of a laugh. But often I'm just letting on.

But who cares about that? Nobody. I'll die and it won't make a bit of difference. A few blokes might say: that's a shame. But that will be it. Another casualty. And just because that stupid cow kept standing in the hallway, asking to be killed.

CHAPTER EIGHT
Carol Murphy

reemerge into the newsroom and realise that I never told Don where I was going. He'll think I've done another disappearing act. He's sitting at his desk, one arm resting on a tottering stack of papers, listening to Tim be outraged about something. The newsroom is open plan and germ-free. It could be anywhere, really, an insurance company or a software firm: lighting set at a level to imitate a spring day; grey carpet tiles which absorb the sound of footsteps; purple screens which afford some privacy, but not too much; windows firmly sealed to prevent the cold air getting in and the employees jumping out. It smells faintly of disinfectant. We keep tidy desks with the occasional plant or picture of the kids; all of us except our boss. Don's desk is almost devoured by monoliths of paper and books. He likes it that way. He says only real hacks have untidy desks; it means they are spending their time out chasing stories: not scanning websites or waiting for some pissed celebrity to write something stupid on Twitter. He says he misses the way it was when he started, with typewriters and phoning in copy. He misses the tangy odour of grease and hot metal.

Don looks over at me, his centipede eyebrows arched. He's already worried that I've screwed it up.

'Sorry,' I say, positioning myself to hide the wet patch on my backside. 'I went out to the park to make a few calls. Talked to the mother. I'm going down to Loughrea to interview her.'

I'm lying already. Other than my father, I haven't rung anyone.

'Excellent,' he says, with perhaps a little too much satisfaction. The centipede relaxes and stretches out. Don glances at Tim, who says nothing.

'I'll need a snappy,' I say.

Don nods. 'Swing past the picture desk and organise it before you leave.'

I go first to my own cubby-hole, the loose heel on my shoe clacking as I walk. I grab my bag and keys, wave goodbye at a few people, stop off at the picture desk and have almost reached the lift when I see Brian bearing down on me, his eyes glassy with concern. He often looks like he's about to burst into tears, which after a few drinks makes me want to mother him. Sort of. I pretend to look busy and vaguely hostile. Yet still he marches over, arriving just in time for the lift doors to glide back, revealing two blokes from sales talking loudly about car troubles. I get in and smile brightly at Brian.

'See ya,' I say.

He follows me in.

The thing is – Brian is a nice guy: tall, broad-shouldered, gorgeous skin and all in that boyish kind of way. How many times now? Four or five, always in my place. I tell him to go home afterwards, and he always does.

He's standing beside me, slightly hunched, hands hidden in his pockets. He smiles cautiously, like he's not sure if he's allowed to do this in a public place.

'I heard about your friend,' he mutters.

'Yeah,' I say, 'it's awful.' It doesn't sound as if I mean it.

'Were you close?'

'Hadn't seen her for years,' I announce. 'Didn't know her that well. She was a bit flaky, you know. Bit of a hippy. I mean it is terrible and everything, but somehow I'm not surprised. You know what I mean? She was just one of those people.'

'Oh,' says Brian. He sounds disappointed. I sound brutal.

The doors peel back and we all get out. The sales guys move off, still shouting about their cars. I pretend to search for my keys. I can't look at him now. I want him to take the hint, but he's still standing there; close enough for me to smell his soap, to hear his slightly-raspy breathing.

'Carol,' he says.

I keep searching.

'Carol, please look at me.'

He's like a little boy squaring up to the school bully.

'You're upset,' he says. 'That's OK.'

'No I'm not.'

'You wouldn't look at me.'

'I was looking for my keys.'

'No you weren't.'

'What?'

My voice sounds like screeching metal.

He opens his mouth and closes it again. To press my advantage, I produce the keys.

'Got them,' I exclaim. 'Now I must run. Have to drive to Loughrea.'

'I'll go with you.'

I'm stumped now.

'You can't.'

'Why not?' He folds his arms and stares at me.

'I'm working.'

'I *know*. I'll go for a walk or something while you're doing the interview. But I can keep you company while you drive. We can talk.'

I feel my face burn. Am I blushing? *Blushing?*

'I'm not coming back up. Staying the night down there.'

'Fine,' he says. 'I'll stay too.'

'No way.'

His head jerks back. I hold up my hands.

'I didn't mean it like that. It's just that I can't. I'm staying in her house. Manda's house. The dead girl. She was my cousin, so it's my auntie's place. You see, don't you?'

His mouth opens slightly.

'She was your *cousin*? My God, that's terrible.'

'Don't tell Don,' I say. 'Please.'

'Of course, of course.'

His hand lightly touches my shoulder and lingers there like an annoying insect.

'I'm so sorry,' he says.

'Well, yes. Thanks. Look, Brian, I've got to go. They are expecting me.'

'Yes, yes. And if there's anything you need, anything at all.'

I'm suddenly gripped by a deliciously irrational idea: behind all the sympathy, he's pleased. I've confided in him, told him something no one else in the paper knows. *Shite.*

'When you get back,' he says. 'Or next week or something. When you feel ready. Perhaps then we could get together and —'

I've half-turned from him, but spin back now. My fringe tumbles into my eyes, so I can only make out his outline as I hiss.

'Brian, do me a favour, like a good chap, OK? Just fuck off and leave me alone. You're absolutely pathetic.'

I walk away, my head filled with an imagined vision of Brian's face. And I know I've done a cruel, crazy thing; but somehow it doesn't register with me: like launching a missile which will kill people thousands of miles away. Instead I think that I really should ring my aunt before I arrive on her doorstep.

CHAPTER NINE

Rachel Belton

'I'm not sure if I was the only one,' says Sandra. 'I used to hear about other girls doing it, but I never met any of them. Didn't matter to me either way, it was just something I wanted to do – something I knew I'd be good at cos me da was a brickee: he used to let me help him when I was a young one. I knew more about it than any of the blokes on the course.'

She slides one leg over the other and gently swings it, flicking the shoe back and forth from her toes. They are mauve, low-heeled pumps with a spat-like purple strap across the sides. Her tights match.

'Daddy, now, he thought I'd be spending all me time fighting off the boys – and so did I, if I'm to be honest – but it was actually the opposite. They didn't know what to make of me, so they ignored it. Me being a girl, I mean. They just pretended that I was one of the lads and they all seemed much more relaxed when they did that.

'There was one or two who were a bit in love with me, I reckon. But that was only if we were on our own would I get them vibes. When the whole gang was together, I was like one of the lads.'

She looks over at me: a direct, pointed stare; as if I might be able to explain this.

'When I think of it now, it was a bit weird. But I suppose it was the only way they could cope with having a woman around. I mean, the stares I would get, the stares *they* would get: it was like it reflected on them as well, as if they did something wrong by letting me into the class in the first place. That sounds a bit paranoid? But that's what it felt like, at times anyway.'

Why am I listening to this women? Her story isn't *that* interesting. When Sandra has breathed the last syllable of her tale, will the world be a different place? Will I be different?

'I was as bad,' says Sandra. 'I met me husband, Pat, down in Galway where I did the course – he's a culchie and I dragged him up to Dublin! And for the first month we were going out I didn't tell him what I did. Said I was a hairdresser. I thought I might scare him off or make him think I was a lesbian or something. Really. In fact, I *didn't* tell him. He just walked past one day, and there was me building a wall. The face on him. But he got over it.'

She falls silent. She seems to be enjoying the thought of Pat's face, all those years ago.

'And did you work?' I ask.

'You know, I did! Never on a site. No one would give me a job on one. But lots of single jobs. There was a developer around here, Denis Hynes, I think he's still on the go. One of the few that are. I worked for him for over a year. I was good at it, too. But then the first baby came along and that was that, you know?

'I did build the extension on our house though.' She tootles a laugh. 'Baby in one hand and a trowel in the other. Not many mammies can do that!'

'Impressive,' I say.

Does that sound patronising? To my surprise, I find myself concerned about this. I want Sandra to *like* me.

'Would you ever go back to it?' I say. She shakes her head vigorously.

'God, no. Out in all weathers? Oh, no. But sure, even if I did, the work wouldn't be there, would it? That's all over now.

'Anyway,' she says, lightly slapping her hands together, 'I shouldn't keep you any longer.' We both stand, though I detect a reluctance in my body. I feel a light rush of frustration: as if there is something here that I'm missing; something to be achieved.

'Still,' I say. 'It was lovely to meet you. I don't often get the chance. Mary, Michael and Agnes keep me well protected.'

This is meant as a joke, but in Sandra it seems to provoke a slightly sickened expression; a distinct drop in temperature.

'Yes,' she says, not attempting to hide the sarcasm. The word lingers between us.

'Do you think they overdo it?' I eventually say.

Sandra shrugs this away. 'Where are they?'

So I tell her: about the girl getting pushed out the window and my picture and the quick evaporation of my electoral machine. Aidan Haslett goes to a meeting and doesn't come back. Mary, Michael and Agnes leave a note. Apologies, but we don't believe in you any more.

'Sorry I didn't tell you earlier,' I say.

'That's all right, that's all right. Sure, you must be in total shock. And all this happened today?'

'This morning.'

'Mother of God. And that's it, like?'

'I suppose. I mean, it's up to me to withdraw, but without any support, well. Not much of a chance.'

'Bastards,' says Sandra.

We both smile.

'Pardon the language. But you know, typical. From what I've heard. I was only doing this for a few months, to get out of the house, really, and because a few friends of mine were doing it and saying it was great craic. But to be honest, I didn't like it that much.'

She points at the table, where Mary, Michael and Agnes would usually preside.

'I couldn't warm to them.'

'Were they bossy?'

'Bossy? It was like being in a cult or something. I thought, like, that we'd get to meet you a bit or be out on the doorsteps, talking to be people about unemployment and that. But we weren't allowed. We'd get in trouble if we were caught talking to anyone.' She picks up her coat, rustles in a pocket, then signals me to sit down.

She hands over a weathered piece of card. 'See that? That's all we were allowed to say. No matter what anyone said to us, we had to repeat one of them things. Learn it off by heart. Mary, Michael and Agnes would have us in here, testing us like we were six-year-olds.'

The card contains a series of bland statements, most of which communicate the idea that I am indeed deeply concerned about whatever issue they have raised, though without indicating that I'm actually going to do anything about it. The key instruction is that canvassers should refer people to the leaflet. *Always, always, refer to the leaflet!*

'I thought it was a bit weird,' says Sandra.

She notices that I'm smiling now.

'What?'

'Well, it is funny because I've got the same thing.' I extract a curling sheaf of papers from my bag. *Candidates' Briefing Notes.* We have to learn this off, whether we agree with it or not. So we all stay "on message".'

Sandra widens her eyes and launches into another rant, though I'm not listening now. When they gave me the notes, I didn't see a problem. Actually, I saw them as useful.

Sandra's ability to keep talking is oddly impressive.

'...but I was interested to know what it would be like, you know? All the politics and that. Can't say I thought much of it. Too much like, I dunno, just telling people what they want to hear, just to get votes. Like, you know the way everyone says that the politicians are all out for themselves? I don't know if that's true, but I'll say this: it's no different to anything else. People say the politicians are corrupt but I think now that it's because the whole country is corrupt. You know the way people say: *I'll look after you.* We all know what that means. And everyone uses pull and all that. There was a family down the road from us when I was growing up and they all got good jobs in the bank cos they had pull. And if you wanted to get a job in the Civil Service, you'd go down to the local TD and he'd pull a few strings. Isn't that corruption as well? Sort of, anyway. That's why I think the country's in the state it's in. Anyone with money now, people always think: he must have done something dodgy. And if he's doing it, then I should do it too.

'All that stuff that the builders and bankers and politicians were up to, sure half the country would have done the same thing if they'd had the chance.'

She gives herself a little shake.

'So I stopped coming in last week. But they,' she nods at the table again, 'kept ringing me. Leaving messages about how I was letting everyone down and making out like I was some sort of witch. I only came in today to give them a piece of me mind.'

She stops now, and clamps a hand to her neck. She starts to chew her bottom lip.

'Oh my God. I'm so sorry, so sorry. All those other people leave you and now I'm doing the same, and you after being so lovely to me with the tea and the chocolate.'

The lip develops a tremor. Sandra is threatening to launch into a full-on blub. I hear myself saying, 'No Sandra, it's fine.' And the day I've had.

So much for discovering inspiration. Instead, all I seem to have found is that Sandra may be a little disturbed. My own fault for indulging her. I should have known better; I, of all people, should have remembered where I was.

I'm forced to coo soothing platitudes while Sandra remonstrates with herself for talking too much and listening too little; for blurting out without considering what calamitous damage her words might inflict on those within earshot. She presents it as a form of social Tourette's Syndrome: one that has wreaked devastation on the lives of those around her. It is something the baker husband has warned her about many, many times. Think before you speak, doll. Think.

I want to smile, to laugh again, but suppress the urge.

She holds up a trembling finger between us.

'I tell you what. I take it back. I don't want to leave. I want to keep on with the campaign.'

'Sandra.'

'No, no, I insist. Rachel, listen.' My name sounds strange in her mouth. 'Wasn't that the problem before? I was campaigning for you but I didn't know you from Adam, except off the telly. But now I've met you and I want to campaign for you.'

'Sandra, there is no campaign.'

She takes the briefing notes and folds them in with her canvasser's card, then rips them in half with her bricklayer's hands.

'Now. No more crap. We go out and say what we think. Deal?'

I pick up Sandra's coat and hand it to her.

'I'm afraid not, Sandra. I'm afraid not.'

Chapter Ten

Maurice Kiberd

The car in front is a bloody classic. She's looking at the workers on the pavement, then at a plane overhead. She's fiddling with the radio and she's talking on the phone. No hands-free; of course not. Bloody Lexus, less than a year old, but she can't afford to put in a hands-free? Some people still have money. She doesn't seem to be holding the wheel at all some of the time. Good thing we're not going fast, though she is going to have to merge into the next lane in a second, so she'd better start paying attention. Stupid cow.

Yeah, yeah, I know: this is the sort of thing taxi drivers go on about all the time. We're all full of opinions. It's a big joke. Not true, though. I know plenty of blokes on the job and they'd hardly say hello to you. But what's wrong with having opinions anyway? Thinking about the world around you? In this job you can't help yourself, what with all the things you see.

People just don't want to hear about it; that's the problem. Because they don't care. They're only out for themselves. That's what's wrong, you know. Nobody cares. That's what I think, anyway, and I won't apologise for it.

This one in front is just dying to cause an accident, so she is. Nearly has one getting into the single lane, waving her arms around like she's trying to take off. Then the phone is back to the ear again as we go round the old Ambassador cinema and she's stopping and starting and stopping; the brake lights are going off and on so much it looks like she's turned on the hazards.

So you see, this is what happens: because I'm concentrating on not running into the back of this idiot, I don't notice anything else, do I? If there's some sort of commotion on the street, I don't see it. All I know is that I'm stopped for about the tenth time on Parnell Street, I see a flash of blue in the right wing mirror and your man is in the back of the car.

He's caught me rightly on the hop. Normally, I don't put up with people just getting in without a word like I'm at their beck and call. They should ask, have a bit of respect. I often park up and tell them to get out. I pull them out if they give me any lip. But I'm stuck in the middle of this traffic, behind her ladyship in her Lexus. So instead I have a good look at the skinny face sticking out of his hood, and I say to meself: *I'll remember you, pal. I'll remember you.* Hard to forget, really. The state of him.

When you've been doing the job as long as I have, you can spot them. If the eyes are glassy or if they want the window open. The ones who say nothing can be bad. The ones who say too much can be even worse. But anyone could spot that this bloke is wrong. Sweat coming off him like he's just got out of the shower. He's looking all around like he's worried who might see him. Talking to himself – talking to himself – muttering and squirming in his seat like it's burning his backside. Doesn't say anything at first – not to me anyway – just gets straight on the phone, then hangs up and looks around again, twisting his body back and forth.

Sometimes I wish other people could do my job; just for a day or two.

Junkie. You can tell from the clothes. And the skinny faces and bloodshot eyes and even in October most of them have tans – from hanging around outside getting drugs or whatever. A lot of them like to go fishing, or so they've told me. Get the drugs and then spend the day staring into a stream. Some of them are all right, I suppose. I'd almost feel sorry for them. But this guy is a scumbag, no question. He's got those sneaky eyes that won't stay still in his head, and even when he's talking to himself I can hear that moany tone a lot of them put on.

Some people like to get all complicated about simple problems. I know what they're saying. Just because I drive a taxi, it doesn't mean

I'm stupid. If your parents were wasters or drunks, then you don't know any better. If you come from a home full of gangsters, the chances are you'll end up one yourself. Yeah, yeah. But what about when they're adults? When they see that most people don't go around robbing or killing or taking drugs? Do they still not know any better? How long do the excuses go on for, that's my question. Every skanger in front of a judge has some sort of a broken-home story to get themselves off. Human nature. People will always try to get away with it.

It's simple. It really is. You're either a wolf or a sheep, and most people are sheep, aren't they? Getting pushed around, getting mugged, getting your house broken into, getting talked down to by the government or all the people you meet every day who think they're better than you, all that; it happens because the wolves know they can get away with it. Because they are let get away with it. Believe me, I know. The things I see.

Don't get me wrong: most people are good, they want to do the right thing; they want to be *kind*. But that just makes them sheep, do you see? The wolves take advantage of that, every time. Only the other night I called into this garage where I like to get a cup of coffee. I like to mix it up between nights and days, just to change the routine, keep meself sharp. And every shift I start from a different rank, move myself around. I have a map in the house and a schedule. I know everyone because of that. Or everyone knows me, anyway. But whether it's day or night I take a break every two hours, to have a coffee or a roll or whatever, make sure the motor is all right, nice and clean inside. I could make more money if I just kept driving, but I'm not like that, am I? So I have these places I like to stop off, all mapped out in me head. They all know me.

Anyway, I stop off at this place, up at the back of Heuston Station where they stuck up all them fancy office blocks. Still half empty. The garage is deserted – it's the middle of the night – except for this group of young fellas banging on the windows and screaming at the bloke inside. No more than fourteen, I'd say they were. Where are the parents? At two on the morning?

So I slipped out the baseball bat I keep under the seat, walked over, cut the legs out from one of them with the bat and gave the other a smack in the mouth. Nothing heavy, but it sorted them, you know? I've sorted far worse, believe me.

They scarpered. The bloke in the shop – he's foreign, dunno from where – said he hadn't even called the guards. I call before but they take long time, he says. But then I turned around and I asked him: why didn't you handle it yourself? Young lads, they were, and you a grown man. Why didn't you come out and give them a couple of digs? He started waving his head around then and going oh no, oh no, I don't want trouble, no trouble.

But that's the problem, isn't it? Innocent people, good people, taking all this and not doing anything to defend themselves – that only makes the wolves worse, makes them braver.

That bloke was right about the guards though. I know all about that. Bloody useless. That's why scumbags like the one I have now think they can get in the back of the cab without even asking.

But it will change. That's what I think. People are fed up with everything. They're angry. Something is going to happen; something bad. I can feel it.

Chapter Eleven

Carol Murphy

The only story about Hazel I can think of is one Daddy used to tell, from which he seemed to get an acidic pleasure. Manda was just about to start a maths exam when she realised that she had forgotten her calculator. She rang home and asked Hazel to bring it in. Hazel arrived with the remote control for the television.

Dad used to tell it to get laughs, though I always suspected that he wasn't marvelling at Hazel's dottiness, but admiring her guile. As if she did it deliberately.

I'd forgotten about my hangover, but now that I have to drive – I have to concentrate – it kicks back in and thumps around my skull. There's a glue-like smell in the car which opening the window doesn't dissipate. I'm sweating, and everything around me seems dreamy and disjointed. My thoughts curl and cascade and every few minutes I arrive at what feels like a tiny moment of realisation: as if everything in my life pivots around Manda's murder and I'm just about to realise why; solve a huge cosmic puzzle. I don't though. I have a hangover. I shouldn't drink so much. I shouldn't lie to people who give me another chance. I should be honest with the people I love. I shouldn't be horrible to people who are trying to be nice.

Why did I scream at Brian like that? Have to apologise.

But I phone Hazel instead. She answers with a tiny, flat voice. She used to near-shout down the phone, as if she were a bit deaf; as if she didn't trust copper wire to project her words. Perhaps it's grief or shock or a few Valium, but it takes her ages to realise who I am.

She keeps repeating my name, Carol, Carol, Carol Murphy: as if she's never heard it before, yet finds it quite impressive.

I embark on a rambling spiel about how terrible it is and how great Manda was, but she doesn't seem to be listening, just emitting the occasional *hmm* until I've run out of things to say.

'You'll stay the night, so?' she suddenly barks.

'Well, if that's OK.'

'Of course you will! Sure, there's loads of room here. Just myself and Juanita. Pack some knickers and we'll do the rest. Bye, bye, bye!'

She's hung up before I get a chance to ask who Juanita is – Hazel, I remember now, has a habit of referring to others as if they need no introduction. I haven't even asked after Conor, or how he's taking the news.

Shouldn't Conor be there now, with his mother?

It's when I get close to Loughrea Town that I realise I've never driven to the Fergusons' house before; at least, with me at the wheel. On every other occasion it was Daddy driving, Mum beside him tunelessly singing some song on the radio and me in the back moaning, when will we be there?

Other than the GAA ground on the way in, I don't recognise one landmark. Nothing. Not that I can think of any, and even if I could they would have probably been demolished by now. Loughrea spread out during the boom years, and is now effectively a suburb of Galway City, subject to bad traffic, graffiti, abandoned half-built housing estates. I can remember when the trip here used to be a drive down the country – there was a distance to be travelled through humourless towns connected by snaky, pot-holed roads. Now it's difficult to tell where Dublin ends and everywhere else begins.

The town is a forest of election posters, the airbrushed faces crowding along both sides of the street. They're trying to look trustworthy or inspirational or angry. As I drive I sound out some of the slogans. *Fight the IMF cuts! We can rebuild! Jail the bankers!* They're not asking for votes so much as belief. *Time for change. A name you can trust. Working for Loughrea. Tom's team. Michael's team. Fergal's team. Making Ireland better.*

We never tried to *create* Ireland; we just assumed it would happen.

I swing onto the road to Galway. All I can remember is that it's on this side of the town, about two miles out, down a boreen to the left, beside a blocky building with no obvious function. Amazingly, I find it on the first go: before I even see the turn I know it's there, and once I'm on the gravel lane and over the railway lines, it's a bit unnerving to find it so dramatically unchanged. The awkward-looking trees choked by unruly bushes, the crudely painted sign, 'Private Property – No Entry'. I park, but don't get out of the car. The Fergusons' home is a crumbling Georgian block which once belonged to a bishop and, before that, some C-division Anglo-gentry. Bob, despite being an architect, never felt the desire to renovate. Any improvements were carried out by Hazel, and consisted of little more than the occasional badly applied coat of paint.

The house is the same muck-green colour, the drainpipes flaking: not more or less tatty than when I was last here (whenever that that was), but *exactly* the same; as if, down this little road, it's still twenty years ago and it's a bit sunnier – though the house is always freezing – and the same stringy dog whose name I never knew is lying outside.

I feel myself shiver: the feeling you get, Mum used to say, when someone walks over your grave. I get out my phone and take a picture; though I don't know who I will show it to. It's like I need proof that this place is the same; proof that it ever existed at all.

Chapter Twelve

Rachel Belton

Before I start the car, I study the walnut dashboard, the discreet assemblage of clocks and dials. This is a car Sandra will never own. She's gone now, but not before watching me slip onto the soft leather seat inside this glistening red vehicle. Doesn't matter what make it is. It's expensive.

She had a wild smile sizzling on her face. I don't know how she can do that; why she doesn't hate me. I would. We come from the same area, with much the same background, yet I can get into a car that costs nearly as much as her house. It's not the only car in our driveway either. It's the small one. From Sandra's point of view, the only difference between us is genetic chance. My life in a sentence: I'm pretty, so I met my husband, Daniel. He pays for everything now.

How can Sandra not resent me for this? She didn't seem stupid; certainly brighter than the usual. She must have read the magazines and seen all the other former models like me. None of them marry bakers. They marry celebrity chefs and playboy barristers. It's a vicious Darwinism, where the pretty and the rich triumph. Another version of the corruption she was talking about. The rich and the pretty, keeping everything for themselves.

Naturally, I was never the same as them. No, I married for love. It just so happened that the guy I fell in love with was the most eligible bachelor in Ireland, the son of a billionaire dynasty built on biscuits and spaghetti hoops in Europe, property in Asia and wireless networks in Africa. Even now, I don't know how much they are worth. Daniel definitely doesn't.

The car purrs into life and I wonder: how can I be sure of my motives? Is it more difficult to love a man who brings you to Cineworld rather than the Maldives?

I didn't know who he was! I kept saying this afterwards. It was at some promotional do for a mobile phone company, where I was required to have my photograph taken while posing beside a man dressed to look like a Blackberry. I noticed Daniel watching me, offering the threat of a smile: as if he had done some modelling too and knew how it felt. He prowled around me for twenty minutes until the over-tanned marketing troll said to my cleavage, 'Rachel, do you know Daniel Gallagher?'

I didn't. I'd never heard of him; though from the way the troll fawned it was clear that I could have read about Daniel in any of the papers; that the mobile-phone company had sponsored him on some expedition and that he was recently returned from Asia. These facts were laid before me while Daniel gently winced.

He didn't look rich, though it's not always that easy to spot. Shabby but rugged, like a gardener or an organic farmer. Eventually the troll went to get us a drink and I was able to say: I know I should know, but what is it you do? He waved this away. Why should you know? He leaned in slightly. I caught a scent of vanilla. I'm a mountain climber.

Well, it's not the usual is it? How many times have you heard that as a chat-up line? But there were other qualities too, apparent even at that meeting. He was confident, without being showy. Witty, in a quiet way. But also sad: not the sort of sadness triggered by a specific event; more a way of being.

I don't know how he got my phone number, but he called the next day. It's Daniel, you know, the mountain climber? He invited me to a reception for the Special Olympics. Not quite a date, but a clever use of neutral territory, to get us a little more comfortable. I liked that. He was careful not to pose in any photographs with me or even to spend too much time chatting while the gossip hacks circled.

Our first proper date was a few days later, at a cosy restaurant in Wicklow, which we always meant to go back to, but never did. It's closed now. Of course by then I'd googled him and knew who he was. Don't know how I'd never heard of him before. There were dozens of newspaper profiles, which at first sketched him as a rich brat, but later on, after he'd led a climb up K2, as an unassuming hero. And was I happy that he was such an interesting guy? Of course I was. Did it please me that he was disgustingly rich? I didn't think about it, not that I can recall. Perhaps I had assumed I would end up with someone like this anyway. Perhaps I had.

Neither of us wanted news of our relationship to end up in the papers, so there were plenty of trips to Paris or Bonn or Amsterdam. He'd tell me about his sprawling family, many of whom seemed quite mad – or as Daniel put it without any irony, steeped in their passions. His mother and several aunts were big into spiritualism: séances, contacting the dead, all that. There was some relation who had known Madame Blavatsky. When he was a child, it was normal to come home and find groups of wild-eyed women in colourful headscarves jangling crystals or chanting at the walls. I asked if he believed in it and he shrugged and said, there may be things we can't see – but we can't see them, can we?

And at the time, this was answer enough. At the time, I was taken more with how the rich are different: how the downy privilege allows them to take a providential view of life and regard those who cannot afford it as somehow cynical. It was charming, in an odd way. Yet Daniel didn't seem like that; at least not entirely. Climbing mountains, I suppose, had taught him that bad things could happen.

I hadn't met any of his family, and he hadn't told them about me. I hadn't told my family either, though there was nothing unusual in that. We both felt that discretion was a good thing: our sacred secret. We didn't discuss it; we simply came to a mutual conclusion – and the ease of this helped us to recognise something in the other: a practicality we both liked. Jetting around the place does sound romantic, I know, but neither of us were romantic people; so I thought. I saw us as people who lived in the world as it was and negotiated around the problems. I told him about my background, about the books I liked to read. To him, I expressed many of the thoughts I had never said out loud before, and he was impressed. *Jesus, you're a brainbox.*

And he was sexy and gently funny and brought with him a stillness I had never enjoyed before. I can't remember there ever being some moment when we declared our love, but I do remember once, sitting in the spring sunshine outside Café Les Éditeurs. We weren't talking. Just sitting, looking around. And it struck me how comfortable this was. I looked over at Daniel, and he smiled back. And that was it.

We'd been together in this way for fourteen months when I decamped to New York. I didn't ask him to follow me. I knew I would be there for at least a couple of years, perhaps even permanently. I didn't have the right to ask. But he came, as I knew he would.

I wonder how Sandra would react if I told her this story. Would she find it romantic or sickening? Maybe I'll tell her, just to see. We will be spending a bit more time together now.

Yes, the bricklayer did it. Not because of her hysterics, which seemed to wash away as soon as they arrived; but because it occurred to her how it *could* be done. The canvassers had volunteered for the Party, and few of them had any affection for Mary, Michael and Agnes. So Sandra rang her friend, who rang another few people, who rang more people in turn, and now we have forty-two of them committed to meeting tonight in a local hotel. I've booked a room. I'm going to use my money now. Daniel's money.

We've agreed to throw away the briefing cards. Tonight I'll run through some of the issues I'm interested in, the ones I wanted to campaign on, but other than that, the canvassers can say whatever they want. That will get us a few headlines. I'll be the honourable candidate, choosing honesty over spin. Aidan Haslett would be proud. The Party will be furious. God knows what the canvassers will start promising on the doorsteps, but that doesn't matter. I know I won't get elected anyway. But at least it won't be an embarrassment.

I'll be giving Sandra and these women what they want, what Aidan told me to give them. I won't solve their problems. I can't. But that doesn't seem to be important. After Sandra the bricklayer had rung her friend and the replies had started coming back and she had jigged with joy, it struck me that all she wanted, what any of these people want, is unfocussed hope: not for anything specific; just the thing itself.

Chapter Thirteen

Carol Murphy

step over the dog, let myself in and hear a sigh crack from my throat as I enter the hallway: still painted a revolting enamel blue, still smelling of thick damp, still dominated by a huge picture of a stern-looking Padre Pio, one gloved and bloody held held aloft, as if dismissing anyone who stopped to look at him. I quickly turn right and enter the kitchen, where there is the first sign of change. The Formica cupboards are badly scratched and chipped. The table and chairs are different to those I remember, though in the same style: nothing matching. There's an arthritic armchair swamped under rugs, a range pelted with dust, and beside that on the mantelpiece, something else which makes me sigh: an old photo of the Fergusons, taken before Bob departed. Conor and Manda are squirrel-faced kids, while Hazel and Bob shyly hold hands, grinning with the confidence of those who have no idea what the future holds. The photograph is faded – it always was, as far as I can remember – but for some reason no one could ever explain to me, it had been turned into a jigsaw. A puzzle, even to themselves.

This kitchen was always far too large for a family this small; it could double as a tennis court, and sometimes did. Hazel, it seems, has continued with her habit of never throwing anything away: years-old bags of sugar, spices, herbs, cake mixes she never attempted, as well as piles of not-very-clean-looking pots, some of them containing unidentifiable vegetables and other substances. Hazel, I now recall, can't cook. An almost pathological collector of recipes, she would follow the first few instructions, get distracted or a bit pissed and burn the lot. The more burnt or inedible the food was, the more she would attempt to distract from this by giving the meal a French name. *Boof Boogy-non avec le pomme de terre de la Galway.* Her French was awful too. Yet never once did the kids, or our family, ever challenge Hazel's ability to cook or her belief that she spoke French like a native. They would gobble up anything put in front of them and cheerfully pronounce it delicious afterwards. Even as a child it was apparent to me that the kids were indulging the adult, not the other way around. The Puzzle Family.

To my right, one of the cupboard doors is plastered with post-it notes with one-word declarations. Bin! Cheque! Dog! There are letters and bills, some of them going back years: a note about a school production of *The Sound of Music*. Manda was in that, I think. Drove me mad singing that song, 'I am sixteen, going on seventeen'.

I get a mental flash of standing in a field – the one on the other side of the house towards the lake – and I'm crying, weeping so much I can barely see, but making no attempt to wipe the tears away. Conor is in front of me. I can't see Manda but I know she's nearby, and even though Conor looks embarrassed or even scared, he's shaking his head. No.

When was that?

I've been looking around the kitchen for a good thirty seconds now without the person at the sink noticing me. She seems to be washing a narrow vase, but having difficulty getting the brush deep inside. She's mouthing resentfully under her breath, as if this process disgusts her.

'Hello?' I venture.

She looks around and makes no attempt to hide her annoyance. She's about my age, I reckon, though it's difficult to tell; she's dressed in a sagging pair of track suit bottoms and a billowing tee-shirt.

But the face: coffee-coloured skin and eyes as black as death. You can imagine her enrapturing any man she wanted. And stabbing him in the chest if he disappointed her. I try to be grown up, but there's a shake in my voice.

'You must be Juanita,' I say. 'I'm Carol.'

She drops the vase and brush in the sink. Not wearing any rubber gloves. Her hands are meaty, like a man's.

'Yes?'

She rolls the S so much it comes out as *yezzz*, like a Mexican gunslinger. She folds her arms and looks at me as if she's already spent half the day dealing with strange women wandering into the kitchen and introducing themselves. You're no different.

'I'm Carol? Hazel's niece? I rang earlier. Is she around?'

Arms still folded, still glaring at me, Juanita says nothing. And it seems as if she's prepared to keep on saying nothing until I either challenge her to a duel or walk out of the house.

'Carol, is that you? My God! Carol! Carol!'

Hazel erupts into the kitchen. She's wearing some sort of fedora-type hat and a huge shawl draped around her shoulders. She looks like a Latin American revolutionary. It's not lunchtime yet but already she carries a nearly empty glass of white wine. She marches to the fridge and extracts two bottles, both open. One she empties into her own glass, the other she uses to fill a tumbler, all the while nattering frenetically.

'Things are bad enough – of course things are bad enough – but now the doctor is ordering me to drink. Good for the stress, he says. And for the heart too. Tannins or something. And just the one glass has virtually no alcohol in it.'

She hands me the tumbler.

'So it actually balances itself out. Go to the Mediterranean and it's what they have been doing since Roman times. Isn't that right, Juanita?'

Juanita says nothing. She's gone back to muttering and washing the vase.

'She's terribly upset,' shouts Hazel. 'She loved Manda. Only met her a few times, but she was crazy about her. Just goes to show, doesn't it?'

She pauses, and I find I'm shocked: astounded that Hazel can say her name so easily; as if Manda died years ago, or never died at all.

Hazel leans up and delivers three air kisses, which provide enough air to suggest that she has already exceeded her wine quota for today. She takes a massive gulp from her glass and beckons me to follow. We take a step into the bowels of the house, a maze of awkwardly shaped rooms, of which only one would be in regular use at any time. The rest were for storage or were, in theory, play rooms or study areas. Once she set up a meditation zone with thick drapes and dozens of candles. Inevitably, the candles set fire to the drapes. Actually, the only rooms downstairs which the Fergusons really used were the kitchen and the room with the television in it. Even before plasma screens and all that, the Fergusons always had a gigantic telly.

Hazel halts and shrieks. 'The cheque! What did I do with the cheque?' She shoots around to face me, as if this is a subject we've been discussing for some time. 'What did I do with the cheque, Carol? We have to leave it out for the man. Oh my God!' Hands to her mouth, wantonly distraught at the prospect of the man not getting his cheque, Hazel rushes back to the kitchen, leaving with me with a smile on my face. She's like a familiar song I haven't heard in years.

I'm surprised that I remember so much. I can only recall a few specific visits. But there must have been more. Standing in a courtyard, waving goodbye to my parents as they drive off in the salmon-coloured Mercedes Dad used to own. He loved that car.

In the kitchen Hazel is still shrieking, but Juanita sounds calm and authoritative. I hear her mumble, and Hazel reply, 'Oh did he say that?' Then silence, clothes rustling.

Hazel returns, looking a bit chastened. Her wine glass is full again.

'Juanita says he doesn't need it yet. And why would he? He knows who we are, for God's sake, known us most of our lives.' Now she seems mildly annoyed. She takes a sip from her glass, sighs, then studies me with furrowed concern. Hazel likes to psychologically assess people, usually guessing at some non-existent upset which she then sets out to heal.

'How are *you* Carol? 'You must be *very* upset. I know how close you and Manda were.'

She says this as if it were a secret she has known about all along.

I consider being honest: telling her that it is many years since I've seen Manda. But that would be cruel; and I've done enough of that today. I consider telling her that both myself and Dad are upset. But that would sound hollow and formal. I want to say something nice about Manda, but all I can think of is when we were little girls playing with our dolls and how in her games she always needed to perform a rescue; give the homeless a home. And I'm just about to say this when I feel it like a cold slap: an internal wrench which shudders through to my stomach.

I shouldn't be here at all. How could I have come? I'm here to feed off Hazel's sadness in the hope of ending my own; of reviving a career I don't even want.

I should leave. But I can't move. And as Hazel awkwardly hugs me, I feel tears trailing down my face and a quake of something like grief: for Manda, for everything that has been lost.

Hazel is hugging and whispering 'let it out, dear' and I keep thinking, though I don't know why: now I'm home.

And I see Conor shaking his head: No.

CHAPTER FOURTEEN

Michael Bourke

When I walk along the street, nudging my way through the crowds, do you know what I see? I see what's not there. I see the eyes of these people misted over by the visions which keep them an inch or two away from reality; the unrealisable dreams that they will get off the dole or win the Lotto or go to heaven when they die. I see the fabulous assumptions that everyone else is richer, happier, has a fully rounded existence. All politicians are corrupt, all policemen incompetent, all priests are perverts. And while these phantoms keep them distracted, they don't see the cracks in the pavement, the cool drops falling from the sky, the slow wasting of their own bodies.

It is a system of belief; though, like much else, it arrives in kit form: it can be knocked together without too much thought or effort. Yet it is enough to provide the spiritual certainty most humans need to huddle beneath. The *ekstasis*, the stepping beyond the physical bonds of the Self, is provided by the marketplace: through alcohol, drugs, sex, deafening music. They think they find God when they are looking in the mirror.

I and my kind are, of course, avatars of much of this; black-suited mystics. Don't be fooled by the ravenous media: our reign is not completely over. The collar still has its power.

Not for everyone, of course. Some are lost to us. The white Irish, the younger ones, still dazed that the warm bath they grew up in has suddenly gone cold: their eyes skate over the priestly uniform when they pass me. They don't say anything, but wonder if they should because, hasn't that sort of thing been banned or something? I mean, like, I was just there and saw this priest. It was so *random*.

Illiterate, spoiled brats.

But at least they are timid: they look, rather than speak. They're too scared now, and fear anything unfamiliar. Before, there were a series of buttons to press; bringing inevitable happiness. Now they have no idea what the outcome will be. The certainty has flaked away.

No, it's the tough working-class ones, the ones from around here who will voice the abuse. When they're drunk or high on God knows what. You're an effing pervert. Ye should be ashamed of yerselves. All of ye.

I occasionally engage with them. Explain the very obvious fact that because *some* priests are paedophiles, it doesn't follow that *all* priests are paedophiles. Because *some* bishops covered it up, it doesn't mean that *all* bishops covered it up. But such scorching logic is usually wasted. It rarely affects a pause in the abuse, a momentary rethinking of their dim world view. Usually, it prompts more of the same: my adherence to rules of grammar providing the final proof that I am indeed the nonce they suspect me to be.

Such is my lot. I am a priest, after all. It is my vocation to accept both the praise and blame, to bring hope to those who haven't found it elsewhere. There are the elderly, who want for little more than reassurance. Yes, there is something after death. Yes, the church is the same. I am the same. They want to see a priest in his collar, somewhat remote, even a bit frightening. Not jolly or casual. I give them that.

But it's the foreigners who adore me. They are the ones who retain the awe, who see the link between me and the man-god; a path back through history to the time the Universe first exploded. To them, I am made of stellar stuff; I know the secrets of its power. Perhaps I activate some speck of tribal memory: a time when religion was not the province of celebrity deities but the impersonal force which preceded everything: Manya for the Aryan tribes, later known as Brahman; Ilam for the Akkadians of Mesopotamia, later known as Elohim to the Hebrews.

Giving It a Name: that's what started the trouble.

For the Africans, for the dusky-skinned, I've probably replaced some malevolent witch doctor. But it's in the eastern Europeans too, especially the Poles, for whom I am Sacrifice and Solace, ready to give up my life so as to spirit their persecuted cousins past vicious barbed-wire borders.

Like the God of the Old Testament, such are the many faces of Me. No: the many visions of Me. For I do nothing to encourage these projections, save wear my collar and conscientiously recite the liturgy. I simply let myself be who they want. It is a passive business. I have no such ambitions for myself. No ambitions at all.

How could I? I have no Self buried beneath these images, no aspect of my being I secretly crave to express. There's nothing there. I have excavated everything out, leaving me as hollow as the smallest Russian doll. No anger. No fear. No passion. I have risen above them all.

Yet, to my surprise, memory had also fled. When I happened upon the girl, I couldn't remember. The Last Rites. Extreme Unction. Viaticum. She fell from the sky, and for a time everything about me seemed to vanish.

Afterwards, I made my way back to the presbytery with relief. But I did not feel a settling, a comfortable readjustment to my *modus operandi*. The manufactured tears still sat in my eyes, and something similar to anguish hovered over me like a bird of prey.

Even physically, I had changed; or more correctly, I seemed to have regressed. Years ago, I put considerable effort into improving my posture, but now that contemptible slump was back. As part of my self-improvement programme, I had also corrected a weakness in my voice, cancelling my tendency to mutter in a curling rural accent. *Look Daddy, it's Pleiades.* Yet when I thought back to the conversations I had conducted at the skip, I realised that this flaw had also reasserted itself. The anguished ladies I had spoken to had to lean in to hear; some had even asked me to repeat myself.

This sudden change in my bearing was not the end of some brief sophomoric pose. I initiated these improvements more than twenty years ago, to better equip myself to deal with a puzzling and hostile world. I am forty-two years of age, a man of some, I like to think, intelligence. Yet this one event has flung me back two decades.

It is a realisation so devastating it brings me to a shuddering halt on the pavement. I stand on the corner of the street which leads to the grey behemoth that is Saint Audeon's church. Across the road, surly-faced young women stand outside their skinny Corporation homes. They smoke cigarettes and hang out washing, and scan the area as if searching for threats. Young people in colourful hats tramp past me. They carry plastic bags into which they have squeezed bottles of cider and tins of spaghetti. In the other direction, the Chinese and Koreans work with the devotion of the ancient Daoists. Every few weeks another premises opens, with a name like *Little Joy* or *Green River*. What was once a huddle of shops and restaurants has swelled to occupy half the street. Their area now: a hamlet of selfless enterprise amidst a city of anger and blame.

I have walked these streets for some years: a visible comfort to those who want it. I know each rusty door number, every drain clogged with burger wrappers. Yet I am a timid boy again, making a poor fist of pretending confidence. I am tempted to immediately recommence the voice exercises I indulged in relentlessly as a young man. I would perform them anywhere and everywhere, just to let the world know how little I cared about its opprobrium. But now I am reluctant to do so. People know me here, and a mad-sounding priest is the last thing they need.

I make for the house at the back of the church, which I share with the parish priest, and my putative superior, Father Jack Kelly. Yes, Father Jack. A man so oblivious he lives as a punch-line. At my age, and with my intelligence, I should have my own parish, but some years ago I came to realise that the latter quality militates against advancement in the Irish church. You can be clever, of course. Sly, cunning, cute as a rat: just never admit to it. The Irish church is in the main run by intelligent men who devote much of their energies to projecting an image of themselves as profoundly unintelligent; something at which they succeed spectacularly well. The rest are genuinely unendowed with brain-power, but have somehow led their colleagues to believe that they are also masking their intellectual gifts.

Thus any member of the clergy who does not take part in this charade is automatically deemed suspect; and at a time when so many of my brother priests are suspect anyway. Intelligence is regarded as contraband.

A foolish and perhaps arrogant young man, it took some time for me to learn this. For a while in the seminary, I even flouted my learning: mistakenly believing that this would please my superiors, that they would welcome debate. I had read too much outside the curriculum. I presented ideas full of doubt and speculation to gimlet-eyed men long since convinced that all questions had been answered.

I had no friends to warn me about these indiscretions, though over the years one or two priests did broach the subject, tangentially: addressing me as if some mind-burning mental illness had afflicted my judgement. *Are you well, Michael? Are you happy? Is there someone you'd like to talk to? For guidance? We all need guidance.* I finally realised what they were edging towards; the poison hidden inside their words. Shut up. Stop talking this way.

The realisation of this truth brought me to address the issue of my own ambition, though happily this was not a difficult question to answer. I didn't get into the priesting game to spend my time blowing hot air at conferences or kow-towing to the pontiff. Indeed, I have taken some delight in informing others that I have no desire for a parish of my own. Few have argued that it should be otherwise. They have left me where I am, largely forgotten, and as far as they know not causing any trouble. I quietly toil at my secret ministry. So we are all content.

Not that my station is without difficulties. Father Jack Kelly – 56, red-faced, former drunk – is part of the school which believes that the only path to inner peace is to admit to some terrible secret pre-dilection. For Father Jack, there always has to be one: drugs, women, boys, gambling or (his specialist subject) alcohol. Father Jack monitors me at all times, waiting for the happy day when I collapse in a howling hump and admit to some appalling secret life, which in Jack's mind will make me all the more human and therefore all the more divine. Addiction is next to godliness.

He is not a bad man, and occasionally I wish I could please him in this regard: I am tempted to make up some demonic compulsion, though I doubt if I could do a convincing enough job.

But these concerns are not foremost in my mind as I stagger back up to our home, wondering if I appear differently now; if a haunted expression has insinuated its way into my features, replacing the stony serenity I have projected for years. Once bathed, I will spend some time in front of the mirror, remaking myself again; remodelling my expression as a mechanic might rebuild a car.

This is all I can think of as I let myself in, yearning for the refuge of my room and bath. But I am ambushed. Here stands Jack, eyeing me with a furious attention; as if he had been expecting this, or something like this; which of course he has.

'What's wrong?' he says, his unruly eyebrows jiggling, his movement towards me so rapid I fear that at any moment I'll be enveloped in a crushing, Old Spice-drenched embrace.

He has tried this before: the direct confrontation. *What's wrong, Michael? No point in denying it. Never kid a kidder.* But on each occasion I've been able to bat away such obvious attacks with a smirk or even a sigh. This time, though, I know my face is failing me. It sits in the old default position of uncomprehending surprise; as if every breath brings with it a new horror. I notice too a tremor in my hands. I attempt to deploy my voice, but nothing emerges save a choking sound. And now, my God, he *is* swooping in wide and low for an actual clinch, his chubby arms crushing me with the raw power of his hungry compassion. Just as he has rehearsed in his mind, I, like a bad actress, blub on cue, smearing snot and misery over his dandruffed shoulder while he whispers to me.

'There now Michael. There now. Whatever it is, we'll face it together.'

CHAPTER FIFTEEN

Rachel Belton

So why politics? Why one party rather than another? Why run for office when I could have joined some moaning, dishevelled pressure group or organised a petition for neurotic housewives? Because I'm not like that. I'm not just passing the time.

Politics is a filthy business. Even in the short time I was campaigning, I heard stories about various affairs and abortions I was supposed to have had. Democracy is not an uncontested good. Do most people vote after they have studiously weighed up the competing fiscal policies or proposals on education or justice? Of course not. They don't have the time; or the interest. They vote for themselves. Because they want a playground built at the end of their street or because they lost their job or just because they like the look of a candidate. They vote having virtually no idea what they are going to get or how it might differ from what they had before. Sometimes a national crisis might bring a large enough group together. But they are Plato's mob, thirsting for blood, not the result of a thoughtful consensus. This is the neat contradiction politicians sell: voting is a selfless act, carried out for selfish reasons.

It's what Sandra said to me, in her own way.

It was a simple calculation. Politics provided the best opportunity to achieve what I wanted. Even for Daniel and I, money didn't solve all problems. And I thought it might be fun. I thought I'd be good at it. I knew I would. You can call that vanity, if you like.

I was guided by simple common sense: if you want something, get to where the power rests. The Party is going to romp home:

everyone knows that. If you're elected, you have power. Straight off, bang. You've moved up the tree to a point where at least they have to pretend to listen to you. *The right to be heard does not automatically include the right to be taken seriously.* I'm full of quotes. But at least they have to listen; and if you're stroppy enough or lucky enough, well.

Such a pity. I *would* have been excellent at it. I even feel it now as I walk into the creamy hotel and see the flushed faces of the canvassers turn to me, energised and intrigued by this revolutionary turn of events. I'm wearing a D&G pinstripe trouser suit which is business-like without being too obviously expensive. You don't want to distract them with the clothes. I'll be calm, and conciliatory. I'll be honest about what happened, but I won't bitch. I'll tell them my hopes of being elected are slim, and they won't believe me: this will energise them even more. I smile gently. I exude unfocussed hope.

I see Sandra waving, but I don't move directly towards her. Instead I circulate among the canvassers, almost all of them middle-aged women, their faces unused to smiling. I thank each for coming and say: don't worry, I'll explain everything. They pump my hand; one or two even hug me. I pose for a picture. Already, they like me.

Daniel proposed a few months after I had moved to New York. He'd just returned from some adventure in Nepal, where he'd nearly broken his neck and lost his little toe. By then we were living together.

I said no; screamed it, actually: which is unusual for us. We are not big on emoting. I said it was because he was a slob who could leave his filthy clothes on the floor for weeks without ever noticing a smell, which is true. Daniel says that spending so much time in small tents with other rancid mountaineers has destroyed his olfactory gear. He likes to refer to body parts as *gear*. I told him I would never marry; I would never be that dependent on another person. And he nodded at me as if he completely agreed. He said yes, yes.

The ceremony was in a small chapel in Nevada three weeks later. They played 'The Wonder of You'. I completed my MBA. I had a vague plan to do something in renewable energy or perhaps to teach, though after the wedding I realised that it was the study itself I enjoyed most; that my sparkling new qualification might not have any connection to the rest of my life. And anyway, I was in my thirties now. Without too much discussion, we both knew we wanted to start a family as soon as possible: something I said I could not countenance unless he gave up mountaineering. It seemed a lot to ask, I know, but our life together would have been torment otherwise. And he agreed. Happily, he agreed.

Was it wise to ask? I don't know. It was part of what led to everything else: to his fevered belief that the world is far fuller than we realise.

The women are standing up to applaud after my little speech. I'm not sure where the words came from. I surprised myself. I said, 'You know how bad things are. We're all looking to see bankers jailed and politicians turfed out of office. But do you know whose fault this really is?

'It's your fault.'

That sent a hum through the room.

'It's your fault, and it's my fault, for letting this happen. For voting and then forgetting about politics; for letting them at it. This election is not about me; it's about you. It's about us. About sacking them all; and all of us starting again.'

Sandra is dewy-eyed. A woman beside her with a plummy accent is proclaiming *About Time! Yes! About Time!* And I'm thinking about how to get away now, back to my baby who sleeps in his room; his breath rasping because he has a bit of a cold. He is watched over by Bob the Builder and Spiderman, and all his dead brothers and sisters.

Chapter Sixteen

Michael Bourke

Naturally, Father Jack can't admit to his disappointment, but the truth of it is writ large across his sclerotic features. Alas for him, my upset was not caused by groping in the trousers of some nonplussed child, but by an event almost completely in the realm of Chance.

He herds me into the kitchen, gives me tea laced with brandy (he seems to receive a vicarious pleasure from dispensing alcohol to others) and demands I relate every detail of this morning's events; which I willingly do; such is my need to make sense of it. But even as I speak I am nauseated by the sound of my nondescript rural muttering; as if my very words are fearful of emerging into the world.

I can see he wants to ask about this dramatic change in my bearing; that his once straight-backed and clear-voiced curate seems to have shrunken in on himself. But he is too taken up with my story, which at first he seems to doubt.

'Out the window?' he says. 'Into a skip? A wedding dress?'

This last detail I am not entirely sure of, female clothing not being a subject I have ever felt the need to pay attention to. I'm mildly offended that he thinks of me as a person who would. I fear he will press me on this, but I am rescued by the sound of the front door bell, and the arrival of two gardaí, here to ask me more questions I cannot answer. Did I see the girl fall? Did I know her? Did I see anyone run from the adjacent buildings? I answer each question in turn, aware of the whiney catch in my voice. Fr Jack is now open-mouthed with amazement. The arrival soon after of some parishioners who have already heard about my drama further deepens his letdown. Not only have I failed to reveal a character flaw today, I have gone the other way: I am made of the stuff of heroes, valiantly battling to comfort a dying girl while others stood around uselessly.

But my radical change of demeanour still needs to be attended to. Saying mass in the morning will be intolerable if I cannot change back, but the sudden crowd in our house (now even more locals have arrived) is making me feel ill. I do not like this attention, this cloying concern. I am vulnerable without the armour of my carefully wrought personality which, if available to me now, would have presented a man almost casual in the face of such horror; such is the strength of his faith: a living example of how the mind is the only bulwark against life's assaults. Instead I mutter and blush, a victim like everyone else.

To escape, I escort the gardaí to the front door: one a gaunt man of about my own age, the other a plump, younger woman who wears a slightly offended expression.

'Father,' she says, rather brusquely. 'Thank you for your time.'

I merely nod, not able to endure the sickly tone of my own voice. The man glares at her significantly; indicating to us all that our business is not yet complete. She says, 'Are you sure you didn't know the girl?'

'Yes,' I say, baffled by this line of questioning. 'Should I have?'

'Well,' he chips in. 'Apparently she was part of a prayer group.'

They stare at me, as if this statement alone will provoke an irresistible tumble of memories.

'Yes?' I say.

'In your church,' he says, nodding towards the front door. They used to meet there every Thursday night. You didn't know that?'

'I was aware of a group.' I want to scream at myself, tear off my malfunctioning mouth. These questions should be answered in bold, precise tones, even with a hint of irony. 'I have met one or two of them,' I mumble. 'But Fr Kelly and I didn't take part. It was their group. They just used one of the rooms. I'm afraid I never met... I didn't know. I'm sorry.' Even my grasp of English is evaporating.

The guards remain mute, their silence apparently thick with judgement: as if by knowing this girl, I could have prevented her death. Preposterous.

I remain in the hallway after they leave, my heart pummelling against my ribs, my breathing shallow and laboured. The sound from the kitchen has swelled to a clamour; the mercy dash to ascertain my well-being seems to have devolved into a party, with Father Jack no doubt liberally dispensing the beer and spirits.

I'm not going back in there. I need to retreat, to reassemble myself. It is rude to simply disappear. Nonetheless, it must be done.

I didn't know this girl. I have no need to apologise for that.

Damn the people. I creep up to my room and lock the door behind me.

CHAPTER SEVENTEEN

Baz Carroll

Loads of times I've been stupid and got meself in trouble. I can do that without trying. But every time I try to sort out meself out, I get the same result. Fucking chaos.

It's like my whole miserable life has been leading up to this, crouched in the back of this taxi and the driver looking at me funny and I'm dialling Martin's number with me shaking fingers – cos he's the cunt who got me into this mess really – but then knowing I can't go to him because that's the first place the Georgians are going to look. Easy to find out where me and Martin live. Half the people who buy off them will tell them that. I run through a list of names in me head and can't think of anyone to help me. My world is too small. They're too scagged out to be of any use or they're stupid or I wouldn't trust them anyway. Scared of the Georgians.

They'll cut my head off if they catch me. I mean for real.

The sweat is pumping out of me and the scabby-headed driver is giving me the dirty eye and asking, 'Where are you going? Have you made your mind up yet?' I keep taking the phone out of my pocket an putting it back again, and for a few minutes I can't talk. This is what it's like: knowing that no matter how shitty your life has been, it's better than getting battered to death with a concrete block by some maniac. At least if you're breathing, there's hope. You just might drag yourself out of the hole, make yourself better, do something, as she always said, *productive*. Over and over she used to say it, until I wanted to punch her. Not that I ever did. I'm not a violent man. But it drove me mad because she was right. She was always right. Even if I do the right thing, I do it wrong.

I don't know if she'll talk to me or let me into the house. But she has to let me see Holly. She has to do that.

So I tell the driver I want to go to Pleasant Lane in Finglas. I say I'll show him the way and he shrugs as if he thinks I've made up the address. Cranky cunt.

I sit all quiet then and try to calm meself. It helps a bit. I'm not panting now, though I still feel hot. I feel like the motor inside me is revving too hard and I can smell it burning. There's a banging pain in me head, like I've got a hangover, though I only had a couple of cans last night. It hurts to look out the window, at the tatty buildings swooshing past and the people on the pavements walking, smoking, standing, talking, waiting. Might never see any of them again. Might never see the roads or the traffic lights or get the smell from those cardboard trees the taxi drivers hang on the rear-view mirror. Everything for the last time. Fuck's sake.

I ring Martin. He sounds half asleep and of course the first thing he comes out with is, 'Did you get it? Did you get it, bud?' Bud me hole. I can't even trust you now. But I do him this favour anyway. I tell him it's all gone to shit and the Georgians are out for my blood and the first place they are going to look for me is the flat. If they catch you there they'll beat you senseless cos they won't believe you if you say you don't know where I am. They'll beat you senseless anyway.

Martin doesn't say anything. I can hear him breathing. He does that: breathes through his mouth, which makes him look stupid.

He's not that bright, to be honest.

'So what do I do?' he says.

I tell him to get the fuck out of there. Run away. Hide where they won't find you. Go down the bog or something. Get out of Finglas. They'll find you in Finglas.

'Oh, OK,' he says, like it's not a big deal. 'What are you gonna do?'

Never mind, I say, sounding like I've got some big plan. Martin's pathetic, but even he would laugh at me if he knew that all I can think of is to go and see me ma.

CHAPTER EIGHTEEN
Carol Murphy

I didn't have to tell Hazel that I was writing about Manda for the paper. She suggested I do it.

Made it easier, I suppose.

It's a standard broken-hearted mother piece, though for the picture she insisted on wearing the hat and shawl, floating back into an armchair and staring dreamily out a window. The photographer whispered to me 'Do you think she could *pose* a little less?' I shrugged, and for a moment I hated my aunt.

It made the front page, along with a four-column headline.

NOTHING CAN BRING BACK MY MANDA

Heart-broken mother speaks of 'overwhelming grief' after daughter's murder.

My first front page in, oh, how long? Can't remember. It's what I wanted, I suppose.

In the car on the way back to Dublin I sneak fearful looks at it while slugging back Red Bull and Paracetamol. The flow of wine was relentless for the rest of the afternoon, followed by a dinner consisting of something burnt and French-sounding. Then Hazel asked, as if it were an entirely new idea, 'Why don't we have a drink?' And out came the brandy.

Juanita didn't take part, at least not much. She kept leaving the room as if there was something far more important she and Hazel should be doing, and would be if I hadn't barged in. At some point I did feel irritated enough to mention it, but Hazel kept distracting me with conversational excursions: about flowers, a bald tyre on her car, John McGahern (about whom she seemed to know a lot), a missing cat, flowers again, the local butcher ('A nancy boy! And him a butcher!'), teenage binge-drinking and the political system in South Africa (about which she seemed to know nothing at all). She didn't seem to get any more drunk – at least, not to my pissed eyes – though her inability to concentrate multiplied with each glass.

Yet she did manage to tell me a bit about Manda. The year of her Leaving Cert she had announced she was going to be a nun, and spent quite a lot of time in a Poor Clares convent nearby. Then she had changed her mind and decided to become a social worker. She had done an 'excellent degree' according to Hazel and was going to go on to do a doctorate but decided to go travelling first. Around Europe mostly, Hazel said, though she was vague about where her daughter had been, or when Manda had returned to Ireland. 'Oh, a year ago, at least.' I was going to ask why she hadn't then gone back to college, but Hazel had already begun to rattle out a story about how a passing priest had given Manda the last rites while she was still lying in the skip. Must talk to him.

My phone clangs, giving me such a fright I wobble the car a little. I clear my throat and hope I don't sound hungover.

'Good piece,' says Don. There's a smile in his voice.

I shoot past signs for Ballinasloe. I was there once, though I can't remember the context. I was working. Standing outside what used to be the pen factory, empty now, but still with the big sign. *Cross. Since 1842.* Yeah, someone is whispering in my ear. You'd be fuckin' cross if you were stuck in this kip.

'Thank you,' I say, trying to sound pleased.

Two hundred and fifty words of tabloidese. I've reduced her; formatted her grief.

'On your way back up?'

'Yeah, another couple of hours should do it.'

'Listen, I'm going to text you a name and number. Tim gave it to me. He knows one of the detectives on the Manda story.' Already it's the Manda Story, as if they all knew her. 'He's expecting your call. He has some good off-the-record stuff on the crime scene. That was the window of her flat she went out.' I feel a bit ill, and swallow to make it pass. Hazel never mentioned it was Manda's flat. I never thought to ask. 'There's also a priest,' I say. 'He gave her the last rites.'

'Excellent,' says Don. 'Talk to them today.' He pauses, as if considering whether to say something else. 'You're doing a good job, kid. Keep it up.'

'Thanks,' I say, feeling sick again. I hang up, then open all the windows of the car.

When I feel a little better, I dial the number Don sent me. The detective won't talk about Manda at first. There's a preamble about how great Tim is, what a fabulous crime reporter he is, what a laugh Tim is and how everyone on the paper must love him too. He seems to be demanding that I prove my credentials as a member of the Tim fan club; he even skirts close to being creepy. 'So how *well* do you know Tim?'

I giggle and agree with everything. I feel sick again.

He finally arrives at the point, though little of what I hear makes me feel better. Pictures of her lying in the skip are already on *Irishscandals.ie*. Someone falls out a window. People take photos with their phones.

The detective thinks Manda was murdered by a druggie. A gang of dealers, eastern Europeans, were living in the flat across the hall from her, though it might have been someone visiting them, perhaps someone who was short of a few bob. The eastern Europeans have disappeared.

He has discovered a lot about Manda – more than Hazel was willing or able to tell. Manda didn't go travelling so much as decide to become a full-time anti-globalisation protestor: a group called the Wombles, who apparently organise a lot of the rock-throwing whenever an American president comes to Europe. According to the detective she had no fixed abode for about eighteen months, moving from town to town to help organise the next riot. Never been arrested though, which either shows a degree of cunning or perhaps she simply chose not to get involved with the rough stuff. Perhaps even with anarchists, women still only get to make the tea.

She returned to Ireland, signed on the dole and appeared to do nothing – no protests or anything political to bring her to the attention of the guards. All they could find was that she had joined a prayer group attached to a church in the north inner city, and through that another group encouraging teenagers not to take drugs. Nothing militant. Christian do-gooders.

I suppose she must have become disillusioned with radical politics and turned back to Jesus. It sounds like Manda. She always wanted perfection; for everyone to be saved.

The cop reckons that the anti-drugs work must have had something to do with her death. She'd moved into that flat only the month before, and her neighbours were well known in the area, so it's unlikely Manda didn't know who they were. There were no signs of a struggle. The front door was open, but hadn't been forced. The television was on (Sky News), and the window was broken. In the hallway outside, they found a small bag of heroin.

'The girl opened the door to some skanger, there was a brief struggle and out she goes. Our boy saw she was dead, panicked and ran off. Didn't even take anything. Dropped his drugs, he was in that much of a funk. We have three people who saw the guy at the window from street level. But all they can tell us is that he was wearing a hoodie. Like half of Parnell Street.'

He sighs, as if disappointed by how predictable it all is.

The M3 toll plaza appears up ahead and I begin to slow down.

'One odd thing, though. She'd written something on the mirror. Used a marker or something. Hang on.' He rustles through his notes. 'Yeah, here it is. "Lucifer's Hammer will bring us together." Mean anything to you?'

'No. Well, I know she was very religious. She wanted to be a nun at one stage. Perhaps it's in the Bible or...?'

'Hmm. Really? That's interesting,' says the detective in a tone which implies someone hasn't told him everything. I hear him writing.

'There's a band called Lucifer's Hammer. Dutch. Anarchist connections, so it might be that. Not anything to do with how she died, probably, but a lot of this now will be explaining every single fecking detail about her life. Pain in the hole. But we don't want some smart-arse barrister making out she beat herself up and jumped out the window. You know.'

'Yeah,' I say, though I'm not quite listening. I can't remember going to bed last night. I remember Hazel screaming *Is that the time?*, then being at the top of the stairs and being grateful that she hadn't put me into Manda's old room. Then seeing Juanita, dressed in a different tee-shirt and just her underwear. She brushed past me without a word and walked into Hazel's room, where the light was already off, and I thought: that's odd.

EXECUTED BY DRUG LORDS

Police believe plucky Manda was watching drug pushers

By CAROL MURPHY

PRETTY Manda Ferguson was executed by drug gangs – that's the belief of gardaí investigating her murder.

Detectives have learned that Manda (30) had been part of an anti-drugs group, and had told friends that she wanted to take on the drug pushers head on by attempting to talk them out of their deadly trade.

Manda plunged to her death three days ago on Dublin's Parnell Street – while still wearing the bridesmaid's dress...

CHAPTER NINETEEN

Maurice Kiberd

So as soon as he gets into the taxi, I know he's dodgy. That's where the story starts.

Though, I dunno. Where does a story start? People I've had in the car yak like they're scared to shut up. Get a bloke in and he starts going on about how he's on his way to get tickets to a match, but then he's telling you about his childhood when he used to be handy at the GAA and how he had the varicose veins out last month but the leg is still killing him so he can't go for the walks like he used to. Used to walk the dog in Fairview Park, though the dog is dead now. Lovely little dog. Bit of company, you know? And we've arrived there and I've turned off the meter and given him back his change but his mouth is still moving and I can't hear what he's saying anymore. It's just mixed in with all the other noise: all the talk and cars and planes and drills and sirens. Yeah, yeah, yeah, come on. Out. I'm losing money.

So maybe I should start with when I was a nipper. Maybe all the things I done brought me to this.

Unlike a lot of people that drive for a living, I take what I do seriously. I know the damage that can be done. I've seen enough of it. Not on me, mind. Nearly twenty years at this job and not a scratch. On me or the car. Proud of that, I am, and not ashamed to say it. Some of the younger lads on the ranks slag me about it, but I know they're only messing. They don't go too far. They know better than that, and they're trying to be professional too, most of them. There are the amateurs: teachers, fellas on short time, guards even. They rent out the plate and you see them at the weekends, sitting at the rank and looking confused. I don't talk to them. If they talk to me – usually with some stupid question – I say: if you were a professional, you'd know that, wouldn't you? They don't bother me much. Word gets around.

So I have to concentrate on the road. Well, no: you don't just concentrate on the road, you concentrate on *everything*. Are the drivers on either side of you paying attention? Are they going to drift into your lane? Is the car behind too close? Is there some idiot or some child trying to run in front of you? I've seen it all. I used to say things. Sometimes, if it was safe, I'd even get out of the car, right there in the middle of the road, walk over and knock on the window. They'd be looking at everything except me, then act all surprised when they'd see me beside them. Only open the window an inch or so, like there was a smell outside and they didn't want it getting in. You'd see the way their chin would tremble or they'd start swallowing a lot or the way they'd lean away from you: scared I might reach in and throttle them. But I wouldn't do that in the middle of the road. Not stupid.

All them people hiding in their cars. They need to find out what's going on, to see what I see. I know I keep saying it, but it's the truth. When I was a nipper, I mean, five or six, me ma read me this story about a little boy lost in the forest at night. The branches were so thick he couldn't even see the moon. Every time he took a step forward leaves brushed across his face and arms, and when he stopped walking he could hear rustling and whispers. He tried running but that didn't work, so he stood still and squinted into the blackness and eventually he could make out that the trees were moving, that they were crowding in around him. Because these trees had minds, or whatever. And eyes. Each tree had one great big eye that slid open every night, with a big black pupil in the middle and squiggly red veins at the corners. Scared the life out of me, that story. Wouldn't let Ma read on so I don't know what happened in the end, if he ever got out of there. But driving around town at night, I often think of that story, you know what I mean? The darkness changes the buildings, the streets, everything. Places that are nice during the day become, I dunno, *evil* at night. Everywhere smells of grease. Like the buildings have eyes, like they're watching the people on the street, who aren't really people any more. They're animals, fighting with themselves. Blood and puke everywhere. They're not having a good time; it's like they're trying to have a bad time so they can get all the poison out of themselves and throw it at each other.

That's what it looks like to me, anyway. You can't get any sense out of them when they're rolling around in the back seat. They can just about remember their address, and all I'm worried about is that they don't make a mess in the back seat or do a runner. It's all about survival. Things I've had to clean up.

When I first started driving, I couldn't believe what I was seeing. I was even scared a bit. Me. Scratching me neck until it bled. But after a while I calmed down and knew I'd be all right. Got through worse. But sometimes you forget and start to think like a sheep, don't ya? Think of yourself as a sheep and that's what you are. I was thinking of meself as I used to be: the quiet kid with the scaly skin who didn't want to tog out for sports because he knew what he'd get from the others. Lizard Boy. Pox Face. Manky Maurice.

Manky Maurice: that's what it ended up as. Everyone had a go at giving me a name, but that was the one that stuck. Manky Maurice.

So I take a deep breath and say to your man, 'Where to?'

He ignores me at first, still poking at the phone.

'I'll pull in so,' I say. 'Just down here when I get out of this traffic. Shouldn't be wasting me time, pal.'

The head springs up now.

'No, no. Sorry, sorry.'

'So where to?'

He gives off this big sigh, like answering a simple bloody question is too much for him. I'm still thinking about pulling in.

'Finglas,' he says. 'Pleasant Lane. I'll show you.'

Pleasant Lane? He must be making that up. In Finglas? I make a show of locking all the doors in the car. Does he think I'm stupid? If he's going to do a runner, he's got his work cut out for him today.

Me ma went down to the school about it and everything – unheard of in those days – and pleaded with the priest to let me off from sport.

But the old bastards didn't listen to a word she said. A few names won't hurt him.

They were right, in a way. I was never really battered, because when it was bad and spread up me neck and onto the backs of me hands, no one wanted to touch me. They couldn't bear to.

Funny, it took years for me to cop on that it wasn't right for them to be treating me like that. Not that it made any difference. Didn't get me a pal or make anyone listen to me. All me life, people don't listen to me, or people like me.

But I don't mind any of that; I don't. They can ignore me if they want. I know what's going on; I know I'm not going to be a sheep like the rest of them. I'm ready. That's the most important thing, you know. I could have stayed at home, scratching. But eventually I learned that you don't have to be like that. I learned that from me father. He was a bastard.

I can't bear to look at you. Get out of me sight.

He wouldn't say it every day: the mood had to be on him for that. Sometimes he wouldn't say anything for days. He'd sit in his chair – and it was *his* chair. Woe betide you if he found you in it. He'd just sit there, all still, one hand covering each knee, his greasy hair sticking out from the bottom of his baldy head. And he'd just stare: like he was watching the telly and the programme was so good it was hypnotising him. Ma would have to talk to him the odd time – to ask for money or to put the dinner in front of him on a tray – and he'd look at her like he'd never seen her before. Everything around him – the walls, the seat, the carpet, the world outside – was a shock.

Very strange, I know. Though to us, at the time, it was normal.

Me ma didn't say a word about it, because I reckon she preferred it that way. With his other mood, you could feel it when you walked in the door: he'd have that bulgy look in his eyes, and he'd be shouting at her, slapping her, telling her she was fat. Which she wasn't. He'd slap me too, if he could, though Ma would usually distract him so I could get up the stairs to me box-room and him roaring at me: you disgusting little freak, you diseased urchin! He was always saying that I wasn't his son, even though I was the spit of him; accusing Ma of all sorts which of course he'd follow up with a few slaps.

I'd get into me pyjamas and into bed, thinking that if I pretended to be asleep, I'd be safe. I was young. The room was tiny, just enough space for me bed and the dark brown wardrobe I didn't like to think about at night. The room always smelt a bit of smoke, on account of the window being so close to the neighbour's chimney. The wallpaper was pale yellow, with all these pictures of bears in a circle, doing a dance around a campfire. Just that picture repeated over and over and over again. One time I tried to count all the bear circles on the wall, but I couldn't do that because some of them were behind the wardrobe and I didn't want to go over there and look. So I counted all the circles of bears on the three walls I could look at. Seven hundred and two. Then I started counting each teddy, but I soon realised that this was stupid because there were six teddys in each circle so all I had to do was multiply the number I got before by six. Four thousand, two hundred and twelve. After that, I tried praying. I'd put the pillow over me head and start saying sorry to God because this was all my fault. I wouldn't even say proper prayers: just sorry, sorry, sorry. One night I said it over three thousand times. Didn't stop him though.

No matter what kind of a battering he gave her, Ma would still come up to me afterwards, so I could have me bath. In coal-tar, you know. Disgusting stuff, but we got used to the smell. She knew the exact temperature that I liked. She'd scoop up the water and pour it over me shoulders. I'd be talking away about school or some comic I liked or whatever, and she'd just say hmm, hmm, yes, love. She was listening to me, I know that – sometimes I used to test her – but she also wasn't there. Scooping that water over me and the lovely tinkling sound it made let her get out of the situation, you know? Go some place else for a while. Hardly blame her for that. We never talked about what happened downstairs. What was there to say?

But soon I was too old to be getting baths from her, and I would miss that little time with me ma. There was something calm about the house after a major screaming match. Him downstairs, chain-smoking and muttering, heading back into his silence; and me and Ma safe upstairs, with her rubbing cream into my itchy skin. My always-itchy skin.

Left by meself upstairs, I wasn't calm. Whether he was having a go at Ma or not, I'd be up in the bath seething. Angry all the time,

I was. I'd think about every dig that was made at me, from that day and going back months. Kipper Face Kiberd. I'd dream about how I'd get them back.

The odd time she'd whisper that Da wasn't well, that he had a lot of problems. He's a very sensitive man. A sensitive man.

I didn't get any of them back. I mean, I did make the odd attempt at fighting, but it was pathetic. I didn't think I had it in me. I thought I was a sheep. But then – I must have been fourteen or fifteen – I started to notice the changes: there was this massive pair of shoulders sprouting out of me, and when I took sly looks at the others in school, I noticed that I was much bigger than most of them.

They wouldn't touch me on the skin, but I would get plenty of shoves going into the class room or if we were queuing up for something. So I started experimenting. If I knew a shove was coming, I'd stand rigid and I realised that it was dead easy to stop them from knocking me off balance. They couldn't do it. Right, I said to meself. Right.

I was never one for studying the books, but I started studying the scraps. Whenever one broke out, and all the lads would be standing in a circle, urging them on, I'd stand there and tell myself to remember what it was the winner did to give them the edge. And you know what? There wasn't much to learn, really. It was simple. Every scrap would start with two lads shoving each other, then swinging their arms hoping they'd connect. They'd usually end up wrestling, still scared of getting a belt. This was the most important thing I noticed: they almost never got a punch in – they didn't *aim* the fist at all. Just swung their arms around in a mad panic.

You also knew who was going to win in the first minute: it was always the one with the most confidence. The other would already know he was finished, but it was better to get a bit of a battering than to run away from a fight. Wolves and sheep.

I'm determined, I am. I didn't know that about meself until then. I spent the next few months practising me punch, figuring out how to make it hurt as much as possible. I already had the big spade hands I have now. The same hands me da had. And I learned it was better to lean into the punch, and not to hesitate. One big punch. Wham.

It's all over. But just in case, I'd spend twenty minutes every day in front of the mirror, slapping myself until tears were rolling down me cheeks. To get used to it; so I'd be able to handle the punishment and keep swinging. Did me the world of good, that. The world of good.

We're out of the city centre now and he's calmed down a bit. He's not saying anything, just leaning his head against the glass and staring out the window at the buildings sliding past. And I can see it in his face: the hardness, you know? The eyes still flicking, looking for the next stroke to pull. Whatever had him upset, he's long forgotten about it now. He's got a big hook nose and that junkie tan, though his skin is blotchy and has one or two little scabs on it. I wonder does he have skin problems too, though I'm not going to ask. There's a meanness to this one. For pig iron, I say, 'Nice day, for October.'

He shrugs, like this is the stupidest thing he's ever heard. Yeah, a meanness.

One morning I went to school and I knew I was ready. I walked in the gate, got a shove from one of the bigger kids, so I did nothing about that. But then this little snotty fella in me own class called me scabby and tried to trip me up. Cool as you like, I turned around and lamped him in the face, hard as I could. One punch. Beautiful.

He didn't fall over. He just bent double, his hands over his face and all the blood dribbling through his fingers. For a few seconds there was no sound, or that's the way I remember it: like me fist crunching into his face had turned it off. And I remember looking up from him and all around the playground, at the dirty red-bricked wall, the black metal bike shed, the fence with the holes kicked in it – and at all the faces. Not looking at him now, but at me. At what I had done. What I might do to them. It felt funny, I dunno, but it was the first time I felt part of the place. All them lads who'd been kicking me out of their way for years, who called me Manky Maurice, they were all looking at me now. Yeah, hello. Broke his nose, I think.

I was dragged off by one of the priests. He gave me a few slaps, but I knew his heart wasn't in it. He knew the score. At the end he gave me the speech about turning the other cheek and if you ignore them they'll leave you alone. I looked him in the eye and said: I've been doing that for years and it hasn't worked. He said nothing. Nothing he could say.

After that, for a while, there was a fight nearly every day. I started to look forward to it. It was like they were panicking, trying to put me back in me place: like they were scared I'd put them where I used to be. I'd say I fought half the boys in my class; gave a few a hiding without them even saying anything. Even the older kids left me alone. They probably could have beaten me, but they were too scared to take the risk, see?

A few kids, the tougher ones, sidled up to me trying to be pally. But why would I pal around with them now? Just because I could stuff them? I'd spent too many nights in the bath, thinking about what they done on me. I didn't need them anyway. There was no more slagging, and I felt good about meself. I was good at fighting, I tell ya. Really handy.

I kept to meself. Sometimes, if I saw a small kid getting a bit of a going over, I might step in; just point the finger and say: leave it. But not much. You can't go fighting other people's battles, can you? The priests should have been stopping them, shouldn't they? I kept meself to meself. I mean, at break time I might play if there was a game of football on. But that was it.

At the weekends I'd read me comics – I loved Spiderman and all that, all the crime-fighting ones – do jobs for me ma and practise me punching. Should have tried boxing, really, but I didn't want to wear the singlet and have people looking at the psoriasis. They wouldn't have said anything to me face. But still.

We arrive at your man's house, and I must admit I'm surprised: it's not like Finglas at all. Lovely little cul-de-sac of bungalows. Not new, but not old or falling apart. Looked after. No litter, no burnt-out cars, no needles. A lot of houses with flower boxes in front of them. There's no one about, but you get the feeling that this is the sort of place where people are happy to stand and chat to each other, to let the children play outside. But in Finglas? I can't believe it. I thought he was making it up.

Don't get me wrong: I'm not suddenly getting all warm and cuddly about this article. As I say, you get a sixth sense about people when you've been driving for a while, and this individual feels all wrong; totally wrong. Especially here. He doesn't fit here.

'Nice little street,' I say. 'This where you live?'

He ignores me and goes into the same routine as all the other skangers: pulling all the change out of their pockets and making out that they're so poor that they'll be starving if I make them pay the whole fare. I never fall for that one. Never. If they say to me: *I dunno if I've got the fare, boss.* I say: *then you shouldn't have got into the taxi, should you? Definitely not this taxi.* They usually cough up after that. This fella is trying to pay me in five-cent coins, thinking I'll let him off. But I won't. I'm waiting for me money. I see your man's eyes flicker as he notices the crusty skin on the back of me hands. But he says nothing.

Some of them mention it. Some of the junkies. *Jaysus pal, what did you do to your hands?* As if I did it to myself. As if I made a choice. Drug addicts, saying this to me.

He gets out without saying a word, but not before giving me this little look that he doesn't want me to catch, but I do: like he'd stick a knife in me and take the money back if he had half a chance. But the look only lasts for a second and I know he's not going to do anything. The junkies are always cowards. They'll only do something if they're desperate. Pathetic.

I don't feel sorry for them, though. Oh, no. No one made them take the drugs, did they? Their decision, so they can't start asking other people to help them out, can they? Not me, anyway.

He slopes down to a house at the end of the lane. Doesn't even notice that I haven't moved away yet. The house is painted white. It has flowers in pots and a child's bicycle outside. There's an election poster in the window. Probably the home of some bloody do-gooder that'll believe whatever crap he's touting around the place. He's definitely heading for this house. He's staring at it.

Now he stops and starts looking around. I pretend to be filling out my call sheet. He doesn't look at me for very long, but he's definitely waiting for me to go. He doesn't want any witnesses.

Would he be here to rob the place? Seems odd, a junkie getting a taxi all this way, just to rob a house. Easier to grab a handbag in town if he wants money for drugs. Here to do worse then?

But no: he isn't the type. And he's stupid. Now he's walking past the house, thinking he's fooling me. Definitely up to something. So obvious.

But what can I do? Can't drag him down to the law just because he looks dodgy. Can't take matters into my own hands. I'm in a taxi. Too easy to find. I know all about that.

This is exactly what I've been talking to you about. Something is going to happen, definitely, but the only person that cares about it is me.

I could just sit here. No that's stupid too: he'll only come back when I'm gone. I could try warning the people in the house – no, that would be crazy. Another mad taxi driver. I don't want them calling the cops on me. Last thing I need.

Your man might be acting all shifty for an entirely different reason. His girlfriend might be in there and he might be shy, or something like that. That's bull, I know, but still. I don't *know*. And I've a living to make. The dispatcher on the radio – the new girl, I keep forgetting her name – she's already looking for me.

So I take another look at him. Blue hoodie. A&F written on it. They're expensive. I'd say that was robbed. Filthy-looking blue jeans, white trainers. Skinny little face with the tanned skin and them sneaky green eyes. He has bushy eyebrows, which makes me think of pirates. The hair is short, I think, though I'm not sure. He never took down the hood. I'm trying to take a picture with me camera phone but I can never get the thing to work. He's too far away anyway. I wait for a few minutes more, because I want him to look at me; I want him to know. But the girl is back on the radio again, Four Seven? Four Seven? Maurice? Where are you? I pull off. I hope that house is empty. I hope he only wants to rob it. He's a junkie. A coward.

Yeah, I know. I'm all talk and then I don't get involved meself. I do nothing. I'm like all the people that get in the back of the car and start mouthing off about the state of the country. *Someone should do something!*

But you can stick your oar in and do more harm than good. Believe me. Suddenly you're the bad guy. This is what I think: the cops or the government or whatever – whoever is really running the shop – they don't want people to get involved, do you see? They want people to mind their own business, no matter what. And they'll make life difficult for you if you do otherwise. Took me a while to realise that, I can tell you.

All you can do is stand up for yourself. Did at school and me life there was completely different. But it never dawned on me that I could do the same at home. That didn't happen for months, or maybe even a year after; can't remember exactly. What I do remember is me, this big strapping lad lying in the bed with a pillow over me head because I didn't want to be listening to the aggro downstairs, and suddenly it comes to me: I can change this. Simple. I started to feel better before I'd even done anything. I think I was even smiling a bit when I got to the bottom of the stairs.

Stopped smiling then, though: he had her up against the wall, his left hand squeezing her throat and with his right hand he was trying to unbutton her dress. It was blue with these kind of wrinkle things across it. Ma liked her dresses. She'd say to me: don't I have great legs, Maurice? Funny, the things you remember. Me ma had long auburn hair, always perfect it was, but now it was sticking out all over place like she was after getting an electric shock. Massive streak of wet mascara down her face.

So I just stood there, until he saw me, until he yelled *go to bed!* But I didn't move. Me ma was looking at me the whole time, but said nothing. I suppose she wanted me to go back upstairs as well, except she knew I wasn't going to. We never talked about it afterwards. But she must have known this was going to happen, sooner or later.

He let me ma go then and yelled *go to bed!* again. Still I didn't move. I wanted him to move away from Ma. I didn't want him to fall on top of her when I decked him.

Christ, he went down easy. I thought I might have to hit him three or four times, but two punches did the trick – and when he stood up after the first belt, I don't think he was even going to try and hit me back. He stayed on his hands and knees then, saying *what? What?* Like he was surprised, like he couldn't understand how this could happen. I turned around and told Ma to go to bed.

The next day things were back to normal, the three of us crowded around the tiny kitchen table slurping our breakfast and saying next to nothing; except this time he had his massive shiner, and I noticed that his hands were shaking when he picked up his mug of tea. And then he stopped eating altogether and started making this sound like he was choking or trying to get sick. But it was neither of them things: he was crying, his face in his hands, his shoulders going up and down and him wailing like a little girl.

I didn't know what to do. I looked at Ma, but she wouldn't look back at me. She was standing beside the cooker, staring at the back of his head but not trying to go over to him or anything. And she didn't look upset or disgusted: more like she was curious, like she wanted to know what might happen next.

I got up and went to school, and when I came home he was gone.

'Your father is gone,' Ma said. And that was it. Never saw him again.

CHAPTER TWENTY

Michael Bourke

My parents were well-intentioned people who, after my eventual birth, were content not to provide me with any siblings. We lived in rural Laois, in much the same manner as everyone else around us: quietly, in a brownish house, once the home of a farmer. The farm was long gone then; the few fields my parents owned leased out to men with caps and a severe deficiency of teeth. During the day the sky was usually a chalky white, though at night a constellation might occasionally reveal itself.

It was this which would rouse my father from his sagging armchair and out into the blackness of the adjoining field. He with the giant tube balanced on his shoulders, scanning the land around him as if we were engaged in some shocking act of sedition: he did not like any of the neighbours to observe him enjoying his hobby. In that grey place and time, as uniform as Stalinist Russia, even an indulgence as innocent as stargazing could be regarded as suspect. Looking at the stars? What would you want to do that for now?

I would come up the rear, carrying the charts and torch. The telescope was built by my father, loosely based on the Dobsonian design and with a 12.5-inch glass primary mirror which he later replaced with a more conventional model made of Pyrex. These details are still lodged in my mind, having heard and reheard them many times. The quest to build the perfect telescope seemed to enthuse him as much as actually mapping the skies. Like my mother, he was never one to squander words. But once in that field, he would babble like an excited schoolboy; while I, the actual school-boy, remained largely mute.

My job was to stand and listen, the charts in my hands, and pro-claim the right ascension and declination. I was required to be adept at reading the charts, to know what constellations are visible at vari-ous times of the year and occasionally to recall the catalogue object numbers of the some of the brighter stars. All these duties I fulfilled with a weary efficiency: for we were not here, I felt, to indulge a pas-sion, but rather to escape. Even to stand shivering in a field was for him a distraction from our daily life of drudge, of wetness, of stale ham sandwiches, of walking in muddy boots back and forth to the house, fingers red from the cold, to find my mother sitting in the darkened, cabbage-smelling kitchen, waiting to be told what to do.

To be in that field was my father's *ekstasis*: a leap outside the foggy monotony of who he had become. *See that star, Mikey? Thousands of light years away, and we're all made of the same stuff.*

At school I would endure the break-times in the company of a small group of lads. The misfits. The fat one, the one with the lump on his forehead, the possible homosexual, and I, the murderously shy young man with the squashed nose, peering up at the world through hooded eyelids. We would stand and talk, mostly, trying to look com-fortable with each other: as if this was the place we chose to be. We helped each other fill the anxious minutes between classes, when the Darwinian nature of the school was most unleashed.

But we were not friends; we never were. Each drizzly evening I would arrive home, relieved to be away from them as much as that rotting husk of a technical school where they ladled out the sorrow-ful drone which passed for education. I would sweep past my silent mother and flee to my room, where the solitude I craved like an addict awaited me.

I have always known that I am different; I have come to admit some lack in me where I do not crave the company of others. Even as a small child I was content to play by myself, and openly resented attempts by my parents to have me socialise with my snot-nosed peers. I was precocious; perhaps frighteningly so. By the age of ten I had consumed every book in our house and demanded more.

Books presented a reality far preferable to the sepia world of my family: one which held out a hope of understanding; of a neatness to life. This is the contradiction I have always lived with: while in my room, buried amongst the books which I devoured without any system or judgement, I loved the world and its inhabitants, despite their flaws. It was living, breathing reality I found difficult to stomach. People disgusted me: each individual coming up with a new reason to prompt this reaction.

I disgusted myself most of all: for my intolerance, and for my grotesque physical form; my short, squat body, my piggy eyes and mangled nose which, my parents proudly informed me, I inherited from some long-deceased great-uncle. I worked hard at reforming myself into a more tolerant person. I tried prayer, confiding in priests, inviting my fellow school rejects to my home, but each attempt only seemed to increase my allergic reaction.

God is the supreme spirit, who alone exists of himself and is infinite in all perfections. I would recite this catechism formula each day, assuming it held out some hope for me.

I eventually resolved to hide these inner failings, to find a way to present another Michael Bourke to the world. Curiously, it was my parents who brought me to this decision. With them, I was never the bookish shy boy, but the over-clever, insolent son who could barely constrain his impatience. Sometimes, to my shame, I didn't constrain it at all. Alone with my parents, I could be insufferable, but with a certain authority; a confidence that didn't seem forced. If I could harness the best aspects of this, I reasoned, while erasing the obvious signs of intolerance, I could transform myself. I wasn't naive enough to believe that such a project could change the trajectory of my life or reshape my inner landscape. But it might make existence tolerable.

Once this decision was made, I managed quite quickly to meta-morphose into a person who was, for the most part, a mature and considerate son. My parents were alarmed at first, but eventually pleased. The other modifications took considerably longer. I estab-lished a regime of speaking and breathing exercises, of walking with books balanced on my head; and from the blinking putty that was me, slowly sculpted a person I could bear.

It took years. It began when I was fourteen years of age and I did not feel I had completed my work until the second year at the seminary. Even after this I would occasionally perform the speaking and walking exercises, just to ensure my standards were not slipping.

All that work. Yet now I find myself in my priestly refuge, waddling back and forth while a thick King James totters on my head; reciting phrases I developed to encourage the *profoundo* in my voice. The oracular oratory howls in the orifice of optimism. It seemed impossible at first, but after a night of walking and precious little sleep, I have managed to regain my former self. Morning mass was tolerable, if somewhat irritating due to the higher than usual attendance. The prurient, collecting there to rubberneck the priest who blessed the face of awful death. The story is in all the newspapers, apparently; even an interview with the poor girl's mother. The obscene intrusion.

Could I have saved that girl?

I sped efficiently through the rites, though a definite frisson ran through the congregation when the time arrived for my sermon. Some of them even leaned forward, hungry for the grubby details.

Naturally, I wasn't about to satisfy such base interest, so instead I merely stood at the lectern, looked about me and quoted Auden, 'We must love one another or die.'

That baffled them, and I must admit to a moment of vanity. I did deliver the line well.

By the end I was enveloped in an emotion approaching optimism. No, relief. I could recapture the self I had previously inhabited.

But this pleasant sensation quickly dissolves when I get back to the house and discover Jack in the kitchen, his face ashen; perhaps a smell of alcohol carrying on his breath.

'The guards rang again,' he informs me.

I nod, feeling my stomach tighten, marshalling all my inner forces so as to maintain my desired shape. Straighten your back and inwardly chant. The oracular oratory howls in the orifice of optimism.

'It's just terrible about that young girl,' he slurs. 'Isn't it? Just terrible. She used to come up here, with that prayer group. I never met her. Did you ever meet her, Michael? I never met her.'

I do not reply, processing the evidence of what I see and the blasts of whiskey assaulting my nostrils. The noise from the kitchen the night before had extended until well after midnight. Is Jack drunk? Has he fallen off the wagon he spent so much time trying to drag me onto?

'Isn't it terrible?' he repeats.

'Indeed it is,' I say, opting to keep my answers short and perhaps significant. I'm pleased to note that my voice is holding up.

Jack looks towards the window, as if he's forgotten about my presence.

'What did the guards say?'

'Oh,' he exclaims, as if waking from a nightmare. 'To give them a ring. You know she was also involved in some anti-drugs thing as well – did you know that? That's why she was in that building, the guards said. To try and talk the drug dealers out of it. Can you believe that? And they killed her for her trouble.'

He swings his head from side to side, then taps his chest.

'Did it all by herself. That's how much faith she had. She had faith. Do you have that much faith, Michael? I don't think I do. She believed God would help her convince those people…'

He regards me with his glassy and bloodshot eyes. Yes, he is quite drunk. But now I am more concerned with what I feel within myself: a deflation; the air slowly escaping. I try to maintain my posture, but the forward movement of my shoulders is irresistible; as if an invisible hand is slowly crushing me.

'I don't know, though,' says Jack. 'Could we have done anything? There's probably no point wondering about what we could have done. What was meant to be was meant to be. Do you know?'

I want to slap Jack across the face; tell him he is in the thick of the superstitious rabble which has once again heaped misery and death upon the credulous. Yet the anger is as much for myself.

Yes, I could have saved her from *Faith*. Because I have no faith at all.

Chapter Twenty One
Rachel Belton

Daniel gives a series of urgent nods as I tell him what happened. We've talked on the phone, but this is the first chance to relate the story in detail: the death of the girl, Aidan Haslett, Sandra Keogh and all the shiny-faced women who are prepared to go into battle for me.

He readjusts his pillows, but doesn't say anything at first. Eventually, he asks:

'Do you think you can win?'

'Probably not. No. Definitely not. But I won't disgrace myself.'

He nods again.

'And why is that important?'

'Because if I do well this time, the Party will back me at the next election.'

'But I thought the Party wants you to withdraw?'

'Well, yes.'

'So you think they'll forgive you for defying them?'

Now I fall silent. I feel a jag of annoyance. I'm tempted to turn over and go to sleep. I am tired. I've spent the last two hours reading the Constitution. But it is a reasonable question.

'I don't know. I mean, this has all happened in one day, so it's been a bit of a blur. The Party might never forgive me. No. This is politics. They're pragmatists. If they think I'm electable, they'll back me.'

I pause. I have a new thought.

'But to be honest, getting elected seems less important now. Daniel, all these women tonight. It was, you know, quite *inspiring.*'

He sits up to look at me. He knows how uncomfortable I would be using a word like that. I'm just as surprised to hear myself say it. For the most part, we're both realists, not given to emotional arguments. We both know that to climb the mountain, you might get frostbite or lose a few fingers. You might break a leg or arm. You might die. But these are not noble sacrifices: they are transactional; the price you have to pay to get to the top.

'Inspiring? In what way?'

'I don't really know. But there's something in it. OK, I admit I didn't want to give up. I don't like failing. Who does? But this evening: you had to see their faces. There was just something that makes me feel different now. I can't describe it to you.'

In the hotel I simply wanted to get home. But now I regret having left so early. These words, these thoughts, are coming to me as I speak them: bubbling up through a new fissure in my mind. Or perhaps I'm simply light-headed from the day's events: succumbing to the romantic idea of some newly discovered pattern where none exists. Perhaps I'm clinging to unfocussed hope. I should sleep. I should think.

'And what about the girl who passed on?'

He looks at me significantly.

'No, Daniel.'

'Come on, Rachel. You feel inspired. You're feeling something moving through you – and you won't even consider that it might be this girl? That she's the unseen force at work here? What's her name?'

'Manda.'

'Manda passes over and suddenly you feel something you can't explain. That's hardly a coincidence.'

'Daniel, please.'

'So shouldn't we ask Manda what she thinks?'

'It's nothing to do with her. It's my decision. I don't feel inspired by Manda. I'm tired, that's all.'

'We'll see about that.'

He's already out of the bed and heading for that freezing little shrine filled with candles; some new, some no more than misshapen blobs which can't be lit; like dead foetuses.

'Daniel, *please*,' I say. 'Not now. Come back to bed.' But he's already out the door and pattering down the stairs.

CHAPTER TWENTY TWO
Baz Carroll

I've been sent to see all sorts of people. Social workers and psychiatrists and counsellors. They wear Wranglers and zippy tops and moccasins, which is probably the height of hippy-fucking-cool in Stillorgan or wherever they're from. A lot of them look unhealthy; sometimes the junkies look better. And they all go over the top to give off this calm-and-fucking-wise vibe; like they've spent years up a mountain with some smelly guru sitting in his underpants and now they've got it all figured out. But you can tell it's bullshit. A couple of years into the job and they cop on that really it's all about filling in forms and not getting blamed and making sure they get all their allowances and tea breaks. No, the world doesn't want to give you a blowjob because you tried to save it.

With some of them you can see the anger, just below the surface; threatening to burst out. But it can't because they're trapped, aren't they? Trapped in their shitty jobs. Not fit for anything else. And sometimes I think they look at me – a junkie waster – and they're thinking: he's having a laugh.

They only ever want one thing: to find out what's wrong with me, just to prove how clever they are. Cos there has to be something wrong with me – I couldn't just be a bad one. There has to be something that made me the way I am, made me the *victim*. So they go through this list of stuff, but trying to make out that we're just having a chat, thinking I won't know what they are up to. Is your da an alcoholic, is your ma on drugs? Any friends or family ever touch you in an in-a-fucking-propriate way?

But none of them really give a shit. They just need to fill out some paperwork, find something they can tick a box for. 'Addict' or 'dysfunctional': something that will fit in the fucking statistics for the end-of-year report.

Usually they think they are on to something when they ask was me da on the drink or drugs or violent in the house. And I say no and they give me the pleased-with-themselves look that means, are you sure, Baz? Then I go: yes, I'm fucking sure. He died when I was two.

Ahhhh.

Oh, they love that, scribbling away.

Was it drugs, Baz?

No, it was fucking cancer.

And do you miss your father?

What a stupid question. How can you miss someone you can't remember? Sure, when I was a nipper I used to daydream about having a da, and I'd go through phases of asking Ma about him. That's natural. But that's not the same as missing him, the bloke who was my father for two years. You can't miss what was never there.

But I copped that this answer only makes them worse: more scribbling and oohing and aahing and then making out that I did miss me father, even though I just said the exact fucking opposite of that. They only hear what they want to hear. That's what you learn.

So instead I look a bit sad and give them all this about how it was hard at times, cos I had no male role model (always surprised when I come out with that one; as if the problem is that I'm thick as well as dodgy), and they hmmm some more but don't write so much. Then they ask – almost licking their fucking lips at this stage, And how did your mother cope with this?

This is what they're hoping for now: the fucking lotto of dysfunction, the ma drugged out of her brains, leaving me in me own shit until one of the neighbours rings up the social workers to complain about the smell.

Except it wasn't like that. She coped brilliant, I say. And because I'm getting bored now; before they can shoot off another *Really? Is that true?* I tell them who my ma is.

Always shuts them up. Has them rustling their papers and staring at each other and then saying *Really*? But in a completely can't-fuck-ing-believe-it way.

When they find out who my ma is, they've nothing left, they've run out of reasons for me to be the way I am; they've no boxes to tick. Because of my ma, I shouldn't be here. I should be in university or politics or even be doing the same thing as these fuckers, trying to figure out the formula for what makes a life go wrong.

The thing is, they all know my ma – they go white when I say Rose Carroll. Yeah, *the* Rose Carroll. And it's not like she's world famous or anything, though I suppose she was on the TV news and the papers and all that for years. They know her because everyone in Finglas knows her. And that's my entire world, has been for years. This trip into town, this taxi ride, this is not what I usually do at all. In an average day I move about a mile from me gaff. Go to the shops, the bookie, the pub if we have cash. No more than that. Can't even do that now. My world is getting smaller and smaller, and soon there won't be enough room in it for me.

So I'd better get a move on. Fix me thoughts. Figure out what I've got to say to her so she'll let me in the door. The last time she ran me, the last couple of times – but, Jesus, that was years ago. That was before she told me to go away.

She isn't the type to shout or lose the head. I could deal with that. She just stands there and talks in this tone of voice like she's having a chat about the weather. She can dish it out, though. Cool as you like, she'll throw back in your face every promise you ever made, going back your whole life. When you were ten you said you wanted to be a teacher, what happened to that, Barry? She won't call me Baz. And like, I've promised to give up the gear millions of times. She remembers every one of them promises. All she has to do is stand in the door and go, you've said that before, Barry. You've been saying it for the last ten years, but look at you still.

You're a liar, Barry. You can't help it, but you're a liar and I can't afford to believe a word you say.

How can anyone cope with that? How can you argue with it? You can't. But I've no bleedin' choice now. I've got to get in the front door or that's it. I'm fucked, and I've nowhere else to go. Taxi fare cleaned me out. I handed out the last euro in coppers, fucking five-cent coins I was giving him, but no chance that the fucker was going to let me off any of it. He looked at the coins like he was offended by them. No notes? He says. No mate, I say. I've a tenner in me back pocket, but he's not getting that. He didn't even say thank you, so I didn't either.

Pleasant Lane looks the same. Quiet. Boring. All the neat houses lined up like they're about to be inspected. One door, one window. One door, one window. We moved here not long after me Da died, though I don't remember that. I do remember being stuck inside the house, bored out of me skull because she wanted me to do me lessons. Torture, that was, though it probably wasn't much of a treat for Ma either. I can't remember exactly when she gave up – or, not gave up, like, but admitted that it wasn't going to work – but I can remember her crying, bawling her eyes out, and me saying, Ma, stop. If it's such a big deal I'll study. But she yelled at me – one of the few times she's ever done it – but you have to *want* to study; you have to realise why it's important. Do you? Do you?

I said nothing. Couldn't lie. That's always been my problem. Couldn't lie. Well, I *do* lie all the time. I'm just shite at it. Can lie to meself, though. I told meself the only reason she was ramming books down me neck was out of snobbiness. Rose fucking Carroll, the Queen of Finglas, couldn't be having a waster of a child. He'd have to be some sort of a saint like her, bursting with community fucking values. She didn't care about me; she was only worried about what the papers would say. And that gave me the excuse to get up to all sorts. All sorts. Broke her heart, I did.

My heart is hammering in my chest now. I could do with a hit of something just to keep the nerves down. I think I have a half a spliff in me pocket, but if I stand out here she's bound to see me smoking it. Probably not too clever to let any of the neighbours see either. Fuck, fuck, fuck. Just walk in, creak open the metal gate I used to swing on. Me and Martin used to do that, him on me shoulders, swinging his arms like he wanted to fall over. He was a mad little fella.

It's hard to get the gate open because me hands are slippery from the sweat and I'm starting to think that this is stupid and even if she lets me in the Georgians will find out and come here and then it's not just me. It's her and Holly. Jesus, Holly.

No, no, no. Anyone that knows – everyone that knows me – knows the story. Me ma could be in the Dáil now, could be a minister or the fucking Taoiseach or president or some shite if it wasn't for me. It's not like it's a secret. In all the papers and everything. That's why I'm here.

That's why she's not opening the door, even now. She just leaves me there, shaking, staring at a poxy election sticker. She still supports that mob, even though they fucked her.

'Ma,' I say to the sticker.

She clears her throat.

'Yes, Barry.'

She says it like I was here yesterday; like she knew I'd turn up sooner or later. But you know what? It's been years.

I hear rustling. She must have the child in her arms.

'Is that Holly?' I say. 'Can I hear Holly?'

She says nothing.

'Look, Ma. I need to talk. I really need to talk.'

'You want something. What is it?'

I look around me. The road is empty, but I don't like standing out here, where any fucker could see me. All it would take would be one, and then the door is getting kicked in at three in the morning.

'Ma, I'm in a bit of trouble.'

'You're always in trouble, Barry. You've been in trouble all your life.'

'Yeah, Ma, I know. But this, like, is serious.'

'Well go the guards then.'

'The coppers? Are you fucking joking me?'

'Language, Barry. I have the child here.'

'Sorry, Ma.'

I can't think of anything else to say. I've tried everything before: tried to make her feel guilty cos I was her son, told her I was dying, told her I'd been evicted. And at first she would open up, even let me in the odd time. But she learned – of course – that I was only look-ing for money and if she wouldn't give me that, something to rob out of the house. *Enable*. That was the word. I'm not going to *enable* you, Barry. Fuck that.

I hear Holly talking. Something like: who are you talking to, Ganny? Can't hear the answer. When I was a nipper, say only seven or eight, every evening we'd sit down in front of the fire and she'd listen to me reading a book. *The Famous Five*, I remember that one. Awful Brit shite. Swotty little kid, I was, the best at reading in me class. Well, half of them couldn't read at all. And Ma would listen to me and correct the odd word and then I'd help her make tea. Pork chops and mashed carrots. The kitchen full of lovely, meaty smells. Apple sauce. I remember once Martin had his dinner in our gaff cos his Ma was sick or something and he couldn't get over the apple sauce. You put apples on meat? Apples? Of course he told everyone at school and I got an awful slagging over it, even from some of the teachers. Poshy Carroll. But anyway, every evening I'd lay the table and, when I was a bit older, when she was sure I wouldn't scorch meself, she let me make the pot of tea. Always liked to drink tea with her dinner, me ma. Still does, I suppose.

She'd ask me what I wanted to do when I grew up, and because I was a sap I'd tell her all sorts of stuff, and she'd tell me I could do whatever I wanted because I had a brain and all I had to do was work hard and not mind all the other wasters and eejits who didn't want to work and who spent all day in the pub. I could do something with me life. It's important to have aspirations. Aspirations. Fuck's sake. Eight years of age and she's talking to me about aspi-fuckin'-rations.

What use is that? What use was any of that?

I haven't said anything for a few minutes, but I know she's still there. I can hear the child moving, singing a bit of a song.

I turn around and say, 'Ma, do you remember when I used to help you make the dinner? I'd read me books and then I'd lay the table and you'd let me make the tea. Do you remember that?'

She doesn't say anything for a while, just makes a noise, like a deep breath.

'Yes, I remember, Barry. Why are you doing this? Why are you here?'

She sounds like she might be a bit annoyed, me bringing that up. I look around again. A car goes past the end of the road, not too slow, but slow enough for someone to have a good look down at me standing here like a fucking twat. I go quiet, to see can I hear it come back. But even if I legged it now, where could I go? This is a cul-de-fucking-sac. I'm trapped by the street I grew up in, by everything I've ever done. An ugly great crow lands in the front garden next door and starts pecking around. He looks at me with his black eyes.

The Georgians will rip me arms off, and if the pigs get me, I'll get a good hammering from them too. Fat sweaty fucks who can't get their wives to ride them anymore, and it's all my fault. They'll get a confession out of me and find me fingerprints in the girl's flat and drag me in front of some crumbling old prick of a judge who'll have me convicted of murder before it's time to empty his colostomy bag.

Then it's Mountjoy or Portlaoise for twenty years, in with all the hard ones. Until some bloke the Georgians know slits me throat in the shower or talks me into hanging meself.

I'm fucked.

I get the shakes then; can't control it. I think I'm going to fall over, so I sit on the doorstep, hugging meself and sobbing like a fucking girl.

'Barry,' she says. 'Barry, what do you want?'

I can't answer, can't say anything.

'Barry, I'm not going to stand here all day. I'm going back into the kitchen now.'

I shake me head, though of course she can't see me. I know she's right. Her and Holly should get away from me. I should get away from here. But she doesn't walk away. I hear her, inches from me on the other side of the green door.

'Ma?' I say.

'Yes, Barry.'

'I'm sorry.'

'Sorry?'

'Sorry, you know, for all the shit. All of it.'

She doesn't say anything about the swearing.

'I'm sorry because I'm after getting into serious trouble. Really serious. Like, this is it. But you're right, you know? For Holly. You look after Holly.'

I start to stand up and I'm thinking: this is fucking weird. This is almost funny. Yeah. This is the first time I've told her the truth in years. Or the first time I can tell the difference, the first time me head has been clear enough. Because no matter what happens, I'm fucked. Why make it worse for anyone else?

But as I get up, I almost fall over because the door suddenly swings open, and there's me ma, taking a good long look up at me and using her hands to stop Holly racing out into the road. I say nothing. I sniff. I wipe me eyes.

'Well,' she says, after what seems like a million fucking years. 'You'd better come in and say hello to your daughter.'

Chapter Twenty Three
Carol Murphy

I get a flash. Just as I'm absorbed into the city centre traffic. I sit in my stuffy car amidst the noise and smoke outside and watch myself. I'm crouched behind a wall – I'm eleven years of age. Or ten. Conor and Manda are on either side of me, crouched also, and I can hear Conor's breath rattling through his snotty nose. The three of us are giggling, though I'm conscious that this was my idea so I should provide some leadership. I shush them to be quiet, then kneel so I can peek over the wall. A stone sticks in my bare knee which I brush off. I'm wearing culottes which I hate, but which Mum made me put on because they are practical. All the mucking around you kids do.

I note that a sprig of nettles is close to my left leg. Then slowly I move towards the brow of the wall, which is newly built, roughly pebble-dashed; not pleasant to touch. It's late, but still bright. We're all sunburned on the backs of our necks. A cow releases a bored moo. A thin skid of cloud sits close to the horizon, like a signature. A bird lazily flaps through the blue-domed sky, crossing the path of a jet much higher above. And I'm aware of all these things, as if they are somehow connected; they have something to do with the three of us sneaking across two fields, crawling on our hands and knees for the last bit – because we're not the first kids to try, and local intelligence has it that Mrs Byrne owns a fierce-looking blackthorn stick which she keeps beside the back door and has no compunction about swinging hard at the heads of nosy children.

We haven't met any children who have had this experience, but Hazel swore it was true and then begged us – she actually used that word – I *beg* you children, for your own safety, never go near the Byrne house. That woman is extremely dangerous, there's no telling what she could do. And you don't want me to have to go down to the guards to identify bodies, surely you don't want that?

We said no, though we weren't too sure what this meant anyway. Conor said she meant having to go to the police station to identify us after Mrs Byrne had cracked open our skulls with that stick, but I doubted if it worked that way. On the telly programmes, they drew a white line around the shape of the body, and if they were going to all the trouble of doing that, then it would only take five minutes to run over to Hazel's house rather than get her to go all the way into town.

Not that we really thought Mrs Byrne had a blackthorn stick. Or that she would swing it at our heads. Or even if she did swing it at our heads, that she would catch any of us. Mrs Byrne was an old lady, older than Hazel, and Conor had already told us that if she came out the door, then we were to run in different directions. Conor said he would wait while we ran to make sure Mrs Byrne followed him, since he was a boy and the fastest runner, which Manda and I thought was very heroic.

Anyway, the whole reason we were here was because of Hazel: she was the one who told us how some of the Grogan kids down the road (who we didn't like) had driven Mrs Byrne crazy by standing at her gate and chanting *Byrne baby Byrne, disco inferno!* for hours and hours until she came after them with the stick. But our curiosity overwhelmed our fear when Hazel told us what the Byrnes did every night.

Apart from the local children, Mrs Byrne also hated her Mr Byrne; had hated him for years. As far as anyone knew, he didn't drink or beat her. He was regarded as a quiet man who worked in a local factory and had a couple of fields beside the house. Other than that, all Michael Byrne did was go to GAA matches. And when he wasn't at a match he would watch it on television. Or any other sport if there was no GAA on. Sometimes he would look at videos of all-Ireland finals or even local matches he recorded himself with a small camera. For close to forty years, Mrs Byrne had sat in the parlour of their house and watched her husband watch sport on the television. Nothing else.

All this was according to Hazel, and even at our age we didn't believe her entirely: not that this stopped any of us speculating on how and why Mrs Byrne came to hate her husband. Perhaps she had spent years begging him to switch off the TV and bring her dancing; or just to watch something else for a change. Or perhaps she said nothing, stewing in her fury, hoping that one day he might notice her feelings, eventually realising he never would. Whatever happened between them, whatever was said or not said, it had given Mrs Byrne the strength she needed to wait: until their three children had grown up and left home.

The day after the departure of the last child, Mrs Byrne took a bus to Galway City and bought an accordion: a large red second-hand Hohner, behind which she was barely visible. This may have been deliberate. Thus obscured, she could sit in the parlour every night and not even have to look at him as she squeezed tunelessly on the instrument; content that she could remain there night after night and ruin her husband's television-watching for the rest of their lives.

Hazel had no explanation as to what kept Mr Byrne going back to the same chair in the parlour. Perhaps it was bloody-mindedness, the hope that his wife would eventually get sick of her revenge; or it was the inability to break a decades-old habit. Perhaps it was guilt – maybe he had finally realised what he had put his wife through. All Hazel knew –from several reliable witnesses – was that every night the Byrnes would sit in the kitchen and eat their supper in silence, after which he would stand, stretch, yawn and plod into the parlour. She'd follow, sit on the opposite side of the room, strap on the instrument and start squeezing. She would play for hours: until her husband went to bed.

This had been going on for a nearly a year at the time Hazel told us about it. So we had to look, of course, which is why we are behind the wall, and why Conor and Manda wait breathlessly as I stretch to peer over the window sill. I feel my right hand is shaking slightly and for a moment I can hear the ticking from Conor's watch, a massive thing with lots of little dials he got for his birthday the month before. But this sound is suddenly obscured by a vibrant wail, and I whisper: *I can hear it!*

The other two don't move, are afraid to, and let me proceed until I have a clear view into the Byrnes' back window. I can only see a part of Mr Byrne, a section of his bald head which has a comb-over slicked on top. From the direction his spotty nose points, I can tell that he is staring stone-still at a television which blazes on the opposite side of the room. But Mrs Byrne is directly in front of me, only the top of her black bun-head visible behind the massive red accordion; her skinny thick-stockinged legs sticking out beneath. She squeezes the instrument slowly, occasionally hitting a button so that now it sounds like wheezing: a beast with asthma.

I use a hand to suppress my giggles, while the others shoot up on either side of me, faces flushed, mouths open. Manda starts laughing and we shush her to be quiet, perhaps a bit too loudly, though the Byrnes don't seem to notice. They don't seem to notice anything: not us, not each other. He continues to stare at the television as if it is the only object of significance in the room; she squeezes on, robot-like.

At first we are amused, snorting and nudging each other, but after a spell we grow quiet. Manda's face, I notice, has twisted into a scowl: as if she doesn't know how to process this information, to calculate what it means. Conor is starting to look as if he has eaten something unpleasant, and for a moment I fear recriminations; that he's going to lean over and whisper: this is *stupid*. Let's go home.

So I reach into my right pocket. After all, no point coming here if you don't have proof.

FLASH!

I gave them no warning, so Manda and Conor are momentarily stunned by the shimmering burst of camera light; as if they've just seen a star die. Then they are amazed I would do such a thing while we are trying to remain undetected, then frankly admiring of my gall. All this happens in less than a second, but it is more than enough time for me to share a quick look with each of them and to relish what it tells me.

Mr Byrne hasn't moved, but Mrs Byrne's accordion has begun tipping over, wailing in complaint as it goes, sliding back to reveal one large brown eye, and then another over a hawk-like nose. She's looking straight at us, though she doesn't seem to register yet what has happened. She squints, mouths some words, but I see no more because Conor is shoving the three of us to the ground, ordering us to scramble along. My knee goes straight into the nettles and almost immediately I feel it throb, and even though I hate nettles I don't mind this time because I'm laughing so much; I'm laughing so much snot is tipping out of my nose, which only makes me worse, which makes the others laugh like mad things as well. And for a moment it occurs to me that I don't care if Mrs Byrne comes after us and cracks my head open. Because I'm never going to feel happier than this, smelling grass and weeds and dung, laughing maniacally under the evening summer sky with my cousins whom I love.

Odd thing for a ten-year-old to think.

A car nearby emits a cranky beep, and I see some space has opened up before me. I drive for ten seconds, then halt, all the other cars moving obediently behind. The woman in the car alongside is staring: probably wondering what I can possibly have to smile about.

But just as quickly, tears are dribbling down my face and I'm scrabbling about to find tissues in my bag. Convulsive sobs thump out of me. The woman in the car looks away.

I've got copy to file. Can't go into the office like this. Not that I wanted to anyway.

I swing into a car park. I'll go to a café with wi-fi. To distract myself, I make a couple of calls. I make an appointment to meet the priest, Michael Bourke. Slow Louth accent, as if he's putting it on. There's also a message from Brian.

'Carol, Hi. I know you're busy and the story must be difficult for you. Actually, it's amazing you can face it. I don't know if I… er, just to say I'm thinking of you and we'll talk soon.'

Jesus. How can he ring me when I was so horrible?

I get out of the car before the tears come again. I find an empty coffee shop, but even as I type the waves of grief sweep up from my stomach. I feel flooded.

I try to calm myself by thinking about ordinary stuff – the sort of things I consider when I'm going to sleep: should I get my eyes tested again? Should I give up drink for a month? Should I emigrate like everyone else? My life is populated with nothing but urges and my attempts to curb them. Go shopping, but watch the finances, cut down on chocolate, the cigarettes, the drink. Eat more salads. Get a pedicure. Walk to work. I don't feel like a person; I don't know what that means. I do things: I shop, I eat, I dress, I drink, I smoke, I have drunken sex, I work. Yet it somehow doesn't add up to anything. A list, not a woman.

I suppose I assumed that at some stage I would achieve happiness or something that looked like it; something like Mum and Dad used to have. I assumed it would just arrive, along with a job and my own flat.

Is that what this is? I'm not *happy*? Is that all?

There are no other customers, so I look up at the squat man behind the counter. He frowns tightly as he rubs a cloth over the counter: as if this is a job of great delicacy, yet brings him no satisfaction.

This place is just off Dame Street. I could leave here now, nip through Temple Bar, over the Ha'penny Bridge, across Henry Street and through the ILAC. A fifteen-minute walk from where she died. I put my face in my hands and wait for the shuddering to stop. The man keeps cleaning the counter.

CHAPTER TWENTY FOUR
Michael Bourke

Jack disappeared afterwards, presumably to drown himself in alcohol. I retreated to my room and remained there, ignoring the house phone or the occasional bleeps from my mobile. When I did venture downstairs, driven by a parching thirst, there was still no sign of him. Perhaps I should have searched, but I didn't have the strength. Once more I had shrivelled back to that hump-backed muttering creature I detested, though this time all hope of reconstituting myself had evaporated. It was beyond me to perform my exercises or even imagine a time or circumstance when I might reemerge.

I could easily have called into the girl's prayer group, just as a courtesy: and if I had I would have quickly spotted the glassy stares of the obsessives. I have seen them before; I have saved them before.

That my collapse has been so complete and speedy throws shadows of doubt across everything I have been for the past two decades. Was my self-improvement nothing more than a pose? Was the confidence I had felt mere self-delusion? Despite my best efforts, was I condemned to be a creature I loathed?

For a while, I was lured into the magical thought patterns so common among my parishioners: torturing myself with the idea that my failure to rescue this girl was a message; a comment from the cosmos. Such egoism in the face of tragedy. Others must die, so that Michael Bourke must learn a lesson. No. The failure was mine. I tried drinking brandy, in the hope of discovering oblivion, but I'm not a drinker.

I was soon vomiting into the toilet beside my room. I peered into the splattered bowl and attempted to make a cold assessment of my worth. Against this one failure, how many have I helped? Do the failures and successes balance each other out? If I cannot recapture the bearing I had so assiduously developed, then should I remain a priest? And if not, what should I do then? Has the usefulness of Michael Bourke come to a close?

If so, why not end it?

Some of these questions I attempted to answer; others, I could not.

Exhausted, I rolled into bed, where I slept fitfully, tormented by visions of angels and dead things, accusing me. I ignored mass the following morning.

I managed to lurch from my room some hours later, seeking only to eat and urinate: even the relief of this I felt I scarcely deserved.

But on this occasion there is an envelope in the kitchen, addressed to me in Jack's sloping hand.

Michael,

I cannot begin to tell you how sorry I am. I have let the church down, I have let the parish down, I have let you down and I have let myself down. Please pray for me. What with all the talking I do about addiction, I should have known, but I didn't. I forgot that you have to monitor it all the time. You have to keep an eye on yourself. But what with everything to do with that poor girl (though I'm not making excuses), I forgot to do that.

So I'm back at square one. The good news is that I realise this and I'm open to getting some help. I've booked into the clinic in Waterford where I was before. A nice quiet place where I can get myself on an even keel again, hopefully. I've let the bishop know. I said you would be well able to run things in my absence, which of course you will be. You are a fine priest, Michael, and I hope you can find it in your heart to forgive me. Please pray for me as I will for you.

Your friend,

Jack

As the letter falls to the floor, I emit the kind of groan a man does when burdened with a final, crushing weight. Would Jack have put the bottle to his lips if I had put self-pity aside and rejoined the festivities that night?

I remain at the kitchen table for some time, I don't know how long; aware only of the rasp of my breath, of how I am a tiny creature, alone in this crumbling house, on this ball of rock spinning in airless space, the stars shooting ever further from each other. One organism among trillions, and all powerless.

All made from the same stuff. The telescope is still upstairs. I never opened the box.

The phone rings, and for a moment I watch this strange, clanging instrument; for a moment I feel as if I have just arrived in this place, that everything is strange to me. I don't know how anything works; or what anything means.

Ah, *meaning.* Sometimes even I crave it too.

My parents died years ago. I gave the house to a local charity, and told them to burn the contents. I have no idea what happened to the boys I used to stand with at school; and since then I have remained purposefully alone.

I pick up the phone. There is a hollow, droning sound, like a train, or a car.

'Could I speak to Father Bourke please?'

A toneless, south Dublin accent. Even the words *Father Bourke* sound strange to me, and for a moment I consider how to reply. Father Bourke, as I created him, no longer exists; he may be irretrievably lost.

'Yes,' I say, as neutrally as possible.

'Ah,' exclaims the woman, as if the very act of speaking to me is reward enough. She prattles on, and to my shame I am content to let her. A journalist, or so she describes herself, working for some tabloid rag I am barely aware of. But I'm far too weakened to point any of this out. The old Michael Bourke would have treated her with flawlessly polite contempt, subtly unhinging all the assumptions of her contemptible so-called craft. But instead I merely listen to her babble, and without having uttered a syllable, agree to meet this virago, to describe for her in delicious detail the thrilling spectacle of life's end.

'Manda,' says the hack.

This, it seems, was her name, and it was a bridesmaid's dress she wore, further amplifying the anguish: to her parents, her friends and no doubt the sibling who expected to see her at the church.

I didn't choose to become a priest, so much as sift through my limited options and realise that it was probably best for me. Only later did it assume the proportions of a mission; or, to use the correct language, did I find 'my calling'. Not that anyone or thing called me. I called myself. Brutal logic brought me to where I am today: the kind which most cannot bear; which would render their lives unendurable.

I had found the priestly life attractive long before I considered it for myself. Like many teenagers of the time, I went through a period of excessive religious zeal, seeing nothing but sin in the faces and hearts of my fellow humans. Our local priest, Father Clarke, a man of massive girth and height, seemed to be a heroic bulwark against all this corruption. I enjoyed going to him to confess my trifling transgressions and asking his opinion on matters public and private. Sensing a possible recruit, he repeatedly suggested that I think of the priesthood. But I politely demurred, never imagining that I could become a creature as magnificent as he. These were in the days before I set out to remake myself; before I fully realised the sinewy beauty of the church: its embrace of the sensual.

That decision came later, when the outward changes in my bearing were already apparent. By then, to further my improvement, I sought ways to display confidence in public, outside my usual routine. So in the summer of my sixteenth year, I asked my father to arrange a summer job for me at his place of work.

I was, like all young men, cruel in my judgements of others. I had come to the unshakable conclusion that my father's indulgence in astronomy (and my being forced to assist him) was prompted by a lack on his part: a desire to escape the realisation of his many failures as a man. But age winnows such extravagant opinions. Now I suspect that he was driven to observe the magnitude of creation as an antidote to constantly thinking about the business of death.

For thirty-two years, my father was general manager of a headstone factory. Yes, such places exist. A corrugated barn, within which granite and marble slabs were cut into shape and then polished, polished, polished: a process which took days and hundreds of gallons of water. As a temporary minion, I was given the most menial tasks: general cleaning-up and replacing the worn tubes of sandstone connected to the giant polishing machines.

It was tedious work, and my colleagues could not be described as stimulating company: fighting, sex and sport constituted their main topics of conversation. Being the boss's son made them all the more wary of me. Yet I enjoyed the place enormously: as if by coming here, I had been made privy to a secret.

My father had often marvelled at how people were uncomfortable with his line of work. No one ever asked: hey Joe, how's it going at the factory? They didn't wish to know that such a place existed: not a *factory* for headstones, an engine of mass production. They would rather imagine that each was individually crafted by some lonely mason, slowly tapping out names for posterity. Or they would rather not think of it at all. Knowing the truth when so many others would rather turn away was a deeply enriching experience for someone of my years. Every day during that summer I witnessed death made visible through the smooth marble and evocative iconography. And I found it beautiful.

This opinion I was wise enough not to share with others. I knew it might be regarded as rather odd; for a time I even thought so myself. Only through observing – or more precisely, listening to – my workmates did these ideas start to take on a greater importance. As I have said, they were conversationally retarded; however, their talk about sex seemed to stem more from need than enjoyment. Every Monday they would regale each other with (I suspected) largely fictional accounts of their amorous adventures, to be retold through the rest of the week. Sometimes, particular highlights from months before would be repeated for my benefit. No doubt, they derived some pleasure from attempting to 'corrupt' the boss's son, so I played along, occasionally feigning shock or lurid interest. The stories were, of course, tasteless and banal, but the more I heard them, the more I realised how uninterested I was in the subject. The pursuit of girls with the aim of groping their body parts held no allure for me; and neither, since you are no doubt wondering, did the pursuit of boys. I had endured puberty, but found the physical changes an annoyance rather than some sort of biological imperative. At the age of sixteen, I came to the conclusion that I had little or no interest in romance: a revelation that I found comforting. Given my unpleasing features, I was unlikely to have had much success.

Once again, it set me apart from others, but by then I was reconciled to the prospect that this would always be the way. Freedom from sex equipped me with a colder eye: to observe how the men at work – who were only a few years my senior – were dazzled by the subject, unable to think of little else. I certainly did not want to be like them.

Their sexual conversation was compulsive, even fearful; such was their need to demonstrate that copulation was a major part of their lives. It made me wonder if my colleagues enjoyed working in the headstone factory as much as I did. They never discussed the final recipients of their work; and once when I asked if they had ever thought of what they would like carved into their headstones, the question was treated with derision: a huge pair of tits, was the answer I received.

By the end of that summer, my transformation was progressing faster than I could have anticipated. It was the beginnings, I suppose, of what you could call confidence. My ability to be alone, without a physical or emotional need for others, I now regarded as a great strength: an opportunity to live in the mind. Heading into my Leaving Certificate, I wondered about an academic career. I was at the top of my class in most subjects and a life immersed in books was hugely attractive.

But the mystery of death kept entrancing me. After my summer at the headstone factory, I saw it everywhere; or, more correctly, saw its denial: through sex or sport or alcohol or whist drives. Life, as everyone else imagined it, would go on forever. Yet how could one view the world without the defining template of mortality? Without realising that the end can be as glorious as the beginning? I could understand – of course I could – how people might want to shy away from the subject. But to consider life without its inevitable end is to not consider life at all.

Thus, by a simple process of elimination, I came to the conclusion that the priesthood was what I should devote my life to. After all, is it not the priest's role to remind us of death? And was this not a task for which I was uniquely qualified? I had no need for children or sex or love or friendship: it would have been a criminal waste to do anything else.

I regretted that it would be a somewhat less bookish existence; and one that inevitably would be crammed with the irritations of other people. But even at that age I knew the value of sacrifice. What is lacking more clearly defines and even sanctifies what is present: the way death sanctifies life.

I did not reveal this decision to my parents for quite some time: I led them to believe that a life of academia was my preference. Perhaps this was due to my natural tendency towards secretiveness, but more likely it was due to my awareness that such a decision would disappoint them. Naturally, when I announced my choice, they did not presume to stand in my way. Yet they fully realised the ramifications: as the only son, I had been expected at some point to provide grandchildren. My decision meant the end of the family line; a continuation of the loneliness which had haunted them for most of their quiet lives.

It was a burden which they shouldered bravely, and which at the time I believed was part of God's plan. On the day of my departure, my father shyly presented me with a gift: a four-inch reflector telescope. Just a small one, he said, that you can carry with you. There might be the odd clear night.

I thanked him, but could not hide my puzzlement. It had been nearly three years since I had declared my utter lack of interest in astronomy, and consequent refusal to accompany him on his trips to the neighbouring field. Thank you, I said. But I will never use it. Back then, I had yet to see the efficacy in certain sorts of lies.

CHAPTER TWENTY FIVE
Rachel Belton

The next day I'm out early to meet Sandra and some of the other women. The story is splashed all over the newspapers, though none of them have carried the picture from the internet. I looked it up this morning, before I left the house. It's still on *Irishscandals.ie*. So the Party didn't get it taken down. Up to 33,000 hits. Far more than I need in votes.

There's an otherworldly perfection to the photo, as if it was staged, as if this girl climbed into the skip, lay in various poses, then smiled, got out and went on with her life. Her arms are spread out like a dancer, her head turned to the side, the bridesmaid's dress fanning out from her waist. Nice dress: the pale pink sheen contrasts with the rubble beneath her. Her legs are covered, though one of her bare feet is twisted sharply to the left, as if it's been snapped off. Her eyes are closed, though not all the way: a crescent of eyeball is visible. She has shaggy brown hair and a ruddy, Irish complexion. There is a small pool of something dark by her left thigh, which could be blood. She was pretty. And perched on top of this is my poster: *BELTON Number 1*. We took so much trouble composing that image: smiling, but not too much, confident but not smug. We wanted it to say: Rachel Belton has the answer. Now it says: look what I did. I made a girl die.

The women are a bit more sober today. No one is smiling or predicting victory. There have been a few drop-outs, though nothing serious. I've put my phone on silent, though it has been buzzing away. Reporters, I suppose. I'll deal with that later.

The papers all use the same phrase. *Her campaign is now in doubt.*

We sip tea and talk politics. I tell them that the Dáil is an elected dictatorship, really. Only a handful of people make decisions or decide on policy; they retain all the power: perfect growing conditions for corruption. The women nod gravely, though I suspect I'm boring them. So I tell them about my son, about his baby vocabulary. Bled for blood. Spuke for puke. Cimemas for Cinema. They smile and tell similar stories. I think I hear traces of my old accent coming back.

After half an hour we disgorge onto the streets. Sandra walks me to a shopping centre which looks like a silver biscuit tin. It presents us with our distorted reflection. She keeps up a steady supply of people she knows, all of whom are told where I grew up and who my parents were. One or two say they knew them; all say they enjoyed me on the television. Some say: it's terrible about that girl.

Daniel was still asleep when I left. I told Renata not to disturb him, to keep Naoise from running in and jumping around. God knows what time he got to bed. I ring him about noon. He sounds excited: the way he does after some exercise.

'It was fantastic, fantastic, fantastic.'

'Really?' I say. Over time I've learnt to modulate my tone, to ask him about his visits to the shrine without displaying any judgement. It's the accommodation we've arrived at. He tells me what he thinks and I give neutral replies. Being the optimist, he thinks he will eventually win me around; make me swoon under the force of his enthusiasm. I find it sweet.

'Yes. Very easy to contact her. She was extremely vivid. Must be a large unresolved issue anchoring her to this plane. I didn't want to ask – we'd only just met – but I will the next time. She says as soon as I put up a flare, she'll come to see me.'

Despite growing up in a house full of mystics and spooks, Daniel still had to devise his own language to describe talking to dead people: something a bit more practical-sounding. Mostly he retreats to his psychic tree house and contacts them by sending up a flare. But sometimes they wade across the river. We'll be in the car or with Naoise at the playground, and Daniel will suddenly sit bolt upright and chant a jolly *hell-o*. The realm of death is not an unhappy place for him. He won't accept any other version.

But grief has made him an extremist, which can be a problem. He makes no attempt to hide his visions, no matter where he is. I have suggested that he be a bit more circumspect; be aware that others are more sceptical. But this only starts the old rows, and neither of us wants that.

'You know, I think she was expecting me to make contact,' he says. 'I should have asked. Anyway, she is aware of what happened to you and she is delighted that you are sticking with it. Had some very complimentary things to say about you. A deep spirit, she said. Like an iceberg. But in a good way – that there is so much more of you yet to be revealed.'

'Well, that's very nice,' I say.

We say our goodbyes and hang up. Sandra raises her eyebrows to me.

'Sorry for eavesdropping, but I heard you say something was nice? Good news? We could do with that.'

I feel a prickle of irritation.

I deploy my best glowing smile: life could not be more content.

'Oh, nothing about the campaign,' I say. 'Nothing to do with that.'

CHAPTER TWENTY SIX
Baz Carroll

We had chops for the dinner, though she made out that it was a coincidence and not because of anything I'd said. She let me play with Holly a bit, though fuck's sake; I don't know how to play with a child. I dunno what you do. I just sat beside her like a total spare holding her dollies and saying, do you like this one? What's her name? The child ignored me, even looked at me once or twice like she thought I was a tool. I would have given it up, left the girl to it and gone for a smoke only for me ma sat in the room with us the whole time. Pretending to read the newspaper, but watching me like a hawk.

I almost said something. Only when it was time for Holly to put on her pyjamas did she leave me on me own, and even then I could see her looking around, trying to think up some way to keep me in her sights. Only gone five minutes, anyway; just enough for me to have a smoke in the back garden.

I haven't told her anything yet. Not much anyway. Told her these Georgians are out to get me, these mad drug dealers. Haven't mentioned the dead girl or any of that. Not yet.

'Would you like to read Holly a story?' she says.

I'd already thought about doing that, but I didn't want to cause a row by asking. So Ma leads me down to the girl's room which is done up all lovely: clouds painted on the wall and loads of pictures from cartoons and all that.

Of course I don't have a clue what you do. Never done it before. Ma hands me a book and I say, 'So she reads this?'

'Barry. Holly is three. You read to her.'

It is deadly to sit with me girl, her still giving off that sweet baby smell, and looking like a cake in her pink pyjamas. And she lets me sit on the bed beside her and put my arm around her while we read the story. Real trusting, kids are. I could be anyone, but she's happy as long as I read her a story.

But Ma is still standing there, and this time I really feel like telling her to fuck off. What am I gonna do? Rob some Barbies?

I give her a bit of a look: not nasty, but asking: what are you doing there? That sort of look. But this time she smiles back. The first time she's done that since she let me in; the first time in fuck knows how long.

'Let me know when you're finished and we can tuck her in.'

So Holly and me are left alone to read the story, though there's not much reading to be done. It's more looking at the pictures and chatting to her and letting her stick her fingers in the holes or stroking the bits of fluff stuck on the pages. Weird shit. Trippy. But the child loves it. The story is about a hungry pig, but it's clever the way they put it together. Jesus, I've been in here for nearly twenty minutes.

But now Ma is standing there again, and I know just by looking at her that the mood has gone sour. She tells Holly to give me a kiss, and the child does, which is brilliant. But then Ma gives me the dead eye and tells me to go and look at the news on the telly.

Shite.

I say goodnight to my little pink cake, then go down to the kitchen to find out that the whole fucking world is looking for me. The description of 'the man seen leaving the building' is total bollocks, could be anyone, but the reporter is almost straight-out saying that I done it, that I killed that girl. Total fucking bollocks. You can't say anyone has done anything until they've had a trial and been found guilty. Fucking legal correspondent on the telly, and he's breaking the law. Cunt.

'Jesus,' I say. 'Fuck's sake. Jesus.'

'So that was you then,' says Ma.

She's standing behind me, arms folded. She's leaning against the wall, beside a picture of the Sacred Heart she's had since I was a nipper. Used to hate being alone in the kitchen with that picture. The eyes following you around the room. Later on though, when I was a teenager, I used to call him *the guy with the tomato on his chest*, just to wind her up.

I say nothing.

'So you're here to hide from the guards.'

'I didn't know about the guards,' I say. 'I'm hiding from the Georgians. You know, they are from Georgia over beside Poland. Drug dealers, Ma. And if they find me they're gonna kill me. I mean, actually kill me.'

'You mean a drugs gang *and* the guards are after you?'

Yeah. I sound like a right genius.

She whispers. 'Sweet Jesus.'

Yeah. Sweet Jesus is right.

She goes and sits at the kitchen table, which is behind the couch, so to see her I have to twist back me head. But I don't. I know she doesn't want to look at me. I know she's sorry she let me in the door.

'And this young girl,' she says. Her voice is shaking, and I know that it's not coming out of anger, or even that she's scared. It's the same shake in the voice I heard when I started playing up about the study; when I told her I didn't want to go to school anymore.

Ma is disappointed, which I find a bit surprising. I would have thought at this stage that she wouldn't be surprised at anything I'd do. She's had some right shite to deal with.

'This young girl,' she says again. 'How was she involved in this? What did she do to you that was so terrible, that...'

She can't talk, and for a minute I wish I could go over to her and put me arms around her, tell her everything is going to be OK. But I can't, of course. Can't say anything now. She wouldn't believe me. Mister Smug Cunt TV Reporter made sure of that.

I look around and her eyes are red. And she's looking at me like it's the first time we've met, and I'm some smelly mad yoke she doesn't like the look of.

She shakes her head slowly and says, 'Barry, how could you do such a thing?'

I say nothing, but I think: I haven't a fucking clue.

CHAPTER TWENTY SEVEN
Maurice Kiberd

can't believe it. In fact I have some bloke in the back of the cab that works for the radio station I'm listening to. So when the news bulletin is over, I say it to him.

'I think I know this geezer. I was on Parnell Street at the time they said, and this bloke in a dark blue hoodie got into the cab. Acting real strange. I knew he was dodgy. Panicking, he was. I knew it the moment I laid eyes on him.'

I'm probably sounding a bit angry. I can do that sometimes.

'Wow,' he says. 'You'd better ring the guards.'

But I start shaking me head.

'I dunno,' I say. 'When I'm driving, I see all sorts, you know? But in my experience the guards don't do anything. Mad isn't it?'

Your man in the back makes a noise, like what he really wants is to change the subject; like he'd prefer to get out now cos I might be a nutter. But there's no stopping me.

'I mean, if I thought they'd do something, investigate; then of course. I'd be in there like a shot. Maybe I've been doing it wrong. Is there somewhere else to go rather than the garda station? You're in the media; do you know anyone?'

He shrugs and starts mumbling; something about we don't do crime on our show. He tells me again to go to the guards, though I know it's just to shut me up. He can't wait to get out of the car.

But he doesn't know what I've been through, does he? He doesn't know what I see.

Life with Ma was quiet after Da left, and that was the way I liked it. I don't talk much really; I'm not that into it. I hear enough of it in the taxi. And people who go on a lot, forever mouthing: what are they saying? Usually nothing. Usually bull. Never trust people that talk a lot. You see, I don't want that much out of life, I really don't. Maybe it's because of the bullying when I was a nipper, I don't know, but I just want to be left alone. I like to get me paper every day and read about the sport or whatever. I make the odd bet on the horses or the football. I watch a bit of telly, mostly the sport. I smoke a few cigarettes. And that's it. I'm happy. I don't go out socialising because I don't want to. Going out and getting drunk and all that? Couldn't stick it. Enough of that on the job. As I said, I know everyone at the ranks. There's all sorts of people there to have a laugh with if I feel like it. Some of the lads there have nights out or play football, but I couldn't be bothered. I was always like that.

I reckon sometimes Ma wanted things a bit livelier. Understandable, I suppose, what with being stuck in the house with nothing to do but cook and clean. I once said to her, would you not get yourself a little job? Who'd want me, she said, who'd want me?

I couldn't wait to get working. Left school and got a job on a truck delivering coal and briquettes and all that. It was all right. I liked being the man of the house. But sometimes I'd get home, covered in coal dust, and she'd be watching the telly – usually some slushy rubbish on some exotic island – and when she'd get up to go to the kitchen, I'd see something in her; like it was breaking her heart to go get me dinner. I'd tell her she could stay; I'd say, Ma, wait until your programme is over. But she never did.

Once or twice I'd come home and she'd be all dressed up, like she was going out. But when I asked, all she'd say is that she just got a notion to put on something nice. She'd go out the back to her bedroom and come back wearing her normal clothes.

I suppose she wasn't getting any younger. I suppose she was lonely. I wasn't keeping her trapped in the house or anything. I handed over nearly all me wages – just kept enough for the paper and a few smokes. There was a social club she went to for a few years. Few drinks on a Friday night, a band, dancing, all that. There was even a boyfriend for a while. Well, I don't know if he was a boyfriend. She went dancing with him a few times, though I only met him the once. Just came home one day and there he was, this ugly little sack of fat, sitting in me chair, bold as brass. You know the sort: convinced that he's dead charming because of the sincere look he probably practises in front of the mirror.

He stood up and stuck out his hand and I shook it; I wasn't ignorant or anything. But I'd been working hard all day, to pay the bills. And I didn't drink or mess about the place. I'd just come home. So I had to say it, didn't I? It was only fair. I had to point and say: that's my chair.

Well, he started stuttering then, his fat belly wobbling with the nerves, and him still holding me hand like he was going to propose to me. But then Ma came in and rescued him. They went out that night and I never saw him again. Never saw any man around the place after that. So I don't know if she ever had a boyfriend. Not really. I never thought it was within me rights to ask.

But that was the way we both preferred it; that's what I think. We both liked our bit of privacy. Like, I knew Da was writing to her. Not much, but every couple of months an envelope would drop through the letterbox with his writing on the front. Understandable, I suppose. The postmark was London, so I imagined him in some kippy flat in Kilburn or whatever, all sorry that he did what he did, that he threw away a nice family and a comfortable house. Well, good. I liked to think he was still suffering: because, if you think about it, two punches weren't enough for him. I liked to think that he was too scared to come home.

I didn't read any of his letters. When the last one came, me ma had only read half of it before she went haring out to the phone. Screaming and shouting on the blower, she was. The letter was on the table in front of me. But I didn't look. No interest.

I read me paper, ignored it; didn't even look at her when she came back in and swooped the letter off the table like it was a pile of cash I was just about to rob. Neither of us said a word. I think there were tears in her eyes, though I didn't let meself look at her for long enough to tell. I wasn't sorry. I wasn't going to be sorry for anything.

Of course I knew something had happened, though I didn't know what. I suppose she might have wanted me to ask, but I wasn't going to do that. It would have been like giving in; giving in to him.

I read me paper, sat up and ate me tea when she served it and kept on eating when the phone rang again and she rushed off to answer. Didn't stop either when she came back into the kitchen. She pulled her chair away from the table and sat. She turned her body sideways, so that she wasn't looking at me. Then she spoke in a voice I don't think I ever heard before or since. It was so light I could hardly hear her. Like a child, telling her daddy that she'd done something bold.

'Your father's dead,' she said.

I don't know what she wanted me to say, or expected me to say. I couldn't think of anything. I wasn't going to pretend to be sorry or burst into tears. He brought it all on himself. All of it. I kept on eating.

'They found him this evening,' she said. 'He hung himself.'

Now she was staring at me; as if there was something I had to answer for.

'Oh,' I said.

'He sent me a letter. A suicide note.'

I said nothing.

'Do you want to read it?'

I shook me head. No.

Ma left the room and I finished me dinner.

CHAPTER TWENTY EIGHT
Baz Carroll

When me da died, Ma changed. That's what all me aunts told me. One minute she was an ordinary bird from Finglas, married to a fitter and with a wee baby. The next thing she was all on her own. Her parents had croaked years before. A few of Ma's sisters called around a bit, but Ma, being Ma, wanted to do it all on her own. She started going to the library. I mean *really* going to the library. Every fucking day, rain pelting down and me just a toddler, she'd march in there and read books for hours. Sometimes with me in her arms, screaming me brains out. It was like a fucking addiction. She'd get narky, really narky, if anyone told her to give the library a miss for the day. Every weekend she'd bring home stacks of books and have them read by Monday. And they weren't Mills and Boon or any of that shite. Fucking complicated stuff. Sociology and politics and all that. The girls at the library were her best friends then and ordered in anything she liked. It was a bit crazed, all right, and at first everyone thought that it was like a hobby: to help her get over the death of me da. But when it went on for a year – and then two years – and when she'd start dumping me with the sisters so she could go to the library, then they all got a bit worried. Would you not give the books a rest, Rose? Just for a bit. Come out for a drink? You're still a young woman, Rose.

But no dice with Ma. She didn't even fight with them. She kept going, and there was fuck all the sisters could do about it. She kept going until three or four years later – out of the fucking blue, with no warning from my ma – and there's this picture of her in the *Irish Independent*, holding this piece of paper like it was a million quid, with this massive smile on her gob. Turns out that she wasn't so nuts after all. Turns out she was studying on the quiet – for a fucking university degree, no less. A correspondence course with the Open University. Stacks of shit was arriving in the post for her every day, but no one saw that, and I was only a kid. And not only did she get the degree, didn't she also get top marks in all of Britain and Ireland. Suddenly, everyone's looking at me ma and thinking: she's a sneaky mare. And a fucking genius.

She couldn't stop then. She was into everything. Residents' Associations and women's groups and community centres – and all the time studying for another degree in UCD that made her a doctor. Doctor Rose Carroll. My ma. Can you fucking believe it? She could have got a job teaching in the university, but she didn't want it. She didn't want to move from Finglas. She was convinced she could turn it into some sort of heaven by having marches and protests and meeting with politicians in the front room every night of the week. She got street lights put in, there's a playground around the corner that Holly goes to, that's down to her, a sports centre and fuck knows what else. If anyone from the papers wanted to talk about Finglas, My ma was the one they called first: the brainbox professor that taught herself.

And no, it wasn't like that. She didn't neglect me, boo-fucking-hoo. I don't know how she did it, but all I remember is that ma left me to school every morning and was there to pick me up in the afternoon. She was the one put me dinner on the table and read with me every evening. And it was always that way. The way I remember it, anyway. There was always people calling in and the phone would be going all the time and I'd be brought to meetings in freezing community centres where Ma would be speaking – but I thought all that was great. There was only the two of us living in the house, but it never felt that way. It felt like we were living in a train station, there was so much going on. Now this is the truth: all sorts of important people came in and sat in the sitting room. All sorts. And not once was I ever sent out or told to go to bed or whatever. I'd be there with me Dinky cars or me Action Man and they'd all be there discussing the state of the universe. Sometimes there'd be screaming matches, but even then I was let stay.

'Jesus, Ma,' I say. 'Remember some of the rows you had in the sitting room?'

She shrugs at me. I've been in the house twenty-four hours – had a lovely kip in my old room. It's full of boxes and books now. It brought back some memories. But she's still dead suspicious.

'What rows?' she says.

'Ah, you know, when I was a kid, when you'd have politicians in there and you'd be trying to get something out of them. There was one time when you slammed the coffee table with your hand – I remember that cos it gave me a fright – and you said, "This will not pass. This will not pass." The others got an awful fright. Went quiet as mouses, they did.'

'Mice,' she says, still correcting me at my age. 'And what were we arguing about?'

'Aw, Ma, I haven't a clue.'

She doesn't smile, though I reckon she feels like it. Instead she shrugs and says, 'That was a long time ago.'

She's pretty much retired now. Apart from looking after Holly.

She hands me over the paper, and there's a big headline about the dead girl and how her mother is in bits and all that. I look at the photo and the headline, but I can't read it. I put it beside me on the couch.

'A mother lost her daughter,' says me ma. 'She's a parent, like you.'

This doesn't come out like a dig. It's more like she's hinting at something, though I haven't a clue what. And she'll keep doing that now, make cryptic fucking comments until I give her the right answer.

'I know, Ma,' I say. 'I know.'

'Yes, I think you do,' she says, which is an odd thing to come out with. Now she sits beside me. She looks at me hands like she's trying to read me tattoos, then stares right into me eyes. She leans back, as if she's suddenly got a fright.

'Barry, you seem calm,' she says.

'Well, I'm not calm. I'm shitting meself.'

'I don't mean that. I mean you're not agitated like you normally are. I mean the drugs. You're not looking for drugs.'

'No,' I say. And even though I told her this already – as soon as I came into the house – only now does it seem to be dawning on her that I'm after telling the truth.

'And when did you stop?'

'About three months ago. I got a bed in the clinic, but I chipped off after a few days, once I'd got over the bad bit. It was staying in there that was making me go back on the gear again, listening to a load of junkies moaning about smack. I didn't need that.'

'I see,' she says, like she has the hump that I didn't tell her sooner. 'So you've been off drugs for three months? Three months?'

'Yeah.'

It was a bastard coming off. Always is. Locked meself in me room for the first month. Then Martin got out of the clinic – we'd gone in together – and he was a total fucking mess. Sick as a pig, he was, fucking weeks later. Until he went back on the gear. Fine then.

'But this girl,' says me ma. 'You weren't on drugs at the time?'

'Ma,' I say. 'Sit down. I wanna tell you what happened. I didn't before because, like, you were upset.'

But she's backing away from me now – backing away – like she's fucking *scared* of me.

I can't think of what to say, so I shut up. I watch me ma back out of the room. I hear her getting Holly and putting on her coat and telling her that they're gonna go down to the playground. Then the door slams, and it's like the noise of the slam is so loud it sticks in me head and won't get out.

CHAPTER TWENTY NINE
Carol Murphy

Manda wasn't one to anticipate horror. There was no sign of forced entry to her flat because there was no need: just knock on the door and Manda would open wide and let you in.

Not that she couldn't be argumentative or immensely stubborn, but she would never have put up a fight over money. Unless she refused to hand it over because she knew it would be spent on drugs. Or money had nothing to do with it. No argument, no struggle. Manda opens the door to two shaven-headed monsters who don't speak. They scoop her up as if she were a small child, not giving her a chance to cry out, only to feel the rub of their jackets against her face, the smell of garlic underneath the tangy anti-perspirant, the confusing jangle, the sudden burst of light, the transient sense of floating; until she realises the end of all hope: nothing left but the opposite of all she has been.

I wonder was this moment worse than death itself, and as I park outside his brooding church, I'm glad this priest was with her. Not that I like priests. Don't understand them. Why do they always *look* like priests? Each one I meet is pale and smooth-skinned and a bit flabby: like an ugly new-born baby. And it's worse when they try to look unpriestly; when there's no collar. It looks like they are trying to disguise who they are. It makes them look suspicious.

Michael Bourke has gone for the white shirt and black trousers combination. He's short and stumpy and looks a bit like a potato.

At least he doesn't act like a priest. No smarminess. No peeking at my cleavage. Just sits on the edge of a seat in his prissy office, staring at the floor; recounting his story as if this was the last in a series of events conspiring to break him.

He didn't see her fall but he heard the thump of her hitting the skip. It wasn't even that loud, he says, but there was something about it that made everyone nearby look around; that made them wince without even realising what had happened. *Horripilation*, he called it, which is a fancy word for goosebumps; the skin shrinking in fear. There wasn't a bang of wood hitting concrete, but a softer sound, like water splashing.

A splat.

'I'm not going to describe the condition of the body,' he announces, anticipating a question I was never going to ask. He sticks his little nose in the air, as if he's trying to point it at something. 'Suffice to say that I assumed she was dead.'

Yet when he whispered the prayer for the dying, Manda's eyes flickered open.

'I don't think she looked at my face. It was my collar – I was wearing it that day – and she smiled. Grinned, actually. Then she closed her eyes again. I shouted for an ambulance, naturally. I didn't even finish the prayer, though that's not important.'

He doesn't sound sure, though: as if completing the prayer was the only useful thing he has ever been called upon to do.

The prayer group Manda had been a member of was connected to Michael Bourke's church, yet he hadn't recognised her, which seems to irritate him. 'It's not as if the church is overflowing every day. Especially with young people.' But he had asked around and was told that Manda felt she could talk drug dealers into giving up their work: an astonishing piece of naivety which sounds exactly like her.

'She thought *faith* would help her,' he says.

He stops talking. He stares at the floor.

Eventually, I stand. He doesn't seem to care if I walk out now or if we continue to sit in silence. There's something annoyingly pompous about him.

But he saw someone die. He saw Manda's life slip from her body. He saw her final smile. He is the last person in eternity to feel her ebbing warmth. I try to remember what her smile looked like. I can't.

I sit again, reach out an arm, then retract it.

'I'm writing about this because I knew Manda,' I say. 'A little.'

He sighs, as if he has been hearing this a lot. Everyone knew her except him.

'I know that she was… I know her faith was important to her. I'm sure seeing you was a great comfort.'

For the first time he looks at me directly. His eyes are dark-rimmed, almost feminine. His mouth curls.

'Fuck off,' he says.

MANDA SMILED AT ME

Priest reveals: Manda smiled at me before she died.

By CAROL MURPHY

A priest has revealed that murder victim Manda Ferguson SMILED at him moments before she died.

Father Michael Bourke rushed to give pretty Manda the last rites after her gruesome plunge from a third-storey window – while wearing a bridesmaid's dress...

CHAPTER THIRTY

Michael Bourke

I opt to meet her in the office, not the house. The church had to be reopened anyway: outrageously selfish of me to have kept it closed. I also hope to project a more officious nature, surrounded by the trappings of ecclesiastical power. Not to impress the journalist – she is bound to be contemptuous of such things – but to bolster myself. In truth, I want to cancel the meeting but lack the strength even for that.

I hear her well before she appears: her high heels clacking down the centre of the church, proclaiming their vulgar selves against the tranquillity around; yobs in an art gallery.

I move to the door of the office and beckon. She's not what I imagine a journalist looks like: far worse, in fact. I expected some power-dressed vamp with scarlet fingernails, but this creature is quite scruffy, her unbrushed hair featuring a vivid slice of red, as if she has accidentally tipped a can of paint over herself. Her suit is wrinkled and seems in need of a wash: rather like its owner, who is making heavy weather of the walk through the church. She smiles as she approaches me, then sighs, then makes what I assume to be a comical face, indicating that this wouldn't take so long if she exercised more.

That is self-evident.

While I wait, I glance around the church, which is empty save the two of us. Been that way for years, it seems. Even on Sundays it is barely half full and at Christmas only reaches the three-quarter mark. But we have kept the place well, Jack Kelly and I, agreeing to avoid all the modernist dabblings many churches go in for nowadays. We have kept it traditional. Rich golds at the altar, with faux-renaissance paintings lined up on either side, marking the Stations. Each pillar is partially shrouded by magnificent velvet drapes which lead to the ornate wooden roof. The roof, however, is badly in need of repair: a task we fear we will never complete. We simply don't have enough parishioners, and those we have are too poor to fund such a project. Jack has beggared himself before the bishop, but the money offered was far from sufficient to bring the roof back to glory; just enough, in fact, for the ugly scaffolding which now holds it in place. The roof consists of interlocking joists, between which are once-vivid depictions of the stars and god-men. Sadly, it will probably be replaced with something plain and modern; something altogether more secular.

The panting hackette finally reaches me. She jabs out a sweaty hand and declares: 'Oh, I need to do more exercise.'

Already, I loathe this woman; but I loathe myself even more. I have the attitude of a willing penitent, ready to submit myself to righteous punishment. I lead her into the office, slump into a chair and wait while she divests herself of her jacket and searches through her massive leather bag for the tools of her sordid trade.

'Well,' she says as she sits opposite me. I ignore this prelude, this marked attempt at charm. I commence speaking. I tell her everything, or almost everything: my experience of this girl's death, followed by my contact with the gardaí and everything they told me about this unfortunate girl, this Manda.

I don't mention Jack, naturally. Wisely, the reporter doesn't interrupt, but scribbles furiously: the sound of a mouse trapped in a small space.

I finish, and expect her to go. It is evident that there is nothing more to say, that I have fully exhausted my usefulness to her. I don't look up. I can't.

But she remains where she is, rustling and groaning and shifting on her seat, as if something has trapped her there and she is struggling to escape.

Then it comes: the softened tone, the elongated vowels which no doubt she imagines sound the same as compassion; a limping totter of words which take their time to stop off at every condescending cliché they can find. She suggests that I was a *comfort* to Manda during her final seconds. It is a vomit of well-meaning insults which reach their zenith with the harshest of all: that she, this bedraggled pimp of words, knew Manda. And of course, believing it would please me, she has to mention Manda's great *Faith*.

Faith. Hundreds of years of mistranslation has the Galilean exhorting all he meets to 'believe' in him. But the word he uses in the original Greek texts is *pistis*: which doesn't mean *faith*. It means *loyalty*.

Now the anger comes. But it is not energising; more as if black walls suddenly partition my vision, screening out all but my failure: not just in relation to the girl, but everything I have set out to do since the seminary. It has all been wrong. Worse: it has been cowardly and hypocritical. I have peddled myths just like the rest of them, hoping that others might sense the music hidden behind my stock phrases. There are no others like me; or at least, none who will admit it. I am alone with a howling truth which for the last two decades I have denied.

This is the truth behind what has happened to me.

I wish to say these things, to declare them, but the words shoot through my mind far too quickly to marshal. Like grabbed raindrops, they splatter against me. I have nothing, but must make her go. So I descend to her level.

'Fuck off.'

She makes a noise, as if she is genuinely surprised by such vulgarity; as if it's certainly not the kind of language she's used to hearing in the salubrious offices of the *Daily Tit* or whatever her rag is called. She stands, picks up her leather sack and flounces out, leaving me to listen to the blood raging around my brain and watching the shake in my hands. I know what I must do; all I can do. I must burn it to the ground.

CHAPTER THIRTY ONE
Baz Carroll

Two days now and she won't talk to me. She hasn't told me to leave, so that's something. But she hasn't told me to stay either. Just ignores me. Puts the meals on the table but won't sit down. Spends most of the time out of the house with Holly. I've never seen her like this before; it's like she doesn't know what to do, and I can't remember me ma ever being like that. She's annoyed, and I know what she's thinking, but for fuck's sake, I'm the one with a price on his head; I'm the one the cops are looking for. If I leave the house, I'm a fucking corpse.

I was hoping she'd calm down, but there's no sign of that. Every time the telly goes on there's more news about that dead girl and how the guards are progressing in their fucking investigations. There's a cop shop just around the corner from this house, so they can't have progressed that much. The papers are even worse. This morning they had some priest who said something to her before she died. Sweet Jesus, they'll have interviewed every fucker who ever met her before the end of this.

All I do is sit around. I go for smokes in the back garden. I watch telly. I sleep. I scratch meself. But it's driving me mad. It's like waiting for something but you don't know what it is.

So this evening, when Holly has just gone to bed and she's banging around the kitchen, I say, 'Ma, I can't stand this.'

She says nothing at first, but then turns around to look at me.

'So what are you going to do?' she says.

'I dunno.'

Fucking genius thing to say.

'You'd better make a decision,' she says. 'You can't go on like this.'

'I know, Ma, but what can I do?'

'You have to go to the guards, obviously.'

'If I go to the coppers, I'm dead. The Georgians will fucking kill me.'

'Not if the guards arrest them. Not if you give evidence against them.'

'Be a nark? Ah, Ma. I couldn't do that. And the Georgians would get me anyway, I'm telling ya. There's loads of blokes happy to do it for a couple of hundred euros and a bag of coke. The guards can't protect their own holes, never mind me. And why would they be bothered anyway?'

'I'd make sure they'd be bothered,' she says.

'Ma, this is different,' I say. 'You don't know what it's like. You can't stop them blokes. And it would feel weird anyway, doing that. Giving evidence. Couldn't do that.'

Her face is getting a bit red now.

'You *couldn't* do that? Why? Because it's wrong? Is that why? Barry, if there's one thing I've come to understand about you, it's that you are capable of anything. Absolutely anything.'

She's not shouting. I fucking hate that.

'Ma, can I explain it to you?'

She's turned around from me again.

'Ma, can I tell you what happened? Do you not want to hear my side? Are you believing the papers over me?'

'Make your own dinner,' she says, and walks out of the room.

CHAPTER THIRTY TWO

Rachel Belton

In the Russian Orthodox Church, a bell is not regarded as a musical instrument. Unlike western European church bells, the Russian version is not tuned to a major or minor chord: each has its individual sound, where the intention is not to play melodies but to produce bone-clanging layers of rhythm. The Russian church bell must be loud and distinctive, because its function is to represent the voice of God.

Funny, the things that stay with you. When Daniel rang from Sergiyev Posad and told me this, so breathy and excited, I remember every word; I suppose because it had been such a long time since he had displayed enthusiasm for anything. The monks had let him touch one of the bells afterwards. The sensation had been like an electric shock.

'The Voice of God. Isn't that extraordinary?'

Giving up the mountains had been far more difficult for him than we imagined. Being Daniel, he didn't issue a word of complaint, but we both had to live with his unease; the unspoken suspicion that he had ceased to make sense. He set up a charity to help injured climbers – to remind himself why he had given up, he said – but he lost interest after a few months and handed it over to someone else. He tried the lecture circuit for a while, but he was never comfortable in front of audiences. He talked about writing a book, but never made it past jotting down a few notes.

The new house in Dalkey kept him occupied for a while. We could have had it all done by builders, of course, but Daniel insisted on doing as much as possible himself. I like it when I'm sweating, he said. When I have cuts on my hands.

I wanted to cry. I wanted to tell him to grow up.

The climbing school was my idea, inspired mostly by my need to get him out of the house. At first he wasn't keen – he didn't feel he had the patience to teach – but soon he realised that at least this was a job where he could be outside, climbing something. Sweating. Cutting his hands. It was a compromise for me: you can break your neck just as easily in Wicklow. But at least he was coming home every evening.

The bell, though: that's what I think brought it back. All the hocus-pocus from his childhood. I suppose you can never escape.

And then I got pregnant, and he was off doing up the bedroom: installing monkey bars so the child could kill itself before getting up for breakfast. I made him take them out and put them in the back garden. He put a sandbox in the bedroom instead; which was also moved to the garden. Life with Daniel, as I'd hoped, wasn't dull. I woke up bleeding a few weeks later and the doctor shrugged and said sorry, you've lost that one. Sorry. I'd been seven weeks' pregnant.

How to react was what threw me: at times I felt the acute pinch of grief, then nothing, then guilt for feeling nothing. So much of our emotions are instructed, and I longed for someone to tell me how to feel, to point to a place on a chart. Like the death of a family member, but less so. You should experience fifty per cent of the anguish that you might feel if, say, you lost a brother.

The gynaecologist said there was no particular reason; these things just happen. Daniel kept asking, yes, but what does it mean? What does it mean? And he kept asking when we got home, as if I could summon an answer, as if there was some secret guide to my reproductive organs which I could show him. Eventually, I screamed: how do I know? He retreated to the cold little room which at the time he called his office. I went to bed.

We spent several weeks at this odd sort of mourning: missing a person we'd never met, who hadn't existed. Is it enough to imagine a person to make them real? By not imagining, do we deny them existence? I don't know what Daniel was doing all this time, though I can guess. I spent much of it infuriated with myself for even being subject to these feelings, and the rest wondering why there was no one I could ask for help. The hospital never rang to see how I was doing. My mother rang once or twice, but was clearly uncomfortable; and anyway, I insisted to anyone who asked that I was perfectly fine. Daniel's mother never rang at all, which didn't surprise me. Odd as they are, they are a family that values fortitude. You don't complain. You don't cry. You get on with it. I have always admired them for this.

Nonetheless, I did start to wonder if there shouldn't be some sort of counselling system for women in my position, something which should kick in immediately. To distract myself, I decided to find out if such services exist in Ireland or in any other country; and then I forgot to. Daniel emerged from his office and seemed fine, and I was strong enough again to present my public face. We got on with it, and I was proud of that.

The second lasted nearly fifteen weeks. I had to have a D&C to make sure I had expelled all the foetal material. Foetal material. Sucked out of me like so much rubbish. This time Daniel shouted at the gynaecologist, who remained impassive, who said this wasn't indicative of anything; said I could obviously conceive without too much difficulty: you can do it again. You don't smoke. You've stayed away from the alcohol and coffee. There are no signs of hormonal imbalances or an incompetent cervix. For some reason, for some people, it happens. Just bad luck.

Bad luck? You call this fucking bad luck?

We went home and argued about the way he had spoken to the consultant. I went to bed; he went to his office, and this time I couldn't help but wonder if all this was due to some weakness in me, some deficiency. Too cold, too businesslike, not maternal. My womb as a hostile environment. Get a move on, kid. I've things to do.

But over a mostly silent breakfast, the slight tremor in Daniel's chin brought me to realise that he felt the same about himself: some problem with his sperm; his milk poisoned. We had no idea how to go about fixing this. We had believed everything could be fixed.

So we both became website junkies, entertaining every half-baked dietary regime, every study which claimed that you should sit for the nine months. Or stand. Or dance. We chose what seemed sensible to us: as a climber, Daniel knows something about body chemistry.

Ten weeks, eleven weeks, twelve, fourteen. A crumb of hope. We can fix it. After fifteen and a half weeks I woke up with the sheets drenched in globs of blood. I didn't even want to go to the hospital, and at first I refused. I lay in the red pools, sobbing, while Daniel tried to coax me up; until he lost his temper and roared, for God's sake Rachel, don't be so bloody *weak*.

I said nothing in the car. I hated him then.

He spoke: rapidly, like a child reciting a poem they have learned by rote. He told me that crying is a good thing, a healthy thing; that I needed to grieve for my dead babies because that was what they were. They were innocent beings who had passed over. But they are happy now, he said. They are in the light, and the only sadness they carry is the knowledge of our pain, of our refusal to think of them as people, the same as anyone you would see on the street. I gave the first two names, he told me. They wanted them. Jane and Tom. They are called Jane and Tom.

When we got out of the car, I smacked him across the face.

I went away after that: visited some old college friends in New York. I didn't tell him where I'd gone or how long I'd be away. I wasn't leaving Daniel, so much as experimenting with the idea; seeing how it fitted. It was unendurable.

I returned to Ireland, to our home. That was barely tolerable either.

But Daniel is a patient man and, like me, almost unstoppable when convinced he's right. While I had been away, splashing around in doubt, he had become more certain that speaking to our dead children was the only way to find solace. There were three now. Jane, Tom and Emily.

For weeks we barely conversed. But he chipped away at me, solicitous and deferential. He would ask how I was, until eventually I returned something more than an offhand reply. We sat in our grand, empty living room, Daniel three seats away. I spoke about what I did in New York, my desolation in a mid-town hotel room, and my fury with him, with our families, with the world. I cried. We hugged. It felt appropriate, nothing more.

Three days later he coaxed me down to his shrine. You don't have to believe, he said. Just see what it's like; if it makes you feel better.

He'd taken out the desk, the seat and any pictures; stripped the room bare, and in their place built a wooden, tepee-like structure. My Dream Tent. I thought: this should be funny. I should be laughing.

Inside, there were dozens of candles, and one of the walls was carpeted with various symbols I didn't recognise: some in frames, some apparently ripped from magazines. The second wall was blank, painted a pristine white, while the third featured three pencil drawings. Each was of a figure in shadow, without any discernible features. It's how I see them, he said. Like shadows. But I hear them clearly, and I *feel* them. That's the important thing.

I said: who? Already knowing the answer.

The kids. They are our kids.

I didn't reply. I dumbly let him sit me down and cross my legs. Relax. Breathe slowly. He set about lighting the candles, pausing before each one as if repeating some secret incantation. The candles threw multiple orange shadows of him against the tent walls, which eventually coalesced into a long-headed, beaky creature. I watched the shadow as he sat back beside me and breathed. Children, come to Mummy and Daddy. Look: Mummy is here.

My first jet of vomit put out half the candles, and as I crouched on my hands and knees, waiting for the rest to come, it again struck me that this should be funny. I should be laughing.

Daniel cleaned me up and put me to bed. I told him it might be best if he moved out for a few days.

I only wanted him out of the house so I could destroy that thing. Set it on fire. Take the rest of the house with it if needs be.

But I couldn't. I didn't have the courage to go down the stairs: just in case he was right. In case some floating grey versions of my children were down there, wondering why I didn't believe in them.

I spent three days cleaning, convinced that the smell of my sick was everywhere, but afraid to descend to the room where I had thrown up. I wrote letters to government ministers and local TDs, fuming about the lack of support and counselling; to organisations in the US and Britain, to mothering websites around the world. Then I rang the gynaecologist and told him I wanted every test he could think of, relevant or not. I wanted them. I was paying.

Daniel returned unannounced, the harrowed look on his face enough for me to let him back in. I probably conceived again that day. They tested me for blood pressure and diabetes, chromosomal abnormalities, nephritis and tumours. They put me on Clomid and prescribed total bed rest for the first three months. I got letters back from some of the TDs, inviting me to meetings. I said I can't. I'm pregnant.

This time I did see the face of my dead baby, squeezed out of me two days before she was due to arrive. She suddenly stopped moving, and I knew. We called her Edel. We had a sort of funeral, which we barely attended. I was zonked on tranquilisers. Daniel had succumbed to a sort of fever, wild-eyed and sweaty, watching our dead family swirling around him. He tried to bring me down to the shrine several times; like a drunken man trying to seduce a woman: half-coaxing, half-dragging. I scraped his face and neck. He left a sequence of black bruises on my shoulders. I flew to London and got my tubes tied. I didn't consult Daniel; didn't feel I needed to. To be honest, I didn't know if I would ever see him again, if he would ever emerge from his astral fog.

But he did, mostly. He texted. I flew home and told him I wanted to adopt.

We got Naoise less than six months later, and we've let him fill the house with his noises and smells. We try not to spoil him.

I'm not a great mother, or at least I'm not one of those who could happily stay at home and watch him grow. I'm not the domestic type. Neither of us is: we become uneasy if we are in the same place for too long; and it must be said, Daniel and I are still careful about how much time we spend together. Grief has made him a dreamer. I don't know what it's done to me. I have one child. Daniel has five. The material and the spiritual. There's still love there, of course; and, for the sake of that love, we work around it. We don't mention it; we don't show our scars to each other.

CHAPTER THIRTY THREE
Carol Murphy

'm in the lift heading up to Conor's apartment and already my stomach is twisting with nerves. But I have to visit. I have to. He's family. My cousin. Manda's brother. It's what families do.

When I rang he didn't even come to the phone. I spoke to his fiancée – Kristel, for God's sake. A blonde American princess, by the sound of her. The type he was bound to go for.

I hate her already.

When did I see him last? Must be a couple of years ago. Some bar in town. End of the summer, but still warm. I was having the last cigarette of the night, about to say my goodbyes when he appeared before me, obviously langers, his shirt half-in and half-out of his trousers; his dress-sense and self-control dramatically ruptured by drink. He spread out his arms like Christ and demanded, 'Smell me.'

I don't think I said anything – well, what could you say? But he kept on insisting. 'Go on, smell me.'

Conor smelt of sweat, mixed with vanilla.

He waved me closer. 'Good, eh? Made it myself. Just back from the South of France with a few of the lads. Ever heard of Grasse? It's where they invented perfume. They have this place there – lots of them, where you can do a tour and then make your own perfume. Forty Euro though – and *two hours* smelling these sticks? I said fuck that, chose a smell I liked and I was out of there in ten minutes. And it's what you smell now. It's good, yeah?'

We didn't speak for much longer after that. He abruptly marched off, presumably to find someone else to smell him. But it was that night he first told me about Kristel – that he had met her six months before at some legal conference in Boston or some such, and then she had visited here and now she was taking a leave of absence to come to Ireland and give the relationship a chance. Obviously, it worked out, seeing they got married. Nearly.

Perfect Conor, with his perfect job and perfect wife: like it was genetically predetermined.

Actually it's not like that at all. He couldn't be more different to Manda now, but as kids they were both wide-eyed and dreamy. After national school, she was educated locally while Conor (like his daddy before him) was dispatched to Gorse Wood Boarding School, where all traces of the bogger from County Galway were quickly rinsed out of him, replaced by a south Dublin-*yah* accent and a devotion to rugby. All of Conor's friends are ex-Gorse boys, the polo-shirt wearing sons of diplomats and billionaires, rightly presuming to be diplomats and billionaires themselves. Over the years I've occasionally bumped into Conor with a gang of them, always screamingly drunk. When he was at school, he never brought any of them home to Loughrea. Not once.

How do I know that?

I get out of the lift, pointlessly poke my fingers into my hair, have a brief panic about my clothes (I'm bulging out of these trousers today) and ring the bell. The door opens almost instantly, and perfectly proportioned light plunges into the hallway, framing Kristel. I almost laugh out loud. Black slacks, a white blouse and a peach jersey thrown over her shoulders. She slides back her lips to expose pristine teeth and extends a slender hand. 'Carol,' she says, in a Kennedyesque voice. 'It's great to meet you.'

She floats around and gently ushers me inwards. We walk down a corridor lined with posters for New York art exhibitions. I glimpse a small, tidy office and black and white photographs of a rugby-playing Conor. We emerge into a long rectangular room full of long rectangular furniture and a nice view of the canal. There's a scent, not unpleasant, of extinguished candles. And I hear Kristel gently breathe the words, 'Conor, don't be an asshole.'

Conor, it seems, has suddenly decided there's something far more important he should be doing than talking to his cousin. He's already halfway out another door. I halt, but before I can start my it's-OK-I-understand speech, Kristel has shot past me. 'Conor, we spoke about this,' she says, firmly, though not in a catty way. I feel a shot of admiration for her.

He's obviously furious about the stories in the paper: the priest, his mother.

Another family death, and another person who can't bear to see me.

She leads a head-bowed Conor back into the living room.

He still won't look at me, his eyes fixed on the oak floor. His hair is starting to thin a bit. I wonder if he has noticed yet. I wonder if Kristel has told him.

I half-expect Kristel to slap Conor across the back of the neck and bark *well? What have you got to say to your cousin?* But instead she deposits him at the edge of the sofa, nods in an it'll-be-fine-now way and pads gently from the room. She points, letting me know her whereabouts in case Conor attempts another runner.

Pitch perfect.

Bitch.

He's standing in a field. Tears on his cheeks. Saying No.

He sniffs and abruptly looks up at me. I shiver.

'Carol.'

'Conor.'

He gestures towards an armchair and I sit.

'How are you bearing up?' I ask.

'Are you going to quote my answer?'

Would Hazel have told him about the story in advance? No; of course not. Probably the first he heard of it was when he saw the newspaper. Just like that time with Manda and the calculator: passive-aggressive venom. *Should I not have done the interview Conor? Do you think? But I had no one else to talk to...*

No wonder he can't bear to look at me.

I don't blame him.

Yet I don't want to admit this; I'm not going to apologise. I'm prepared to sit here and come up with any trite argument I can.

It must show in my face. He sighs loudly. 'Sorrysorrysorry,' he breathes, as if he's been saying it a lot today.

'It's OK,' I say.

'No, it's not.'

He stands, straightening himself. Conor always had good posture. There was something militaristic about him, which gave him an air of authority. It was why he was the leader when we were kids. He puts his hands behind his back, like a general about to address the troops.

'I remember all those summers. I know you loved Manda.'

There it is again. People reminding me of feelings I can't recall: of a version of my childhood that didn't happen.

Yet I don't feel like contradicting him. I'm suddenly aware of blood rushing through my veins: I can hear it, and find myself thinking what it must be like for tourists just before a tsunami hits. One second sipping cocktails in the dreamy sun, then only a few seconds to wonder if your life has been a waste. Like Manda, sailing through the air. Another shiver passes through me. Conor sits down again and takes on a softer tone.

'It's just, you know, seeing it in the paper, and it's there beside a picture of a drunk celebrity or whatever. As if they were of equal importance.'

I nod. I consider offering, *better me than someone else*. I haven't written about her sex life or about her wanting to become a nun – and any other reporter would have been all over that. Slightly-slutty, slightly-fruity murder victims are perfect for tabloids. But I've kept her bland and distant, pretty and blameless.

Well, aren't I great.

'Fuck!' Conor is standing again, as if suddenly electrocuted. 'I'm sorry, Carol. I'm trying not to blame you. It would have happened anyway, I know that. But it was you who put Mother on the front page in that ridiculous hat. For fuck's sake.'

Mother. Long gone is Conor calling her Mammy. Gorse Wood knocked that out of him.

'She insisted on the hat.'

'Oh, I'm sure she did, while Juanita did an inventory of the house. Fuck it. Kristel and I should be in Boston, having a proper life. You did know that, didn't you? As soon as we were married, we were off to Boston. I have exams scheduled for the American Bar. We're paying rent now. On a home over there. Our new home'.

He stops to rub his face.

Inventory of the house?

'And here I am going on about *myself* and we haven't even buried Manda yet.'

'Yes,' I say, as neutrally as possible. 'Is there any word? On when the autopsy will be finished?'

He doesn't reply.

'Did you see much of her since she came home?' I try my best not to sound as if I'm interviewing him, though I doubt it will do any good. He fears me a bit now. Meet Conor in any other setting – for a brief chat or a long lunch or even a few pints – and you'll see a man who is perhaps a little distant, but always polite, interested in you, consummately self-possessed. But it doesn't come easy to him, and it's at times like this that the effort of being the daily Conor, the nice marketable Conor, uses up most of his resources. He's nothing left in the tank to cope with a disaster. Perhaps he'll get some therapy in Boston. He and Kristel could get a family rate.

He pulls at the leg of his too-well-ironed jeans. He long ago stopped being comfortable in casual clothes. Out of his suit and he's not sure who Conor Ferguson is, how he should be.

'No,' he says, as if answering an accusation. 'I didn't see much of her. Before she left or after. What does that mean, anyway? What are you getting at, Carol? Is that why you're here? To drag up all, you know…'

Conor pauses, panting, then drops his voice to an edgy whisper. He doesn't want Kristel to hear.

'Did *you* see much of her, Carol? Think you're going to waltz in here and judge me?'

'Conor, I didn't mean –'

'Oh, fuck off.'

I don't know what he's talking about. I've done more harm than good by coming here. Should have phoned or sent a card. Anything but this.

He leans back on the sofa, leather squeaking beneath him. He puts his hands to his face, causing his black top to rise up a little. Belly still nice and flat. Kristel probably kicks him out of bed every morning to do a few miles around Herbert Park, along with all the other flawless Dublin 4 jocks and skinny-neurotic middle-aged women fleeing death and collapsing marriages.

I'm fat and lazy and judgemental.

Conor starts talking, but still can't look at me. He drapes an arm over his face, like a shy child.

'Look, I did try to keep in touch, but you know what it's like. Everyone's busy. You have to organise things weeks in advance. But then, I dunno, in the year before she went away there was this constant niggle. All she wanted to do was argue about bloody politics, which was just a way of getting at me for working in corporate law. Suddenly I'm evil incarnate and all the ills of the world, the country going bust, global warming, Iraq, Palestine – it's all my fault.'

'Hmm,' I say. 'Well, it seems like when she was in college she did get involved in radical –'

'And it's so bloody unfair! I worked hard. Manda of all people knows that, *knew* that – I deserve what I have. And it's not like I'm, I dunno, promoting child labour or something. What I do creates wealth, creates jobs. And isn't that what we need now most of all? That's a good thing. Isn't it?'

I shrug, trying to make the gesture seem sympathetic. 'You know what it's like in college, Conor. It's an insulated world.'

'Exactly!' he yells, stretching out his hand towards me as if I had just won a prize for giving the right answer. 'And even when I explained myself she still took it to mean that I'd got all cynical and had compromised my principles. But I was never left wing, she knew that. She had this really, really annoying habit of assuming everyone agreed with her.'

'Yeah,' I say. 'I know.'

I smile at the memory.

But this seems to deflate Conor, past his annoyance and around to his dead sister, lying in a skip. He sighs and leans back again. The succulent couch and the silvery view of the canal were probably the main attractions when he was showing the place to prospective tenants. Now he'll have to ring them and delay. Or perhaps he's done that already. How long though? How long do you postpone a wedding after the bridesmaid has been murdered?

'All I was trying to get her to understand was that I like what I do. I think it has worth, and that – if you understand economics – what I do helps people down the line. But she wouldn't even consider that. And when she seemed to understand what I was saying, that I believe in what I do, well then it was like, like she looked at me with disgust. Real disgust.'

He gestures, to see if I can explain. I shrug back. His voice deepens and becomes slower.

'I just thought it was one of her dopey phases, that it would pass like everything else. But she was the same when she came back from her travels. Worse even. We hardly ever spoke. She seemed to find it difficult, like I was physically making her ill, and every time – every time – she'd end up screaming at me. Or chanting slogans like a zombie. People before profits. As if that would change anything. And what does that mean, anyway?'

Now he looks at me directly, for the first time since I've arrived. His eyes are red-rimmed, his skin broken and blotchy. He slowly shakes his head.

'Fucking hippy politics,' he mutters. 'That's what killed her.'

He switches his gaze to the large window, all his talk gone.

'Did you ever meet any of them?' I ask. 'Her political friends?'

Without looking at me, he curtly shakes his head.

He keeps looking out, silent; hardly moving now.

'But I do wonder,' he eventually says, and already I know that this will be more question than statement. He wants to know what I think. 'I do wonder. I know you're not supposed to say it. It's not PC or whatever. But, you know, she was *sick*.'

He looks at me now, as if I'm his co-conspirator. I don't know what to say.

'I mean, surely it's reasonable to ask if that had anything to do with it. Maybe that's why she got involved with these people – maybe they saw she was vulnerable and exploited her, you know?'

I shrug. I feel a burning at the back of my neck. My mother calling me into the kitchen – no, ambushing me as I swept through, on the way to some friend's place or the pub. I was in college then. She wore a pained expression: part of her routine aimed at letting me know that I was an adult now and therefore it gave her no pleasure – *no pleasure at all* – to say I was a selfish cow who used her home like a hotel and treated her parents like members of her staff. All of which was true. But this time her tone was without that tight-mouthed quality: it was soft, uncertain; she'd never had to speak to me this way before. It halted my rush out the door: just one word, spoken like a desperate prayer.

'Please.'

I paused, just to stare at her, to wonder what new tactic this could be.

'Car, something to tell you.'

Despite my objections, she still reserved the right to use the abbreviated version of my name, though only on special occasions. *Car* meant: this is serious. I don't want to fight.

Everyone still goes on about how much I look like my mother. But she had a grace I never possessed, which as a child I quickly gave up trying to copy; a languid way of picking up a cup or sliding on her coat, and I often caught men looking at her. She was slimmer than me, she had better skin and could easily have passed as my older sister. Even in the weeks before her death, the days before, the day. It was sudden. She died. Just like that.

She'd pulled her sleeves over her hands, more the nervous teenager than me.

'It's just, well, about Manda. She's had to go into hospital.'

It was almost as if she was asking my permission to tell me this.

'Oh,' I said. 'What's wrong?'

For the life of me I can't remember where I was going that day, only that it was something I was late for. I desperately wanted to peek at my watch or even tell Mum to hurry up, but I knew that wouldn't go down well.

I hadn't seen Conor or Manda for years.

My mother bit her lip.

'It's a psychiatric hospital,' she whispered.

'Oh,' I said again, careful to inject a little shock into my voice. 'That's terrible.'

'Yes, yes.'

I knew I was required to ask.

'So what happened?'

'We don't know. She had some sort of breakdown. Can't start college this year, apparently, which is a terrible shame. Perhaps it was the strain of the Leaving Cert?'

She stared at me, ready to scoop up any evidence of upset.

I think I said OK or thanks, made some excuse and left.

As far as I can recall, Manda's breakdown was never mentioned in our house again. And I know this is difficult to believe – I scarcely believe it myself – but I never thought of it either. Not until now, with Conor staring across at me, wondering if it was the poor wiring in Manda's brain which killed her.

'No,' I say to him. 'All that was years ago, wasn't it? And she was in hospital just the one time, wasn't she?'

Conor nods.

'She got better,' I say. 'Just because she had problems once doesn't mean she couldn't become a big strong woman able to make her own decisions.'

He is looking away again, but still shaking his head.

'Yes,' he says. 'Yes, she could certainly make up her own mind.'

He smiles at me.

I smile back, and for a moment I love him intensely.

She had a nervous breakdown, and I forgot about it? I never thought about it? How could I do that? Perhaps there's something else going on here; perhaps there's something wrong with me.

We both fall silent again, like exhausted boxers. I sense that Conor has more to say, though this time I don't want to hear it; I don't want him to pin me with a glance.

Kristel wafts back into the room. I assume she's been listening to our conversation. She gives me a look – not unkind – to indicate that Conor's had enough now. We idly chat for a while about the coverage in the other papers (a few reporters have rung), my job in general, when the wedding might take place (she doesn't know), what part of the world Dad is in. We talk as if we are waiting for something to happen, which of course we are: we're waiting for me to leave. But there are ways of doing these things, especially in such circumstances, especially in Ireland, and I appreciate that Kristel is prepared to take her time. She offers me a cup of tea or coffee, and even though I'm more comfortable than I would have imagined, I decline. I need a cigarette, and Conor and Kristel are – of course – non-smokers. They would probably let me if I asked, but in trying to accommodate me they would rinse all the joy out of it: looking for something that resembles an ashtray, trying to keep the slightly appalled look off their faces when I light up, even falling briefly silent, as if it is not possible for me to smoke and speak simultaneously. And of course they'd be poised to rush to the big windows and fling them open the moment I leave.

Still. I've got to give them up.

I say I have to go and Kristel nods in a business-like manner. No *are you sure?* The visit has reached a natural end and I find myself warming to Kristel for not trying to disguise this fact. An Irish person would drag it out. They'd want you to go but feel guilty about it. Then again, that sort of thing is dying out. The guilt has been replaced by blame. Listen to the radio any day of the week. It's like our guilt points outwards now, at everybody else.

Conor doesn't say another word, but hugs me tightly. I feel him shuddering; internal winds sweeping through. Kristel leads me into the hallway.

She gives me a sympathetic look and drops her voice.

'The Fergusons aren't great for talking about stuff. But I guess all families are a little weird.'

I realise I like Kristel enormously. People are surprising me a lot lately. And I want to tell her so right away. I want to suggest we go shopping or invite her to one of the girly nights in my flat (the next of which is tomorrow tonight and I've done nothing). But instead I give her a hug, to prove that we Murphys are emotionally balanced people who are totally alive to their feelings. I silently promise that I will invite Kristel out. Perhaps after the funeral, when things have calmed down. Perhaps we'll become friends. Perhaps.

Chapter Thirty Four

Maurice Kiberd

I went to the funeral. Not for him; I didn't give a damn about him. I went because Ma wanted me to. I got the body over and arranged the funeral and the plot in the graveyard. Paid for the whole thing. I did it because she's me ma, and she wanted me to. That's what you do, isn't it?

If I hadn't gone, she could have been all by herself. Me da had a brother in England, but we hadn't a clue how to find him.

Yet the church was packed. Full of old ones shaking out their umbrellas from the bucketing rain outside, talking into their bony hands when they saw me. I hadn't thought about the neighbours. Me da was born here, you see. A fair few of them old ones would have known him; one or two might even have remembered his parents. The Irish love funerals, don't they? So that was enough reason for them to turn up, to crowd around Ma afterwards, hugging her and telling her that me da was a lovely man. A lovely man. Always polite, always clean. A great singer. And there was me ma, in tears, saying: yes, he was.

I suppose it was easier for her to go along with it.

They said nothing to me.

But that's what happens, isn't it? They'd probably seen him with the shiner all them years ago and thought: that young fella is a bad one. Driving his father away, keeping his mother like a slave in the house.

Killed his own father. That's what he did.

But they didn't know the truth, like me and Ma did. All they listened to was their own yak yak yak. They heard what they wanted to hear. They thought: oh, that young fella is a bit dodgy. And that was the whole story.

To hell with them. I didn't care.

We buried him, and we went back to normal. Normal life, the way we both liked it. Never talked about him again. Me ma left some mass cards over the fire place, but I suppose that was just her being religious and that.

I forgot all about him. I can honestly say that. I was busy driving me taxi, and didn't give him another thought. No reason to. But it's funny isn't it? You forget something, and then one day it comes back to you – and then you realise how long it's been since you thought of it. Years. Just like that.

She didn't do much afterwards. Every now and again one of her friends from the street would whisper to me: Maurice, would you encourage your mother to go out a bit more? It would do her good. And I'd promise to say it to her. Sometimes she said she would, other times she said she didn't feel like it. I'd say, OK, Ma. Whatever you want.

You do the same things, day in, day out, and you're happy doing them, but you don't keep count, do you? I didn't know how many times I'd eaten me dinner or gone to work or started me shift on the Stephen's Green rank or said to me ma: are you going out this Friday? Why don't you go out?

Only it struck me one day that Ma had never really been the same since the funeral. She'd gone into herself, you know? She'd let herself get old. Me ma, with her lovely auburn hair. She was an old lady.

It seemed like it happened all of a sudden. I don't know. The hair was nearly white and she had this stoop like her chest was hurting her and it took twice as long for her to get up and down to the shops. She was nervous as well. The area was getting worse for the crime and vandalism. Really bad.

I'd been driving the taxi for years by this stage and saw it all over the city, but I'd still get a shock when I'd come home and see the smashed bottles and the graffiti. Young fellas, a gang of them, terrorising the place, hopping rocks through windows and shouting abuse at some of the old women. Robbing stuff. The guards were useless. They'd be called, night after night, but the young fellas would be long gone by the time they arrived.

There were residents' meetings: with a garda, with a councillor. We put community alert stickers on our windows, as if that would do any good. And for a long time – a long time – I went along with it. I went to all the meetings; I even stood up and spoke at a couple of them. I knew it wasn't going to do any good, even though I suppose I hoped it would. But I had to for Ma's sake. I knew she didn't want me to sort it out my way – which I could have done at any time. But she didn't want that again. She wanted me to be a sheep, along with everyone else.

So I did nothing. I tried me best – I really did, even though she knew how angry I'd get when I heard the stories: urinating into letterboxes, and walking away, laughing. Some nights I'd be shaking, I'd be so furious. Have to go to me room and smack meself; the way I used to when I was a kid.

I don't have to tell you what happened. There were more meetings. I didn't bother going. There were empty promises from the guards to patrol the street. The place got worse and worse: even the postman refused to deliver letters once or twice. It was that bad.

I don't know if it was the postman that finally made me do something. I don't know if it was one particular thing. Can't remember. Could have been just that the opportunity came along: a night when I was home early and Ma was in bed and I could see them waltzing about the place; like no one could touch them.

I parked the car a little bit away from the house and waited. One of them actually kicked it. Can you believe that? With me inside. That would have been enough, because I like to keep the Merc spotless, so I do. Pride in me work. My car is a 1991 Mercedes 500 SEL V8. Metallic blue. Leather seats. Beautiful. Can't tell you how many times people have got in the back and looked around it said, nice car. And I like that, you know? They enjoy the taxi ride: it's not just getting from A to B. It's a pleasant experience. Who wouldn't like that? I use this special stuff to clean the seats that keeps up the leathery smell, you know? I'm real careful about washing, drying and waxing – got a paint job five years ago with original Mercedes paint that turned out brilliant. I bring her in for a regular service, though I can do most of the jobs meself: changing the brake fluid, bleeding the fuel lines, cleaning the air box, all that. I thought about buying an old Merc and doing it up, I know so much about them now. Not for the money, like. Just for the love of it. I'd enjoy that. I need to get a place to do it though.

Luckily, he didn't put a dent in the car, but I put a few dents in him. One of the little bastards even had a knife, but I sorted that quickly enough with the baseball bat.

A couple of them got a good going over: the bigger ones, the hard men. But the others I only gave a few slaps. I wanted them to carry their mates out of the road while I followed, so I could show them the line they could never step over again. And they didn't.

Ma knew what I'd done, but what could she say? I think everyone knew, the way the neighbours looked at me after that. But the kids never grassed me up. They knew what was good for them. The cops called around and gave me all this earache about how two of the poor boys ended up in hospital and all that. But I reckon the guards were only doing it cos they had to. I saved them the bother. Did their job for them.

What are you telling *me* for? That's all I said to them. They'd nothing to say to that.

No one came up and thanked me. All that complaining about living in fear, about the guards doing nothing. But when someone grew a pair and sorted it out, all I got was gossip and dirty looks. People want it both ways, don't they? They want the problems solved but they don't want to do anything about it. Would it have bothered them too much if the guards had done what I'd done? Would it hell. Bloody hypocrites.

Doesn't knock a feather out of me, though. Really. I'm well used to people only being concerned about their own little patch, not caring about the community or even the people next door. Things have changed, changed more than you'd realise. Years ago, when I was a kid, like, those young fellas would have got a few belts from the guards. Problem solved.

But not any more. That's what I learned on the job. Like a mug I couldn't believe that the cops weren't bothering to do anything about all the chaos. Every Saturday night it like was Baghdad on the streets of Dublin – and you'd hardly ever see a guard. And I thought this must be because the guards didn't know, that no one was telling them. What a dope.

I'd say for the first six months I was driving the taxi, I must have gone up to the law nearly every night I was on: I saw people getting the tar beaten out of them. I saw cars getting robbed, windows getting smashed, graffiti, pissing and puking and worse on the streets. Disgusting. I was up so often that that a fair few of them got to know me. *Hello again, Maurice,* they'd say, with that sarcastic tone – like I was wasting their time – and them in their comfortable stations with their feet up on the table.

Not once – not bloody once – did they ever ring me or follow up on anything I told them. And it wasn't like I was a nutcase or I was looking for attention or gratitude or something. I was doing me bit as a citizen like you're supposed to. Like you're supposed to.

So what I'm doing back here, I don't know. But I have been thinking about it. Before when I'd come in it was about scraps and vandalism and that. This is murder. Poor young girl, pushed out a window. Probably put up a struggle when that little bastard was robbing her. And he has the brass neck to take a taxi home afterwards. My God. They can't ignore that.

Just thought: what did he pay me with? Was it *her* money?

'Maurice,' says the guard behind the counter. The place smells of tea and toast, and I see your man has a crumb hanging off the edge of his moustache. I don't remember him. Maybe I reported something to him in the past. Maybe he was there for the other trouble. Doesn't matter: all I know is that he's already taken on a sarky tone before I've even said anything. Suddenly I get a fierce itch on the back of my hands. But I resist it. It's cleared up a little lately.

I tell him I think I saw the fella who murdered that young girl, and he waves a finger at me.

'Now don't you be using that word,' he says in a big culchie accent. 'We don't know if anyone murdered anyone yet.'

What a dipstick. I tell him my story anyway, and in return I get even more sarcasm.

'Really?' says this idiot. 'So you happen to have the home address of the alleged killer? Well aren't you the one-man crime-fighting force, Maurice?'

This fella is younger than me, but I'm not old. I can still feel the power in me shoulders. This fella looks wrecked. Round blotchy face; a big gut pushing against the buttons of his shirt. I could leap over this counter before he put his mug down. Give him a shot in the head to make him dizzy, then a couple in the belly to bring him down. Then work away at my leisure. I could make his uniform more red than blue.

But I don't. I stay calm; I don't scratch. The guard is writing down what I say, but doesn't seem that interested in where I brought this bloke. I have to *suggest* that he takes down the address. Pleasant Lane. He looks at me like I'm making it up.

That's it. I walk out and I know that's the last time I'm ever going into a garda station. That's it. I feel like something has broken inside me. I shouldn't have bothered. All I get is ignored. Treated like I'm wrong in the head. There are a lot of selfish, lazy people out there; people who want to be sheep because it's the easiest thing to do. So they get what they want. They get anarchy.

CHAPTER THIRTY FIVE

Baz Carroll

Me head feels like it's gonna fucking explode now. She was out of the house again today, and this time I got the feeling, you know? The *itch*. Came at me all of a sudden, and it started to make sense. Bit of skag and it would all go away. At least I'd be able to handle it better. The stress. The long boring hours. Nothing to do. Telly is shite. She doesn't have Sky. Or even a PlayStation. Of course I can't ring anyone or stick me head out the door in broad daylight, but this idea came to me, like a vision: I could order a taxi, then skip into town and tap up some of them blokes who hang out around the DART station, blokes that don't know me. Get a taxi, score the gear, be back before anyone knows I'm gone. Then I'd be all right. But I've no money. Well, a tenner, but that's not enough.

So I start searching the house for cash – and I'm in Ma's bedroom, pulling out drawers like a mad thing. Back to the same old habits, except if she copped on – and she would – I'd be out of the house for the last time. Nowhere to go except down a dark alleyway.

I tidy up after meself and get out of the room. I go into the drinks cupboard and knock back a load of Baileys – it's the only fucking thing she has – and then I go to bed. At least I can sleep for a few hours.

They're back when I wake up. I can hear Holly and Ma chatting away downstairs, and now I want to be there with them, in the warm. She hasn't told Holly not to have anything to do with me, but the child gets the vibes. If I say something to Holly now, she looks over at

Ma, like she's asking: can I talk to the crazy murdering junkie? Fuck's sake.

I go downstairs, and the two of them go dead quiet, like when a gunfighter walks into a bar. Holly is having her tea. Macaroni cheese. I used to get that when I was a kid. I sit down beside her and ask does she like what she's eating and she nods at me, her little gob full of grub and her eyes all shining up. And I ask can I have a bit and Holly slides the bowl over to me and I say yum yum yum. She smiles at me like I'm a bit mad. Which I am.

I can tell this is winding up Ma. Talking to me own daughter, having a laugh with her. This winds her up.

So when she's finished, I tell Holly to bring the bowl over to the sink, just like I used to do when I was her age. And she does, like the good little girl she is. Ma takes the bowl off her and says she can play with her Bratz before her bath. So Holly runs off, leaving this massive fucking silence behind her.

I'm trying to think of what to say first, but Ma beats me to it. She seems calm, but a bit like a robot. She talks slowly, like I'm an idiot that can't understand. And she tells me that for years and years I've been taking drugs, and that this has probably changed me brain, damaged the way I look at things. Even now, when you're off them. Drugs made you a liar and a thief, she says. Drugs made you selfish. You'd get into trouble but always blame other people. You'd come here and steal to get money for drugs. From me. From your mother. Even though I gave you every chance for a decent life, for a happy life. But you were the one who chose to throw that away. You chose to become a hopeless drug addict, like Martin and all the others. But unlike them you can't blame poverty or having a bad home or an alcoholic parent. I gave you everything, Barry. Everything.

'Yeah,' I say.

I wasn't expecting her to speak to me at all, so now I don't know what to say. It's like a speech she's been rehearsing.

'Yeah,' she says back. 'So perhaps because your brain is so addled by drugs, you don't realise what you are doing now. What you are doing now, Barry, is far worse than anything you have done before. Far worse.

'By staying here, you are putting your daughter in danger. If these men found out that you were here… And you're giving her a memory, Barry. She's old enough, she'll remember. She'll remember that after her father murdered an innocent young girl, all he did was come here and hide. No remorse, no worry, no concern for anyone else. When she's older, when she remembers all this, how do you think that will make her feel? You had no reason to become an addict, Barry. But you're giving Holly one.'

I'm fucking stunned by this. I'm stunned because I never thought of it; because it might be fucking true.

Ma never once asked why I started taking drugs. Not that I could have given her an answer. But still.

I should be thinking about what to say to her, but already I'm blurting out: 'Ma, this isn't my fault. Serious.'

'Barry,' she says, in that teachery fucking tone she has.

'Ma, I didn't do nothing. I swear to you.'

'Barry, for God's sake.'

'Ma, I'm not lying. She was gone out the fucking window when I got there. I only went in cos I heard glass smashing and her door was open and…'

'Jesus, Jesus, *Jesus*, Barry.'

She's fucking screaming at me now all right; something she's never done before, even when I was younger and driving her mental. She's crying too, and even though I'm yelling meself – I'm saying, Ma, I'm telling the fucking truth – I can't help thinking that I've only seen her cry a few times, and that's going back years. The tears don't come out of the corner of her eyes like with most birds, but right out of the middle and down her face. Like her eyes aren't used to it.

'Ganny,' says Holly. She can't say the letter R yet, which I thought was so fucking cute a couple of days ago. Now the sound of me daughter saying that word, all scared and shaking, is like a bullet in me brain. I'm a cunt. A total cunt.

Ma looks at me and I hold up me hands. I'm not going to say anything else. No point.

'What is it?' says me ma as Holly runs towards her and snuggles into her lap.

'Shouting,' says Holly.

'No. Me and your daddy were playing a game.'

'That's right,' I say. 'And I got a bit excited and started shouting. I'm a stupid daddy, aren't I?'

Holly doesn't answer that one. Instead she aims her big eyes at me.

'You said fuck.'

CHAPTER THIRTY SIX

Carol Murphy

I sit on the bonnet of my car and light up. *Ahhh*, thank God. Could do with a coffee now. Where Conor and Kristel live is a nice, oldish development, overlooking the DART line and some tennis courts. The parking area is enclosed by trees, muffling noise from the traffic chugging through Ballsbridge. Conor was cute enough to buy some years back, but I suppose even he could be in negative equity now. No option but to rent, and get out.

The cigarette makes me a bit dizzy, or perhaps it's been the whole experience. It was exhausting coming here. I was almost out the door when Kristel suddenly wanted to talk.

'This thing about Manda going to live beside drug dealers. Isn't that just a little, you know, crazy?'

I hmmed, not sure what kind of response she wanted.

'I mean, maybe it wasn't politics or religion or the family disintegrating that caused all this. Maybe it was just…*her*.'

I suppose it's the story which makes most sense. What's that thing? Occam's Razor. The simplest explanation is the most likely. She was nuts. That's what got her killed.

'What do you mean, the family disintegrating?'

She put a hand to her mouth.

'Oh, I'm so sorry, Carol. Sometimes I can be a bit over-frank. The yank, you know?'

'No, not at all,' I said. 'I prefer frankness.'

From years of interviewing, I've learned it's always best to say as little as possible and let the other person blather on. I waited.

Kristel flicked back her blond hair, then smoothed it down. She has brown roots.

'Well, you know,' she whispered. 'Conor's dad hasn't been in touch for years – something else Conor refuses to talk about – and there were issues with you. Conor and Manda, well, that was always difficult, and neither of them seemed to have had any contact with Hazel. Conor won't go down to Loughrea, he can't stand to be anywhere near her. After the wedding – whenever that is – we're heading to the States and Hazel will be gone to Spain, so…'

'Spain?'

'Yeah,' she said, as if she assumed I already knew. 'With Juanita?'

Juanita doing an inventory of the house.

'Conor doesn't approve?'

Kristel made a face, as if Conor's disapproval was a subject she had tired of long ago. 'Well, you know Conor.' She glanced over her shoulder. 'I guess it's tough to accept when it's your own mom, but I think he's a little homophobic. He needs to work on that.'

'Yes,' I said, though it was less a word and more a sound to give the impression that I'd taken all this in. My mind felt viscous, like an over-boiled pot of milk. I thought again of the tourists on the beach, watching that gigantic wave sweep towards them.

I think I mumbled something about going for a drink – a suggestion which seemed to surprise Kristel, though I can't remember her response. I had to get out then. I felt woozy and slightly panicked that she would never stop talking. I near-stumbled out the door and into the lift, and for some reason had to cover my eyes.

But back out here, a ciggie in my hand, I feel calmer. I will think about everything Kristel and Conor said, and why there appears to be so many things I have forgotten. *The issues with you.* But not now. Can't do it now. Got to work.

Yes, I am my father's daughter. Not that it's easy to avoid unpleasant thoughts: it requires effort and discipline. But at least I realise I'm doing it.

Manda wasn't crazy. No way.

I chain-smoke into a second cigarette when my phone rings, and for a few seconds I debate whether or not to answer; it's the office.

Don sounds pretty happy about everything.

'Rachel Belton?' he asks.

'Yep,' I say. 'On my way there now. She's not campaigning today so she's out in her squillion-euro house in Dalkey.'

'Great. Have you seen the picture?' says Don.

He means the picture of Manda, dead in that skip.

'No. Tried, but couldn't get it to open for me.'

This is a lie.

'Sick stuff,' says Don. 'Anyway, Belton's campaign is finished. The Party have told her to withdraw. She hasn't made the announcement yet, so see can you get her to do that but agree to keep quiet about it until tomorrow morning.'

'Right. So no pressure then,' I say.

'Easy for you. No problem.'

Don giggles, a throaty snort that's a bit girlish. 'Oh yeah, and will you ring Brian? He was mooching about, looking for you.'

I feel a tightness in my chest. *Jesus.* I half-expect Don to inform me that it's about time Brian and I formalised our relationship, because you obviously have feelings for each other. It's what you want. It's what Brian wants. It's what the entire office wants because *of course* we've been talking about little else. Brian is very open that way.

'Right,' I say warily. 'I will.'

'Yeah, yeah,' says Don. 'He was around a couple of times. Fucking annoying actually. He has two stories he should be chasing. But he puts on that baby face and thinks he can get away with it. He's much cuter than he lets on, that one.'

'Oh yeah,' I say emphatically, though this is not a thought I've ever had about Brian: he is exactly what he appears to be. Most of us are, I think; we just don't always realise it. Brian is hard-working and reliable and, as far as I know, everyone at the paper feels the same about him. I'm mildly appalled and thrilled that Don should be saying such things.

He has no doubt said all this to Brian's face – and thus considers saying the same thing to anyone else not to be gossiping. Don is one of those rare creatures who, without being stupid about it, actually says what he thinks.

I wouldn't be able to.

Don is rabbiting on.

'Do you know how old he is?'

The tightness clutches my chest again. Here it comes now; here comes the lecture about what you do in your own time is your own business, Carol, but fuck's sake, it's starting to effect his work and, you know, he's only a kid.

Does Don know? Like a lot of hacks from his generation, he had to give up the drink entirely, so he never comes to the pub. Someone is bound to have told him. But would Don care? No, a lecture isn't coming. The tone is all wrong – it's conspiratorial. Don knows the answer but assumes I don't.

And he's right. I don't know what age Brian is. I've never asked. I've never asked him much of anything.

'Twenty-three?'

'He's fucking thirty-one. Would you believe that?'

I feel like screaming, but swallow hard instead. Brian has been working on the paper for about a year, maybe less. I'd assumed he'd come straight from college. In fact, I'm almost sure I've heard him talking about lectures and projects as if it was in the recent past. But perhaps not.

'Noo,' I finally manage.

'He is,' says Don. 'Worked on some paper in Westmeath for years. And you know, I'd forgotten all about it until today when he was moping about here. He acts as if he's still a kid, so people will help him out a bit more. He always has to be told what to do. But at his age, well, he should be like you. He should *know*.'

Don says goodbye and hangs up. I feel myself glow.

Brian, you sneaky shit.

Yet I understand why he did it. It's not exactly telling the truth, but it's not an outright lie either. All he wanted was for people to be nice to him, and who doesn't want that? If he looked his age he'd probably have been left to fend for himself; I probably wouldn't have looked twice at him. So why not? Brian is capable of deception. Just like the rest of us.

This, I decide, absolves me of any pressure to ring him; to apologise for being nasty.

I've finished my cigarette, yet I'm reluctant to move; to talk more about my dead cousin and pretend it means nothing to me.

I wonder how much longer Brian will go on trying to contact me, and I wonder about Conor and Kristel's life together. They seem to fit; to have worked out a system. Relationships are all about habit, I think. Remembering to talk, to show affection, to make love. You train yourself to love a person so you can cope with those days when you come home and would rather hate them. Not because they've done anything wrong, but because your boss is a prick or some BMW just cut you off on the Merrion Road. Or you're angry. Simply, unaccountably angry and you don't know why except that suddenly you can't stand the face of the man you live with.

It's not easy to love someone. You have to force yourself.

Oh yeah. I'm a real expert.

His name was David, and I met him crossing the road.

This was during the boom days; when it seemed like there was nothing to be scared of.

Well, I was crossing the road. He was standing on the other side: looking like he just happened to be there and had no plans to be anywhere else; looking as if he quite enjoyed standing at the corner of Baggot Street and Merrion Square. It was such an odd picture that I smiled as I walked. He caught me and smiled back, and by the time I'd reached his side of the street the smiles had turned into grins. Out of embarrassment we were forced to speak to each other.

He was an architect, he told me. Not a partner or anything, but he enjoyed the job and was on his way to an interview with a much bigger company where the pay and prospects would be better. But just as he reached this street corner it had struck him that he had never planned to go for this job: he had applied out of habit; because it's what you do, isn't it? When he asked himself: will this new job make me any happier, the answer was he didn't think it would. I asked would going for coffee make him happier instead. He said yes, it would.

That's how it started, simple and easy as that. Did I love David? I don't know. I know everyone else did. He was gorgeous and funny and clever and always wore lovely shirts. And everyone said he was *perfect* for me, as if I suffered from some one-in-a-billion abnormality and by some astronomical stroke of luck, I had managed to meet someone similarly afflicted. I suppose what they meant was that he was patient and kind and good for me. He calmed me down.

And it felt as if we didn't have to do or plan anything: that we simply slipped into the sweetest system: where everything would come to us. Without even talking about it much, with just a look or a squeeze of the hand, we knew we would eventually move in together. And the rest would follow.

I can't remember what set him off the first time. Something trivial anyway; it usually was. *You never told me you ate broccoli? Are those boots new? Are you listening to me? Are you? Are you?* The anger would pop and spasm through his body, forcing a spill of accusations about how I was lying to him, how I had another, submerged life which I would never reveal. His face and eyes would bulge magenta, like some inner monster was clawing to get out, and he'd be on his feet and slamming the walls and howling and grabbing my arm; wrenching it so hard that five blood-red scrapes remained.

It would pass just as quickly. He would be prostrate with apology: putting it down to tiredness or insecurity or the strength of his feeling for me. So of course I forgave him.

And we'd be fine, for a while. Especially in public, when others were around, expecting us to be golden. In public, we believed it too.

But when it happened again, and again and again, all the available excuses had already withered up.

He never hit me.

We went to a counsellor, a couple of times. But this only seemed to make us weary, as if we'd been doing this for years.

He went to visit his parents one weekend – he was from Carlow – and that was it. Never heard from him again. I was relieved. I wasn't surprised.

I know David had some sort of problem, yet when he would bellow at me, have me cowered in a corner, hands covering my face, I'd be unable to answer back. Not just out of fear, but because I agreed with him. He was right. There were cavernous areas of my life that I'd never show to him, that I was barely aware of myself.

Sooner or later, wouldn't that drive anyone mad?

Since then; well, I haven't bothered.

The weird thing is that my parents' marriage was the best I've ever seen. They had rows, of course, but I always knew that nothing could sink their partnership. It made me happy to see them together; I can still remember the feeling. It was the kind of steadfast love which is far rarer than we like to admit; it's what anyone would want. Anyone but me, and I don't know why.

CHAPTER THIRTY SEVEN

Rachel Belton

Sandra brings me to a ramshackle place in Stoneybatter which I suppose has a certain cosiness. *A Slice of Heaven.* We sit in the window and watch the people walk by. I start talking again, babbling really: about clientelism and multi-seat constituencies; an infantilised electorate; the weak committee system; an ineffective civil service; the poor regulation; the lack of transparency; the matey culture between business and politics which has left all the power in the hands of a few people...

I look over at Sandra. She blinks back. I'm not sure if she's following me; I don't know if I care. I just need to speak it out loud. For the last two nights I've been reading compulsively: position papers, policy documents, economic studies, the Constitution; ideas have been bubbling from my mind. *And seeking to promote the common good, with due observance of Prudence, Justice and Charity.*

The cold part of me looks down on this and asks: *what are you doing? Why are you wasting your time?*

I don't know.

Sandra cocks her eyebrows, then smiles.

'You know, I never thought I'd be having conversations like this.'

'But do you follow it?'

'Ah sure, yeah.'

I change subject. I tell her about the miscarriages, the rows, Daniel and his shrine to the dead. It takes three cups of tolerable coffee and two slightly stale meringues.

'My God,' Sandra says. Her eyes are watering. 'And you, you just don't talk about it? Contacting spirits and all that?'

'Daniel mentions it to me. Does that quite a lot. I don't make any comment one way or another.'

I lean forward, and for a moment catch my spectral reflection in the window. I look different, though I'm not sure how. There's something compelling about confiding in Sandra. She has a receptive quality, and we're both a bit giddy from a morning of calling at houses. People swing open their doors and ask: what are you going to do for me? I say: probably not that much. What are you going to do for yourself? For your neighbour? One or two have volunteered to canvass for us. A few slammed the door in our faces. Most look puzzled and ask: what am I paying taxes for? They retreat into their houses, stunned. The other canvassers are saying the same, or something similar. No cards, no notes.

I am aware that I have never done anything like this before, with this degree of abandon. On the canvass, and here, with Sandra. I've never felt the need to tell others my business. I suppose I would have regarded such a need as weakness. Foolish too: people always betray secrets. It's in their nature. It's why nothing works the way we wish it would. We establish moral codes, economic systems, institutions, religions, laws and states and submit ourselves to them in the hope that they will take on a life of their own, that they will achieve a perfection we cannot. But they are built and run by people: flawed, venal, self-serving people. Like people, they will always disappoint.

Why am I talking to Sandra this way? I don't know. Perhaps it's better to talk than not.

'Between ourselves,' I hiss, 'Daniel had a séance with the dead girl, you know, Manda.'

Sandra's forehead scrunches up in mild disgust.

'Oh, no.'

'He couldn't wait to do it. According to him she's fully behind the campaign.'

Sandra is smirking. 'Sorry, sorry,' she stutters.

But I'm smiling too. 'I know, I know.'

'I suppose everyone is a bit mad in their own way,' says Sandra. She stops talking. It's probably difficult for her to know what to say, after a story like that. She'll think about it for a while, and come back with supplementary questions: does Daniel believe in God? Is this a religion? What about when your son is older? What's Daniel going to say to him?

An excellent question; to which I don't know the answer. But if it's a choice between protecting Naoise and keeping Daniel, well...

'Best get back to it,' I say. Sandra giggles, as if I've just suggested that we open a bottle of champagne. We've been enjoying ourselves enormously on the doorsteps. If someone wants to give out, we let them: in most cases, we agree. Yes, politicians are all in for themselves. How can I convince you that I'm different? Well, I can't. Sometimes I give a little spiel on modern geo-politics, about the European Union and global economic tides. We are part of a giant web, and the strands of that web only grow stronger and more complex. We have less power over our own country now; there's no point in pretending otherwise. We need to decide what to do about that. Sandra loves when I give this talk. Wow, she says. Wow.

We've spoken to dozens of people, but I can't think of a single instance where we reckon we've won a vote. We've left most people puzzled, I think. Funny: some of them even seem disappointed that I don't act like the other candidates; that I'm not trying to sell. They want a sales pitch, even if they don't believe it any more.

Sandra leads me across the road to a series of criss-cross streets with Nordic-sounding names. She says we'll do it for another hour. She knows I want to get home early tonight; put Naoise to bed.

My phone rings. 'Rachel? Hi.'

The tone is fake-chummy. Must be a reporter.

'Rachel, my name is Carol Murphy.'

CHAPTER THIRTY EIGHT

Carol Murphy

The traffic out to Blackrock is gruelling. It's gone five o'clock. There are road works at Sydney Parade. Around me I can see scarlet-faced motorists texting radio talk shows. *What kind of muppet schedules road works on a Friday? On a bank holiday weekend? At rush hour?* But I don't mind. It gives me a chance to recompose, to store away various matters. And there are worse places to be stuck. I don't mind saying it now (though this wasn't always the case), but I'm a Dublin southside girl and I like it. My apartment is in the centre of town, but I can understand why so many of the people I grew up with chose to stay. It's a dreamy place, especially like this, on a crisp October day, with so many of the landmarks comfortingly unchanged, the large Victorian houses peeking out from ivy coverings, like children in a forest. Remaining in Blackrock or Sandycove means never having to grow up, not entirely anyway, because there seem to be fewer hard edges here. It might sound cheesy, but that's comforting: there's something solid at the centre, like our idea of Christmas, of home.

My father sold the house. My family. Her. All the little-girl-and-Mum stuff. I was nine when we had our first harvest-moon day. That's what she called them, though I can't remember why. Must have been around April or May, I think: it was certainly spring. A fine day, and at breakfast she announced: it's much too nice to waste it on school. Let's go to the Zoo instead.

We laughed at the penguins and screamed when an orang-utan made to throw his poo at us. Then we had ice creams and went to town and she bought me a pair of jeans with zips at the bottom.

From then on, every birthday would be a harvest-moon day, along with the occasional surprise. We did it until I went to college and suddenly resented having to live at home, with *them*.

I was in Brussels when I heard: on some junket aimed at proving that the European Union wasn't all about expense accounts. They brought us for a series of very nice dinners. I was recovering from one of them in my room when Dad rang. Your mother is very unwell. You'd better come home now. She slipped into a coma last night. We don't know why.

The words were delivered levelly, and slow enough for me to take them in. It was all he knew, and all he wanted to say. I said, 'OK.'

I dashed out of the hotel, leaving behind half my clothes and my mobile phone, but I did manage to get back to Dublin within three hours. By then, my mother was already dead.

It was her heart, though the friend of Dad's who explained it kept calling it SADS. Sudden Adult Death Syndrome. Terrible, literal name. She had an irregular heartbeat, or a long QT interval: a flaw which many carry throughout life without realising it, without it affecting their existence at all. Mum certainly didn't know. She had a couple of fainting spells when she was a teenager. That might have been a clue, though at the time they were put down to heat or exhaustion or puberty. No one thought to check her heart, to see if that treacherous organ might one day fail to supply enough blood to the brain, lulling my mother into an unconscious state so deep she wouldn't even notice Death wrapping its bony fingers around her throat, wouldn't hear us screaming please, come back.

Were Manda and Conor at the funeral? They must have been. I'm sure they were. I remember little of that day. I was spaced out through the whole process. It was a slideshow of faces, of my hand shaken, my cheek kissed, of people telling me to eat something, of Dad nodding as others described *their* grief to him. How ridiculous.

I stuck it out because I had to, because it was my duty. I stood in the room we hired in the Burlington Hotel and shook my head and smiled and waited until the very last person had left. I spent that night in the house with Dad, though we didn't say much. We sipped whiskey and watched TV: something we'd never done before. The following morning I couldn't wait to leave, to get home to the flat I live in now, which I'd bought only a few months before. Buying it was a very adult thing to do, I'd fancied: though now it struck me that by moving into adulthood, I'd lessened my dependence on my parents, on my need for them to be alive.

I visited Dad a couple of days later. He already had the For Sale sign up.

'So?' I said.

'Yes,' was all he said. Yes.

He ran away. And while I'm angry with Dad for deserting me, I also can't blame him. Why remain in an empty house? His life had been severed by Mum's death. He had no option but to invent a new one. I had already gone.

Yet there are days. Especially when I'm out here on the southside, where years of my life still seem both vivid and unreal: all the evidence has been swept away. Who can tell if the three of us ever zipped around Dublin Bay on the *Shooting Star* or sat in the kitchen eating pasta or drove to Galway, counting away the towns? Sometimes I want Dad to be here, just to nod and smile and say yes, Princess, it did happen. It's all true.

CHAPTER THIRTY NINE

Michael Bourke

When I walk through the streets, do you know what I see? I see people with no choice. From the moment of conception, DNA strands have plotted their hair and eye colour, their height, what deformities they will carry. They arrive in this world as a pink lump of genetic switches. They learn language and how it is wielded; they sit in the kitchen and absorb the prejudices of their parents, which mammy and daddy also sucked in from the breast.

Yet despite all the years of careful programming, we are free. Free to vote one way or another, free to sin or transgress; free to change mobile phone operator, free to turn over the channel or not go on holidays this year or pick Cornflakes over Rice Krispies.

We don't want freedom; that's the truth of it. It's too much hard work – and for very little benefit. Why think through every decision rather than copy others? Why make choices which could render you pacifically alone? The herd doesn't want that. We want to belong: to our lovers or families or political parties or football teams or book clubs. To our religions. And each time we become part of something we willingly, happily surrender freedom.

I knew this before I entered the seminary, and like most young men, concluded that this was all there was worth knowing. I had read widely in sociology, history, psychology, theology: and everything had reinforced this idea; an idea which, of course, had come originally from God, via Freud. Our desperate need for a Father to solve our problems, to tell us what to do.

Yet even religion claims we have free will. But how can we when an omniscient God knows exactly what we are going to do?

This was one of many conundrums I hoped to hear solved at the seminary. It was my first great disappointment. Instead of elegant theology, I endured a daily trek through a wasteland of mangled ideas. God knows and doesn't know. Conditional contingencies. God limits his omniscience. *Simplex intelligentia.* God is there and not there.

Ridiculous.

So catastrophic was the failure of my teachers to explain this obvious contradiction, I was tempted to pretend it hadn't happened. Like a child who discovers parental adultery, I had a self-protecting reflex: to loudly continue as normal until the problem would miraculously self-correct.

But this was impossible to sustain for long, and finally a phrase which I had read and heard many times before presented itself to me and refused to be ignored.

God is unknowable.

It was these three words which exploded light into the dark caverns of my ignorance. For if there is an animating force in the Universe, existing outside the limitations of time and space, outside language and human reason, then how can we say anything about it at all? How can we say *He cares* in the way we do or *thinks* about us or even *exists* in the way we understand the term? As in modern physics with its poly-layered dimensions, rippled space-time and particles which simultaneously exist and don't exist, *God* does not make any sense. It is not something we can understand or intuit. *To find the maker of the Universe is hard enough*, wrote Plato, *and even if I succeeded, to declare him to everyone is impossible.*

As I delved into texts outside the coursework, I discovered many thinkers, Christian and non-Christian, freely admitting this problem. Yet still many of them would waste thousands of words attempting to describe the indescribable, and failing to make even a millimetre of progress towards the ineffable.

When these thoughts first forced their way into my mind, naturally I resisted: the alternatives were not just unthinkable, but ridiculous. Was religion no more than a conspiracy, an instrument of control?

Or simple superstition, dressed in modern folk-mass clothing? Or the creeping accomodationism of modern life, where everyone gets to be right?

It was only when I began to examine other religions – Hinduism, Buddhism, the creation myths honestly fictionalised by the ancient Greeks – that I began to detect a pattern. These religious stories were never intended for literal consumption, but as metaphorical guides to life: to aid exploration of the injustices and mysteries. The question is not: does God exist? That cannot be answered. The question is: how should we live?

While my admiration grew for the wisdom of these ancient authors, so too did my contempt for the well-fed clerics continuing to hawk two thousand-year-old tales from the Middle East to explain a world of iPods and professional sports.

Even worse, they were betraying the authors of the tradition. Ezra, the father of classic Judaism, always insisted that the *Torah* be constantly reinterpreted as the ages passed; the Cappodocian fathers taught that the Dogma of Trinity was not to be believed literally, but used as a method of expanding the mind past rational thought and language – for within rationality God does not exist. Only centuries later, in a church bloated with power and threatened by the po-faced posturing of Martin Luther, did an insistence on *belief* in this mystery become the norm; and it was only in the third century that the rabid Constantine, through the Council of Nicene, chose to enforce the idea that Jesus was God made man: a belief that the Apostles almost certainly did not share.

For a time, this process of discovery was obsessional. I could not help but squeeze every pip of faith from myself. While my peers prepared for what they fancied would be fulfilling religious lives, I secretly gorged on the despairing knowledge of what the Universe is really like. Every night, sweating in the stiff sheets of my bed, I would consider leaving the seminary. But to go where? And to do what? I was a custom-built machine with no other useful function.

So I remained, hoping that these dreadful thoughts would be shattered by subsequent events: that I would witness in the faces of my teachers genuine faith; genuine belief in the literal truth of Jesus.

I did find it, in some. But now that I had entered this dark cell in my mind, I could not leave. I found my own belief irreparably broken. I felt myself gravitate towards the other teachers: the ones who presented a messier, subjective picture; and over time I came to suspect that these men represented a church-within-a-church: a fifth column which knows that the entire Christian project is built on a fiction.

I still resisted. I spent hours in my room or in the small chapel down the hall, meditating and praying: desperately attempting to feel the presence of the personal God they had told us about. But nothing revealed itself. The Universe presented only my own reflection.

But if this was the case, then why remain? Why maintain this monstrous untruth?

Simple self-preservation. I may have been cloistered in a seminary, but I wasn't a fool. I knew how the world worked. To make public my ideas would have only led to my departure, and this I could not bear. I attempted, repeatedly, to edge towards discussion of my heretical notions with others whom I suspected might be sympathetic. But they were unyieldingly wary, so blatantly that what began as a suspicion grew into a certainty. There *must* be a group, possibly a large one, which knows the truth but remains within the church.

I had no evidence of this. Even one admission from another would have sufficed, but I'm hardly the sort of man, then or now, in whom others confide. Yet – or so it seemed then – it was the only logical explanation. I could only further conclude that these people had chosen this barren road because they knew that the material existence of God was not important: merely that *God* be available when people need *Him*. If humans created the Divine out of a fundamental need, then is it not in the service of humanity to fulfil that need? To keep telling the stories? Perhaps, in time, to present new ones? To maintain the fiction, even at great personal cost?

This, dare I say it, was the Christian thing to do.

To my mind, it was infinitely preferable to ceding ground to all the other fictions: of fame, money, sex. Of course religion, like any belief system, can become the source of murderous intolerance, given its head, but wasn't that even more reason to continue on the priestly course? As a denier of formal religion, I could influence at best a handful of people, but as a priest I could spend every day clipping the thorns from the spiritual urges of my flock.

So I remained at the seminary, relieved by my decision and consolidated in my purpose. If anything, my mission was now greater than ever, and with precious little adjustment required to my personal theology. The basic messages of the New Testament remained, on a common-sense basis, as pertinent as before.

My mistake was to assume that there were others like me. Even after the seminary I would, occasionally, broach the subject with colleagues, but all I ever heard were the same ponderous platitudes: doubts are natural. We all have them. Talk to Him, pray for him. It will come back.

It was a ridiculous fantasy to indulge in, a childish conspiracy theory to which I am now embarrassed to admit. Stripped of a God to believe in, I shifted my ardour to an imaginary brotherhood of priests in the same situation as myself, and over the last two decades, the thought of such a group did give me comfort. I can see that now. I needed to belong with them; I needed to fill the God-shaped hole in my life.

I thought I could walk through life alone while staring coldly at its realities. I thought that I, above all others, could be free.

Since the journalist visited me, I have worked on regaining some equilibrium. When her story appeared in the newspaper, I was once again besieged with parishioners wanting to wish me well or even bringing small gifts: apple pies, the occasional lasagne. There is a small group, mostly widowed women, who haunt the church, and it is they who have been most active in the supply of food. They also seem aware of Jack's departure and the reasons for it. Quite a few, I suspect, were present for his alcoholic implosion. They are kind to me, and I am grateful for it.

I am perhaps permanently changed, and in the process of discovering a new self. The realisation of my myriad failures tempts me to retreat to my room and never emerge. But there is also a sense of responsibility: to Father Jack, to this group of women; anyone who comes to the church is performing a small mercy. So I go on with my duties, while realising what an abysmal coward and hypocrite I have been; that I am. But what to do about this, I have yet no idea. I know I cannot go on like this much longer. I say mass, I hear confession; I've done a few home visits to the elderly. I fulfil my functions. I stand in front of people who believe me and lie through my teeth.

CHAPTER FORTY

Maurice Kiberd

A whole day after me visit to the guards, and there's nothing on the radio about them arresting anyone or anyone helping them with their enquires. Whatever that means anyway.

All they had to do was go out there and take one look at this bloke. They would have known straight away, even they would have known.

But they didn't bother. Of course not.

For the life of me I can't understand why. I never could. I started to think that it must be something about me. Maybe it's the scaly skin. Maybe I come across as a bit strange, I dunno. Doesn't help that poor girl, does it? Or her family. They might never get to see any justice, and all because the cops are too lazy to go out to Finglas? Because they're too busy having tea and toast? Makes no sense, no sense. The papers are saying the girl was done in by drug dealers from Eastern Europe, but the fella in the back of the cab was as Dublin as you can get. Bit odd that, isn't it? First they say they are looking for a bloke with a blue hoodie, but now it's immigrants? Like they're looking for an excuse to do nothing.

I don't know what to do now. I shouldn't have stuck me nose in anyway; I should have known better.

But I can't get it out of me head; it's like the world won't let me forget it. Every time I put on the radio people are going on about that poor girl. I even know her name now. Manda. Never heard that one before. Another name I keep hearing is Belton. Rachel Belton.

The girl landed with an election poster on her head or something, and now the papers are saying Rachel Belton won't get elected because of it. Don't understand why. Not that I care – politicians are worse than guards, if you ask me.

But I'm in Rachel Belton's constituency – so every time I head out the door, there she is. Everywhere. *Belton. Belton. Belton.* There seem to be more of her posters than anyone else, though I might be imagining that.

So it's hard to forget about the girl when I keep seeing pictures of your woman Belton, you see? I feel like I'm being nagged about it. Doesn't that sound a bit mad? It does. It feels a bit like the other time when them lads got into the taxi and I knew I couldn't ignore it; because it was like they had been *sent* to me. Do you know?

I've caught meself buying more than one newspaper, just so I can read more about it. And it is strange. I mean, apart from the guards doing nothing, the media have gone absolutely mad with it. There's interviews with the girl's mother, a priest that met her, stuff about Rachel Belton, then about Rachel Belton's husband. It's like they all knew this girl, like they can't get over her dying, like no one ever will.

I'm not one for any of the hocus-pocus stuff. Once you're gone, you're gone, I reckon. But something is *going on* here. Very strange.

But it's like I'm the only one that knows that Manda was chucked out a window by a filthy drug addict. Simple as.

I don't know why I bother, but I ring up the radio station, the one that I had that bloke from the other day. I get some snotty young one, who sounds English to me; tells me I should contact the authorities. *Lah-de-dah.* When I tell her I did but they ignored me, she says, 'Well, perhaps they are investigating but doing it quietly. Perhaps they don't want to draw attention to their enquiries. Have you tried ringing them again? Did you get a name? Perhaps they might give you a quiet heads up.'

'A what?'

'A heads up. A private briefing on the investigation.'

I start laughing. I can hear from her breathing that she's narky now.

'Well, that's all I can advise,' she says. 'I have to rush to a meeting now.'

I feel like saying: oh, yeah, me too.

Instead I let a roar: dog's abuse; all sorts of ugly names I'd rather not repeat. Not like me. I don't like to lose me cool. I like to stay in control. All them scraps I've had over the years, and not once did I lose me temper or act all pleased with meself. When they went down, I was like, professional. Yeah, that's the word. Professional. I'd be a bit worried if I started losing the head. I'd be worried what I might do.

So I give meself a few slaps in the face, sit down, take deep breaths, look out the window and tell myself not to move until my heart has slowed down, until me breathing is normal. I try to think calm thoughts. I think about Ma giving me baths when I was a nipper.

It's like a dream.

I don't know for how long I'm sitting there. Must have gone into some sort of doze or something, because next thing I know the light outside is different. It's gone from bright to kind of dirty; the way it can be on summer evenings in the city, when there's been lots of cars driving around.

I'm sitting here, wondering if the cars really make the light look that way, or if I'm just imagining it, when she walks past the window: just there; a few feet away. And I know she's come to see me, which, if you think about it, isn't that surprising. But still it gives me a start, like seeing a dead person.

The doorbell rings then, and for a moment I don't do anything. I feel like I can't do anything; I'm frozen. I have to force myself to stand, to drag my legs across the carpet and towards the front door. She has this big thick smile on her face.

'Hello,' she says. 'My name is Rachel Belton. I'm running in the election.'

I fold me arms.

'I know that,' I say.

There's a woman standing behind her. She doesn't say anything. She just nods and smiles like a mad thing, like that will encourage me to love Rachel Belton as much as she does. I know this woman. She's a local. Knew her when I was a kid. Rachel Belton says, 'Have you made a decision on who you are voting for?'

'I'm not voting,' I say. 'Don't believe in it. Don't believe it will make any difference. You're all the same. I've had dealings with your sort before, and nothing gets done. You're not going to get elected anyway on account of that poor girl.'

She nods and gives a kind of a smile at this, a sad smile. Nothing disrespectful.

I look at the other woman.

'Sandra,' I say. 'Sandra Connolly. I was in the same class as your brother Tom.'

Maybe I shouldn't have mentioned that. I beat the tar out of him a couple of times. But she doesn't act like she remembers.

'Yes, yes,' she says. 'Though it's Sandra Keogh now.'

For a few seconds the three of us say nothing, as if me knowing Sandra Connolly might make some difference. My neck is tingling. I'd love to give it a good scratch. But instead I point at Rachel Belton and say, 'I'm not going to vote. Not even registered to vote. But there's one thing you can do.'

CHAPTER FORTY ONE
Carol Murphy

I press the buzzer, announce myself and the grey metal gate trundles back. As I drive up the curling driveway, I get another flash: the tree house. We'd go through phases when we called it the den, or our base and, after she'd read *Lord of the Rings*, Manda wanted to call it Lothlórien. But mostly we called it the tree house.

Conor and Manda's dad disappeared when they were kids, and once he got himself a younger model and a new baby on the other side of the world, he didn't exactly make strenuous efforts to stay in touch. Occasionally Manda wrote him long, resentful letters, some of which he replied to. Conor refused to talk about it, and would walk away from any attempts to bring the subject up. It seems he still does.

Hazel never mentioned him either, and the only pictures I remember are a few Manda kept in one of her many diaries. Stringy, unremarkable man, dressed in clothes that seemed slightly too big for him. One of the few remaining traces of their dad in the Ferguson home was the tree house he constructed. Hazel claims she can't remember when he built it or even why, given that he did so little else around the place, though I sensed an unspoken suspicion that she found it preferable to spending any time in the house with her.

Or he simply wanted to use his skills as an architect to make something nice for his kids; perhaps he recognised that it was all he could ever do. And this wasn't a glorified shed near some trees – this was a house *in* a tree. It had a balcony and a central room which curled around where the trunk split in three. There was a spiral staircase and glass windows and even a slate roof. He had begun work on a turret, but never completed it. We spent hours, days, months, *years* in there: having wars, playing schools and hospitals, eating, arguing, laughing. I can remember sitting in there by myself, crying, though over what, I don't know. I can remember us standing on the balcony and cutting back the branches so we would have a better view of anyone coming. I can remember sleeping there, more than once, and the thick smell of damp and leaves and our whispered conversations which would stop each time we heard some small animal rustling through the branches above us.

Another flash: Manda has her hair long. She must be a teenager. She's sitting cross-legged and saying, if a tree falls in a forest and no one is around to hear it, does it make a sound? And Conor and I groan and say, Manda, shut up about that, will you?

Two days ago, I was unaware of any of this.

Even when she looks a bit wrecked, which she does, Rachel Belton is radiant. She's wearing an off-white trouser suit, the silk obediently following the line of her still-toned body. No make-up either. She was about to put it on when I arrived, but didn't bother when she realised that I don't have a snappy in tow. She shrugs in an embarrassed way before gliding onto the armchair opposite, one leg girlishly curled under the other. She stands again. 'Actually, do you mind if we go into the kitchen? It's more comfortable.' She glances around balefully. 'We never use this room.'

I don't blame her. Even though the house is fairly new, the room is decorated to resemble a Victorian library, full of weathered hard-back books; the sort of place where you'd expect to meet Sherlock Holmes. There's a grand piano in one corner and paintings of old-fashioned-looking men and women: one of whom, I realise, is Rachel herself, gusseted into an aquamarine ball gown, a look of vague regret on her face. This room is too big, too pristine, too much like a film set to be believable as a real room used by real people. It's creepy.

'I mean,' she goes on, 'we use it if we are "entertaining".' Her fingers hook in the air. 'You know, pressing the flesh, all that.' She's not talking like a politician, or at least not the way a politician talks to a hack. It's as if I'm her best friend. Or perhaps it's because she doesn't need to be cautious any more. I follow Rachel Belton as she pads down a glass hallway with gold-tinged views across the southern sweep of Dublin Bay. She kicks off her shoes and makes a slight ummm sound. Under-floor heating, I presume. I feel like doing the same.

The kitchen is larger than my apartment, though it's still rather snug. There's a scrubbed kitchen table and a squat, old-fashioned Aga, which on closer inspection isn't really old at all. On the breakfast bar there's a few used breakfast bowls (porridge) and a coffee-maker shooting rich smells into the air. Toys are scattered around the floor. She whips up a stuffed elephant and cuddles it.

'My son is in the park,' she says, beaming. Must be more than a decade ago now, but there was a time when Rachel Belton was famous for being famous: her picture in the Sundays or a few reality shows. I can't remember what programme it was, but there's Rachel in a one-piece bathing suit. And her body is fabulous, of course, but I can't help noticing the cellulite on her legs.

Then she stopped. Turned off the publicity. Got married, went back to college, eventually rebirthing herself into a candidate for a north Dublin constituency. Bit of a PR mistake to invite a reporter to her gasp-inducing south Dublin home, virtually carved out of the cliff-face. Some of the voters in their two-bedroomed terraces might not be too impressed. Even if she is about to jack it all in, the party won't be too thrilled with her either. Not for the first time, she might be about to give up a good story.

For a moment, I feel sorry for her.

Rachel is one of those well-tailored vaguely liberal Party types. No, scratch that: one of those well-tailored females who all sound and look the same and seem terribly, terribly earnest and bright and energetic. Yet you're still left with the suspicion that they only entered politics because they'd grown a bit bored with the voluntary work for *charidee*, most of which consisted of organising fancy piss-ups in upscale hotels around town. They're always gorgeous and well-preserved and married to a zillionaire. The pretty and rich shall inherit the earth.

Without asking if I want one (which I do), Rachel pours me a coffee, slides over sugar and milk and perches on a stool at the breakfast bar. She watches me sugar my coffee, then gently suggests, 'You can smoke if you want to.'

'OK, thanks,' I say as Rachel reaches for something which approximates an ashtray. An old saucer is the best she can do. Only as I pull out the packet does it occur to me: how did she know I smoked? Do I look that wrecked? Do I stink of tobacco?

I consider asking, but she's already pointing to the packet and saying: 'Can I have one?' I pass the box over while she says, 'I don't normally, or not any more. But it's been a tough few days, you know. And I kind of admire people who still smoke. It probably takes courage to keep it up now, what with all our tut-tut culture.' I nod heroically. She lights up with relish.

'What would you like to talk about?' she says.

'Well, obviously, the election and the, you know, killing of Manda Ferguson.'

'You want to know if I'm going to withdraw.'

I root in my bag and extract my digital recorder. I don't usually record interviews – my shorthand is pretty good – but with politicians you can never be sure. Especially ones who are upset and might want to retract what they say later on. Rachel Belton nods her agreement.

'My first instinct,' she says, 'was to do just that. That picture of the girl lying in the skip with my poster across her chest. All over the internet now. Thank God no newspaper published it.'

There's a slight upward tilt at the end of the sentence – it's as much a question as anything else. I shrug because I really don't know if anyone is going to print the pic. I doubt if Don would go for that, though you can never be sure. She pulls gently on her cigarette. The smoke emerges from her nose in neat lines.

'My difficulty is that everyone will associate me with that poor dead girl, which lumbers me with a *yuk* factor when it comes to voting. I know politicians all say it has to do with policies and principles, but the reality, Carol – as you know – is that it is a popularity contest. People vote for the candidates they like, or at least the ones they respect. It's an emotional decision.'

I go to open my mouth, but she waves me silent.

'Yes, yes, I know what you're going to say. People might not vote for a socialist or someone who's a heavy republican or something. But other than that, we're all the same, to be honest. The candidates, I mean. In office, we'll do pretty much the same things.'

This wasn't what I was going to say. What I was going to ask was why she is talking this way. It will make her sound bitter. Or crazy. I hear myself whispering.

'Is this on the record?'

She smiles and nods.

'Yes, of course.'

She smiles again, almost joyfully, and I wonder if Rachel Belton has gone a little bit off her rocker. She doesn't seem that way. She's made quite a few campaign gaffs; she's come across as aloof and arrogant. Yet now she seems calm and rational, even serene. I feel gripped by an eerie sensation, as if I'm not quite inside my body, as if the edges of my physical self and some other version of me don't quite match. It's not unpleasant.

She doesn't look quite right smoking; like a child pretending.

All this is a bit too much for me: the casual splendour of the house and its setting, which Rachel Belton doesn't seem to notice. I'm dehydrated, hungover. My cousin has been murdered. Her brother acts as if it was my fault. My aunt may have become a lesbian, my father pretends none of this is happening and for some reason everyone is under the impression that Manda and I were really close. Which we weren't.

I'm sure we weren't.

No I'm not.

There's a huge inky blotch covering years, as if someone has painted over my memory.

I hold up a hand to stop Rachel Belton speaking. I take a breath.

'Rachel,' I say. 'Hasn't the Party told you to withdraw?'

She grinds the remains of her cigarette into our makeshift ashtray, squinting into the residual smoke.

'Not *told* me, no. Well, they can't, can they? That's up to me. They want me to. They've made that plain. But I've decided not to. *We've* decided. I have a lot of people supporting me; far more than I imagined.'

I lean forward.

'But do you honestly think you have a chance now? How can you get elected if you say all politicians are the same?'

'Why not?'

'Because, because… It's like saying people shouldn't bother voting at all. The result will always be the same. The Party will go mad.'

'Oh, I know that.'

She looks at her hands and starts plucking at a cuticle.

'Before my little boy, I had four miscarriages. I had problems hanging on to… you know. The only reason I wanted to get involved in politics was because I became aware of just how little support there is for infertile couples and for women who miscarry. It's scandalous, really. I mean, we had a really hard time.'

She peeks over at me through her long lashes.

'Do you have any kids?'

I shake my head, and as usual when asked this question, feel inexplicable guilt.

'Well, you're younger than me,' says Rachel, 'and I don't know, maybe it hits women at different times in their life, or it hits some and not others. But everything about me wanted a baby.'

She squints at me for some hint of understanding. I say nothing.

'And you can say there are other things in life, and there are, of course, but when I was going through the miscarriages, I was dying along with those babies. I began to feel that if it went on like this it would be, you know, the end of *me*.'

'In what way?'

'Not suicide or sickness or anything like that. This felt like nature taking over, it was primal? It was like everything in me – every second of my life before that – had really been bringing me to the point when I would be a mother. My whole purpose was nothing but that.'

She looks out at the sparkling sea. The sound of waves washes into the silence.

'I don't know, Carol. Each time it happened, I could feel the life ebb out of me. Every time it got harder and harder to get out of bed.

'I suppose I was depressed. We both were. And now we have Naoise and it's brilliant. But I'd say, yes. I'd say we still haven't got over the others. All those lives gone.'

She shakes her head; as if to get the Death out of her hair.

'And Daniel, my husband, felt it just as badly. I mean, he was strong, as men feel they have to be. But still, you know.'

I don't know, but I nod and smile anyway.

'So,' she says, slightly embarrassed now. 'That's what got me started. To help people who have been through the same.'

She waves a hand towards our surroundings. 'And we've money. For people who don't have any, well, I can't imagine.'

'OK,' I say. 'OK.' Her face has become angular, more pointed. She might start crying, or shouting.

'And that's it,' she says. 'I mean, it's not the only issue I'm interested in, of course. But after what happened to that girl, it struck me that to get elected, I'm required to say certain things and be a certain way and to some extent, not tell the truth. Or not tell all of the truth. I had these people around me – and they meant well – but every single syllable had to be considered on the basis of how it would *play* with the electorate and the papers, and they gave me these things to say which were so vague, often *I* didn't know what they meant.'

She smirks. 'Well, I don't have them around me now. They all thought I should withdraw. Assumed I would. My *friends*.' Rachel shakes her head. She seems genuinely amused.

'But now, I feel liberated, you know? And I suppose I won't get elected, I may come bottom of the poll. But I'm going to keep campaigning. And I'm going to say what I think, even if that means people won't vote for me. Because I said that's what I was going to do, so I'm going to do it.

'It's the women. The women in the constituency. They've been campaigning for me and knocking on doors, and when the Party was involved I'd met hardly any of them. But we had this terrific meeting and they want to keep going. Not for me, but for themselves. To try it without all the spin and premeditation. To see if that works.'

She shivers.

'I'm not explaining this very well. I'm not sure if I understand it myself.'

We sip our coffee and sit in the quiet. An orange sun is starting to slide into Dublin Bay, shooting horizontal rays through the kitchen.

'And if, you know, this girl Manda hadn't died, I would have done what I was told and spouted the party line. I might even have got elected. The polling was reasonably good, you know.'

I say nothing.

'You think I'm mad?'

'No,' I finally say. 'Not mad. But I don't know what you'll achieve.'

She shrugs, then cocks her head to one side, squinting at me.

'Why are you smiling?'

'Well, it's just Manda,' I say. 'She would have *loved* that you're doing this. Loved it.'

Controversial candidate finally admits it...

'WE'RE ALL THE SAME'

Distraught Rachel vows to tell the truth.

By CAROL MURPHY

TROUBLED election candidate Rachel Belton has shocked party colleagues by claiming that 'all candidates are the same'.

Former model Rachel's campaign is in doubt after a number of gaffs and the brutal slaying of constituent Manda Ferguson...

Chapter Forty Two

Baz Carroll

She was a bit more civil to me after that row. Not throwing her arms around me, but talking; the basics. Here's your dinner, that sort of thing. Jesus, what a pain. Her son turns out to be a fucking killer, that's all the she needs.

I sit on me own in the dark sitting room where all the politicians used to come. I have a few more gulps of the Baileys. Disgusting shite, but it has a kick. She has a load of pictures lined up on the big brown sideboard. Me in a superman suit. Me in a brand-new school uniform, me face all smooth and optimistic. I keep jigging me leg; I can't stop it. I try to think of what to do. The cops won't listen to me. I'll be guilty, and that's that. I'll always be the bad guy. Yes, I'm fucking scared. Perfectly natural.

I was never brave, you know, like her. Or smart. She wanted me to be, but I suppose I got the old man's brains.

I walked out of school on me fifteenth birthday; actually a few weeks before that. But I knew I was safe by then, and all me mates loved the way I just stood up in the middle of class, said *Fuck this* and walked out, never to return. It was legendary.

The school went mad and rang Ma, but I'd already done a deal with her to do an apprenticeship if I could give up school. No one knew that, though.

So I went to do this fitter's course, but it was shite boring. I just stopped going, until she found out and I was sent back again. Then there was another course, some electrical bollocks, then some shite with art and computers. But I never stuck any of it. I always felt like something better was going on, somewhere else, you know what I mean? Fun, crack, wildness. None of us thought we would live forever. I'm fucking astounded I'm still here.

It wasn't until I was seventeen that I first got lifted by the law. Not cos I'm clever, but because I'm a bit of coward. I'd be there when there was robbing and stuff going on, but always be cute enough to make an excuse and go home early, or pretend I was sick from the drink and not get in the car. Still though, after the first time, after me ma came around to the station and calmed everything down and convinced the cops to let me out, I was fucking delighted with meself. Felt like I was a man. No stopping me then. Funny thing, though: I can't remember me first time with heroin. There was always drugs – smoke, coke, pills, whatever – suppose I just smoked some without thinking about it.

All I do remember is that we fucking loved it. We'd talk about it, think about it, plan how to get it, plan how to get the money to get it. And then there was nothing else.

I can't remember half of them years. I can't remember first signing on, or when I moved out of the house (or was I kicked out?), or even getting arrested for the fourth or fifth time and finally getting a sentence. Like, a real one.

Seven months in the Joy, I did, and do you know what? It was a fucking laugh. Sure, there were loads of mad geezers and queers and bad fuckers, but if you stayed out of their way, you were fine. No shortage of gear either – it was easier to get in there than outside.

I was out of me bin for all that seven months, in a warm, happy haze. That's what did it for me, I reckon. I was let out on a shit-grey, miserable day and came back here to the ma's and her full of plans for rehabilitation and how she hoped that I had learned me lesson. Fuck that. I wanted to go straight back in.

And I spent years – fucking years – chasing that good feeling again. But I never got it; dunno why. And I changed – from a bit of a mad cunt that most people liked and could have a laugh with, to this bloke that was scared. All the time, scared. Scared of everything. Scared of not getting me gear.

Of course I got in trouble again and went back inside. Did a year that time. Fucking grim. The gear was harder to get, and one or two of the screws were right cunts. I had a bit of hassle. Sick stuff happened. Stuff I never want to talk about.

I tried to give it up; loads of times. Got into clinics, tried it on me own. One time we got that film out, *Trainspotting*, and did all the things your man did in the film to get off the gear. Doesn't fucking work. Leaves you howling for drugs.

It's time, isn't it? For most people out there, unless they're bleeding loaded, every day is the same. Get up, go to the shitty job, come home, fall asleep in front of the telly. Few pints and ride on a Saturday night. But with smack every day was different: you never knew what kind of shit could float through your mind. Even though you might be living in a hole with no money and you're stinking and everyone around you is stinking; even though you know you're killing yourself, you still feel like a king.

A fucking king.

Most of the time I stayed out of Ma's way. I knew she wouldn't want to see me around the place. Or have the neighbours see me. But still I'd go down to her occasionally. Jesus, she is me mother. Get a hot meal, bit of a chat. Sometimes I would be off me tits, or I'd have the shakes and be looking for money. And she'd sit me down and we'd talk about this and that and she'd always ask me what I was doing. She was good at that. Had the patter for everyone. Made them think she cared even if she didn't give a fuck.

No. That's not fair. Dunno why I said that. Ma is genuine, and I never asked her anything about what she was up to. But as I say, I was out of me tits. Not all the time, mind. But a lot of the time.

I didn't even know that she was going for the election, and I can't remember talking to that reporter or getting me photo took. There was always blokes coming by where we used to hang out, chatting us up, thinking we'd suck their cocks for a few quid. We'd say yeah and scarper as soon as we got the cash.

It's funny the things you remember. I can see meself sitting on the wall around from the row of shops. Beside the road and the playing field so we could always see people coming, and there's me, Martin,

Johnser Finnegan, he's dead, whathisname, fuckhead O'Toole. He was a prick. He's dead, and somebody else. Can't remember him. And this bloke, fucking Carl or something his name was, we didn't know him that well, and he comes waltzing over and holds the paper in front of me: and there's a picture of me sitting on the same fucking wall. Fucking *weird*, it was, like the drugs had brought me to a whole new level.

And this guy Carl, he was delighted about this, he thought it was hilarious, giving it all this: you mad cunt Baz. Your mother will be fucking raging, I'd say.

Now, I'm not violent. I'm not. But only for the fact that I'd done some gear and I was out of it, and I would have beaten the fucker to death. Even in the state I was in then, I could still fucking read. *Secret Shame of Candidate.*

I went up to the house to say sorry. Big fucking mistake. And me completely out of it. In fairness now, I didn't know that the house was full of people, all these bleedin' big shots, all freaking out over the druggie son, and that she was sitting there, cool as you like, and giving them all this gas about oh, he had problems with drugs, but he's making some progress now; and it gives me great insight into the problems of the area. All the shite politicians come out with. They were probably believing it too, until I turned up at the front door, crying me fucking eyes and telling her how sorry I was and that I didn't know and that I'm going to give up the gear. She tried to steer me into the kitchen, but I wasn't having any of that: I burst into the sitting room and told them that my ma is fucking brilliant, fucking genius she is. And it's not her fault that I have a few fucking issues. She did her best, but I'm a mad cunt, do ya see? So don't be sitting there with that fucking snobby look on yeer faces. My ma is better than all of youse put together, and if you don't know that ye're a bunch of stupid cunts.

Oh, yeah. That helped. That did the trick.

Can't remember what happened after that. Had a cup of tea, I think, and fucked off. Only the next morning did it hit me what I'd done. Felt a bit shit about it, so I stayed out of her way. Didn't go near her for months. And even when I did visit again, I only went at night, when no one would see me.

But she knew what I was into, didn't she? If she was that ashamed of me, she shouldn't have tried going for the fucking thing in the first place.

Funny though, she never mentioned it after that. Never said a word. We went back to the same old routine, me turning up at the door and her taking me in for a few hours, and trying to talk me into giving up the gear and me saying yes Ma and not meaning a word of it. Weird. If she'd done something like that on me, I'd go fucking mad.

I'm sick of sitting here, drinking fucking Baileys, waiting for something to happen. The sweet smell of it is stuck in me nose and I feel like puking. So I go back into the kitchen, where's she doing the tidying up. I dunno why I say it. Maybe for the sake of something to say. Maybe I want a row.

'Ma, that time you were in the election and I fucked it up on you. You never said nothing about that. Not one word. Didn't give out or anything.'

She shrugs. 'Would it have changed anything?'

'Suppose not,' I say. 'But still, you know...were you not that pushed about it so?'

She smiles, though not in a friendly way.

'It's what I had wanted for years. Ever since I finished my degree, I suppose. No, Barry. I was extremely pushed about it. But we can't have everything we want in life. You just have to accept it.'

'Oh, right,' I say, though I don't really understand.

I say nothing for a few minutes.

'Ah, but Ma, you must have been raging with me coming in that time? Embarrassing you in front of your friends?'

She sighs, like this is really annoying her, but she doesn't want to let on.

'No.'

'But you must have been.'

'No, I wasn't.'

'Come on, you wanted to do it for years, you said that, and then I fuck it up by being in the papers out of me box? You must have been raging.'

'Barry, what do you want me to say?'

She's narky now. Right narky. I feel a bit of a tingle.

'You were annoyed but you never said it.'

'And what would have been the point of that, Barry? Could you have understood it then? Can you even understand it now? You were a drug addict, you had no mind left.'

'I have a mind. I understand loads of stuff.'

'Really? What do you understand? What do you understand?'

'I ruined your life. And you can't forgive me for that. And I don't blame you, Ma. I can see where you're coming from. But go on, just say it.'

Sunlight is banging through the window so I can't see her properly; can't see her face. She's like a shadow or a ghost that fires the dishcloth into the sink and marches over to me. For a minute I think she's going to give me a belt. But instead she drags over a chair and sits opposite me. The chair makes a screeching sound that hurts me teeth. She sticks her face right up to mine.

'All right, yes. I hate the person who did that. I hate that ugly monster for what he did to me and what he did to my son.'

She's poking me in the chest now – hard – it fucking hurts. And the weird tears are coming again.

'I used to have a son, a lovely little boy who was sweet and kind and bright and was going to do great things with his life. But the monster took him away – *I* let the monster take him away. I –'

She stops talking, stops poking me. She stands up, goes back to the sink and dries her eyes with the dishcloth.

'Anyway,' she says, 'that's all in the past. It's far too late. All that's left, Barry, is for you to make a decision. You have to go to the guards. If you think you have a choice about it, you're fooling yourself.

'And so far, I've been patient. I've been hoping that if anything of my son remains inside you, that you'll do one decent thing in your life and go up to the garda station. Don't make me call them, Barry. I couldn't face having to do that. But for Holly's sake, I will. Please, Barry.'

I say nothing. I'm not feeling any tingle now. That again. I can't stick this. And I decide: fuck the risk. I'll go out of the house.

CHAPTER FORTY THREE
Rachel Belton

I didn't tell Sandra that Naoise was adopted, of course not. His birth mother was a college student. Could still be as far as I know. Yet still I feel a twinge for not mentioning it. All this being honest is addictive. That reporter seemed quite alarmed by what I was coming out with, though in a nice way. I liked her. I didn't expect that.

I feel different. I don't know why.

She knew the girl who died. That was disconcerting to hear. I'm glad Daniel wasn't in the house. God knows what he would have made of it; what he might have said.

The next day Sandra asks, *how did it go*: in the way you do when someone may have bad news. She seems surprised, even suspicious, when I tell her I enjoyed the interview and liked the journalist. Strange, heady days that I'm living in now: it feels as if I'm slightly drunk all the time, or on some drug where I don't know what's going to happen, and this lack of knowledge frees me from concern about the future. The people on the doorsteps ask: what are you going to do? And I say: whatever I can. What promises? And I say: no promises. No promises at all.

I have no idea where any of this is leading, yet I'm gripped by an illogical conviction that it is leading *somewhere*. We're not wasting our time – me and all these women. I may even get elected. We're starting to think that now. We've already heard whispers that Head Office is taking notice. They're saying: these women are *doing* something. New people are joining them; people who aren't involved with the Party.

This is something like a revolt.

Yes, that does please me.

There's been a gestation which at first I wasn't aware of; which the others recognised long before me. We talk now of what will happen afterwards. *Afterwards.*

In between the doors I talk out loud to Sandra. Today it's participation. How do you get voters to be more involved? To shake them out of the idea that they have to do more than vote every five years? To stop being passive consumers and become active participants?

You can't force them, says Sandra.

No? Not even a little?

They need to want to do it, she says.

It is in their interest.

Yeah, but you know people; you know what they're like.

I know. And I don't know. What do I want? What do *we* want? To make society better? To improve ourselves? I don't know if we are all here for some particular issue; sometimes it feels as if it's more about being together, about presenting ourselves to the world as much as remaking it. It's about Us.

And Sandra: she's my friend now. This is how she's introducing me. Not Rachel Belton, the candidate. Rachel Belton, my friend.

Has it made any difference? Everything I've done? If I'd stayed at home and married Tommy or Jack from up the road and befriended Sandra twenty years ago, would I have arrived at this point anyway?

I'm getting surprised by gulps of emotion, as if another person is trying to climb her way out of me.

She leads me around a circular sweep of cottages, mostly populated with old people who are happy to chat. Many don't even know there's an election on. Some of them admit to being lonely, or scared. They have a haunted look; of people who are barely here, feeling the life dribble away from them. Some of the houses stink rather badly. We talk about the pension. Will the government reduce it? I don't know. About meals on wheels and young fellas causing trouble and the Irish language. One or two dismiss us. Some of them smile; as if they think we're mad. Others present their shining faces to us, full of hope and faith, and no matter what I say, all they hear is: I'm going to help you; I'm going to make your life better. They believe with a desperate fervour; they have to. *Croyance Utile*, Voltaire called it. Belief in a God or an enemy or a better future is what motivates the public: and what they believe in doesn't even need to be true. Useful belief.

Perhaps it's more than useful; perhaps it's essential. Perhaps it's why I'm here.

This one is a bit younger. Could be in his thirties or forties; it's difficult to tell. He is blocky and pugnacious-looking, and there's a crusty rash up the side of his neck and on the back of his hands which is difficult not to stare at. His eyes dart between Sandra and I as if he's been waiting for this, as if he really wants to have an argument.

'I don't vote for your shower,' he bellows. 'I don't vote at all.'

He looks at Sandra then, and says he knows her. They establish a brother of hers he went to school with. But this connection doesn't soften him. His glare returns to me.

'You're not going to get elected anyway. On account of that poor girl.'

He stops talking then, hands dug into his trouser pockets, presumably to see what our reaction will be. He seems quite pleased with what he has said.

'Well, if that's the case,' I say, 'then why did you answer the door?'

And he smiles. Not because he likes me, but because the audacity of my answer seems to stir something in him: the way a teenage boy might delight in the prospect of a scrap.

He leans back on one leg and studies me.

'Right,' he eventually says, 'OK.'

He swoops a thick arm in front of us.

'I'll tell you something. About that girl that got killed. I'll tell you something. Let's see what you do about it.'

CHAPTER FORTY FOUR
Carol Murphy

My phone rings. *Rachel Belton* shimmers on the display. *Shit.* Now it'll be *you quoted me out of context* or *you twisted my words* or *I thought you were a decent person.* But I recorded it. She said what she said.

I don't have to answer if I don't want to. After suffocating in traffic for an hour, I finally got to my apartment and filed the copy from there (still can't face going into work). Don was so pleased he let me take the morning off, to make up for a few of the late nights I've put in lately. I could ignore this. Take a message and ring her back. Or not.

But I can't. I admire what she's doing. A little. And I'm worried – *Jesus* – I'm worried that she is upset about the story. I didn't use any of the quotes about the miscarriages, even though I should have. I pick up the phone and try to sound tough.

'Rachel.'

'Carol, is that you?'

On the phone she sounds older; like a dotty aunt. 'Sorry to bother you,' she says. Not the kind of thing angry politicians tend to say.

'That's OK.'

I hear wind whipping around, forcing her to shout a little.

She sounds happy.

'I'm back canvassing today. About twenty minutes ago I knocked on the door of a taxi driver who said he thinks he picked up the man who may be involved in the death of your friend. He picked up this man right outside the building, a couple of minutes after it happened. Brought him to Finglas. He says he thinks he knows where the chap *lives.*'

'My God,' I say.

'Well, yes. And he says he's been to the guards and the media but no one will listen.'

'Hmm,' I say, doubtfully.

'That's what I thought too,' says Rachel. 'At first. You do get a lot of, er, troubled people on the doorstep. But this chap seems pretty normal. A little intense, but taxi drivers are all like that, aren't they? It's up to you, of course, but would you like his phone number? Check it out?'

I can't say no. She reads it out with the verve of a bingo caller, so happily that I feel I have no choice but to ask.

'Did you see the piece?'

'The piece?'

'The article in the paper. After our interview yesterday? It's on the front page.'

'Oh! Yes, I saw the paper but haven't bought one yet. Saw the headline. Seemed OK to me. Anyway, I'm sure you presented me fairly, Carol. Gotta go.'

She hangs up, and for the umpteenth time my eyes fill with tears.

Chapter Forty Five

Maurice Kiberd

Now that I've said it, now that something is actually happening, well, I don't know what to think.

I couldn't believe it when she rang me. It was like she was getting in touch from this other world: where things happen, where people won't treat me like a lunatic. Or she's made a mistake: she'll talk to the guards and they'll give her a nod or the secret handshake or whatever it is, and that will be that.

I dunno though. She made an appointment. She said she was coming. She seemed, like, *pleased* to have got a hold of me.

But I don't want me picture in the papers. I don't want to be making out that I've got anything to do with Rachel Belton or politics or any of that. I'll tell her. I will.

But will she pay any attention? I mean, the media and all the people you see there, all the politicians and singers and people off the telly – it's like that's the Real World, and the rest of us are just watching it through a window. Except for maybe the odd time when one of us gets out of the Grey World and into the Real World for a few minutes, and we're supposed to be grateful for that, to not mind what's said about us in the papers. Because didn't you get to be in the Real World for a while? Out there, in your unemployed grey houses, with only your colour telly for a bit of comfort, you barely exist. You think there's things like justice and fairness, but that's only for the Real World. Out in the Grey World, youse are just sheep.

So I sit down in me chair and wait for her, trying me best not to go mad scratching, and wonder what all this stuff in the papers has to do with me. Do I fit into it? If they put me in the papers, will I feel different?

I see some young one drifting past the window, looking a bit lost. Reckon that's her. I'm waiting though. A minute later there's a knock on the door. Why knock, when there's a doorbell?

I'm nervous, I don't mind admitting it. It feels like years since I met someone who wants to hear what I've got to say.

But does she really? What's she up to? Why didn't she use the doorbell?

I stand up and go to let her in.

CHAPTER FORTY SIX
Carol Murphy

It's a part of Dublin I haven't been to for years, if at all. It looks a little familiar though. Perhaps I've seen it in photographs. A ring of tiny cottages; probably one-bedroomed, mostly with ramshackle extensions in their dank backyards. No. Never been here before. You live in a city, but not really. You follow the same invisible dreaming tracks every day.

Odd little place. The cottages form an almost perfect oval around the centre square of grass. Well: some grass with a few weeds, punctuated by muddy gashes. A makeshift goal lies upended like a dead animal. But what grass there is displays an eye-popping range of greens: from almost-white to sluttily verdant, all of it recently washed by rain; the clinging drops carrying just a hint of purple from the clouds which bubble up overhead, getting ready to put on a show. And the question slides into my head: when we were kids, did Conor and Manda ever come to Dublin? They must have, though I can't think of a specific visit. I have a jagged image of sitting with them on Sandymount Green, drugged with boredom. They must have come to Dublin more than once, though all I can remember about those visits is that it was never the same. I'd be trying too hard to make them like it, and they would be withdrawn and sulky, and eventually I'd succumb to feeling the same way. We had to be in Loughrea for it to work. We had to have the shambolic home, and Hazel charging around the place. We had to have the tree house.

Don't know why being here makes me think of this, except it has the feel of some place I've been before, and seems much smaller now. It's tiny compared to the sky, and I feel Gulliveresque standing beside my little red Toyota, with me dressed – I only now realise – in crinkled tracksuit bottoms and damp-spotted runners. My hair isn't brushed and a few of the nails on my right hand are filthy from having to pick congealed gunk out of the bottom of the dishwasher. At least I've brought my bag, in which I locate a pen and some paper: things to make me look reporterish. People like you to look the part.

I shouldn't be here. It's a Saturday. This guy is almost certainly deranged, but I reckoned that if I did it today, I could avoid working on Monday, a bank holiday. Having the girly night tomorrow so I'll need the Monday to recover.

No. That's not the reason at all.

I don't know why I'm here.

Even though I know this interview will be a waste of time, it still feels better than doing nothing. I had a good week, work-wise. I may have even saved my job. I could have stayed in bed today or gone shopping or done a million things, but I couldn't settle – and even talking to someone who never met Manda suddenly feels better than any other choice.

On the phone he had sounded curt and unsurprised, as if he had been expecting me and was a bit miffed that I hadn't got in contact sooner. He said little more than his address, though he repeated the house number – 19 – as if this alone had a significance which I was bound to pick up on, as if I would share his annoyance at having a house with such a low number.

I've no idea where number 19 is in the oval of homes, so I've guessed about halfway and then parked the car. For some reason, I hope I haven't stopped too near; I'd like to have a good look at the outside before I knock on the door. Not that a house exterior can tell you much. But I still want to have a cautious look.

Of course, I shouldn't be looking for the house at all, but the taxi, which is about fifteen metres from where I stand. A Mercedes. Old, but gleaming. I walk towards it, my runners squeaking like a siren across the estate.

I'm the only person here. No kids playing on the grass or signs of movement behind net curtains. Just me, squeaking along for anyone who wants to hear. The Merc is about the same length as the cottage it's parked outside. The house is clean too. It's probably the cleanest here, and the one with the greatest pretensions: painted a meticulous light pink, and topped off with a row of multi-coloured hanging baskets. In the window squats a large statue of some religious figure I don't recognise. Perhaps Mr Taxi Driver is older than he sounded on the phone: old-style dacent Dublin working class, brought in up communities which have all but evaporated and with a set of values which are now mocked. Yet he and Mrs Taxi Driver still try to maintain some standards, despite the crumbled conditions of the other homes. That, or he lives with his mother and she's responsible for the house. Or he's gay. Or all three.

I quickly tie up my ratty hair and knock on the polished door.

It's wrenched open: as if he was waiting just behind. He points and says, 'There's a bell. Why didn't you use the bell?'

I have no answer. 'Oh,' is all I manage.

The taxi driver sighs, as if heartily sick of having to explain this to people. He's small and blocky, perhaps mid-forties, bald but with wispy hair at the sides. He hasn't used a brush today either. He wears grey trousers with a few small stains around the lap; a striped shirt under a cardigan with frayed arms. Below all this he is sockless, his feet in a pair of cheap transparent flip-flops. His toes are gnarly, and the big toe of his right foot carries a birthmark so angry-looking it almost glows. There's a white crust around it which extends in a trail up under his trousers and emerges behind his shirt collar, spreading along the left side of his neck. Nasty psoriasis. I'm a doctor's daughter. I know a thing or two.

I've glimpsed as quickly as I can, but he's caught me looking. He glares back, almost challenging me to do it again.

There's something about this man.

He takes a series of quick sips from the mug of tea he carries — as if tea is far too valuable a resource to waste, no matter what the situation.

'I suppose you'd better come in then,' he says. I follow, taking the chance to look again at the scrap of paper in my pocket. I'd forgotten his name. Maurice Kiberd. He doesn't look like a Maurice Kiberd. Maurice Kiberd sounds like a history professor or a government minister.

No sign of a Mrs Kiberd. The inside smells of turf mixed with farts. It seems tidy, but so dark it's difficult to tell if the place is clean or not. From the furniture and some of the ornaments, I reckon a woman has lived here, though not for a while: the place seems abandoned. Maurice Kiberd strides to a corner of the room and without looking slumps back into a sagging armchair flanked by an outspread tabloid on one side and an over-full ashtray on the other. He gestures towards a chair opposite for me to sit in, then almost yells, 'You don't want tea, do you?' I'm almost tempted to say yes, given the massive inconvenience this would obviously cause. But instead I shake my head. I sit. The springs poke at my back.

'Well, Maurice,' I say.

'Mr Kiberd.'

'Mr Kiberd. Sorry.'

He grins, rather pleased with himself.

'Sorry, sorry, sorry,' he says, as if to another person in the room. 'They're always sorry. But it's respect, do you see? It's manners. Manners are gone. Children are not taught manners, and that's what starts it. That's when they start to turn into little animals. Wolves.'

He looks directly at me.

'I'd say you know what I mean.'

'Yes,' I say, neutrally. 'So Rachel Belton told me –'

'Oh!' he exclaims, as if he's sick of hearing this. He points.

'Write this down. I'm no supporter of *that* party. Or any other. I wouldn't vote for her. I wouldn't vote for any of them. I'm just a citizen trying to do me bit, you know? So don't be putting me on the front page alongside that one, OK?'

'Absolutely,' I say.

He seems slightly taken aback.

'All right,' he says, more warily now. 'You want to know about that fella that got into the taxi.'

'Yes.'

'But you don't believe me, do ya?'

I say nothing.

'You think I'm some mad bloke looking to get into the papers or whatever. Looking for attention. That's what the guards think. And do you know why? Because they know me, because I've been down to them before reporting things, doing my civic duty.'

He points to the window. A sliver of spider web hangs from it; dancing to unheard music.

'I drive at night. You wouldn't believe what goes on out there at three o'clock in the morning; you wouldn't believe it. And when I call into the guards to tell them, or if I give them a bell? "Oh yes, Mr Kiberd, we'll send out a car." But they don't. Or they make out they know about it already. But if they did, why don't they do something? You don't read in the paper about any of the things I see, you know what I mean? The guards don't give a damn, or they're scared or they don't have the whatdoyacallit, the resources or whatever. I don't know. But out there at night they're eating each other alive, I tell you. And nobody is doing anything about it.'

He pauses, panting, his eyes glassy. I stay quiet.

'My mother. Old lady. Scared to leave the house. Used to walk down to the shop on her own every day, no bother, until she was mugged for her purse. Bloody young fellas.'

He extends a hand. It's wide and flat. The knuckles are covered with flaky red skin.

'Pardon my language, but you know what I mean? In broad daylight they did it, no bother. *I* knew who they were, but the guards?' He roughly pounds the hand on his knee. The tea on the floor beside him vibrates. 'Nothing. And my mother was never the same again after that. Wouldn't leave the house. Terrified, she was, especially with me out working. But what could I do?'

Maurice Kiberd leans back in his seat; as if challenging me.

'OK,' I finally say. 'OK.'

I leave a long pause. He's staring at the ground, perhaps a bit embarrassed by his outburst.

I look around. The mother must be upstairs, shivering under her duvet; just as scared by the rage shrieking inside her son.

The rage. This is like with David.

In a quiet voice, I eventually add. 'That's really terrible.'

He rouses himself, shakes.

'No,' he says. 'It's all right, it's fine. That's my sad story, we all have them. All I'm saying is like, you know…'

'Yes, Mr Kiberd. Absolutely,' I shoot back, with what I hope is enough sincerity. Because I mean it now. Or I think I do. I mean it when I promise that I will definitely get back to him and let him know what I've found out; even if I've found out nothing. I want to take this man seriously because I suspect no one ever has before; because that's all he seems to want. Even if he's wrong.

Why? Because of my angry, sick ex-boyfriend? To somehow make up for my failures?

Stop, Carol. Stop.

I'll bring the story to Don who will peer at me from under his eyebrows and ask: 'Is this man a nutter? Looking for attention?'

CHAPTER FORTY SEVEN

Maurice Kiberd

No, I didn't tell that journalist everything that happened with me and Ma. Why should I? None of her business. And why should I trust some young one who walks in me door? I'm not stupid. I know what the media is like, twisting everything. I like to be honest and upfront, of course I do, but I learned from experience. If I'd told her everything she would have been the same as everyone else, same as the guards. Oh, this guy Maurice is dodgy. He's a bit mad. He doesn't lie down and take it like everyone else. He fights back. Must be something wrong with him.

I don't know if she believed me. We'll see. I don't know.

I didn't tell her Ma was dead.

They waited for months. The street had gone back to being quiet again. No noise, no vandalism. Kids could go out and play on the grass. I suppose word had gone around. It *had* got around. One night I was leaving a fella home who lived about five minutes from here, though he didn't know me. Young bloke, nice suit, a bit drunk. Not from the area – only bought his house for some crazy price a couple of years before the bail-out and all that. He was trying to make out that he knew all his neighbours and it was great and everyone is so friendly: you know the rubbish yuppies come out with. Anyway, as we were passing our street he pointed and said: see that road there? Few young lads caught doing graffiti by the Provos. Broke their legs.

Provos? I said. I thought they'd gone out of business.

The stories that get around.

Going to the cops all them times did have one thing going for it: at least they had me number and were able to ring straight away after Ma was mugged. Mugged. Would you call it mugged? They took her purse all right, but how hard would that be? Taking a purse from an old lady? They broke her nose. Broke her bloody nose.

They didn't need to do that. Of course they didn't. That was a message. We can't get you, but we can get your ma.

So when I arrive at the hospital, does anyone ask how are you, Maurice? Would you like a cup of tea, Maurice? Don't worry, Maurice, we'll catch the scumbags. Instead two plain-clothes coppers won't even let me see her. Instead they insist – we *insist*, Mr Kiberd, real sarcastic, like – that I talk to them first. And all they do is start quizzing me about who did this and why. I'm not stupid. I said nothing, and at first I was furious. Shaking, I was. They knew to be careful when they saw that, especially the younger one. Trying to act tough, but I could see his bottom lip trembling. Pathetic. Eventually, they got to the point – to warn *me* what would happen if you take the law into your own hands, *Mr Kiberd*.

All I did was repeat over and over, can I see my Ma now? Can I? Can I? But they wouldn't let it go, kept going on and on and on about it; as if they seriously thought that nagging me would make a difference. I stopped listening, tuned them out. An old lady gets her nose broken and I'm the bad fella? Even from the stupid guards it was a bit much. Beyond the pale.

Cruel. That's what went through me mind: how cruel they were being, and for no reason. They could have said it to me after I visited me Ma or the day after or anything. And the more I thought about it, while they droned on, the funnier I started to feel. It was like, I dunno, a *weakness*, and the next thing I had me face in me hands and I was crying. *Crying*. Shoulders pumping up and down and tears streaming out of me. That shut them up, though they must have loved seeing me like that. Loved it. *Mr Kiberd*.

I couldn't take me hands off me face until they left the room, I was that ashamed. And I swore to myself that if I saw them outside, and there was even a little bit of a smile or any of that, then they'd get it. Tear them apart. Cops or not. Hospital or not.

But then I remembered me ma and that I had to pull meself together for her. She was in an awful state. Big black rings under her eyes. Her nose looked like it had exploded and was only held together with bandages and metal plates. Started crying again in there. Don't know what come over me. Stress or something. Ma looked terrified, then looked away.

'Go into the bathroom son and wash your face.'

That was all she said to me.

My God, the fury. I felt stuffed with it. There was no room for anything else in me brain. Nothing. But the funny thing was that, even then, I knew I wasn't angry with the guards or even with them lads so much; couldn't expect any better from them. I was livid with meself; disgusted that I hadn't protected her; that I hadn't seen this coming; that all I could do was cry like a bloody homo.

For about a week I didn't work. I had a feeling the cops were watching me, so when I wasn't visiting Ma, I'd stay in the house. Didn't talk to anyone. Didn't go to the shops or anything. Just sat there, looking out the front window. At all hours. Slept on the couch, when I did sleep. Lived on Ritz crackers and oranges. Even Ma noticed that I'd lost weight. But I couldn't risk going out, do you see? I was scared of what I might do out there, to anyone who looked at me sideways; innocent or not. I'd crush them.

But eventually I got meself under control: I knew that losing the head wouldn't sort things out. The guards were right about that. You have to be cool; you have to take your time. Just like they did. Anyway, in the meantime I had to look after me ma, which was tricky enough. If I'm honest, it was something I wasn't really able for. How do you look after your parent when they're suddenly acting like a child? Came as a total shock to me.

She couldn't do anything when she came home, or wouldn't do anything. She'd sit in the chair and that would be it. Wouldn't go out or cook dinner or anything. Suddenly I had to do it all, and to be honest it's not the sort of thing I know much about. Didn't know what to buy at the shops; didn't know how to cook. Had to get a book for that, after I'd nearly poisoned us a couple of times. But I muddled through, and after a while I was all right at the cooking. Not that Ma ever ate much of it.

As for the cleaning and all the rest, I wasn't really great. I'd keep the outside all painted and neat and that. But I couldn't get the hang of the housework. So eventually the GP arranged for a nurse to start calling around. She'd clean up a bit and change me ma's clothes and tidy up her bed and all that. And she'd talk to Ma. Great at that, she was. Chat away, even though Ma hardly ever said a word back. I was glad of it, because I tell ya, I found that bit hard to handle.

I had work to do anyway: there were things that needed paying for. So I stayed out all the hours I could; I needed the money but also, I have to admit, I didn't like being at home. I couldn't bear to see her.

Isn't that terrible? I couldn't bear to see her.

It was four months before I did anything. I spent four months digging the fingernails into me hands. Some days I'd say to meself: forget about it. You'll only make things worse, like you did before. Then I'd think about them swanning around the place, delighted with themselves, telling everyone how they sorted out that taxi driver down the road, and how they're the real hard men cos they beat up an old lady. They never came back to our street – they weren't that stupid – but I knew well that they were doing the same in other streets about the place. Terrorising people, and with no one to stop them. That really stuck in my craw. Really did.

But I did nothing. I couldn't decide.

What happened instead was that it fell in me lap; and then it felt like I should do something: I was *supposed* to do something.

I don't believe in God or any of that. Not in Jesus in Heaven look-ing down and looking after you or any of that guff. Never looked after me. Never looked after Ma. But sometimes I wonder if something might be going on, behind the scenes: like there's clues you have to look out for, and if you spot them you'll do all right.

Or maybe that's all guff. I dunno.

But how's this anyway: one Saturday night, in town, and don't the two of them get into my taxi? The two I put in the hospital. Needless to say, no one ever got arrested for attacking Ma. Don't know if they even got questioned.

Rotten drunk, this pair were. Dunno what age they were by then. But hardly eighteen. Too drunk, anyway to recognise the taxi they kicked and the man who got out of it. Too drunk, or too cocky. I don't know.

So how could I ignore this? When it was put in front of me? What would anyone do?

One of them gave me an address and called me *Pal*, thinking he's dead smooth. Real charming. Not so clever to notice that I didn't bring them anywhere near to where he said, but out to the Phoenix Park where it was nice and dark: the part where the queers go to meet each other. I liked that touch.

They were so easy. My God. For hard men. Just told them to get out of the taxi and they did. Sheep: squealing when I hit them with the bat, one of them even begging, offering me money. Pathetic. Not men at all. Animals.

I didn't kill them. I'm not a murderer. But I didn't want them to walk away from it this time. I broke their ankles – I mean, smashed them to bits so they'd always have a limp, so every time they took a step they'd always remember who did it to them, and why. Then I left them in the dark to crawl on their hands and knees. Animals.

It was so dark, and they were so drunk, there's no way they saw me face, even though afterwards they made out that they did. I cleaned the car inside and out the next morning so the cops couldn't find any mud or anything when they looked. Some CCTV camera did get me though: going along the North Circular Road when I said I wasn't there.

That didn't prove that I did anything, but the cops didn't care. All they wanted was to put me away, even if it was a stitch-up; the two of them lying through the teeth they had left when they stood up in court, moaning about how much their poor little legs were hurting them.

At least the judge was a bit sympathetic. Turned out that the two have a fair load of form, while I have none. The judge said this probably wasn't as straightforward as they were making out; that I wouldn't just attack them for no reason. Yet still he sent me away for three months. Three bloody months when I never felt warm or safe, when the stink of shit was never out of me nostrils, when I don't think I slept for one whole night.

But I stuck it out. It was during my final two weeks when they told me that Ma was dead. The nurse had been going to see her every day, cooking her meals and cleaning and all that. And suddenly Ma started speaking. Had hardly said a word for weeks, but now she was all chat, telling the nurse that she was feeling much better, though she was finding it hard to sleep at night. So could the nurse get something off the doctor for her?

I suppose it wasn't the nurse's fault. She didn't know what Ma was planning. She found her in bed two days later, an empty bottle of brandy beside her, and all the pills gone.

I wanted to go berserk when I heard; I wanted to wreck the gaff and everyone around me. But I knew if I did, they wouldn't let me go to the funeral.

What a miserable day. Rain coming in at an angle and stinging my face, but because of the handcuffs I couldn't wipe it off or stop it flooding into my shirt and down my body. Shivering I was, but I didn't care. I was alone now, but I still remembered the way Ma couldn't look at me that time when I cried. Have to have pride, even now. All the neighbours were stood around the grave. Not looking at me, of course, but gawping at the screw who came with me and muttering to each other: that's it now. Now he's killed off his mother as well. What will he do next? They knew nothing. All alone, I was. But I didn't back down.

I didn't tell that reporter that me ma was dead. I talked like she was still alive. Isn't that a bit strange?

CHAPTER FORTY EIGHT

Carol Murphy

Around the time Manda went out the window, Maurice Kiberd was driving along Parnell Street. He was aware of some sort of rumpus, but not what it was. He probably would have stopped to look, only for this guy jumped in the back of his car. Skinny, blue hoodie, stud in his eyebrow, perhaps in his thirties though it's hard to tell with junkies. And there was no how are ya bud or any of that, just drive. Please. Drive.

According to Maurice Kiberd it took the guy some minutes to decide where he wanted to go. There was one brief phone call, and a mention of a girl, though Maurice didn't catch the rest of it. The junkie seemed to be in tears, and finally announced. *I wanna go home. To Finglas.* Didn't utter a word after that. Doesn't make him the culprit, but at least it sounds like he saw something. Perhaps Maurice isn't a crank after all.

I'm tempted to go straight out to the address he gave me, but I need coffee and cigarettes and I've been diverted by a text from Don.

Have you seen the tabs?

Don refers to all the others as *tabs*, as if our paper is some sort of Harold Evans-style broadsheet. Though I suppose we're not the worst. This isn't a happy text though: probably means they have a story we don't. *Shit.*

I buy my papers but don't look at them, then find a place that does coffee and cakes. *A Slice of Heaven.* Before I go in, I light a cigarette but throw it away after two drags.

Inside, I hear my voice wobble as I order. The café seems to darken and I have an odd urge to run out of the place. I get a flash of Manda, yelling at me. She's a teenager. *What would you know about*

241

love? What would you know? I spill a bit of my coffee as I bring it to a table beside the window. It's started to shower outside: that misty rain which swirls around and which we don't seem to get as much of in Ireland any more. The cars going past switch on their wipers. A fat, agitated bee buzzes up to the other side of the glass and starts bouncing off the window. It sounds like knocking.

What would you know about love?

I don't want to think about this. I don't want to look at the newspapers either, but they've rolled open and already I can see the name Belton sprawled across three of them. Probably appeared as an exclusive in a first edition, but since then all the others have picked it up.

I 'SEE' MANDA

Husband of candidate claims he 'sees' ghost of murdered bridesmaid.

I feel like retching, but take a slug of coffee to keep it back. The coffee burns my throat and makes me pant like a dog. The bee outside the window keeps knocking. Pat, pat, pat.

THE husband of controversial election candidate Rachel Belton has claimed to have seen the 'spirit' of pretty Manda Ferguson – brutally murdered by Drug Lords.

Former mountaineer Daniel Belton says the spirit of Manda wants his wife Rachel to continue running in the general election – so she can tell people the truth.

But this isn't the first time former mountaineer Daniel has had close encounters from beyond the grave. A keen spiritualist, he told...

I groan; loudly enough for everyone else in the café to hear. I wrench the newspaper shut and throw it on the floor. Eyelids flicker. Don will think this is a story that I missed – and I suppose I did. I wouldn't have written it anyway. I had Rachel Belton down as a bit naive, but trying to do the right thing. Not *crazy*.

I stand up quickly, step outside and violently pull on a cigarette. Things like this never happen by accident. Someone made a call, someone set this up. We all do it, day in, day out. The fiction of *News*. Yet we still believe.

I throw my half-smoked cigarette on the pavement. It lands beside a the dying bee.

But why would she do it? A few religious types might vote for her now, but that's it. She'll be a laughing stock; a nutcase.

Perhaps she was just stupid after all.

As I return to my table, everyone in the coffee shop is looking at me, or trying not to, though I don't think about that until much later. I haven't really studied my surroundings, and am only aware that the place is small and that most of the others are female and elderly, whispering and tutting, doling out judgements on a world which doesn't care what they think anymore. Without realising it I have my phone out and I'm dialling Rachel Belton's number. I have one eye closed, like I'm aiming. I can feel blood swelling through the veins behind my ears, though I don't feel agitated: cold, if anything. No, that's guff. The emotion is always there, sloshing around inside me, registering every slight and compliment, pressing to come out and shout Fuck Off. I Love You.

He answers the phone almost instantly. An Anglo-Irish twang, which sounds English, really, except that he'll occasionally use words like 'grand' in a non-intentional stage-Irish voice. In Meath, where he grew up, where his family have lived for hundreds of years, he's still the Brit. The contradictions of imperial history. Millions of people who don't really belong in any country: whites in Africa, Russians in Eastern Europe, chaps with English accents in Ireland.

'Hello?' he says, as if not entirely sure that this is the correct way to start a phone conversation.

'Daniel Belton,' I say.

'Er, yes. Who is this? This is Rachel's phone. She'll be back in a minute.'

'What does Manda look like?'

'I beg your pardon? Sorry?'

'It says in all the papers that you've seen Manda. So what does she look like?'

'Sorry, who is this?'

'Carol Murphy. A journalist. I interviewed your wife yesterday.'

'Yes, yes, she mentioned that.'

'Did she say I knew Manda?'

'Yes, er. I can't remember. You knew her?'

'If you saw Manda, what does she look like?'

'Well, Carol, I don't know if you know anything about spiritualism, but it's not quite the same as seeing a person on the physical plane. And the papers have blown the –'

'How did you know it was Manda then?'

'Well, she identified herself.'

'She *spoke* to you? And what did she say? Specifically.'

He sighs, probably frustrated that his media-course phone manner isn't working (engage the interviewer by using their first name); probably looking for an excuse to hang up. But he doesn't.

'It's not like…Carol, I know you may be sceptical about this, but it is something I have a belief in. And yesterday this person who turned out to be a reporter asked me a question…'

'What did Manda say?'

'…and I answered it in good faith. I'm not going to deny what I know to be true just to suit a cynical media…'

'What did Manda say?'

'…and I certainly didn't ask for it to be splashed across all the front pages. That's your profession…'

'What did Manda say?'

'…not mine.'

It builds in steps: he raises his voice, then I raise mine. There isn't a word from anyone else in the café now. They are openly staring, though I get a fleeting sense that this is not without sympathy. My eyes spurt tears.

Perhaps Daniel Belton also suspects I'm crying, because he's finally stopped talking, at least for a moment. He tries to reset his tone to one of compassion.

'Carol, I understand that this girl was your friend so you must be grieving her loss. You must be devastated. And Rachel and I would in no way want to...'

'What did she say?'

He sighs again.

'Spirits don't *say* things. Not like you and I. It's more that one gets a sense from them.'

'A sense of what?'

'Well, a sense that things will be OK.'

'That Rachel should continue with the election?'

'Well, yes. It was a question in my mind at the time, and she would have been aware of this. But as I say, this reporter...'

'So you *saw* something that didn't look like Manda and didn't say anything, but you reckon it was her. And you reckon that Manda Ferguson went to all the trouble of coming back from the dead or the other side or whatever you fucking call it, so she could do a bit of ghostly canvassing for the Party – the kind of political group she hated in life, which she spent most of her adult life working against.'

'No, Carol.'

'You're saying she was murdered, went up to heaven and God turned out to be a Christian Democrat? That's what you're saying?'

'No, Carol, it's got nothing to do with politics.'

'But you're on the front page of every newspaper in the country saying exactly that. *Exactly that.*'

I'm screaming into the phone now, jabbing my finger in the air. Even people on the pavement outside are pausing to look at me. Yet it doesn't feel as if I'm speaking, as if I'm forming sentences or even thoughts: it's as if the words are assembling themselves into the proper order, slickly juggled by some invisible force. I have a sense of watching myself, of observing this process take place, and I'm reminded of these old gentlemen I used to meet when I first started out as a reporter: they'd be covering the courts, been doing it for years, and wouldn't need to write out their copy like me. All they'd need was the charge, the plea and perhaps a quote or two and they could recite the story off the top of their heads. Like Michelangelo, one of them told me. He didn't think he created statues. He merely searched for blocks of marble with the statues already inside.

Now I'm waving my left hand like an orator.

'Oh, I love the way that you've convinced yourself that this is some sort of religious belief. No chance that you're delusional or, heaven forbid, just *pretending* to get your wife elected.'

He's still on the line. I can hear him breathing. I don't know why he's taking this.

'But I suppose you're not the first person in the world to do it. I just wish I hadn't been involved. I actually thought she was genuine.'

'Carol, she is genuine. Look, she's just come back now, would you like a word?'

This is why he hasn't hung up on me: he's been waiting for the boss to return.

'No, I wouldn't.'

I'm on my feet, though I don't remember standing. My face is drenched with tears and spittle hangs from my chin, dropping onto my chest. I must look a sight, though at least there's no make-up to ruin. Not that I care anyway, because it feels as if, with the tears, something else has come; something has broken or exploded and I can hardly get enough breath into my scorched lungs.

'You *evil* fucker. You didn't know her, didn't know what she was. I knew her. I loved her.'

She's looking at me, mouthing the words.

What would you know about love?

Oh, God.

Something else is coming back now; a glimpse of something.

Oh God.

What would you know about love?

I can't talk anymore; I'm shaking too much. I let the phone drop onto the table and for the first time take in all the old ladies sitting around me in ones and twos. They stare straight back. I don't see any hint of disapproval, of wishing I would leave. Instead the looks are concerned, are kindly; as if they have lived through similar times as well, and are glad for me that I responded the way I did. I sense that if they were a little more forward, they might even applaud.

CHAPTER FORTY NINE
Rachel Belton

walk into the kitchen, brushing my wet hair, and see a deathly white Daniel placing my mobile phone back on the kitchen counter. He's wearing a wrinkled mauve shirt. All his shirts are this way. They are washed and perfectly ironed and he puts on a fresh one every day. Yet it always appears as if he has slept in his clothes. I have accused him of crumpling them on purpose, but he denies it.

'Was that my phone?'

'Yes. It was that reporter you had out here.'

'What did she want?'

He pauses, considering what to say. I feel my throat tightening.

'To abuse me, it would seem. She was screaming, completely out of control. That girl must have a few problems.' He stands up, as if he's about to leave.

'She was screaming?'

He sighs, as if it's an annoyance even to speak about such trivial matters.

'I forgot to tell you. I'm sorry. I just forgot. Some reporter rang here yesterday. Not *that* one,' he says pointing at the phone. 'Another one. A man. Can't remember his name. And he was asking for you, of course, and we were chatting a bit, that's all. I didn't know it would end up in the newspaper.'

'What did you say to him?'

'It was completely under false pretences. Is that not illegal?'

'What did you say to him, Daniel?'

He looks directly at me now, and seems to deflate before my eyes. He knows what he's done. And it's not just because of what it will do to the campaign or the public ridicule it will expose us to, but where it leaves he and I. We sit on the kitchen stools, already exhausted by what's to come.

'I mentioned that I had spoken to Manda.'

'Jesus, Daniel.'

I put my face in my hands. He makes no attempt to come near me.

'Perhaps it's only a small story,' he offers.

'It won't be.'

'How do you know?'

'Oh, grow up, Daniel!'

My phone rings. I don't look at it. Then the accusing chime of a text message, followed by another. And another. I turn off the phone and hold it up to him.

'It's on the front page. That's what the texts mean. Which means it's probably on all the front pages. And you *forgot*? You were prepared to let me walk out the door without knowing this? To spend a day making a fool of myself?'

'I don't see how this makes a fool of you. It's something I said.'

'Oh, for God's sake, Daniel. You're my husband. Everything you say reflects on me. If you have nutty beliefs, then people think I do too. Do you not see that?'

He flinches.

'Nutty?'

'OK, not to you, but to most people they are a bit weird. Surely you see that?'

'Most people are wrong.'

'So I just tell people they are wrong? That's what I tell them? I tell them that my husband chats to dead people every day, and they'll accept that, they'll vote for that? Daniel, don't you see the damage you've done?'

'I thought you got into this election because you wanted to stand up for what you believe in. That's what you've been saying.'

'But Daniel, I *don't* believe in spiritualism. You know that. I never did.'

He seems surprised.

'I knew you had doubts. I knew it unnerved you. But you never said.'

'Yes I did. Lots of times.'

'But that's when you were angry.'

'So? It was what I thought. I don't believe in it. I don't believe you can talk to dead people.'

'I'm imagining it then? I'm making it up?'

'No. Yes. Actually, yes, you're convincing yourself that it's real. And all it's doing is driving you mad, Daniel. Your grief, it's…'

We both have tears in our eyes, though I know Daniel's will be more difficult to restrain. I haven't spoken to him like this in a long time; I was hoping never to have to again. But it's what I have to say; the words I cannot escape from. The author of my own life.

He backs away from me, waving his arms as if trying to get rid of a bad smell. He disappears down the stairs, and for a moment it seems as if his shadow lingers behind; as if it's reluctant to follow.

I turn on my phone. Seven text messages, most of which address me in the same slightly embarrassed tone, like attendees at a funeral who can't find the right words. *Have you seen the papers today?* The only deviation is the text from Sandra. *Saw the paper. Fuck.* There's also a message from Aidan Haslett. *Rachel. Ring me as soon as you can.* I can guess what he's going to say; what he thought he didn't have to say the last time.

I don't ring him. Can't do it; not yet anyway. I think about Sandra and all the other women, getting ready for another day of asking people to vote for me; wondering should they continue, wondering what they can say about the candidate with the mad husband. And it had been going so well. Yes, Sandra. Fuck.

I think too, about that reporter, Carol. I liked her. Smoked her cigarettes. I think she liked me too. Now what does she think? What else will she think I haven't told her? Funnily enough, it's this that makes me weep.

Is murdered young woman trying to tell us something?

'WE SAW MANDA TOO'

'Visionaries' claim she has a message for Ireland

By MATHEW FULLER

Following controversial claims by an ex-mountaineer that he has spoken with murdered Manda Ferguson, several other people have come forward to claim that they have seen her too...

Chapter Fifty

Michael Bourke

A group arrives at the door of my house. Some are regular attendees at mass; others I have not seen before. But they are of similar type. They wear the static gaze of the true believer; they ooze the impregnable smugness of those convinced that they have cracked the problem of everlasting life.

I invite them in, a jab of anxiety shooting up my spine: this is different from the usual drop-ins. Generally, people don't stay long: *I won't bother you*, are the first words from their mouths, and I don't dissuade them from their declared intention. They leave their gift or have their mass card signed and are gone. Or they avoid the problem altogether by dispatching a child to make the delivery. This visit, though, is more formal: it has the feel of a deputation; of urgent night-time meetings where it has been decided exactly what should be said.

For a moment, I wonder if they are here to accuse; if they come armed with incontrovertible evidence of my lack of faith. I feel my face grow red, and curse it.

They seem to have nominated one to do the talking: Sharon, whose surname escapes me. She is a chubby, pleasant-faced woman of middle-age who over the years has been in this house many times. She's organised race nights and pub quizzes to raise funds for the church and the nearby school, and is one of those who seems more interested in the church for its community rather than religious applications. Sharon is no zealot.

But today she is stripped of the battle-hardened look of a practical woman. Normally her black hair is scraped back from her face, and her *de rigeur* dress code one of trainers and track suits. She wears a woollen coat spotted with dog hair which is obviously reserved for more formal occasions. Her hair is untethered; she has the appearance of someone who has spent the night standing in the rain. They all seem this way.

My offers of tea are refused with a certain urgency: what they have to say is too important to be prefaced with the usual chat about the weather or the consistently poor fortunes of our under-12s soccer team.

'Father,' she says. 'Did you see in the paper about the girl? The girl that you knew?'

It would be churlish to pretend that I don't know what she's talking about, or to point out that I didn't know the girl at all. As for what was in the paper, I am truly in the dark. I must confess to glancing at the headline which referred to myself, but disgust prevented me from reading further. Since then I have steadfastly avoided all media, and for the same reason.

Detecting my puzzlement, Sharon adds, 'Not the one about you, now. All the other ones. About the appearances.'

I shake my head. 'I'm afraid not,' I say. 'I don't like to read about it. You know.'

They seem amazed by this admission.

'But it's been on the radio and everything,' says an elderly man whom I don't recognise. He has a lightening-shaped scar above his right eyebrow. 'And the telly. Did you not see it? The angel?'

Again I shake my head, further adding to their astonishment that anyone could not only be unaware of this news story, but wilfully insulate themselves from the all-penetrating eye of the electronic media.

'I listen to music,' I say.

They stare at me, blank-faced.

'Sure no wonder,' Sharon snaps at the man. 'Didn't Father have an awful traumatic experience? I don't blame him.' *Traw-mak-ick*. I often hear music in their speech.

The elderly man seems happy to accept this logic, leaving Sharon to resume her role as spokesperson.

'Father, the girl, Manda – she's been appearing under lampposts. All over the country. The papers and everything are full of it. We saw her, we all did. In the Phoenix Park.' She points at the elderly man. 'Tom and few others go to the big cross there and she appeared to them under the lights. If you pray, she appears. Do you know what I mean?'

I don't know what to say. But finally I ask, 'Under lampposts? Why?'

The group seem phased by this question.

'Is it so people can see her?' asks the scarred elderly man. He looks towards me, as if I can provide theological guidance on this point. The role of lampposts in religious phenomena.

'Maybe it's something to do with the elections,' says Sharon. 'You know the way you found her with that election poster on her chest? Didn't that woman's husband say he saw her? He was the first, I think.'

'Or there is no relevance,' I say. 'It could be a simple trick of the light.'

'Oh no, Father,' pipes up Tom. 'There's a group in Finglas. They saw her too. I was there as well.'

He seems proud of this fact; as if witnessing more than one miracle gives him a certain cachet.

'Have many people have seen this?' I ask.

As one, the group nods and mumbles. 'Loads of people,' says Sharon. 'Hundreds, I'd say. Yeah, hundreds.'

'Under lampposts?' I say. More nodding.

Once again, I want to run screaming to my room; I want to grab Sharon and shake her until common sense reasserts itself; until she remembers that she never really believed any of this supernatural clap-trap: that the only theology is a theology of people, looking up at the stars and creating their own stories.

But of course I don't. Instead I say, as neutrally as possible. 'I see.'

'You have to see it,' says Sharon.

I don't reply.

'You could come to Finglas,' says Tom, the scar on his forehead gently undulating as he speaks. 'They'll be there again tomorrow night.'

'No,' says Sharon. 'Why would he need to go to Finglas? Sure, can't we do it here? She knew the Father. She's bound to come here.'

Many times I have been presented with situations similar to this. Not the recipients of visions, granted, but individuals convinced that they had received a signal from God: a postcard from across the cosmos informing them that yes, they should go back to college or buy that house they couldn't really afford.

Normally, they are quite simple to handle: people can easily be swayed by superstitious arguments, especially from their priest. I would baldly state that any decision made was theirs and theirs alone: and this was the way God wanted it. Rather than a sign, perhaps this was a *test*. After all, if God put you on this earth to make your own choices, then isn't it a little proud to assume that he should help you as well?

I used the illusion of freedom to give them a freedom, of sorts.

Yet I quickly see that this strategy has little chance of success. I can't recall ever having dealt with a group of people claiming to have had the same experience: and it is obvious they are not here seeking confirmation of what happened, or even interpretation of what it means. They are convinced.

I am reminded of the story of the Buddha, and for a moment I consider telling it to them. Pestered by a follower who wished to know if God existed, the Buddha told him he was like a man shot by a poison arrow who refuses all medical treatment until he learns the name of his attacker and what village he came from: details which will do nothing to aid his healing.

I imagine their faces as I relate the tale. The who? Is that the fat bloke?

Instead, I'm stuttering. I hear myself saying that I don't know, that I would have to check with the bishop. The group continue to stare at me, like children trying to understand some difficult concept.

'Would ya?' says Sharon. 'Why?'

'Well, because, you know. The church takes the view that such matters need to be investigated. The hierarchy would be cautious.'

'Why?' she says again.

'Because of the danger of hoaxes. And we would need to be sure who is appearing and why. I mean, how can you be sure it was the girl?'

'She looked like the picture in the newspaper,' says another woman with mascara shooting from her eyes. 'And we all saw her. We all saw the same thing.' There's an edge of anger in her voice.

'Yes, yes, of course,' I say. 'But the church, as I say, is cautious on these matters. They would be reluctant to call it a miraculous event until all the other possibilities have been exhausted. Sometimes it can be a natural phenomenon, or some sort of mass suggestion.'

The more I speak, the more their disappointment balloons around us: they had assumed that I, of all people, would accept their story, that I might even be pleased. I pause, glance at the ground. I ask, 'Why do you think she's appearing?'

'It's a sign of hope,' says the elderly man.

'Hope for what?'

'You know, what with everything going on in the world. She's here to tell us that things are going to get better. That's what I think anyway.'

'But is she going to make it better?' I say. 'Surely that's up to us? That's up to people.'

'Yeah,' says Sharon, as if this is an obvious point. 'But we have to feel better before we can do that. She's telling us not to give up. And look at the state of the country, Father. There's loads of people giving up.'

She regards me evenly. Sharon is a clever woman. And perhaps she is right. Perhaps hope is good, no matter how ridiculous the source. It strikes me that if I agree to their request, and then attest that I have seen nothing, this might put an end to it. It sounds like an opportunistic media invention anyway, preying on the delusions of desperate souls. Another few days and it will be over. Until the next expenses scandal or sporting row.

I hear myself agreeing, but insisting that the arrangement remain private; just between us. We'll spend half an hour this evening, I say. They nod fervently, like children who have finally won permission to play on the swings and now have to endure adjuncts from their parents to be careful and wear a coat. Although I am issuing these instructions – although I quite enjoy the hint of authority which has crept back into my voice – I'm already wondering if this is a monstrous mistake; if control has already slipped from my sweaty grasp.

I trudge up to my room, and some urge I do not understand brings me to search underneath my bed and extract the dusty cardboard box, the top of which declares in breathless, futuristic typography: *The Super Space Conqueror!* He probably had to send off to the United States for it. Remarkable that it travelled all that way and arrived undamaged. Even now it seems to function: there is no mould on the mirrors, no scrapes. The eyepieces and finder scope wait faithfully in their cardboard housings. I run my hands along the cool white enamel exterior of the instrument, and although I know that this is a six-inch reflector, that there was probably a more expensive model with an electric clock drive, that the mirror is probably made from Pyrex, I still find it strange and wonderful; a numinous thing. I find myself hugging it; as if it contains all the belief I have ever needed.

Chapter Fifty One
Carol Murphy

We were teenagers by then. I could have been as old as fifteen, and even though we spent a lot of our time sleeping or watching TV, we still made our way out to the tree house every day. *Jesus*, the memory is *so* vivid. I can smell the just-fallen rain pattering from the leaves and onto the roof. We have posters on the walls now. One of Nirvana, though I can't remember any others. Manda has her hair blonde and curly and she's wearing a dress that looks like an oversized grandfather shirt. She's sitting on one of the beanbags we got, leafing through some magazine. Conor is on the floor, legs stretched out, in Levis and a striped top, jerking his legs in time to whatever is playing on the ghetto blaster, and I say to them, because the thought strikes me there and then: isn't it amazing that we still come here? They look at me, slightly puzzled; as if I'm about to point out all the other great places to go in Loughrea which for some perverse reason of our own we have chosen to ignore.

I mean, I say, that we're all grown up, or pretty close to grown up, but we still fit in here, there's still plenty of room. Manda and Conor study their surroundings and nod in agreement. It's like he planned it that way, I say, for the future. Referring to their father as *he* is about as much as I can get away with, if I want to avoid Conor disappearing for half the day.

Hmmm, he says. I dunno. Even if it was too small, *I'd* still come.

Me too, I quickly add.

And me, says Manda. Of course.

There's a pause while we consider this.

I've come here by myself, says Conor, as if admitting something terrible. He looks at Manda. And we've come here?

Two or three times, says Manda to me.

But it wasn't the same, says Conor, staring at the ceiling again.

I should be thrilled at this compliment, but I realise I'm not: because it's not intended as such. It is a statement of the obvious. It would not be the same without me. Or Conor. Or Manda.

Is it because we are cousins? Manda says. That we love each other so much?

Out of anyone else's mouth, a statement like this would be quietly ignored. But it is as normal as air coming from Manda. Conor curls his lip, then says, I know people who hate their cousins. Fight with them.

Then we're very lucky, says Manda. Very lucky.

I suppose it just happens, I offer. Chemistry or something.

The others give silent agreement: a near-miraculous combination of DNA and personality and circumstance has brought the three of us together. It has given us something billions of others might never experience; such is the blind chance of the universe: which makes us want to hope that there may be some governance behind it all.

Yes, says Manda eventually, though a little doubtfully. While Conor and I have already opted to be atheists, Manda has declared her belief, though she doesn't know what sort yet. She's read a bit about Buddhism and Islam. She likes Shinto in Japan, but still goes to mass. Sometimes it makes her cry, though she can't explain why.

Perhaps, she says, we were *meant* to be together. Conor rolls his eyes. Manda gives him a shove. You know what I mean. This does feel like it was meant to be. We have each other for the rest of our lives. Isn't that amazing?

And we trade smiles, because we know that this is true.

Chapter Fifty Two
Baz Carroll

I didn't tell her I was leaving; just waited until it was dark and slipped out. Of course I'm going to go back. I took a key. Not that stupid. Have to be smart, because she doesn't give a fuck now.

A monster, she called me. Her own son. Like, for your own ma to say something like that to you, Jesus. I know what she meant: that the drugs were the monster and that. But still.

It's a nice night. Not that cold or anything, and not that many people around. I walk to the end of Pleasant Lane and turn right, away from the cop shop. If I see anyone coming I'll just cross the road. Walk around the park, get a bit of air into me lungs. Jesus, it's nice to be out, and already I can feel it doing me some good. But I'm nervous as well, out here, all alone. Maybe they've been waiting for me to leave the house. Maybe I'm the fucking tool that's walked straight into their trap. No, don't think so anyway. They'd have grabbed me by now. But I stop walking anyway and look around the street, all the houses cuddled up together. It makes me feel – I dunno. Reminds me of something. Being a kid, I suppose. When I felt safe. Be nice to feel safe.

I start walking again, get onto the grass, which is a little bit wet. I have a fucking mad notion to lie down on it, feel the wet, lick it. Must be losing me marbles, if I have any left. But it is sweet to be walking on the springy ground, looking up at the millions of stars and trying to pretend I haven't a care in the world.

I wonder what happens when you die. Does anything happen?

How could she be saying the drugs was the monster? I'm the one that took the drugs. So it was me she meant, really. All that shite about there's no point talking about it? Fuck's sake. I'd prefer a bollocking, bit of screaming, bit of emotion, get it out there. The way she's going on now, it's like I was just another of her projects; the playground or the community centre. I'm the one that didn't work out.

You know why I took drugs? Because I liked them. Because they were a laugh.

There's a bench up ahead covered in graffiti tags and cigarette burns. Still no one around, so I sit down and have a smoke. Running out of fags now, even though I've been rationing them. Can't risk going into a shop, but. Maybe she'd get me some. Still have a tenner.

I've had me mobile off since this started. But now I turn it on. There's a ton of bleedin' messages, all about the same, of course. A couple of blokes warning me about the Georgians. Fair play, and three from this cunt I wouldn't trust one bit, saying he wants to meet me. He has something for me. Prick.

Two are from Martin. He doesn't sound too good, but he's surviving. Says he's over on the southside, sleeping rough. Good lad.

I know I keep saying that it's Martin's fault for getting me into this, but it's not really. I was off the gear, yeah, but I knew I'd be going back sooner or later. Done it loads of times before. You get straight and what have you got? Fucking reality. Who wants that?

I remember seeing *Star Trek* one time – used to love all that sci-fi – and there was this one about this bloke that's all disabled and fucked up, can't talk, can't move a thing. Sits in this wheelchair and all he can do is make these lights go on and off: green for yes, red for no. But in the end he goes to live on this planet where they can plug his brain into this machine, into his mind – and he can't tell the difference – he's all young and good looking again and he's running around the place with this smashing-looking bird that's real, like, but also plugged into the machine cos she's fucked up as well. And he wants to do it. Who wouldn't?

That's what I've been doing all me life. I'd plug into the machine, then after a while get all stressed out because I got lifted by the law or took some bad gear and got sick. Then I'd go off it for a while and realise why I was on it in the first place. There's only been one time when I was gonna give it up for good. But that's another story.

I said to Ma I'd been off it for three months, but it's more like two. I got cleaned up, even got a few bits of work here and there, cash jobs, painting and gardening and that, which I don't mind if the weather is good. And it was all right, for a while. It was a change. But I started to get bored. I knew I'd get bored; I always do. I'd come home in the evening and there would be Martin all happy and wet-eyed – he wouldn't do the gear in front of me, out of consideration. We'd have dinner, a few spliffs and some beer if we had the money. Play *Grand Theft Auto*. And Martin, being Martin, would start telling me how great I am to get off the gear and how he reckoned that this time I'd be off it for good. He could feel it.

That's when I got bored, listening to that. And sitting in the flat on that plastic-covered sofa with chips and fag butts and fuck knows what else down the back of it. And looking at the spotty black damp stain on the wall, and the fucking smell of the place: like someone hid a turd somewhere and you can't find it. It was only a matter of time.

Martin gave me the excuse I needed. I found him lying on the couch, sweating like a fucking pig because the gear he took turned out to be baking powder or some shite, and he's starting to hurt because he can't find the usual bloke, or any other bloke. Even in Finglas it's getting hard to score drugs these days; things have changed. And because my best mate is hurting, his little ginger head waving around the place, I volunteer like the hero to go and get him some: because I know these Georgian blokes in town. Been in that flat loads of times. I'll sort you out.

But I wasn't being a knight in shining fucking armour; I would have taken half of it before I got home. All of it if half didn't do the job.

So only for that young one going out the window and I'd be back on the gear right now. Service as normal. Fuck's sake. Don't even have the stuff: I got such a fright I dropped it after the big hairy Georgian runs into the flat behind me and starts yelling fuck's sake, Baz, what you do? What you do? I ran for me fucking life.

I think about giving Martin a bell, but that would get his hopes up – he'd start asking me when it will be OK to come back. And I haven't a fucking clue when that will be. Jesus, maybe it never will.

Instead I text him. *I'm OK. Still hiding. Take care Bud.*

I sit quietly after that.

Martin is my best friend, me oldest friend, and I got him into this. Sort of, anyway. Wouldn't hurt a fly, Martin. Totally fucking harmless.

The sound of voices makes me stand up. But it's not shouting or laughing or fighting; the usual things you hear. This is like mumbling, or people whispering secrets to each other. And at first I dunno where it's coming from, but after looking for ages, I make them out. Just the black shapes of people on the playground. They're not moving, none of them: like their all hypnotised. Or they're zombies. Or they're all listening to someone giving a speech. Except I don't see anyone doing that.

I creep over, just until I'm close enough to hear, and I see that some of them are fucking kneeling. That's when I cop what's going on – these mad fuckers are praying.

But I don't see a priest, and anyway, they're not praying together; they're saying their own prayers or standing quiet in the dark. All of them are doing this – looking at fucking nothing. One or two of them are even chatting – real softly, like. One old one says: isn't she beautiful? And the other old one is agreeing with her, nodding her head off and going on about how her dress is shining in the darkness. Now I see some other mad cunt holding his arms up and making noises like he's at a fucking rave and out of his tits on drugs.

I walk around them and still can't see anything. These people are all old, most of them anyway. And mostly women, the sort of old ones you see outside church tut-tutting because the priest needs a fucking haircut. But from the smiles on their faces, it looks like the lot of them just got the ride.

There's no one around who looks dodgy, so I amble up to them. They're not paying attention to me anyway; too busy staring into the darkness and looking like spacers. Even when I'm up beside them I can't see what they're looking at. This old geezer with a big red scar on his face clocks me and says, 'Isn't it wonderful?'

I walk over to him.

'What are youse doing?' I say.

'The angel,' he says.

'Sorry pal. Don't see nothing.' I nudge him, friendly like. 'Have you been putting too much whiskey in your cocoa?'

But he's not amused by that. Not amused at all.

'There,' he says, like I'm blind and stupid.

'Sorry pal,' I say.

He points with his bendy old finger.

'Do you see the streetlamp?'

'Yeah,' I say.

Ma had those lights put in.

'Do you see the election poster?'

'Yeah. Connolly. Number 1. You praying to Connolly, are ya?'

He does this massive sigh.

'Do you not see a figure floating just in front of the poster? Look hard now.'

And I do it. I'm leaning forward. I'm squinting at the fucking lamppost. And for a second I'm thinking of saying I do see something, because he seems like a nice old geezer. But instead I feel a fit of the sniggers coming on. I have to turn me face away so he can't see me smiling.

'Sorry now,' I say. 'Maybe it's gone home for the night. Maybe it's me. I'm not into politics or any of that.'

He sighs again. Like he's really fucking sad.

'*Perhaps* you don't see her because you don't have enough faith. What's your name?'

'Baz.'

'Baz, the power of prayer is an amazing thing, and the proof of it is right there. Will you pray with me Baz, so you can see her?'

'But like, who is it ye are seeing?'

'The Angel of the Streetlamps. The girl who died. You must have heard about this? It's been in all the papers and the television. She's appearing everywhere. It's a sign, Baz.'

He talks like I must be from the fucking moon if I don't know about this. But now I don't want to know. I feel sick in me stomach, and I feel like I might wet meself; like when you're a kid and the big-gest, maddest fucker in the class, who has beaten up everybody else points at you during Geography and says: after school; you're next. And I'd imagine that me house was a spaceship, but that it also had a force field all around it, so all I had to do was run like a mad thing to Pleasant Lane, just into my street, and I'd be safe there, protected by the force field and everyone around who knew me.

Your man puts his hands together, and nods at me to do the same, and I'm so fucking addled I do it. He closes his eyes and starts chanting *Our Father*, and I remember who I am and what I am. I turn and leg it for home.

Chapter Fifty Three

Michael Bourke

I follow the ritual which, until his departure, Father Jack and I observed together: the strict order of tasks bringing to mind the careful recitation of coordinates from my father's curling star charts. *Six hours Right Ascension. Forty-five degrees Declination.* For each set of numbers I would declare, my father would utter a clipped yes. *Now give me Regulus. Corvus. Puppis.* He knew where they were, but he liked to be told.

It is mostly menial work, the days of such clerical luxuries as a housekeeper having long since passed. In our home I do the washing up, the laundry and some hoovering if required. Today, it is required: I have been more than a little lax of late. But now I clean and tidy with a particular urgency; almost a sense of desperation: like a house vendor hoping that this time, the people who view will want to live here. It occurs to me that perhaps this is what I am doing too; perhaps this will be my last night here. I am not afraid though; I feel, indeed, like God: at a remove from the events of the world, impervious to harm; vulnerable only to passing tides of sadness as He witnesses some fresh folly from the beings he has created.

There is a swelling pile of post to be opened; and more than a hundred emails in the parish inbox. I work through it diligently. Most I file for future reference, for someone else to deal with. I reply to some, but only to refer them on to others or to state that I cannot help at this time. I seem like a man tidying up his affairs; a man preparing for death. It is not an unpleasant sensation.

265

Why do I feel this way? I do not know. I have not come to any conclusion or formulated any plan. Indeed, I seem further than ever from such a goal, falling back on my default strategy of doing nothing; of letting the decisions of others carry me along. I should, of course, have said no to the zealots: I should have told them that apparitions are nonsense. I should have been brave.

Once finished, I make my way over to the church. Our house and Saint Audeon's share the same plot of land, encircled by a high and rusting iron fence: rather like a compound in some foreign territory. Naturally, this was not the intention of the design: the spendthrift use of land was a brash display of power and wealth. Yet now it feels as if we do indeed live in an enclave, with savage natives clamouring outside. When myself or Father Jack are not there, the church is rarely unlocked, having been victim to repeated break-ins and vandalism – some of it unspeakable. We abandoned evening mass some years ago, mostly due to a lack of demand, but also because those who did turn up were invariably the worse from alcohol and drugs. Drunken brawls during the consecration had become commonplace. The high gates also have to be locked up before the light fades as many of the local young people would otherwise use the grounds for *al fresco* drinking parties. They still attempt to get in, though they are usually too inebriated to clamber over. Thankfully, no one has been seriously injured while attempting this, though one or two have come close to being impaled.

When the weather is pleasant, as it is today, I like to stroll the perimeter before entering the church. The sun sits high in the cold blue firmament, and there is only the merest hint of a breeze. Speaking from a meteorological point of view, Ireland is not a country to raise the spirits. But Autumn always has a mournful beauty. There are regrets for the summer it could have been. If only.

I inspect the railings and tarmac, picking up beer cans and burger wrappers which have been flung inside. Occasionally, there are syringes and used contraceptives. All of these I place gingerly inside a black plastic bag. As usual, I notice the severe rusting of the ornate ironwork, and realise with sadness that we will probably never raise sufficient funds to fix this, or even to paint over it. The collapsing roof is the priority.

Today, though, most of the rust is covered up by a wide sweep of variegated election posters jammed through the railings. Each one depicts the gurning head of a candidate, along with a slogan which defiles the laws of syntax and logic.

Odd, this Irish synthesis of politics and belief. Canvassing outside mass for the votes of believers is an unbreakable custom. The posters appear on the church railings every four years as if by magic; and never is permission sought. Never is their presence objected to. Even if I had the urge to complain, I would not know who to contact.

It's healthy, I suppose: a secular alternative to what we serve up in here. At least the customers come to it armed with plenty of life-giving scepticism.

Today, though – I don't know. I don't know why today, of all days, I take the posters down and stuff them into the green recycling bin at the rear of the house. I am not angry or frightened. I have no point to make. The posters just seemed to be blocking the light, and on a crisp Autumn day like this, there should be as much light as possible.

I lock the gates – it is now about four o'clock – and finally enter the quietude of the church.

Why do I genuflect when I enter? Why do I bless myself? Because I always have. I know there is no Man-God to take offence at my lack of observance; but that does not take away from the beauty of these gestures: their physical grace projecting the magnificent idea of something greater than ourselves; greater than everything. Isn't that idea worth a genuflection? I happily bow my head to it; to the Universe.

Yet after this moment of reverence, my duties here are similar to those of the house: Jack and I are, in truth, glorified skivvies, our service to God entailing a lot of polishing and hoovering. Good for the soul, Jack was fond of saying – though he was scrupulous about never being caught cleaning the altar. It would dispel the magic, he said. He is not without his little deceits also.

I think of Jack as I clean. Sometimes I would gently tease him. Was Jesus a carpenter or a carpenter's son? The word used in the original Greek is *tekton*; which could mean a stone mason or even a day labourer. What do you think, Jack?

He would shrug such questions away; perhaps suspecting what I was up to.

I miss him.

For any other human this would, of course, be perfectly natural. But for me it is a staggering revelation. I am quite happy to be alone; I'm not lonely – though I'm not sure what this feels like. Yet I realise that now, if given the choice, I would prefer Jack to be here, standing out by the bins, suckling on a cigarette. His presence is what I miss, rather than the man himself: the way he yabbers can, at times, be infuriating.

It takes me nearly two hours to tidy up the church: a process which I find has given me an appetite. I can't remember when I was last hungry, or even when I last prepared a meal. I've been surviving on what the parishioners have brought me, or failing that, biscuits and scraps of salad. I eat only out of habit, out of a sense that this is required to maintain the human system called Michael Bourke. Now I find myself anticipating the sensation of food on my tongue, of it shifting into my stomach. Peanut butter. Crunchy peanut butter on crusty white bread. Mammy would sometimes make me a sandwich. For a treat, if she'd been into the shops in Drogheda.

Such is my desire for peanut butter that I glance at my watch as I lock up the church, calculating the possibility of visiting the shop and constructing a thick sandwich before Sharon and her group arrive in the hope of seeing visions.

It's ten past six; they are not due until seven. So it's possible, yes: and this simple prospect gives me a rush of joy.

Joy. How odd.

I look up and find myself locating Orion; barely visible in the evening light. The Hunter with his dogs. The Three Kings. *Shen.*

I hear voices: chatting, laughing, shouting out names. Even without seeing them, I can sense their expectation: like people going to see a particularly good film. Where I exit the church is at the back, right beside the house and not visible from the road, so I am able to snatch a clandestine view of this commotion.

It is a crowd: starting at the locked gates and spreading back as far as I can see. They are armed with cameras or mobile phones.

There is even what appears to be a television crew slouching near the front.

I duck into the house, scamper up the stairs and from behind a net curtain see that the road is full in both directions: so full that traffic has to crawl through the glut of people. There are dozens, possibly hundreds. I extract my *Super Space Conqueror* and use it to take a closer look at this mob. At the gate, I spy the elderly man with the scar who accompanied Sharon this morning. He seems quiet, but not displeased with the hoards swelling around.

My instruction to keep our meeting private has been flagrantly ignored. Perhaps by this man, perhaps by them all. Not that it matters.

I go downstairs and check the messages on the house phone, then on my mobile which I hadn't bothered to switch on. Two from the guards, about the prayer meeting I am due to hold this evening. One from the bishop's secretary, asking me to ring him urgently; and three from various journalists: one asking about *your attempt to summon Manda*. Almost as soon as I am finished listening to these, the phone rings again. I ignore it.

I sit by the kitchen table, afraid even to turn on the light. I listen to the growing human hum.

I do not know what to do.

I can't go out and refuse them admission: a rabble of that size, here to see miracles, would be impossible to control. The few who visited me this morning ignored my words.

Perhaps I didn't make myself clear; perhaps my infernal muttering made me difficult to understand. Or perhaps they didn't feel the need to pay much attention: after all, if you are communicating with the Eternal, why listen to some shrunken, sceptical priest?

It strikes me that Jack would be pleased with this. He's old enough to remember when large congregations were the norm. When the crowd numbers winnowed, he seemed to take this as a failure on his part. Even if it meant telling the most shamefaced lie, I suspect he would be content with a full church again.

But I cannot.

If I was one of those people clamouring outside the gate, I would doubtless see a pattern in these events. Ever since that girl belly-flopped from the sky, the architecture of my life has been subsiding. I have been forced to see the lie in the strategies of the past twenty years and have been edged inexorably towards making a decision: towards declaring my true beliefs; taking a revolutionary stand.

Much as He did.

The Man Jesus was irascible: he was willing to squash po-faced convention and embrace muddy morals; explode the bullying, craven notions of right and wrong. He wasn't an ascetic guru but a blood-filled mortal who feasted and drank with thieves and whores and heroin addicts.

He was alive.

I wonder: was he ever as reluctant as I am now?

I watch the last tubes of light slip down behind the kitchen windows. I am in almost total darkness now, which only seems to magnify the sounds from outside. The combined chatter is almost a roar: as if they are about to start chanting.

The phone rings again. I sit still and allow tiny globes of sweat to glide along the length of my nose. Here in the darkness, I feel invisible. But of course it can't last. It's almost seven o'clock, and soon Sharon's group will be ringing the presbytery bell at the side gate, demanding entry for their frenzied followers.

I cannot keep them out. All I can do is destroy the temple I have sought to protect.

CHAPTER FIFTY FOUR

Carol Murphy

I don't know what I'm doing here, only that I can't go home. I'm scared to go back to my own apartment, my own life in the present tense. I have a few of the girls coming over tonight. I have to buy food and drink and scrub the bathroom, yet here I am driving around this dump looking for the address the taxi driver gave me.

There are lots of places like Finglas; with the same unfinished quality. It's like a refugee camp: everyone seems to be waiting, and are driven half-mad from the boredom of it.

Yet I was expecting worse. You know: burnt-out cars and boarded-up houses. I haven't seen any of that. It is vast: rows of jagged boxes spreading out in all directions, interspersed with choppy fields. I see horses in the distance, and people everywhere: as if no one can stick being in their own house, so they stand out on the street, chain-smoking, their blotchy bodies stuffed into cheap tracksuits.

It's mostly women. The few men are formed into small, urgently striding groups: as if there's some terribly important business they have to complete. They annoy me.

I won't be asking them for directions, so I glide past, throwing the men a judgemental look. One of them waves back.

It feels as if nothing has changed here; it was always like this.

I didn't look at a map before I came: I expected the street to present itself to me, to leap up and say Carol! Over here! But I don't want to stop. I continue to move through estate after estate, around the spreads of grass where children chase each other, past more women laughing and shouting, clumps of men conspiring. Some of the streets are neat and quite well laid out; others look as if they've been through a war. I'm exhausted: asking for help would be far too much for me now, to absorb all those convoluted directions, the snotty kids, the yabber yabber yabber.

My family were quiet, really. *Were*: did you notice that? I mean, we could all talk, none of us were shy, but speaking was something we *chose* to do, rather than something that was compulsive or vital. There were times when my parents would opt to chat, to me or each other; other times we would sit in silence – a very comfortable one, it should be said; one that seemed to bring us closer, in a funny way. We studied a world full of pointless yakking.

I don't remember my parents ever saying this to me. It was simply something I knew about them. It was a shared view of life: that not all human problems can be solved or discussed away; that sometimes, it's even better to keep secrets. Too much truth, like too much sun, can burn you.

But, there were times.

Driving home, don't know from where. We were close to the house. Somewhere around Ringsend, I think. The traffic had slowed to a stately crawl. An anxious huddle of cars and people up ahead, the traffic slowing to take in whatever horror was on offer. Except it wasn't horrible. As we slid past, it looked serene, like a renaissance painting: a sudden burst of sunshine throwing exquisite light upon the people standing around, all of them frozen, all looking towards the centre of the tableau where the man kneeled. Beside him an expensive bicycle lay twisted on the ground, as if shot. The kneeling man was dressed in priestly black, his face turned away from us, his shoulders moving steadily up and down.

The other man lay on the ground just beyond him, and to my young eyes could well have been asleep. Certainly, he looked serene, his eyes closed in a Jesus-like swoon, his beard and long hair suggesting a Christ who had remained on earth, lived on into his fifties. It was only as we went past did I realise that the kneeling man was pumping his chest.

I went to speak, but stopped, already catching my parents exchanging a look. My father pulled in. They got out of the car, Mum sat in behind the wheel and we drove off.

Where's Daddy gone, I asked; even though I knew this was a stupid question.

He'll be home soon, said my mother.

Dad returned home some time later. We said nothing.

It was the sort of thing we didn't speak about, and even now I don't think this was a bad thing. My dad got enough misery and loss at work. Why continue it at home?

Or so I assumed the logic went. It was never explained to me.

But why this particular event sticks in my mind is because the following day, or sometime soon after, I did ask. I can't remember why: probably revenge for some perceived slight or rebellion over something I wasn't allowed to do. It was calculated: by saying the words I knew it would plunge a brick into the still pool of our family life. See what I can do if you take me for granted.

He was working on the boat. It had been parked in our driveway for years, for most of my life, and I'd come to assume that its only function was to provide a place for my father to let off a little steam. It never occurred that every evening he went out to work on it, he was planning his escape from here. From me.

I asked so loudly and clearly that I was rather pleased with myself. Daddy, what happened to the man who fell off the bike? Did you help him? Did he die?

My father said nothing. He put aside whatever tool he was using and came down the stepladder. For a moment he stood in front of me and wore a puzzled expression, as if he was trying to understand what I had just said.

How old was I? Nine or ten.

Finally, he shook his head.

No, Princess, he said – though in such a way that I still have no idea what he meant. No, the man did not die; no, I could not help him. Or simply no, Princess. No.

He walked back to the house, leaving me crammed with a feeling I didn't understand, which I would have done anything to get away from. I tried ignoring it for a while, pretending that I planned to be outside the house anyway. But this made me feel even more foolish, and lonely. I tried converting it to anger, furiously stomping up the stairs to my bedroom. But this didn't work either. I got into my bed and hid behind a mound of teddy bears, careful to turn their eyes away from me. The next morning I couldn't bear for Mum to look at me either, though I don't know if he told her what I had said. Of course, it was never mentioned, along with all the other hurts and embarrassments we would rather forget. Daddy kissed and tickled me when he came home from work, and showed no trace of hurt or resentment. And I was thankful for this.

A car horn bleats at me, and I realise I've been sitting at the traffic lights as they slid from red to green. I wave my apology at the car behind, but the driver has lost patience. He pulls out and roars past, yelling something I can't hear, his face thunderous. Unthinkingly, I move off and turn left.

And there is it: Pleasant Lane. More a wistful hope than an address, I imagine; named by some long-deceased town planner with a vision of lives so well lived, there would be little regret when the time came to leave them.

The house is in the far corner. It is a neat, brick-faced cottage, perhaps a bit over-decorated with potted plants; as if not entirely confident of its prettiness. I ring the bell. I have no idea what I'm going to say. Maurice Kiberd didn't know the name of the man he picked up. Hello, are there any murderers living here? Oh yes. I'll just get him.

A woman emerges. In her sixties, wearing a purple sweater and a grey woollen skirt. Her hair is tied in a bun and reading glasses hang from a chain around her neck. She has the air of a university professor. A quizzical smirk hangs around her mouth as she takes me in. This one looks out of place, it says.

Between stutters and pauses, I explain myself: I'm a reporter, looking for a man who got into a taxi and came to this address and who may have witnessed the death of a young woman a few days ago. She fell from a third-storey window. You may have heard about it. She makes a slight *tsk* sound. I'm hoping she'll interrupt me or volunteer some information, say: oh, that's the people next door. Bad sorts, or even tell me she has no idea what I'm talking about. But she doesn't. She continues to listen, continues to smile.

Despite my discomfort, I find myself warming to this woman. She seems familiar. I run out of words.

She peeks up at me.

'So?' she says.

'Well, you know, I was wondering if that man lives here? Does what I'm saying ring any bells?'

She gets me to run through some of the details again. Dates, times, what this man looked like. But she's shaking her head before I finish.

'I'm sorry, dear, but I can't help you.'

'Hmm,' I say. 'Might the neighbours?'

She shakes her head again, gestures to her left.

'The woman here lives alone and is very old. Probably wouldn't answer the door to you.' Her hand moves in the opposite direction. 'And Jane who lives there has two young children, but there's no man on the scene.' She puts a hand on my arm.

'To be honest, a lot of people here might not be open to speaking with a journalist. They might be a bit suspicious, you understand?' She says these words kindly, then lowers her voice. 'They are good people, but some of them have had problems with the gardaí or the social services, and a stranger coming to the door asking questions? Hmmm... even if they knew something, they probably wouldn't tell you. It's instinctive. It's sad, I know, but that's what happens when communities are neglected.'

I'm certain I have seen this woman before, heard her speak like this before. Perhaps we haven't met though: it could have been on television. But I don't want to appear foolish by asking.

'And you came out all this way to ask me?' she says approvingly. I shrug, blather something about following all leads.

'Well, you're great,' she says. She makes the *tsk* sound again. 'Terrible about that young woman though.'

She fiddles with her glasses, as if they are some sort of religious symbol. 'And it's *very* odd these stories about her ghost.'

'Yes,' I say a bit too quickly. 'But that's just Daniel Belton.'

'No dear,' she interrupts. 'It was on the news. On the radio. The guards have been getting calls all day from other people who claim to have seen her. In the bridesmaid's dress, and under lampposts, for some reason. All over. Louth, Mayo, Kerry. Poor souls. It's hysteria. Times that are in it, I suppose. Funny: we think we've changed, but then the old superstitions come out. No offence, but sometimes the media…'

'Yes,' I say. 'Yes, I know.'

She allows me a moment of silence while I take this news in. I wonder if Conor and Hazel have heard. I consider phoning Rachel Belton again, but what would be the point? Not much she could do about it.

Apparitions? This is insane.

I never texted Don back. *Shit.*

'Are you all right, dear?' she eventually asks.

'Yes, yes,' I say. 'Bit tired, you know.'

'Oh yes, I know.' For a moment our eyes lock and we smile: as if we have led similar lives; as if we have so much that links us together.

'Well, good luck, and it was lovely to meet you,' she says, extending a hand. 'And what's your name?'

'Carol. Carol Murphy.'

'I'll look out for it in the paper.'

'What's your name?'

'Rose Carroll.'

She waves her hand at me, as if her name isn't important; as if she'd like me to forget what she just said – and for a split second something sweeps behind her eyes. I still can't place where I know her from, but it occurs to me that Rose Carroll might be lying.

We say goodbye again and I walk back to the car. Our family grief seems to be spreading like a mushroom cloud, enveloping everyone around us. *Our* family grief. I'm part of it, it's part of me and I have a sudden, intense craving for this to *mean* something. Not just another random movement of atoms around the universe.

But apparitions? This is so *Irish.* Anything to dodge reality, to pretend the normal rules don't apply. The papers will be jammed with it for days, along with every loolah claiming it as proof that we never should have joined the EU or legalised homosexuality. Anything to get to our minds off our failing country. We haven't changed. We're still sacrificing goats to make the thunder go away.

Conor will be apoplectic. Must ring him. Must ring Don. But what can I say? He'll want me to find some of these loons. The story is out there now, so he'll demand mock-up photos of Manda floating under a lamppost in Westmeath. He may even feel the need to publish the pictures of her lying in the skip.

I can't. Once again, I have to let him down.

My phone rings.

I roll my eyes and look towards the sky: a reproach for the God I don't believe in. A being, I now imagine, which takes a giggling glee in plotting my life like an episode of *Coronation Street*. We'd be cutting to the end titles now, or just after I say in a small, scared voice: hello Don.

But it's not Don. The caller is my father. Who never rings me; who, not once in the years he has been away has seen fit to pick up a phone and dial my number.

So I don't do anything. I stare at it until the ringing goes away.

CHAPTER FIFTY FIVE

Michael Bourke

Jack is in charge of the central heating, though he has drilled me often enough on the eccentricities of the church's ancient system. It is rarely turned on: usually on occasions when children are present, such as christenings and communions. Yet Jack was assiduous in making sure it worked, that there was at least enough fuel in the tank to keep it going for a couple of hours. He'd even shown me how to bleed oil from the tank connected to our house and transfer it to the church's supply, a skill I have never used until today. God help me, Jack would be horrified by the use I am putting it to now.

But I am past teasing out the rights and wrongs of this action. In truth, I have not considered them at all. It feels more as if this is a proposal which has lain dormant in my mind for some time, pointedly ignored by me until I could do so no longer; until all the other, hypocritical options had been exhausted.

I am almost relieved.

I know it will appear insane.

The church is close to perfect for the execution of my plan: the scaffolding which supports the sagging roof is conveniently placed at each corner; right alongside some of the velvet drapes which extend from floor to ceiling. The preparation, though, is arduous. I must fill every container I can find, a task which takes the best part of thirty minutes. As I dart back and forth, I run the risk of detection from the road and have to endure the nagging of the doorbell and phone. I should rip both from the wall, but cannot afford the time.

Dividing equal amounts of oil in each corner is also a problem, given the irregular sizes and shapes of my various receptacles: which range from cups to buckets. I hear the noise of the engorged crowd and the tone changing also: the jolly expectation has gone, replaced with a crawling impatience. There are occasional shouts; I think I even hear my name. The phone in the church office begins shrieking. This, I turn off.

I was never one for physical exercise, even at school, where I found sport to be savage and repellent: sublimated homicide. But now as I attempt to clamber up the first scaffold, I realise the disadvantages of lacking murderous impulses as a boy. A quarter of the way up, my muscles and joints are so seized with pain that I become briefly convinced I will not make it any further; especially as I am forced to make this climb with a bucket in one hand.

It is the sound from outside which spurs me on. Now they are chanting.

Open up! Open up! Open up!

They are growing angry; demanding that the witch doctor give them their magic. The thought of being caught up here by the frothing hoards, and having to explain what I am doing, motivates me further, and, after a last scramble during which I seem to lose the ability to breathe, I make the summit.

I pant for a few moments, then carefully pour the oil down along the drapes. I reposition some of the planks on top of the scaffold so as to form a path between the drapes and wooden roof.

Miraculously – and I am so desperate now I would almost hope for one – I also discover a rope: a piece of equipment which enables me to make my next ascent unencumbered by the bucket but able to haul it up when I reach the top. Some of the oil spills, making my descent particularly treacherous, but at least it has aided the speed of my progress. The mob has grown louder still. I wonder if Sharon and the others are encouraging this; making wild speeches about the marvels that await.

Finally, all four corners have been drenched in oil. I am sweating so much my shirt appears to have changed colour, and as I make my way back to the first scaffold, matches in hand, I find myself dizzy from even this simple exertion. The drape doesn't explode into flame as I feared it might, but makes a stately progress up the line of the velvet, bringing out its deep redness. The second comes alight with more of a vulgar whoosh, while the third needs some encouragement to take light at all. As I approach the final scaffold, I see the flames are already starting to guzzle parts of the roof, spinning out curls of thick grey smoke. Despite the darkness now fallen, this may already have been spotted outside. I must hurry.

The heat is already extraordinary, as if the air I breathe is ready to ignite. I run to the final scaffold, but find that the oil has not seeped down to ground level. Once again I have to mount the hot steel poles and clamber my way up to where the oil ends, where it has also dripped around, making the scaffold particularly difficult to grip. I slide and slip and finally have to loop my arm around one of the poles as I struggle to extract the box of matches from my pocket: a process which is conducted as much by feel as sight, so thick has the smoke become. Yet I can make out the ravenous glow of the fire spreading across the roof, the thunderous crackle of the flames masking the noise from outside. A massive snap announces the opening of the first fissure. Shards of flaming wood sing-song to the ground.

Hurry, hurry. They are on their way now.

I cough, light a match, cough and light a match. The drape ignites immediately, shooting upwards and back: along the drape but also across the oil-smeared poles and onto my right arm.

There is no pain. At first, there is even a moment of puzzlement as I contemplate one of my limbs bathed in shimmering orange. I notice how tiny holes are opening in my shirt sleeve: peeling back to reveal the flesh inside. But now the heat of this prompts a more instinctive reaction. I attempt to slap out the flames, but find I cannot do so without loosening my grip on the scaffolding: and I am too far up to risk jumping. I comically wave the flaming arm around, but this only nourishes the fire. Then my footing slips again and I have to use this arm to resecure my position. I get the smell of cooked breakfast. My own flesh.

Having no option, I have to risk balancing on the pole while attempting to slap out the flames with my functioning hand. I am able to do this for perhaps five or six seconds, until I feel myself falling backwards, into the puffy clouds of smoke. And I see the flame has almost engulfed the roof now: a writhing orange blanket which will soon cover me with its stinging caress.

CHAPTER FIFTY SIX
Carol Murphy

If you're a speck of dust, viewing the fathomless universe of my apartment, then you probably look at me the way astronomers view the death of stars or fearfully watch for some rogue chunk of rock which might slam into our planet. To the speck, I am a force too large to calculate or imagine; one that can move the structures of the observable universe at will; one which doesn't seem bound by the physical rules the speck of dust must adhere to. The speck is wondering: is this God?

Too late – nanoseconds before it is sucked into my Dyson – it will realise that I am merely large rather than all-powerful; that my actions have been caused by other forces which cannot be seen or measured. And perhaps there are, in turn, greater influences than those: an infinite stretch of them, each knocking against the other, like in those world-record domino arrangements they always have in Holland.

The force controlling me at the moment is the clock. It was a bit of a relief to realise the time, giving me more than enough reason not to answer my phone; to say I'll call Dad later. I don't know what he wants; only that, whatever it is, I don't have the resources to deal with it. I'm depleted; a dry lake.

No. That's not the reason at all. How can it be? I resent him for not calling me for two years, yet when he does, I freeze. All I can admit to myself is that the sudden materialisation of my father provoked a sort of terror within me; I was scared of what he might say.

And if I'm too busy to ring Dad, then I'm certainly too busy to text my boss… but I change my mind on that one. No point being rude. I text Don: say that I'll speak to him on Tuesday. I know what will happen, so why go through with it now? He'll want me to write about the lamppost visions of Manda. I'll refuse. Back to the charity ball stories for me. If I'm lucky.

I drive to the shops, stabbing at the radio to avoid news reports. I fail to do it. My cousin is now the most famous ghost in Ireland, already the subject of celebration and satire. More counties claim sightings. Galway. Cork. Leitrim. Waterford. Nervy witnesses tell their stories in machine-gun voices. *Just there. All of a sudden. Floating. Beautiful, she was. Just floating. And serene! She looked at me. Turned her head and looked. At me.* A psychologist comes on to speculate. Perhaps the combination of street lighting and election posters is causing an optical illusion. Suggestion is very powerful, he says. But he sounds unconvinced. I stab the buttons again. A sniggering DJ says, coming up next, *Ghost Town*... followed by... *Angel!* I shut off the radio with my fist.

In the supermarket I hurriedly stock up on wine and nibbles and salad. It strikes me that I'm the only member of my family left.

I move past a rack of newspapers, and can't help but look.

THE ANGEL OF THE STREETLAMPS

My mother dead, my father drifting around the Mediterranean. Yet I remain in this emptying city. I'm a ghost too. What happened to us is now happening to the Fergusons. Perhaps it's genetic; perhaps my father and Hazel passed on the coldness gene: an inability to love anyone truly. Maybe that's why I'm in my thirties and alone.

Somewhere around the cereals, this thought brings me to a halt; and for a second or two I worry that I'll make a scene beside the Crunchy Nut Flakes. But I manage to shake it off. I take deep breaths. I try to sing to the piped music, which I usually enjoy when I'm here. *I wanna know what love is.* Yes, I do.

Back at the flat I attack the dirt like a mad thing, prepare most of the food and finally check my watch. I would have liked a bath and a glass of wine, but there's not enough time. Instead I throw back a G&T while watching the television news. The election stories are dull enough – I'd almost forgotten there was one – everyone blaming everyone else for the economic sinkhole. There's a twang of disbelief in the politicians' voices, as if they'd rather cry than argue; as if they'd rather be doing anything else right now.

There's been a stabbing in Galway, a bad car crash in Limerick. A church burned down in Dublin, and more sightings of Manda. A magenta-faced woman with trembling lips calls her the Angel of the Streetlamps: as if she's already a well-known religious figure, not a tabloid headline. Yet another shrink on saying it's a societal reaction to the recession; to a nationwide crisis of confidence. Like people who see UFOs or the moving statues in the 1980s.

Hmm, says the interviewer. But why this young woman? Why now? What was so special about her? Why the lampposts?

I don't hear the answer. I turn off the TV and get into the shower.

I'm an efficient showerer, if there is such a word. In, scrub, and out. I'll stay in the bath until it gets cold, given the chance, but there's something about standing in a cubicle that makes me feel vulnerable. Yet this time I do want to stay for a bit. I feel I can hide in here, and hopefully the hot jets can work out some of the shrieking cramps in my neck. I keep my eyes closed. Looking down at your own body is never pleasant. So I place my hands against the tiled wall and stand as still as possible, my eyelids jammed shut, and wonder what the girls will make of Manda's sainthood. Of course they don't know she's my cousin, so I've decided to tell them. I have to talk to someone, and it'll make a change from the usual who-has-emigrated or lost their job conversation. Probably best to get this nugget into the conversation early before one of them says something stupid.

They could. Anne-Marie might. We studied journalism together, though afterwards she went into PR which suited her better. Anne-Marie has the baffling ability to see the best in everyone and ignore what arseholes they can be. She's exhaustingly enthusiastic, in a hilarious sort of way. Without a man at the moment, but not a woman you'd worry about being able to get one if she felt like it. She's effortlessly gorgeous and looks about twenty-three and we have an affectionate toleration of each other. I can be as cynical as I like and she can spout rubbish like *it was meant to be* or *he's a typical Leo* or get excited because she had a *feeling* something would happen. Ghostly sightings? She must be lapping it up.

Normally, I would find this hilarious and enjoy a bit of an argument. But not tonight. No.

Then there's Annette and Elaine, both of whom I used to work with. Elaine is on a broadsheet now while Annette gave it all up to churn out chick-lit novels. It's going OK for her, though she's yet to hit the big time. Both have men: Elaine's is new, so I expect to hear a lot about him tonight. Annette has been living with the same guy for the last ten years, a fat lump who keeps switching jobs or giving up work altogether to go back to college or take some personal development course. They've no kids and no intention of getting married. They seem deliriously happy.

I get out of the shower, make a G&T, dress, throw the food together, pour another G&T and let the girls in, all of whom, conveniently for me, arrive within two minutes of each other. We hug and admire each other's shoes and haircuts and move into the living room where, to fit in with everyone else, I switch to wine. Anne-Marie gives me the chance to bring up the subject almost immediately by putting on her sad face in the middle of a story about some press launch where *everything* went wrong but no one really noticed because everyone there was talking about that poor girl who died in the bridesmaid's dress. And isn't it *interesting* that now all these people are seeing…

Well, I intone.

It's in a voice loud enough to cut across Anne-Marie and portentous enough to let them know that I have Major Scandal. Their faces turn to me as I pour more wine and say again: well.

'Manda Ferguson – the girl who died – is my cousin.'

'Yes!' exclaims Anne-Marie, as if she knew this already. 'Were they the ones who lived in, where was it? Galway or some place?'

'Loughrea,' I chip in, slugging wine.

'Oh my God. Were they the ones you knew really, really well? Like you practically grew up with them?'

I feel a stab of annoyance, and again the temptation to deny it. When did I tell this to Anne-Marie?

One thing I'm not going to mention tonight: girls, I have a massive hole in my memory and I think I may be a bit mad. Bad enough knowing that these memories are creeping around my subconscious, ready to leap out in front of me like a mugger.

The smell of stale things, mixed with grass.

I don't know what to say to Anne-Marie, so I finish off my wine instead, making a neutral sound as I do so. I pour another glass for myself and top up the others, and then I begin: I tell them about going to see Hazel and her new girlfriend, about speaking with the detective. They make puzzled and disturbed sounds when I tell them about the words on Manda's mirror. *Lucifer's Hammer Will Bring Us Together.* They'll want to come back to that. I tell them about the creepy priest, Conor and his girlfriend, Rachel Belton and her mad husband, the taxi driver and the trip out to Finglas. Every now and again, one of them stops me to clarify a point, but for the most part they listen, sometimes open-mouthed at my story.

Finally I speak about the Manda apparitions; and how I will refuse to write about them, even if it does mean returning to my pointless career path. The others make pained faces, though I notice Elaine is nodding. She's impressed.

There's a satisfying silence when I finish. I drain my glass and pour another, though I notice the others haven't touched theirs. I realise I'm tired: even reaching for the bottle has left me slightly woozy.

'My God,' says Elaine, the only other working hack out of the four of us. 'So the paper let you follow the story, even though she was your cousin?'

I look at Elaine. She already knows my answer.

'You didn't tell them?'

I shrug.

'Oh dear,' she whispers. She won't say she disapproves, of course. But she doesn't have to. I should have known she would react this way. Elaine was always a bit too po-faced to work in a tabloid and operated on the assumption that everyone around her should feel the same. That I choose to work in one, that I said I liked it, was always a source of puzzlement to her; perhaps even evidence of a lack of moral fibre.

'OK, Elaine. Just say it. You think that was unethical.'

'Well, it's not a *huge* deal, to be honest.'

'You *do* think it was unethical. Look at the face on you.'

That face swirls red. Annette shifts in her chair, ready to make conciliatory gestures. But it's still quite civilised: the voices are moderate.

'Why is it unethical?' asks Anne-Marie. Everyone ignores this.

'Well?' I say.

Elaine sighs; like a complaining child.

'I just think you should have told them. You know: things aren't going so well for you there. So if it comes out that you lied as well...'

'I didn't lie. I just didn't tell them.'

'Hmm,' she says.

I have my arms spread out as if I'm holding an enormous cake, and although I know I shouldn't be justifying myself to Elaine, I can't help it. It's compulsive.

I don't know why I lied. Not really. I thought it was to please Don. But I could have told him. Of course I could.

'Did it affect the story? Did it affect me? I think I did a better job because I knew Manda. I was a valuable resource for the paper.'

I know I sound pompous. I know it will annoy Elaine.

'But now you won't report on the sightings.'

'You of all people should appreciate that. I can't report that crap.'

She pauses and moves her head, as if swallowing.

'Yes, they are crap. But some new-agers and religious old ladies think they are seeing these things, and that makes it a story. Part of your cousin's story. You can't start choosing which parts to report and which to ignore. You know that.'

She's speaking slowly and deliberately, as you would to a particularly stupid elderly relative.

'Fuck off, Elaine.'

'Now girls,' says Annette.

'So I have to write things I know aren't true – I have to lie? First you accuse me of lying and then you criticise me because I won't lie. Fuck's sake, Elaine.'

She makes a gurgling, frustrated sound.

'Carol, calm down, will you? All I said –'

'Don't tell me to calm down. You said I should be prepared to exploit my family for a few headlines. Write lies about them when they are so hurt, when they are falling apart.'

I wipe my eyes and reach for my glass. In one movement, the others go for it too. Annette gets there first.

'I don't think you should,' she sings.

I smack her hand away and drain the rest of it. Elaine sits back and folds her arms. I slam down the glass and stare at her. Anne-Marie gingerly touches my shoulder.

'You've had a traumatic few days,' she coos. 'You're bound to be upset with all this going on in your life.'

I continue to stare at Elaine. Anne-Marie keeps talking. 'Maybe people really are seeing your cousin. I think they are. I think she's trying to tell us something. She must have been a really special person.'

'*Do you?*' I say. But then I can't remember what other words are supposed to come. I opt for, 'Don't be stupid.' It comes out sounding kinder than I intend. To Elaine I manage, 'Always looked down on me. Don't you realise that you're so, so, you know, so –'

'Carol, please,' whispers Annette.

I have a sudden urge to close my eyes, but I don't want to do that in front of Elaine, who I hate now. I know she wants to get up and leave, but that would be a sign of defeat. I say nothing; sit back and wait.

My phone rings.

At first I ignore it. But the four of us are silent: the insistent chirp fills the room. I answer.

'Yes?'

'Princess,' says my father. 'How are you?'

'Fine,' I say.

Only now does it occur to me that I'm completely pissed. I'm slurring my words slightly and wonder if he notices.

'No news on the funeral,' he says.

'No, not yet.'

'OK.' I hear him inhale.

'And how are you coping?'

I try to sound calm, but my voice is rough and shaky.

'Coping? Of course I am. The story is hard work. But I'm fine.'

Now I wish I had walked from the room. They're all listening; they all know I'm a mess. I'm a mess.

'I didn't mean that, Princess. I meant how are you feeling? You know, you may be more upset than you realise.'

This is not convivial everything-is-all-right Dad or distant-professional Dad. This is a voice I've never heard before. Or not heard for years. Something else I've forgotten. He'd read me a story and tuck me in and give me advice about the bullies or the mean girls or the stupid teachers. 'Are you talking to anyone about this?' he says. 'I mean, professionally? A counsellor?'

I hoist myself out of my chair. The others give an involuntary start, convinced that I'm bound to crash over one of them. But I don't. I make my way into the hallway and try to sound jaunty.

'Jesus, Dad, I'm a big girl. It's all very sad, but I'm fine. I mean, I hadn't seen them for years, you know? And I know we used to visit there a lot, but, I'd forgotten all about that. You know, you move on? Where are you anyway? Are you in still in Italy?'

'Ah, Carol,' he says, gently chiding. 'Don't say that. You know how close you and Manda and Conor were. And perhaps we should have talked more about it at the time. But what could we say? That doesn't take away from how close you were, though. You should talk to someone, Carol.'

'Dad, you've got this completely wrong.'

I'm insistent: my father has just interrupted me on a girls' night out; I'm having the most wonderful time.

'Carol,' he says. 'I'm going to get you a few names. I think you need to talk about what happened, you know, back then.'

'What are you talking about? *Nothing* happened back then. Dad, have you got a girlfriend?'

They smashed it up. It's in pieces around me.

'Daddy,' I say again. 'Have you got a girlfriend?'

The words come out so distorted I barely recognise them. There's a rushing in my ears which drowns out everything else. I reach out for the wall, but it moves. I know I've dropped the phone too, and I can't see it now. The world seems to be tipping over, fading from grey to black. I see Manda's face, then nothing.

CHAPTER FIFTY SEVEN
Michael Bourke

I am first aware of a rasping sound which I feel as much as hear: it launches a shudder through my body.

My body?

I am alive then? Or have I been wrong all along? Is this growling blackness what constitutes the afterlife? Please, no. Don't let me be subjected to the face of a smug, vengeful God.

Who am I saying this to?

The panic is momentary. The rasp is my own breath. I straighten and curl my fingers, though this is more difficult for my right hand, which seems tightly wrapped in a hard substance. My face also feels strange; something hard is pressing into it. I jerk with sudden claustrophobia and crack open my eyes.

There is light, but not too much; like summer evening twilight. I make out a ceiling criss-crossed with metal strips, a plain room with nothing on the walls save some announcement entitled SAFETY and a poor painting of a hordes. The chubby face of a nurse hoves into view, her round cheeks swelling as her smile widens even further. She removes the oxygen mask from my face.

'There you are,' she says, as if she had been searching for me. 'Don't try and speak yet. Your throat will be parched.'

Now that she has mentioned it, I do feel murderously dry. She wields a plastic cup and straw and murmurs encouragingly as I gulp down.

When I'm finished, she shows me a button attached to a wire. She slips it into my left hand with a reassuring pat.

'My name is Marie,' she says. 'If you need me, just press that button, OK? You're in Beaumont Hospital, but you're fine. You have a broken arm and a few burns, but nothing to worry about, all right?'

She delivers this news with a jolly finality; as if she is certain of how delighted I will be to hear it.

'All you have to do is get plenty of rest. Tomorrow we'll get you up and talking.'

I make a noise to indicate my assent, but she waves a scolding finger.

'A-ha! Enough of the heroics from you now, Father. More than enough for today. We've had the phone out there ringing off the hook with people asking after you. The newspapers and everything. And you in here almost after killing yourself trying to save your church.'

She tuts her obvious disapproval for this kind of activity, then grins once more.

'So everything is fine. You'll sleep so?'

I nod gently. My head hurts.

'Good man,' she says as she replaces my oxygen mask and stands, her white outfit rustling electrically. She turns off a light and leaves me in the bluish dark, the distant sounds of hospital commotion already fading as my weighted eyelids slide down.

Heroics? If I had the energy to smile or even laugh out loud, I would. But instead I find myself in the field beside the house, my father and I tiny against the blazing night sky as he swings the telescope upwards.

CHAPTER FIFTY EIGHT

Carol Murphy

I've been drooling in my sleep, which is disgusting, and when I stretch my legs I realise I still have my clothes on. I open one eye and immediately shrink back from the scorching light of my bedside lamp. Elaine leans forward.

'How are you feeling?'

'What time is it?'

'About three in the morning. The others have gone. I said I'd stay to make sure you were all right.'

'OK.'

I can think of nothing else to say. I feel robbed of all context. This could be a million years from now, in some strange future where we exist in beds. My memories are so fuzzy I can barely retrieve them. My apartment, the girls, my anger. *Jesus*. Dad called. *Jesus*. I hated Elaine. Jesus.

'I can't really remember.'

'You passed out, love. Anne-Marie got all hysterical and wanted to call an ambulance.'

We share a smile.

'But I'm afraid you did hit your face on the way down.'

There's a soreness around my right eye. I gently prod it.

'Shit.'

'You're going to have a bit of a shiner, Carol.'

I want to get up and have a look, but I know I haven't the energy. Instead I roll onto my back. 'I'm such a stupid cow.'

Elaine doesn't attempt to contradict this, which reminds me why I like her. I was horrible to her and she's still here.

'I'm sorry,' I whisper.

'Forget it,' she says. 'Why did you get so drunk anyway? What's wrong?'

I feel Elaine take my hand. 'Is this something to do with your cousin?'

'I just remembered a few things tonight. That's all.'

Elaine doesn't reply. Eventually, she whispers 'Go back to sleep, yeah?'

'Yes,' I say. 'And you go home. Go off to that new man of yours.'

It's so quiet, it's as if there's only Elaine and I left in the world; the two of us talking softly, knowing how much we need each other. I wave my hand at her to go and close my eyes. I hear her stand, the snap and swish of her coat, then her lips brushing my forehead. I try not to shake.

The lamp by my bed goes off, and immediately I get that smell of damp leaves, feel the static rub of the two sleeping bags we would zip together. Occasional raindrops thud on the roof. The wind hisses outside.

Conor is asleep, his mouth slightly open, air gently rattling past his teeth. Conor likes his sleep. We've kept him up half the night, Manda and I on either side, resting our heads on his arms, just underwear and tee-shirts. And we've talked about our families and music and what's life all about and finally arrived at our favourite topic. Not that we give it a name; we're careful about that. Usually it would start with Manda peeking at me across Conor's chest and asking: is there any-one you like? And I usually had some story about a boy (though once or twice I made them up). Invariably, he was someone I worshipped from afar, because good-looking guys didn't normally go for book-ish, chubby girls. But sometimes there might be a bit more than that: a look, a conversation, even an awkward kiss. And of course I would have to detail how the kiss went. The boy got it all wrong, naturally, so I demonstrated with Conor, flicking our tongues together like lizards and snorting with laughter.

People didn't understand how much we loved each other; that love made us different.

We laughed so much: cuddled into Conor, Manda and I caressing each other's arms. We'd talk about what it might be like, what we'd like to do and have done to us.

But when Conor spoke: we were enthralled and appalled by how easy it was for him, how mechanical – how even speaking would have an effect. He would usually end up having to lie on his belly, because we'd be nagging. *Is it up now? Is it up now?* We came to regard it as a separate being: Conor's pet. And when he eventually showed us, Manda and I were rapt as we saw how it transformed: from a small animal nestling in a bush, snaking out into a bulging, veiny thing. We shrieked in delight and horror every time it jerked, as if reacting to some of things we said; as if it had ears.

He wouldn't let us touch it though. He said it would make a mess. Conor didn't like mess. He told us he only did it to himself in the shower because the water washed all the stuff away. Otherwise dried bits of it would stick to him and it smelled: he was convinced people would know. But he did show us how he did it, at least the first part, which Manda and I reasoned might be a skill we would have to learn.

We laughed so much.

He would study our breasts and we showed him how a squeeze or even a touch could make the nipple stand up. On the night I'm thinking of, Conor was asleep, but Manda and I were still giddy, still squirming in the sleeping bag on either side of him, our hands between our legs. We studied his snoring, until Manda whispered: shall we have a look?

She got the torch and we slithered downwards until level with his boxer shorts, which we carefully eased back. There it was: lying like a fat worm on Conor's stomach. We clamped hands on our mouths to stem the laughter.

Shall I kiss it? Manda whispered.

She gave it a peck, prompting a low moan from Conor. More giggles. She kissed it again, and now I reached forward, hooking my fingers around the stem as Conor had shown us. But the touch of my cold hand gave him a jolt. He half-sat up, groaning in sloppy complaint, then rolled away from me, his thing swinging away and smacking Manda in the eye.

We succumbed to muffled shrieking as Conor settled back down to sleep. Eventually Manda clambered over him and slid in beside me, our bodies glowing. We slid hands under each other's tee shirts, our tongues tasting sweet and meaty until we came to the brink of sleep. I don't want to be anywhere but here, Manda breathed.

Yes, I said. Yes.

Chapter Fifty Nine

Baz Carroll

I turn around to her and I say:

'You never asked me why I took drugs.'

She looks at me as if I'm after saying something completely different; like I'm after paying her a compliment: there's almost a bit of a smirk on her mush. Or maybe it's relief, like she's been waiting for me to ask.

She said nothing about me coming back to the house. Maybe she never noticed I left. I'm not gonna say anything, anyway, and there's no way I'm gonna tell her about what I saw. People praying to that girl? Fucking sick.

'No, I suppose not,' she says in this tiny voice. 'Should I have asked?'

'Dunno,' I say, like a eejit.

Look: I don't know why I took drugs. Not really. Loads of people go through their whole lives without thinking about them. Maybe they don't know what they're missing, but I suppose they must have some other reasons. When I was running back to the house, away from them mad fuckers, I was wondering what it would be like if everyone did drugs. And do you know what? It'd be terrible. Nothing would work, because everyone would be like me and Martin. Me ma would be like me, and I'd have nowhere to go. I need everyone else not to take drugs so I can.

Amn't I a cunt?

Now she's definitely smiling, like she's got me.

'And would you have been able to tell me, Barry?'

295

'I dunno,' I say. 'But you never asked. Why not Ma? Did you not want to know?'

She sighs.

'Barry, you've spent years in and out of clinics, giving up, then going back on them again. I've lived through that too. Hoping, then running out of hope. I mean, are you going to stay off them this time?'

She doesn't wait for me to answer.

'I think you took drugs because you didn't want to give them up.'

'Oh,' is all I can think of to say.

'Am I wrong?'

She sits down, but doesn't look at me.

'Every day, Barry, every day I think of what has become of you and know that I had a hand in it. I was so busy trying to save Finglas, I didn't bother to save you.'

She shakes her head.

'No. That's trite.'

I wonder what *trite* means. It rhymes with shite.

'I was unable to save you,' she says. 'With all my education, I simply didn't know what to do. I so wanted you to be different to all the other boys around here, I made you worse than any of them.'

'Ah no, Ma,' I say. But it sounds like I don't mean it.

She smiles at me; half-hearted.

'Here's something you never asked *me*, Barry: why did I start studying? Why did I work to get all these qualifications?'

I shrug.

'Boredom, Barry. I got married, had you, and one day realised that this is all my life would ever consist of. And I hated it. I loathed it.'

She looks at me now.

'I mean, I loved *you*. But I felt trapped. Do you understand?'

I point to the front door.

'Ma, I can't leave the house.'

She smiles.

'Yes. So you have some idea. I didn't say anything – you couldn't in those days – but every day I fantasised about escape: travelling or going to college or becoming an artist – I had a dozen different scenarios in my mind.

'Your father was a good man, and I loved him. But he wouldn't have understood. No one would have: everyone around here, my family, his family, would have thought I had gone mad if I announced that I wanted to go to college.'

She looks at me closely.

'So I was sad when he died, but, God forgive me, I was also relieved. Because it gave me a chance to change things.

'I didn't think of you as much as I should have. I mean, I did think of you, but you always had to fit into my plans. Be the son I needed you to be.

'And you know, I didn't fully realise it until that day you staggered in with all my election people in the sitting room.'

She starts smiling, like she's been tickled; and then the smile spreads across her face into a big laugh.

'You scared them to death, Barry.'

'Did I? I didn't mean to.'

'The chairman was as white as a sheet by the time you finished your little speech. His hands were shaking so much he dropped his car keys into a cup of tea.'

She goes all quiet for a second.

'Such a thing to be laughing about,' she says.

We look at each other, and we're still smiling, and for a minute there it feels like I'm a nipper again. Having tea with me ma, looking forward to kicking a ball about on the street afterwards. Safe inside me force field.

She looks down at her hands. They are old now, and a bit bent in on themselves from all the writing and cooking and cleaning and tucking me in at night. Night, night, little Barry love.

'I didn't ask, I suppose, because it seemed unfair. Wanting you to come up with *one* reason. Who can do that? For anything in their lives? And I was also selfish, I know that. Even if you had reasons to tell me, I didn't want to know them. Didn't want to know how much it was my fault.'

'It wasn't your fault, Ma. Don't talk shite. I took the drugs. Nobody forced me.'

She smiles, a bit sad. I'm thinking of giving her a bit of a hug – dunno when I last did that – but then the doorbell rings. I hear Holly pounding along the hallway to see who it is. The doorbell has gone loads of times since I've been here, but Ma is pretty good at getting rid of people without pissing them off. Charm, she's got. Buckets of it.

But I wish it hadn't happened now. I wanted to hug me ma.

She goes out and I sit back, slug on me tea that's gone cold and think about all the times she took me in, no matter what state I was in. And all the time thinking that it was her fault. Fuck's sake.

I hear a bit of a chat going on, then the door close. But then no movement, like me ma is waiting for them to walk off. This doesn't sound good.

She comes back in, and just by looking at her face I know I'm completely fucked.

'Barry,' she says. 'Did you get a taxi here?'

'Oh fuck,' I say. 'Was that the cops?'

'No, a reporter. Nice girl. But she's tracked you down here. And if she has, then it's only a matter of time before the guards do. Or worse, Barry.'

I put me face in me hands. Fuck.

She points at the radio in the kitchen. 'Actually, I'm not surprised. Whatever about the guards, the media won't let it go. The stories on the radio today… insane, insane.'

Ma sits beside me. She puts an arm across my shoulders.

'I'm sorry,' she says.

She doesn't have to say any more. No choice now. The cops are better than the Georgians; she's right about that. And she's right that it's better for me to go up there than have them dragging me out in front of Holly and all the neighbours.

'All right,' I say. 'Can I have a cup of tea and a smoke first? Just to get me head together?'

'No,' she says, but in a kind voice. 'One more day probably won't make any difference. Go tomorrow. Spend the day with Holly. You can spoil her a bit. Be a dad.'

I nod again, cos I can't talk. Cos big girly fucking tears are pouring down my face now, and now it's Ma that's hugging me, and I can smell her smell and I know that I'm home.

CHAPTER SIXTY

Carol Murphy

I'm knackered, but I can't sleep. It reads just after nine on my alarm clock. I have to get up, do something. The flat will need a clean after last night, but I find that the girls have already done this for me. I sit on the couch, unable to imagine how I can say sorry to them; how it could be enough. Yet I know they've forgiven me already. They know the way I am.

After two coffees and two cigarettes, I start to feel a bit better. No more Manda sightings mentioned on the radio, though Rachel Belton has withdrawn from the election. She's released a statement saying her husband *has issues to work through*. At least that's something.

Can't sit still. I go to shower, and only then recall the glowing tenderness on the side of my head. Purple-black skin writhes around my right eye. I look like some condemned creature in a documentary on domestic violence. I experiment with foundation, but this only makes it worse. For the next few days, no matter what I say, everyone will assume that some man has hit me. I'll be watched with pity and fear. I decide to regard it as a penance for all I've done, for last night, for all the lies I've told others and myself.

Were they lies? It doesn't feel like that. It feels as if I've awoken from a coma; or that I've suddenly discovered I am a completely different person. Another Carol Murphy was here all along. War is raging over who I should be. This knowledge leaves me empty. I need to fill it up with something, anything. Work.

I shower, and even though it's my day off, opt for a pin-stripe trouser suit which I rarely wear. If I'm going to look like a battered housewife, at least I can offer people the added zing of looking like a professional. Fancy job, but the husband still hits her. The pleasures of judgement. I make sure to pack a notebook, voice recorder, pen, phone and cigarettes in my handbag, then head to the car and drive to Finglas. It's my job. It's normality, what I have now. I need a break before I think any more of the past. I find Pleasant Lane and park up in the only spot available, beside one of those little electricity hut thingies. I light a cigarette.

It's a beautiful autumn day: crisp and super-real. A single cloud curls like the smoke from a post-coital cigarette: perfect, the radio is saying, for the Dublin Marathon. Seven miles away in the city centre, thousands of runners are swarming. Another thing I meant to do once. I downloaded the guide which had all the details about how to build up your fitness. I printed it out and stuck it on the fridge. It's still there, I think. But I did nothing, didn't even start. It wasn't so much the exercise, but the thought of all those dark nights, pounding the road. Too lonely.

The street is airlessly quiet, as you'd expect on a bank holiday morning. I notice that the house I called into yesterday has an election poster in the window. Is that why the woman was familiar? This seems to fit: I have a cataracted image of her speaking – at a public meeting, I think. She was good: relaxed and not showy like so many of them are. Or am I making this up? Her name: Rose Carroll. Is that familiar? No. Nothing there.

I finish my cigarette, then wish I had brought a coffee. Too early to be knocking on doors. I should go and get a coffee, then come back.

Shouldn't have come at all.

Now I want to get away before anyone sees me, before they think: what is wrong with that woman's life that she sits in her car on a bank holiday when everyone else is still in bed? When they are cuddling with their lovers or pillow-fighting with the kids? What is she hiding from? What does she lack?

My phone rings. I give a yelp of surprise, of relief: perhaps I wasn't wrong to come here. Without thinking I pick it up, keen to show my non-existent watchers that I have a reason to be here, to be anywhere.

'Hello Carol,' says Don.

'Hi,' I say, trying to sound sprightly. 'I see Belton's withdrawn.'

'Yes,' he says, in a quiet voice. It sounds as if he's just woken up, or he'd prefer not to talk to me at all. I decide to take the initiative.

'Don,' I say. 'I know you're annoyed with me. I know I didn't ring you back. But all that crap about sightings of Manda, I just couldn't.'

'Carol, I know,' he blurts. 'And I know why.'

I don't answer.

'Why didn't you tell me?' he says. 'No, that's stupid. I know why you didn't. If I'd known she was your cousin, I would have left the story with Tim. That's what is so fucking tragic about this, Carol. I know you lied because you wanted to get back to doing some good work. And you did, you were great. Until I find out she was your cousin.'

The sky seems to grow darker, and now I am thumping along the pavement; training for a marathon I will never run.

'You know what it's like here. You were already being watched after the warnings and the suspension. They were looking for an excuse. Jesus, Carol.'

I hear the click of his lighter.

'Look, kiddo. If it was just me, I would have said nothing. But the Suits are going ape about it. I've no choice. The shite they come out with. *Unethical*, they say to me. Probably had to look it up in a dictionary.'

'But how,' I say, then pause, realising I already know. 'Brian told you?'

'Yes. Of course. Told you he wasn't as innocent as he makes out. He rang pretending to be all concerned because he's been leaving you messages and you weren't getting back to him. And he was *so* worried he felt he had to tell me that Manda is your cousin and that, you know, you might be going off the rails or something. Of course he's already told Upstairs the same story. Little shite.'

I make an involuntary sound, half sigh, half-laugh. Don doesn't say anything else, perhaps to let this sink in. Which, eventually, it does. He's already said he's sorry.

'You have to let me go.'

Let me go: such an odd phrase; implying that I wanted to go anyway, that by paying me and sending me out on stories and giving regularity and purpose to my life, Don was somehow holding me back. But I don't want to couch it in any harsher terms. I know Don is sorry. He'd had high hopes for me.

'Yes,' he eventually says. 'I'm sorry, Carol. It's just fucking, oh, you know. Fuck!'

'Yes,' I say. 'It's OK.'

We're both quiet for a few seconds, unsure of how to finish our conversation. I hear a door slam nearby. Somewhere in the distance, boys are shouting. A football thuds.

'I'll do you a reference, of course,' he says. 'And I'll make a few calls. I'm sure there are a few shifts going around town. Must be, with so many people getting laid off. Oh, yeah, and you haven't been fired. It's a redundancy. There was going to be a few of them anyway, so there is a few bob in it for you. Anyway, in six months or so it will have blown over so, you know, I can get you in back in then.'

'It's OK,' I say again. Don has been babbling, which isn't like him: and now that's the most important thing. I don't want him to be upset. Because I'm not.

'It's fine,' I say. 'Really. I screwed it up, Don. I know I did. But, you know, this might be the best thing for me. Maybe it's time for me to do something else, anyway.'

'Like what?'

'I don't know yet.'

I tell him he was the best boss I could ever have had. He stutters in response. Don isn't comfortable with affection, but that's OK. I know he likes me; he always did. I don't need to be told.

We promise to talk during the week. I remain sitting in the car, puzzled by my calm, knowing that I have not one clue as to what to do next. Maybe I have failed so much, this is a relief. Maybe now I can be somebody else.

Poor Don.

Brian: what a shit indeed. But Don won't forget it.

Poor Brian.

A knock on the car window makes me jerk. And there is Rose Carroll, holding hands with a curly-haired toddler who stares at me with frank puzzlement. The toddler points at me and says: Mam.

Rose smirks.

'She says that to everyone. Even men.'

A slight quiver in her eyes betrays that Rose has spotted my shiner. But she isn't going to mention it.

'So you're back again? Still working on your story?'

Now I smile.

'Actually, no. Not any more. It just ended.'

Rose pauses, obviously wondering what I mean by this; what I'm still doing here. Her cheeks shine in the brisk October air.

We both look at the child, who eventually points again, this time at my bruised eye. Rose gently presses her arm down.

'Shouldn't point, Holly. It's rude.'

'How old is she?' I ask.

'Oh, three and a bit, though sometimes I think she's a lot older. Thought I'd finished doing all this a long time ago. But then grand-children come along, you know.'

I nod, as if I understand.

'She can be a handful, our Holly. But we wouldn't have her any other way.'

I feel there is something else Rose might like to have said, but I don't press it. We are little more than strangers to each other, after all: yet right now this strikes me as the best sort of friend to have. We offer what we want, but don't push for information we are unwilling or unable to give. We have respect for secrets; for what we have both chosen to forget; for the parts of each other which are unknowable, even to ourselves.

Little Holly starts singing. Rose says, 'She loves Bob the Builder.'

I smile, then ask, 'Is it good for kids? Around here?'

Rose slowly nods.

'Actually, yes. There are swings in the park, just up there. There's a playgroup in the Civic Centre that Holly goes to sometimes. And there's a couple of other little girls she plays with. Holly, don't you like playing with Ciara?'

Holly thinks for a minute, then solemnly intones a yes and goes back to singing.

'The area has problems,' says Rose. This sounds like a spiel she has given before. 'Lots of unemployment – and that's only going to get worse with the state of things. So you have drugs and crime. There are some streets in a terrible state. Terrible state. You wouldn't walk down them. But there are just as many like this one.'

She looks around.

'Most of my neighbours have lived here for, oh, at least ten years. Some much longer. I'm in that house thirty-five years now. Would you believe that? I know the names of everyone. Everyone says hello to each other and they might have a little chat. Not too much, but enough. I mean, we're not in each other's pockets, but we don't pretend we don't know each other like they do in lots of places nowadays.'

She hmms, as if repeating a truth which she hasn't considered for some time.

'Yes, it is good. It feels like… it feels like I live in a place where I'm surrounded by people. Not houses.'

We lapse into silence again, though this time I suspect Rose senses the agitation in me.

'Better get going,' she says. 'We're off to the swings. Nice to meet you again, Carol.'

I smile, and off she goes into the bright day with her tottering, chattering grandchild. I haven't said goodbye because I can't. I'm scrubbed of words, and it's nothing to do with my lost job or Manda or Conor or what I have denied to myself. It's simply because Rose Carroll remembered my name; because she went to the bother of reserving some mental space for the name of a woman she'd probably never meet again. My name and face, carried with her.

I check myself in the rear-view mirror. One red eye, one black. Out loud I say, 'You're fired. Don fired you.' Yet still there are no tectonic shifts within me. If anything, there's a lightness now. I pick up my phone and text Conor. I tell him we have to meet as soon as possible.

CHAPTER SIXTY ONE
Rachel Belton

I can hear Aidan Haslett pulling on a cigarette; which makes me wish I had one too. I'll buy some. To hell with it.

'So,' he says. 'This is a bit of an odd one, isn't it?'

I don't answer. I'm not going to explain myself to him.

He sucks again.

'You took your time getting back to me.'

'I was considering my options.'

He makes a sound approximating a grim laugh. Options, yes.

I know I have none. But I wasn't going to make the decision alone. I've spent the last twenty-four hours ringing all the women who have been campaigning for me. Every single one. Sixty-two phone calls. Three thought I should keep going. Several burst into tears. We've decided to get everyone together again in a month or so; after the election, when everything has calmed down. We have more than just politics now.

'You had a good run,' he says.

'Did I? No thanks to you.'

He makes the strangled sound again.

'I thought you were a good candidate. But I'll be honest. I didn't think you'd get elected. Even if this hadn't happened. The numbers just weren't strong enough. I thought my experience could be better utilised elsewhere.'

'Sorry for wasting your time.'

'Don't be snippy, Rachel. You had a good run. You showed determination. After that girl was killed, it was all over, really. But you kept going; you got the constituency machine behind you. Crikey, you hijacked it. Head Office didn't like that at first, but they respected what you did. You proved you have the Right Stuff. So next time out, who knows?'

He's trying to be generous, in his slithery way. As if he's reading my mind, he says, 'I'm not trying to be kind, Rachel. This is how I see it. That interview you gave, that was very slick. All politicians are the same. Risky, but clever. I'd say you got quite a bounce out of that. For a while there, you were the only honest candidate in Ireland.

'But after this business with your husband… that's the thing about the media; that's what you learn with a bit of experience. They are the real opposition. They lionise you one day, cannibalise you the next. Obviously, you have to withdraw now.'

'Why?'

I only want to be contrary. I'd like this to end in a row, though I don't think I have it in me. I'd love to tell Aidan Haslett to fuck off; to be the working-class scumbag he's always suspected I am. I see my shadowy outline in the marble splashback. I'm holding my hand to my mouth, like I'm about to sneeze.

'You know why,' he says. 'Don't be obtuse. This is a tough business and you have to be realistic. Apparitions? Crazy stuff. It's an embarrassment to the party. And you. You know that. Every loony right-wing Catholic in the country has scurried out of their burrows. They think their time has come again. John Charles McQuaid, back from the dead.

'I'm sorry Rachel, but whatever you say or do now, you'll be associated with *them*. Even if by some fluke you did get elected, no one in the house would work with you. Not with that kind of political stink.'

'Hmm,' I say. Even Daniel has been shocked by what's happened. He's in our bedroom, trying to sleep. He hasn't spoken for hours.

'Right now you have a bit of sympathy,' says Aidan. 'Even admirers, for how you turned things around. Don't blow that. Resign gracefully, thank everybody. Then get your husband sorted out and in a few years' time, when all this is history, you're in with a good chance.'

'Yes,' I say, neutrally. He is right, of course: this was what I signed on for, what I was prepared to do. Daniel was a liability. I should have known that from the start.

'OK,' I say. 'I'll issue a statement.'

Aidan Haslett's tone warms, swelled with the satisfaction of winning his point once again.

'OK,' he says. 'Send me a copy. And take care. Take a holiday, if you can.'

'I plan to. We've already booked.'

'Excellent.'

'Aidan?'

'Yes?'

'Fuck off.'

Chapter Sixty Two

Carol Murphy

We've agreed to meet in Howth, even though it's miles away. We've come up with some comfortable excuse about the marathon; that the traffic in town will be chronic.

We've chosen a location as far on the northside of Dublin City as it's possible to get. And by this simple choice, we've opened it all up again. I feel wisps of guilt writhe around me; a nervy excitement which seems to make everything I hear and see more acute.

Yet when I arrive, I'm glad we've chosen here. It's on the sea. The sea. It's always there, always has been: always waiting for me to remember. Which is daft: that I'd forget about the sea, I mean. My family is there. Mum and Dad and I sailed into Howth so many times, it's like we lived here too.

I stand by my car and study the fishing boats leaning against each other like drunken friends, at the stretch of green beside the empty car park. The smell of fish glides past my nostrils. Further up, the yachts sway gently, as if saying hello. I hear bells clanging.

The place we've agreed to meet is easy to spot, though I think it's new since I was last here: pretend-old-fashioned; prefabricated cosiness. I march towards it as if this is something I regularly do. I need another coffee.

I consider what to say to Conor. I'm stewed by contradictory emotions: I'm anxious, yet calm; wistful yet furious. My first instinct was to confront him: to say that what happened with us could have made Manda what she was; that we unknowingly herded her towards that window. But that's unfair. On her and us. She was more than just a victim of events.

So am I, come to think of it.

I pause outside the bar to light a cigarette, paying no attention to the wet slick on the pavement where, about twenty minutes previously, five bottles of some obscure German beer exploded on the ground. The glass has been efficiently swept away, but the shimmering patch remains.

I take a step, and my left leg goes from under me, skidding sideways and forcing me into what looks like an attempt at the splits: something I was too scared to try even as a girl. I wrench my right leg over to correct myself, but it rockets out and up, pitching me backwards; and for part of a second I am in the air, flailing; and it occurs to me how rare it is to have no contact with the earth: even for a millisecond, to be *free* of it. Scary, but calming also: to be rid of the din, of the constant press of other people. Perhaps this is the way to think of death. Perhaps it's not so bad after all.

I suppose astronauts must know what it's like. Do they ever get lonely? They must. When they sleep, do they dream of being back on earth? I'll never visit a space station, so it strikes me that the only way to reproduce such a sensation would be to jump on a trampoline. So as to have no contact with anything, I'd have to be naked. Me, naked on a trampoline. I could do that. As long as the trampoline is a thousand miles away from any other human.

And I think of the brain – of what an astounding organ it is, of how it routinely defies physics by cramming so much thought into this speck of time; a speck which will end with hurt.

It's as much loud as painful: the smack of my head and bum hitting the pavement; the wet immediately rushing into the wool of my fancy suit.

I'm ruined.

My thoughts about space and death and the mind are swept away. Now existence is smelly and grubby and gigantically unjust. I already have a black eye; and now this.

Why do these fucking things always happen to me?

I sit up gingerly, smacking the dirt from my skinned hands. I intend to sit for a moment – I don't care who sees me – because I need to catch my breath, I need the pain in my back and head to fade and most of all I need the courage to want to stand again.

But then a shadow falls across me, and I find myself being scooped up. I feel a smile, and by smell alone I know it's him. It's all anyone could ever need.

Chapter Sixty Three
Maurice Kiberd

The next day I don't want to go to the shop. I don't even want to get up. I feel like – I don't know what I feel like. Like I don't own myself any more; that I sold meself to that reporter and God knows what she'll do with me, how she'll show me to all the neighbours.

Ma wouldn't like this.

Not that I care. Why should I care? Bit late to be worrying now. I don't need to explain meself to them, or anyone. It's not that. It's all this media, you know? The way it's all connected. I just thought: bit of an interview, story about that young girl in the paper might help, you know? But how do I know that's going to happen? I can't control it. It's in the paper, but then it's on the telly and the radio and the internet, even, and then everyone has an opinion about what I said and they have an opinion about me, even though I've never met them. I listen to the radio on the job. I hear all the people that text in or ring up, giving out, giving out, giving out. And it seems to me that the point is to get all excited about nothing – and it'll be about me, this time. It's like that reporter took a few of my words – that's all she needs – and like some sort of a witch she can make a person out of it, or something that looks like a person. And that other Maurice Kiberd will be floating around forever. But he's been made up by the reporter and made up by all the people ringing and texting and talking. It's a big machine and me, like a sucker, offered meself up to it.

Nothing I can do now, though. Can't make it stop. When it's out, it's out, and nobody cares. Nobody cares about what's true. They just want a good story. Not just the media, now: everybody. Religion, sport, politics. They're all stories.

Such things to be thinking. Especially when there's worse off than me. Far worse. I'm not dead. I wasn't pushed out a window. It's only a story in a newspaper, after all. Not even a picture. The girl didn't take a photograph of me. What am I moaning about? It might help. That's why I'm doing it, after all: to bring that girl's killer to justice. To give that girl's family some peace.

There's no story.

When I finally get up and go to the shop, there's no story in any of the papers. Nothing. Not even a mention. There's more about Manda, all right – about all the religious old ones saying they can see her and that. But nothing about the investigation. Nothing. I read the paper twice, just to be sure. Nothing.

I tell meself to get into the cab and drive. Do a bit of work; take your mind off things. Done damn all work for the past few days.

I tell meself that it might appear in the paper tomorrow. Maybe she missed the, you know, the deadline or whatever. But I know that's not true. I offered myself to the Real World, and it wasn't interested. Too ordinary, too straight-talking, too honest. Whatever.

I'm driving around Dublin, picking people up. Bringing them to work or the court or to a cancer screening. I don't have the radio on; not today. I don't want to hear all that chatting, all them people being angry when they don't really give a damn. People get in and out of the car. Some of them want to talk, but I don't say much. Some of them ask questions, the usual rubbish. Are you busy? Have you just started? Lovely day. They want to talk about the election and the IMF and all that. But I don't answer, and I can feel them getting uncomfortable, squirming in the seat and wondering should they ask to be let out here. They don't, because they're too scared to do even that. Sheep. I'm sweating, even though it's not that hot, scratching my neck until it bleeds, my fingernails black from doing it. I don't care. Let them look. Let them be disgusted. I grip the steering wheel until it hurts and I tell myself to wait until tomorrow. Just wait until tomorrow.

CHAPTER SIXTY FOUR

Carol Murphy

So what happened in the end? We arrived at the house in Loughrea as we had a million times before, except this time Hazel was waiting by the back door, her face colourless. My parents told me to wait in the car and disappeared inside.

I stayed where I was until my feeling of foolishness overwhelmed my fear of what I might find. I crept across the courtyard and towards the tree house, hoping I could hide there until whatever was exercising the adults had blown over.

But there in the bottom dip of the field, in a place where we had never sat before, were Conor and Manda. My memory of this is dream-like. They noiselessly rose out of the long grass, as if levitating, back-lit by a low red sun which rinsed out the colours of the sky, yet which made Conor and Manda appear more vivid: the three of us alone in a fabricated universe.

Their appearance gave me a start – I may even have yelped in fright – yet they didn't speak. We all looked at each other.

'Hi,' I eventually said. They didn't reply.

None of us moved.

'What's wrong?' I said.

Conor looked at me incredulously and then shook his head: No.

'What's wrong?' I said again.

'Don't play innocent,' said Manda. 'You know what you did.'

'I didn't do anything.'

She looked away.

'I didn't do anything.'

'You betrayed us,' Manda said.

'No I didn't. What are you talking about?'

I was telling the truth. I hadn't betrayed anyone. Yet I knew my protests sounded desperate and reedy; the more I denied, the guiltier I sounded.

'What's going on?' I shouted. 'Why is Hazel looking so serious? What happened? Why do you think I betrayed you? Please tell me. I wouldn't betray you. I love you.'

At this, Conor glanced at Manda: as if I had made a fair point. Manda glared at me.

'What would you know about love?'

I ran to the tree house; head down, gulping air, but soon found myself staggering over spiky slabs of wood: brown nails showing like rusty claws. The ladder was gone. Chunks of the roof had dissolved and what seemed liked rocket holes had punctured the walls.

I crumpled to the ground and only now saw the shards of wood fanning out around me, as if I was sitting at the epicentre of an explosion; as if I had somehow caused it to happen. I looked back down the field. Conor and Manda had gone.

Like a broken DVD, the world seemed to freeze then jump forward in staccato image-bursts. Hazel appearing in the field to call her children in for another burnt dinner. Hazel standing at the base of the tree, hands pressed to her face as she listens to the sounds from the tree house. Hazel running back inside; Hazel ringing my father, screaming at him. Hazel sitting with her children, trying not to see them as monsters, telling them she knows all about their sick games. Manda shouting, Conor looking away, and now Manda also falling silent: both of them swept with a sudden, inexplicable disgust.

She could have come out any night and discovered what we were up to. But this never occurred to us; even after Hazel confronted them. Discovery could only occur if one of us broke our magic trust: and that person, they had concluded, was me.

I sat where I was for a while. Even though I couldn't see them now, I yelled at my cousins to fuck off: not because they had accused me in the wrong, but because they had been coming out here without me. They'd said they didn't like to. They'd said it wasn't the same.

I remember Dad coming to the field to get me, but saying nothing. There was a trip home which was largely silent, and then life as normal. They never spoke to me about it, perhaps fearing what I might tell them. But I wouldn't have said anything. I didn't want to. Even in the car back to Dublin I began the process of constructing a new image of my world, in which Conor and Manda hardly existed; where they were merely some cousins I used to play with once, long ago.

It must have been three or four years before I saw them again: at some wedding, I think. By then we were all young adults and quite capable of ignoring what had happened.

All this comes back to me in scorching detail as Conor and I sit in the window of the café in Howth. We're holding hands, sipping coffee and Conor is failing to suppress the smirk on his face. I've already spent fifteen minutes in the toilet, trying to dry the wet patches on my clothes. The trousers are OK, but the jacket is destroyed.

We've talked about that day, the words finally released after years. I had only gone a couple of hours when they realised the truth. Hazel let it slip that she'd been out to the tree house the evening before and heard them. Manda went berserk; Hazel ran screaming from the room. Manda wanted to go after her, still convinced that she could explain what had happened, that we had done nothing wrong. She wanted Conor to come too, but he refused: now unsure what his motives had been; suspecting some sickness in himself. Conor and Manda argued, and said some things which even today Conor won't repeat. For weeks afterwards, a deep silence clung to the house.

It's my first time hearing this from Conor. Yet it feels as if I already knew.

They were forbidden from any contact with me, and for a while, each other. They tried, of course, but somehow my parents managed to intercept their letters and phone calls. I don't know if Mum and Dad read the letters, but I reckon not: they didn't want to think about it any more than I did. We all got on with our lives in Dublin.

Conor had to stay in boarding school at the weekends, and in time he and Manda erected fences around what happened. Eventually, neither wanted to speak about it. All that was left were unexplained traces: in Manda, a certain rootlessness; in Conor a muted fury towards his mother; and in me, well: take your pick.

Now he's grinning and saying, 'You're a klutz. Always were.'

He points.

'I've got to ask. The shiner?'

'Self-inflicted. Drink.'

He smiles again, then looks at our entwined hands.

'It's so strange,' he says. 'Seeing you again. Like this, I mean. Every other time it's just been, you know.'

I get a flash of leaving the church behind the coffin, watching them slide it into the back of the hearse. Conor, Manda and Hazel stand at the edge of the crowd, dressed in immaculate black and washed by a sepia light. They look like strangers. I glance at them, then get in the car.

'I know.'

It suddenly occurs to me what it is I need to say to Conor. And I'm relieved that I don't want to shovel out recriminations or calculate the past against the present.

'I'm sorry,' I say. 'I wanted to say I'm sorry.'

'For what?'

'For forgetting. About the three of us, I mean. For pretending it never happened. I filed it away and never wanted to think about it again. I'd convinced myself that we had just played together as kids, years ago, but that it was nothing special. How could I have done that?'

Conor nods, but says. 'You did nothing wrong. We did it too. But this.' He holds up our entwined hands. 'This is a relief, you know?'

He falls silent: probably because, like me, he realises that it can't be the same as before; of course not. Now we have to try to understand what we are to each other.

'Kristel,' he says. 'I never told her about us. Just that there had been a rift.'

'Yes,' I say. 'Of course. What would be the point?'

Conor squeezes my hand.

'She's a good woman,' I say. 'I like her.'

And we sit in silence, staring out the window at the twinkling sea.

CHAPTER SIXTY FIVE

Michael Bourke

Having a scorched throat and some minor smoke damage to my lungs proves to be an advantage over the next twenty-four hours: it means I am not required to speak when the guards arrive. They ask questions and I nod yes or no: constructing a scenario almost totally of their own imaginings. *Heroic priest finds church on fire and rushes in.* By the time they leave they have all but admitted that it was probably the work of local thugs, full of narcotics and discontent. The chances of catching them are remote, they inform me.

I know little about investigative procedures, but I find their incompetence astounding: they seem to have simply chosen to believe me, almost solely on the basis of my profession. Unless this is some shrewd tactic on their part. Yet all they had to do was make the accusation, and I would have admitted my guilt.

Once again I find myself riding a wave of events outside my control. The bishop visits, though briefly. He has never been comfortable in my presence – perhaps sensing that I am different – and is all the more discomforted by having to praise my heroism. I, of course, play the role of the humble cleric, honoured by his visit.

I also take a brief phone call from Jack, who seems to be doing well. In typical fashion, he is more concerned about the state of my mental health rather than the church or my shattered arm. I reassure him that my spirits are good, which they are. I feel a lightness, an unburdening; as if I am not a priest any more.

Marie, my nurse-guard, keeps all the other visitors at bay: journalists and politicians, the grim-faced women from the parish. I receive a card from Sharon, full of high-blown concern for my health whilst making no mention of how she and her cohort turned a private meeting into a near-riot.

Yet if there had not been a large crowd present, I would probably not be here now. When the fire was spotted, they managed to knock down the gate simply by pressing against it; the rusted hinges aiding their efforts. I was rescued within minutes of my fall.

After two days in hospital, I have had quite enough. Enough hiding. They want me to remain, of course, but I am adamant, and after signing all sorts of waivers I emerge again into the joyous, bustling world; buses and people shooting past.

Unknown to anyone, I return to the house Jack and I inhabit. Miraculously, it is undamaged, save for a curious lack of heating oil in the tank. The bishop has already arranged (because the insurance company will pay) for a clean-up of the church. I wander in and greet the workmen, who regard me and my slinged arm with mild alarm.

The walls are encrusted with soot, which gives the interior an otherworldly aura. The Stations of the Cross are completely destroyed. The four scaffold towers are mangled into abstract shapes, while the roof has completely disappeared: as if carefully removed by a giant scalpel. But most of the pews are intact, so I instruct the men to leave them there. I tell them I would like the church to remain much as it was, albeit without a roof. They shrug and say OK. If that's what you want. We don't care. We're getting double-time.

We discuss some more details of the clean-up, until there are no more details to discuss; until the foreman informs me that they should be finished by tomorrow evening. An impressive turnaround, I tell him. He shrugs again.

As I leave, one of the men approaches me. He has the embarrassed air of someone not used to speaking to priests. He nods. 'How's your arm?'

'Nothing serious,' I say. 'It will heal.'

He points to the west.

'You know, I was in Parnell Street the day that girl died. I was just going into the ILAC with my young fella. I saw you getting into that skip.'

'Yes,' I say.

'Terrible, terrible. That poor girl.'

I don't reply. If this man wants me to confirm some magical pattern in these events, I will not do so.

'It's funny,' he says. 'Well, not funny, but strange. I was out of work for six months, but the day after I got a job with these lads. You know, it makes you appreciate what you have, doesn't it?'

'Yes,' I say. I find I am smiling. 'It certainly does.'

Overhead, clouds drift lazily by, constantly changing the configuration of shadows around us. We are both within and without. I feel liberated by this contradiction. The planet brims with potential.

I walk back to the house and consider how long I have got. There was no sign of the utensils I used to transport the oil to the church, so perhaps the police were shrewder than they appeared. On the computer, I check the weather forecast for the next few days. All is as it should be. Then I pick up the phone and dial a number given to me by one of the guards investigating Manda's death.

'Mrs Ferguson,' I say. 'My name is Michael Bourke. Father Michael Bourke. I was with your daughter the day she died.'

'Yes,' she says in a shrunken voice, as if fearing what I might say.

'I'm ringing because I'd like to extend, to you and your family and friends, I'd like to extend an invitation.'

CHAPTER SIXTY SIX

Carol Murphy

We hugged tightly, but awkwardly; avoiding lips and bodies. I make him promise to ring his mother – to go a bit easier on her. He said he would try, but I don't know.

On the drive back into town, there's one final task. I ring the taxi driver. He doesn't answer, so I leave a message. I say I wasn't able to discover anything in Finglas, and anyway, I'm off the story now. I've been made redundant from my newspaper. I'm sorry.

I can't think of anything else to do, so I head for home. I'm trying to figure out how to avoid the mobs and shut off streets in the city centre when it strikes me that this is exactly what I want: to be among people as they walk around, squinting in the sunlight, chatting, laughing, shouting into their phones, shivering with cold. I nip across the toll bridge and in around the back of the Pepper Canister Church: a building which has been used in so many adverts and films it doesn't seem real; part of a genteel, post-Georgian Ireland that we never managed to achieve, but miss all the same.

Mount Street is gently quiet, apart from a few clumps of numbered runners sitting on steps, either finished already or reluctant to start. I leave the car there, but have to double back when I see a traffic warden marching towards me.

'Miss, Miss,' he squeaks, just as I reach the ticket machine. Tiny little fella, bulging out of his brown uniform. 'You don't need to buy a ticket today. It's free.'

'Oh,' I say. He grins up at me, revelling in the tiny victory of a day when he gets to give people good news for a change.

I make my way up to Merrion Square, dodging around the barriers which funnel me towards Nassau Street where crowds have congealed on either side of the road. Runners sweep past me, their shoulders hunched as they concentrate on the next piece of road to be conquered. They scoop plastic cups from tables, making only the briefest gesture of thanks: they can't afford to expend any more energy.

I've been standing here for some minutes before I register that most of the crowd are applauding. Tourists from Padua and Marseilles and Des Moines, day trippers from Leitrim and Offaly and Sandycove: they've all come to clap people they have never met, for doing something which, when you think about it, has no real point. They are running for the sake of it and being cheered by strangers, as if they too have managed the twenty-six miles. And I find myself smiling because of this; I find myself cheering and clapping too.

CHAPTER SIXTY SEVEN

Baz Carroll

I don't like to think about her. I don't like to say her name. Nobody around me mentions her. They all know.

So I dunno why I'm thinking about her now.

OK. Fuck it. Her name is Jackie. Her name *was* Jackie.

I met her on one of my trips to the clinic. It was hard that time. I was sick as a pig. Puking and sweating and thinking: this is not gonna get any better. As soon as the pain is over, I'll have to sit in a room with a load of miserable fuckers talking about our feelings and moaning about the world and their parents and society and how it made them put a lighter under some tinfoil. Fuck's sake.

I knew exactly what would happen, knew what every fucker would say before they opened their mouths. To move the attention off me, I'd always get one of the others to talk. We'd be sitting in our groups, and as soon as one of them would start mouthing off, I'd be all, yeah? Jesus, that's interesting. Tell us more. And before you know it, the hour would be over without anyone else having to say a word. If that didn't work, I'd start a row about something. Or if that failed, I'd start going on about how brilliant smack is and this really good stuff I could get me hands on and how brilliant it would make you feel. The counsellors would hate that. After ten minutes, half of them would be screaming to get out the door and get their hands on it. Total laugh.

They were all so up their own holes, no one ever copped to what I was at. Tossers. Except for Jackie. As soon as I opened my trap I could see her putting her hands to her mouth to cover the smiles, and then she started joining in: me and her, making out that we were fascinated by some dumb culchie who was only on the gear for three months and was all weepy about it. Fuck's sake. Probably not even addicted.

Afterwards, she looked at me with these big brown eyes. And that was it. Thick as thieves, we were, and with the same stories: in and out of clinics, bit of trouble with the law. The only difference was that her family would have nothing to do with her. And she wasn't from Finglas. Fucking *Glasthule*. I'd never heard of it before. It's on the southside. She showed me her family's gaff one time. Huge. She was posh.

But she didn't put on airs and graces or anything like that. She was just like you or me, apart from the accent. I liked that accent.

She was a small bird, tiny, with long brown hair and these wrinkles that would appear on the side of her nose when she smiled, which I thought was weird at first but then I couldn't get enough of it. I'd tell her jokes, just to see them.

In the clinic they don't like fraternisation so we had to be careful, which made it even more of a laugh.

We reckoned afterwards that she was pregnant before we got out. Bang. Just like that. With all the drugs, I wouldn't have thought I was able.

We were totally stunned. We got on great and all that, but we only knew each other a few weeks at that stage. The whole thing was crazy.

But the more we talked about it, the more real it got, until we had talked so much that we could almost see the baby. We could imagine what it would look like and what it would do when it grew up. Weird, I tell ya. And that changed us. Like me and Jackie weren't the two mad junkies any more, but two other people who have a baby and make plans and think about what will happen years from now. Never done that before. Thinking about this afternoon would usually be all I could manage. Suddenly I was that other bloke, with the other life.

So it wasn't like I asked her a question or got down on me knees or any of that shit. We just started talking and the next thing she was telling me stories about her sister's baby that she'd minded a few times and how Jackie would do things different; and I was talking about getting a job – a regular fucking job – and organising us a place to stay. We were like, obsessed with it for a while. Suppose it kept our minds off the gear.

In the end though, Jackie did all the organising. Fucking brilliant, she was, at talking to social workers and getting loads out of them. Got us bumped up the queue, somehow, so that we ended up with this lovely little place in Ballymun. You know, one of them new places they built up there. Two bedrooms and a big sitting room with a kitchen at the end. Even a fucking balcony. I remember telling Martin and him getting all excited. *A bangly? That's deadly.* Dunno why, but he just couldn't say the word properly. Balcony, not fucking bangly. I'd keep bringing it up in conversation, just to hear him say it. I'd be laughing me hole off, but Martin wouldn't mind. He's cool that way.

Brand new when we moved in; spotless, though we had no furniture to put into it. But Jackie sorted that out. Straight down to the Vincent de Paul, turned on the waterworks and got the place kitted out. Sweet.

As for me, well, getting a job wasn't that easy. Never was, come to think of it. Around here anyway. Always a fucking recession here. I worked in a garage for a month or so, but that was shite, then did a couple of courses. I've done more courses now than I have spots on me arse. And they're just as useless. In the end we decided, fuck it. Went back on the dole and did a few odd jobs here and there. At least until the baby comes.

Jackie tried telling her family, but they still didn't want to know, the cunts. So Jackie was mad keen to meet my ma. Because Jackie had a bit of an education and that – she used to read books in the flat – she knew all about the Queen of Finglas from the papers.

But they never got on. Funny that. I thought Ma would be delighted that I was off the gear and settling down. She said she was pleased, but it didn't sound that way. She was always polite with Jackie, but it was like she didn't trust her, you know?

This drove Jackie fucking mad, and I got a load of *your mother doesn't like me*; as if there was anything I could do about it. And after a while she started to refuse to go over to Finglas for the Sunday dinner, making out that Ma was looking at her funny. Jesus.

That's something else I never asked Ma about.

Now me and Jackie got on, but I'm not making out it was Little House on the Prairie. She had a temper and a vicious tongue on her. Vicious. And in fairness I suppose I could be a bit of a pain in the hole. I'm not what you'd call dependable. I forget things. Especially when the baby was close to coming and she was as fat as the Michelin Man. Jesus, she ate the shite out of me sometimes. And sometimes I deserved it. Most of the time I wouldn't argue back. I'd read a bit of the book she'd got me, so I knew a bit about the hormones and the swollen ankles and all that. It can't have been much of a laugh for her. Well, I know it wasn't. She told me every fucking day.

But this is a weird thing to say. I was happy. That nine months shot by without me noticing. And after the baby arrived – little Holly with her Ma's eyes and hair – I couldn't believe that we'd spent all that time together. In our flat, paying our rent. Not fucking up. Amazing.

And I'm not blowing me trumpet or anything like that, but after Holly came, I wasn't lazy. For the first time in me life, I got off me hole. There wasn't much choice, was there? Jackie didn't want to do the breast-feeding, so I was able to muck in with the bottles in the middle of the night and changing the nappies and all that. Knackered, we were. Spaced out of it most of the time, so I suppose I didn't really notice – I just thought Jackie was quiet cos of the tiredness. It was all baby, baby, baby. *I* was all baby, baby, baby. Feeding Holly, changing Holly, bringing Holly for walks, putting Holly into her cot. And if I wasn't doing that, I was talking about Holly to anyone that would listen.

But Jackie just got more and more quiet, more into herself. I suppose she didn't like being a ma, I dunno. But after a while she's started refusing to do her bit, getting up in the night or putting the baby to bed. She never carried her around or talked to her. Looking back now, it's like she hated Holly. I dunno. Can a mother hate her own child? Is that possible? I know there were one or two times – more than that, actually – when Holly might be crying or having a bit of a shitfit, and

Jackie would say to me: you shut her up. Shut her up or I'll throw her out the window. At the time, I put it down to her being tired.

So I ended up doing everything. If I left the flat, I brought Holly with me, to give Jackie a bit of space, like. I'd go to me ma's or down the park or the shops or even when I was signing on. It was like the pram was stuck to me. Which was good too cos it kept me on the straight and narrow. People don't offer you drugs when you're pushing a pram. Not a lot, anyway.

But you can fucking see it coming, can't you? Got back to the flat one day and she was gone. Bags packed, and off. No note, nothing. I rang around but no one knew a thing. I even tried her stuck-up family on the southside, but they slammed down the phone on me. Cunts.

So I said to meself: fuck her.

I can do this alone. Ma wanted me and Holly to move in with her; went on and on about it. But I said no. Wasn't I doing it all meself anyway before she left? Only difference was that I wouldn't be listening to any fucking moaning. Just me and Holly. We'll be fine.

But it wasn't the same. Of course it wasn't the same. Every time I looked at the baby I thought about her, and I thought: what the fuck happened? What did I do? Could I have done something else? How could she be such a cold bitch? I tell ya, it drove me fucking mad.

So of course I started using again. Just a little bit in the evenings, when Holly was asleep and it was so quiet I wanted to scream me brains out, cos I knew that if Jackie appeared at the front door I would have taken her back. Begged her to come back. Even if it was to do all that moaning again, just sit in the corner and say Baz, you stupid cunt. I would have taken her back with a huge fucking smile on me face.

But that never happened. To this day I don't know if she's dead or alive. Not knowing; that was torture. I'd have all these conversations with her in me head, then realise what I was doing and start crying; then do some smack to cheer meself up. If that didn't work, I'd take some more smack.

It was a lucky thing that I gave Ma a key to the flat. She's the one that found Holly sitting in her cot, screaming because she was starved and covered in her own shit. And me passed out in the kitchen, after taking so much smack I should have been dead. Maybe that's what I was trying to do. I dunno.

Ma got Holly up, cleaned her, fed her, then packed all her stuff, and with me still on the kitchen floor. She was just about to leave when she got a saucepan of water and poured it over me head. That woke me, for a few seconds anyway. Ma told me in that calm voice she has that she was taking Holly away, and that if I came to the door, I wouldn't be let in. And all I could do was nod cos I was so fucked. But do you know what? I was relieved. At least Holly would be safe with Ma, and I could go back to doing what I do best. Killing meself with drugs.

That was two years ago; more.

I did what she said. I stayed away. Moved back to Finglas and into that shitty flat with Martin. Told everyone that me ma didn't want to have anything to do with me; that she wouldn't even let me see me own daughter. Baz the Wild Man. I'd have a few drinks and I'd be calling me old one a snobby bitch, but all the while I'd know that, really, she'd done me a favour. She done Holly a favour. Saved her life, probably.

And I didn't go near the house, didn't go near either of them. I know that sounds cold, but it was easier. I'm a coward. I didn't want to think about losing me daughter; about letting down me own flesh and blood. I'd do anything but think about that.

I should be dead. But now here I am back in Ma's house with my beautiful little girl. For a few hours anyway. It's only temporary. That's the word, isn't it? Yeah. I always felt me life was temporary. Waking up in the morning has been a total fucking surprise to me. What? Still alive? Even without drugs I always felt like that. I suppose it will get me in the end. It always does.

CHAPTER SIXTY EIGHT
Carol Murphy

Hazel almost sings my name; pleased that I've called, but pleased also to tell me that her phone has been going constantly.

'Father Michael rang me,' she screams, 'Father Michael!' as if the name and the very fact of his calling is enough to set me screaming as well.

'Who?'

'You know, you know. Father Michael! The priest!'

I want to slap my head, like a cartoon character. I *do* know Father Michael: the priest who found Manda in the skip; the self-pitying weirdo.

I'm sitting outside a coffee shop just off Grafton Street. I found a scarf and an old pair of shades in the car, so my black eye and ruined jacket are at least partially covered. The Marathon is over now. Glowing runners mill around, sipping water, hugging themselves inside blankets and posing for photographs.

They seem excited, or perhaps relieved to find that they could do something: that the gap between reality and their imaginings could be crossed. They seem reluctant to leave, some of them even pausing to speak to the purple-haired election candidate waltzing down the street. The vote is tomorrow. I'd completely forgotten.

'Yes, I do know who you mean,' I say. 'Of course.'

'Well, Father Michael wants to say a special mass or a service or something like that. In Dublin. In the church she used to go to. It's on Wednesday, so you'll be coming? Of course you'll be coming.'

'Yes. Yes.'

'Now it's nothing fancy, and even though you represent the media I won't be expecting you to speak. I might say a few words though.'

I smile. Hazel loves to say a few words.

'Father Michael says it's not really mass. I suppose it's because the church caught fire, but he says not to mind about that. There's no roof left but he says that makes it very atmospheric. And sure that wouldn't stop us, would it?'

'That was *his* church that burned down?'

Hazel pauses.

'I suppose, dear.'

Another weird coincidence, though I'm encouraged that Hazel isn't pointing this out, isn't investing it with any meaning: that she's brave and sane enough to accept the world as it appears to be.

I say, 'Have you been following the news?'

'About what, dear?'

'All these, you know, sightings. Of Manda.'

'Oh, for God's sake,' she squeals. 'Isn't that ridiculous? What is wrong with people? And what is wrong with that man who says he talks to her? Conor thinks it's just a stunt to get his wife elected.'

'You were talking to Conor?'

'Yes,' Hazel says, as if this is an unremarkable thing. 'Few minutes ago. But you'd know, Carol. Is it a stunt?'

'I don't think so, now. The wife withdrew from the election.'

Hazel pauses, then with as much drama as she can muster (which is a lot), she breathes, 'Really?'

She talks as if I have imparted some highly scandalous secret; as relishable as chocolate.

'I think she was embarrassed,' I say.

'Yes, yes. Though *these people*, do they get embarrassed at all?'

'Some of them do…'

'You know the way they are always going around getting botox done or having affairs with air stewardesses and all that. And then it's all over the papers? But does it stop them? Not at all.'

'Well, I don't think Rachel Belton…'

'And why are they so obsessed with their pubic hair, Carol? All these, you know, Brazilians and all that. What's wrong with what God gave them? And why do they have to tell everyone about it? It's disgusting. It's not funny, Carol. I'm serious.'

I'm laughing so hard I narrowly avoid shooting coffee out of my noise. I notice the shy smiles of some of the people around me. They are eavesdropping, but hope I don't mind. I'm enjoying my conversation with Hazel, and they are too. It's like the reverse of the normal rules: what I would consider no one's business but my own, today I don't mind sharing; I actually want to.

'Anyway, you'll be there on Wednesday?'

'Yes,' I say. 'Of course.'

'And bring your father,' she says. 'Two days is enough for him to get home. It's about time he got off that boat. Tell him it's not a funeral so he doesn't have to see anyone crying. I know what he's like. It's just a service. I need him back here; you do too. And he needs to come back to the real world every now and again.'

Hazel drops her voice: as if what she's about to say is a secret; or perhaps she's not entirely sure how true it might be.

'It's funny that something like this might bring us back together.'

Hazel tells me she loves me and hangs up.

'And I love you,' I say.

I put down my phone and lean back. A delicious exhaustion floods through my limbs. I feel I could sleep now, could sleep for days. I close my eyes and imagine being outside my body, looking back at this overweight, black-eyed woman dressed in a badly stained, probably smelly trouser suit. Amazing I'm not getting more looks. But this is who I am, or part of it anyway. It strikes me that how I see myself from the inside is almost irrelevant. What's important is how I push out into the world, what indentation I make upon it. How I sound, how I touch, how I kiss, what I say; all these things and more define how I exist, what trail I leave behind myself, even after I'm gone. Without everything and everyone around me, I am reduced; I barely exist.

Perhaps this is obvious. Perhaps you and everyone else have always known. But for me, it is the first time.

I look at the people slowly moving around me, and for a moment it feels as if I'm staring in the windows of Marks & Spencer or gently nodding to what's on my iPod or sending a *Wher R U?* text or looking at a mime artist who pretends to be a statue or linking my boyfriend or dodging the charity muggers or dragging my child or sitting here, watching. I am them, and they are me.

Funny that something like this might bring us together.

'Fuck!'

I'm getting looks now; some mildly shocked, some quizzical. I stand, gather up my things and rush off.

I think I know what happened to Manda.

CHAPTER SIXTY NINE

Rachel Belton

The aeroplane swoops along the southern French coast and banks towards Nice Airport. The sea glows and glistens beneath us, while the land is brown, gently scorched by the months of summer. It's autumn, but still warm here: warm enough for us to rent a house with a swimming pool in Eze-sur-mer. We'll eat barbecue and do cannonballs into the pool. Crannonballs, Naoise calls them. Daniel promises he'll have him swimming by the end of the week.

Naoise peers out the window, open-mouthed. 'Likkle cars,' he says. 'Likkle houses.' Daniel shoots a grin. 'They'll be big when we get down there.'

'No,' I say. 'Didn't you know? France is the country of tiny people. We'll be giants there.'

Naoise rotates his black eyes; first at his father, then me.

'Mammy,' he says, as if shocked. 'You made a joke.'

Daniel leans across and takes my hand, gripping it so tightly it almost hurts. The counselling is going well, he says. He thinks he's been feeling guilty for years.

He can go for hours now without hearing them. *Daddy. Daddy. Why don't you talk to us?* He doesn't think they will go away completely, but perhaps they will be quieted enough to give him some peace: so he can live in this world, with Naoise and I. And that's enough.

We all look out the window, our three bowed heads reflected in the wispy clouds.

'Whooo!' cries Naoise as the plane bumps onto the tarmac. He's excited now, and as we step outside he holds his hands up to absorb the blanket of heat. Then he joins his hands together.

'Dear God. Thank you for the sun.'

Daniel and I exchange a look.

'He didn't get that from me.'

At passport control, the man can't pronounce his name, but after some coaching, purrs *Bonjour, Na-sha. Bienvenue en France!*

While Daniel collects the car, Naoise and I sit outside the terminal. I light up a cigarette. Must give them up. Again. Difficult here, though, where everyone makes it look so graceful. When we go home, then.

The others wanted to wait for me to start the discussions on what to do next. But I insisted they press ahead. It is about the group, not me. They don't quite believe that yet. But they will. They have to. I may not rejoin them for some time. I have Naoise and Daniel to think about.

And there's plenty of help now. We've got offers from academics and journalists; people and groups with various ideas. There are invitations to speak at public meetings; there's an inaugural convention to organise. The press have picked up on us too, casting me as the unlucky candidate with the crazy husband, but our group as a unique new force in Irish politics, untainted by the old habits. *Belton's Women. Belton's New Model Army.*

There will be rows about policy and strategy, about what exactly to call ourselves. Are we a pressure group, a movement, a campaign, a political party? I've been clear about what I want: that it has to be about changing the system; about making it work better; about getting people involved.

We won't have votes to back up our case, but did we really need them? After I spoke again with Sandra and some of the others, what should have been obvious all along became clear to me: we have the most destructive weapon. We have money.

Daniel says I can have as much as I need.

The rich and pretty; getting everything they want.

For a while it all seemed new to me; now it feels like a pattern of events which has played out dozens, hundreds, millions of times before: we'll be angelic in our first enthusiasms, but the grinds of failure and success will eventually render us petty. We'll squabble and gossip and end up fighting over the kingdom we have established; eventually destroying much of what we've created, but hopefully leaving some small, enduring good behind. It's the Irish way.

Our group wants to change the systems and institutions. This will be our public mission. But it's not really about that at all. It is people we want to transform.

How do you change a heart?

My phone beeps, to inform me that I have one new voice message, and even as I dial it, I get a strange sense of knowing who it will be. Aidan Haslett has that smug laugh in his voice again, though this time it's not so annoying. It's warmer, even amused.

'Well, Rachel,' he says. 'Well, well, well.' He chuckles, and for a moment I wonder is he drunk.

'Sorry, sorry. I know you're away. Sorry to disturb. But my God. My God. You've really done it now.'

CHAPTER SEVENTY

Maurice Kiberd

What are you, except yourself? That sounds a bit, I dunno, stupid, I suppose, but what I mean is: all you can be is yourself, do you know? I don't know what makes you what you are – whether it's God or because your old fella gave you a slap in the head when you were young. All I know is that I've spent me whole life standing up to the wolves – fighting them and beating them. And just because no one else seems to care, should I stop now? Should I stop being who I am? Just to fit in with people who don't give a damn about me?

It's all I've got left, really. Don't have a wife or family or any of that. Yeah, that might have been nice. I can admit that. But don't think I've spent years at home worrying about it. I haven't. I've been too busy. I'm not a moaner. Look, let's be honest. What woman was going to want to touch me? With the psoriasis and all that. Best to be straight up about it. And I'm not looking for pity. It's just the way things turned out. That's life. I mean, I am a man and all that – don't get the wrong impression, now – I've even gone to women who, you know, let me pay them for it. Never enjoyed it though. And even then I'd catch them glancing at me skin. Even then.

I suppose I could have made an effort. Done that internet thing. Found meself a woman with psoriasis. That would balance it out. But I've got to admit there was another thing bothering me: that I might turn into me da; do all that to her. You never know, do ya? You never know.

The one thing I can say without fear of any contradiction is that I did all I can. I rang the guards and the radio station and talked to the Belton woman and the reporter. Did everything. To hell with them. Do it my way now.

Too old now to settle down. Set in me ways. I couldn't do all that sharing me feelings and compromising and being nagged. Did you put out the bins, Maurice? Did you pay the electricity bill?

No, couldn't be getting on with that.

But I don't know. I've knocked off work early so I can hang around the house on the off chance that the phone will ring. Maurice! So sorry! There's been a huge mistake! That bloke was arrested this morning and we have you to thank for it. I'm waiting to hear from that reporter to tell me I'm great for coming forward. I even lift up the phone to make sure it's still working.

Yeah, right. I'm pathetic.

But I'm looking at the phone so much I don't even notice the answering machine, blinking away there. Sure who ever rings me? Who ever leaves me a message? The thing is covered in dust and I have to think for a minute how to work it.

So I listen. Then I listen to it again.

At first I'm saying to meself: well at least she rang back. She kept her word. But suddenly she's not doing this story anymore? Suddenly she's been laid off her job? She gets made redundant on a bank holiday?

For a minute there even I don't want to believe what's going on; it's just so bloody brazen. She talks to the wrong bloke; she wants to tell a story no one wants to hear, and that's it: she's out.

I sit quietly for a while and take deep breaths. I think about ringing this girl, but it's probably best not to involve her.

This is what I decide to do: I tell meself to go for a drive. Just a drive. Out to Finglas, to where you dropped him off.

Just see what happens.

But I already know what that is.

I give the car a good wash beforehand; haven't given it a clean for nearly a week. It helps me to get back to feeling normal; get my own life moving again. Haven't been working, haven't been doing anything; that's part of the problem. I was obsessed with that poor girl.

Well, that's it now. Won't think of her again. Why should I? I'm not an old man. I need to think about what I'm going to do. Can't be just driving a cab and reading the paper until I drop dead. Maybe I should try the internet thing. I could find out how it works, anyway. No harm.

Before I get in the car, for a brief moment a voice in my head tells to not to go; to forget all about about it, find out about internet dating instead. But I know I wouldn't be able to do that. I'm not made that way. If there's unfinished business, I've got to finish it. I'm the only one that can.

It's an odd thing to say, but it's a beautiful drive out to Finglas. The roads are nice and clear and the weather is lovely: the sky is so blue it's like it's not real – like I'm driving into a film. I'm glad I've cleaned the car because in the bright light it looks great; it looks classy. I wonder if it's like this for all them people who exist in the media, who don't have to be looking at graffiti or crime or fellas living on the street. Does everything seem new to them? Do even simple things like a driving a car seem that bit more exciting?

I dunno. I'll never know.

I get out to Finglas in no time at all. Pleasant Lane. Still can't get over that name.

It's funny what I'm doing: I'm not looking out for landmarks or trying hard to find the place. I'm just going to drive for a while and see what happens: see does Pleasant Lane come to me. And if it does, then that means something, doesn't it?

Loads of people outside, like there always is here. Gossiping and playing football and shouting across the street at each other. Loads of them standing in their doorways, just looking around. They do that in our street too. *Our* street? I suppose not. Though I'd never move away. It would be like leaving Ma behind, somehow. Couldn't afford to anyway.

I go around one big massive park with nothing on it, not even a dog. I reckon I'm getting close to Ballymun now, so I turn back, then turn onto another park, this time with a load of swings and slides and that. This looks familiar.

And there it is. Right there. Wasn't hard to find at all; like it's been waiting. It knows what's needed; what I'm here for. No getting around that now.

There's even a parking spot, just in the right place: at the end of the street, with a good view of your man's house and right beside an ESB sub-station, so there'll be no one looking out their window at me.

Maybe this is the way things are; maybe there is no choice. Maybe someone came up with a plan for me millions of years ago and there's nothing I can do about it.

I push back me seat, glance at me watch and still I say to meself: give it an hour. One hour exactly. If nothing happens, then I'll go home. This seems like a nice street, after all. Don't want to be causing trouble when there's no need. In fact, there's a good chance nothing will happen. Maybe that's the reason I've been brought here: because this isn't where this bloke lives. It could be a friend, or the place where he gets his drugs, you never know. Or it might be a nice street that he heard about where he could do a bit of robbing. I could find myself getting lifted by the cops, accused of being his accomplice. Now that would be funny.

Whatever happens, I'm glad I came. This feels like the end of the story – and I don't just mean the one with the skanger killing that girl. I mean my story, I suppose: the one with all the fighting and all the wolves trying to eat me up.

I'm yawning. With all the sun today I could easily fall asleep. Another couple of minutes and I would have, but the door opens and there he is, bold as brass. Totally pleased with himself.

Just as I remember him too – wearing the exact same clothes. He stops outside the house for a minute and lights up a cigarette. Takes his time about it too. Then he starts to stroll towards me, looking this way and that – and this is the mad thing – not a bit worried about being pulled by the law. He only has this huge smile on his face, like he's been having the time of his life. Murder some innocent young girl, get a taxi home, then pull a few strings or grease a few palms to make sure everyone forgets about it. Everyone except me.

I know why I'm here. I have little doubts, of course I do. I reckon everyone does; that's natural. But I can't ignore all the signs, can I?

It's like me life has been all about this: by doing this little bit of justice I'm making up for letting him out of the car in the first place, for all the bad and stupid things I've done before. I'll be bringing a bit of balance back into the world. And how many of us can say they'd done that?

I get out of the car and try to look relaxed. I don't want him getting spooked or nothing. Doubt if he will though, with that big grin on his face. King of the world, Ma.

I won't take the bat out yet. Give him a few digs first, until he goes down.

I'm no murderer. But this isn't murder, is it? It's an execution. It's justice. How could it be anything else? A fella that throws someone out a window, and then he's laughing about it a few days later? He's not a person. He's an animal. A wolf. He'll kill other people if he gets the chance. If they get in his way. Probably doesn't even think he's doing anything wrong. Probably thinks he's allowed to kill anyone who annoys him. How could I feel bad about ending that life? My conscience will be clear. No matter what happens to me.

But a few digs first, yeah.

CHAPTER SEVENTY ONE
Carol Murphy

I slip my arm through his and he gives it a squeeze.

'Ready?' I ask. He nods and I tell him, 'You look handsome. Nice suit.'

He glances down at it.

'Yeah. Been a while since I wore one.'

We walk through the high gates and up towards the church. There's no electricity, so braziers are lined up outside, the flames throwing out grabs of light in the purple dusk, illuminating the faces around us in photographic moments: talking, smiling, hugging. There is a comfortable hum of conversation which swirls around us and we around it. My father squeezes my arm again and points out people he hasn't seen in years. Decrepit aunts he thought were dead, alcoholic cousins, mad cousins, a multi-millionaire, a suspected bigamist. We try to remember their names. Some recognise us and rush over, pumping his hand, kissing me and describing over and again how small I used to be. The commonplace miracle of growing up. And because, to them, I'm still barely more than a child, they feel free to ask what I'm doing with myself and make impressed noises when I tell them I'm a journalist. I don't mention that I'm unemployed. Most ask about the election. They forlornly speculate that the new mob might not be as lazy and corrupt as the old mob and might do something to sort out the economy; and by saying this, I know what they really want to talk about. So I mention Rachel Belton first, allowing them to shake their heads and marvel that this woman could top the poll, despite having withdrawn, despite a clearly mad husband. I explain that her name was still on the ballot papers – there wasn't time to print up new ones – and due to some bureaucratic short-circuit, her votes were counted. They ask me does this mean she can take a seat now? And I say I don't know. I don't think so. They ask: do you think she got votes because of the husband? Because of what he said? I say I don't know. Perhaps. Perhaps it was because of the other things she said. She tried to tell the truth. She tried.

They all keep saying: it's funny, isn't it? It feels as if something has changed; we' just not sure what it is yet.

My father watches me as I talk. I catch him smiling.

'What?' I whisper.

'You know,' he says. And I do. I sound like my mother.

It was easy to get him to come home; all I had to do was ask. Yes, he said, sounding chastened. It's about time.

Last night we drank a bottle of Colli di Luni which he brought back from Liguria, and he wearily told me that he has seen one or two women. Nothing serious. He couldn't be comfortable with them: eventually, he found them irritating. He doubts if he will ever settle down again, but he's not self-pitying about it: he's my dad. It's just the way it is.

Later on, I lay in my room and listened to his settling-in noises as he got ready for sleep on my couch. Groans, creaks, a cartoonish yawn. Night, Princess, he called out.

Night, Daddy.

We make our way to where Hazel is standing. She's wearing a massive, saucer-shaped hat and is flanked by Conor and Kristel. Conor winks, rolls his eyes and goes back to pretending to listen to his mother. Hazel is in full flight, talking to the priest I interviewed. He tentatively nods at me. Hazel extends a hand towards us, but continues explaining her theory about why Bulgarians have a longer life expectancy. We respectfully wait. The priest shuffles in discomfort. Dad nudges me.

'See over yonder.'

He's directing my gaze towards a skinny, white-haired man attempting to calm a wriggling toddler. He's with a pretty though sour-faced Asian woman many years his junior.

'Who's that?' I ask.

'You don't recognise him?'

'It's not Bob, is it?'

As if to confirm this, Conor makes his way over to the couple and extends a stiff hand to his father. I can see Bob is tempted to pull his son into a hug, but decides not to push his luck. Conor shakes hands with his father's wife and finally greets his tiny half-brother. The toddler shrinks back into his father's arms. The four of them pause, unsure of what to do next; or if there is anything to do next.

'Oooh, painful,' says Dad.

'Robert,' he declares and strides over, patting Conor on the back, shaking Bob's hand and of course, kissing his wife. They seem relieved, and grateful.

Dad and I have already discussed when to tell them, and decided that afterwards is probably best. We've booked a table for dinner. Perhaps we can get Bob to come too.

Then again, all I have for them is a theory: one they may not want to hear. But it does fit; it is what Manda would do. *Lucifer's Hammer will bring us together*: what she wrote on her bathroom mirror. I should have done it sooner. Sky News had been on her television the morning she died, and all it took was a call to a friend to find out what she may have watched: a report on a group of Christians in Ohio who believe that in 2035 the earth will be struck by an asteroid named Lucifer's Hammer.

My friend sent me a copy of the report, and there in the middle is an interview with a young, pretty guy who even looks a bit like Jesus, and he's saying that we should end all our petty domestic and international squabbles and come together, given that we have so little time left. He's convinced that once the asteroid comes closer, and we realise it is going to hit, that this will actually happen. He's got a huge smile on his face, and says it may not be so bad if Lucifer's Hammer kills us all: at least for a few weeks or months or even years beforehand, we would live like the people we want to be. And wouldn't that be good? Might that not be worth the risk of extinction? To finally realise ourselves?

I can almost see Manda watching this, wearing that bridesmaid's dress which I'm sure she hated, miserable because she's about to take part in a ceremony which will put an end to her family: Conor and Kristel off to Boston, Hazel to Spain, her father and me already gone. In the hodgepodge theology Manda subscribed to, she may well have seen this as a sign from God: an instruction.

And it would have been the contradiction of her sacrifice that she would have found the most attractive: by extinguishing herself, she became the lynch-pin of her reborn family: by dying, she achieved a new sort of life. The act of smashing through her window and falling to the ground would make her more like the God she prayed to.

Of course, it's just my theory, and I don't know if anyone else in the family will believe it. I've already rung that detective and told him; though I couldn't use the word. Suicide.

Hmm, he said. Possible, I suppose.

But I know it's true.

My father wanders back over, this time with Bob and Conor in tow.

'Bob is going to join us for dinner.'

Bob kisses me and says: the last time I saw you...

The priest is herding us inside now. I take Dad's arm.

'You know what you should do,' he says. 'You should write a book. About... all this.' He waves at the squash of people. 'I mean, Manda had a hell of an effect, didn't she?'

I scowl.

'No really. You could, you know. You're far smarter than you give yourself credit for.'

'We'll see,' I say, suddenly parental.

My father looks up at the scorched remains of the church, the streaks of smoke from the braziers barely discernible in the emerging moonlight.

'Well, this should be interesting,' he says. 'Shall we go in?'

CHAPTER SEVENTY TWO

Michael Bourke

Some of the people swirling around still refer to tonight's gathering as *mass* or a *service*. I smile and tell them that it is neither: it is a non-religious event. It is people coming together to remember Manda, and to puzzle over what is out there, and what is our place in it. To puzzle over what it might mean.

Such waffle. In my eagerness to express what tonight's proceedings are not, I have not told them what they are. But this is because I do not know; I have no name for it. At least the girl's mother, Mrs Ferguson, seems to understand; indeed, she seems to heartily approve, and tells me so at tedious length.

This confusion is, I suspect, a good thing: to come together in spiritual doubt rather than religious certainty. Definitions, after all, can be divisive. Let us see what happens.

The church looks magnificent. I engaged some local lads to position braziers outside, while the men who performed the clear-out lent me some of their portable arc-lights for the interior. They criss-cross the darkened church, creating crepuscular patterns along the walls. As I usher the people inside, I hear many of them gasp.

Some of the locals have turned up: the grim-faced women, of course, but there's no sign of Sharon or any of the others in that group. Off to seek wonders elsewhere. I notice too that one of the detectives from my hospital interview is also in attendance, which I am unsurprised by. It's only a matter of time before he makes his arrest, which is as it should be.

I let everyone go before me and take their seats. They remain quiet; uncertain as to what will happen tonight, and awed by these strange surroundings: the alien shapes on the walls, the gash of unfamiliar sky.

I walk in, barely visible among the glaucous shadows. The echo of my footsteps ping-pongs from the walls. Apart from the whisper of wind, it is all that can be heard. I take my time, letting the silence develop. I'm tempted to say *sacred* silence, but I cannot; not any more. The old words are redundant, their meaning extinguished by centuries of smugness and tyranny. We need new words, though I don't know what they might be. How foolish, how naive to expect that one story could explain it all.

I move through the concentric circles of darkness, and hear the breathing around me, shuffling, the odd cough. Yet no one speaks. I take my first tentative step upon the altar: as if this is a new place; as if I am a stranger, newly arrived. Perhaps I will speak of my quiet, faithful parents: her at home, him in the factory, preparing for the deaths of others. And the day I left, and the present they shyly gave which I didn't want, but now makes me weep and smile; which compels me to ask the question: when there is nothing left to believe in, what should we believe?

I establish myself behind the lectern and look out at the people, huddling together against the approaching cold. *Right*, he would say. *Now give me Alnilam, Hatsya, Zeta Ophiuchi*. I take a deep breath.

'Good evening,' I say, before gesturing upwards.

'Let us look at the stars.'

CHAPTER SEVENTY THREE
Baz Carroll

But the weird thing is that I feel relief this time too. Not the way I did before, mind; when Ma took Holly. Rescued her from me. I feel relieved because at least I've made a decision. Finally. I was hiding here hoping it would sort itself out. Jesus, what bullshit.

And I'm after spending a great day with Holly. Playing with her dollies, out with a ball in the back garden. We made her favourite dinner – she likes chops too – and had ice cream after. I read her a story in bed and we had a little chat about this and that. She told me the names of her dollies and names of everyone in the street. Knows them all, she does, and a fair few of them were around in my day.

She's lucky, living here with my ma. I was lucky too but I fucked it up; that's all it was, pure and simple. Don't see any going back now. But that's life, isn't it?

Still, when I was watching her playing away, chatting to herself, I couldn't help feeling that there's always a bit of hope, you know? Maybe things will be different for her. Of course they will. I know they will.

Me and Ma decided not to make a big deal about me leaving, just in case Holly got upset or wanted to come with me. I was due to go this morning, just slip out while Ma brought her to the swings. But that reporter was outside again, so Ma texted me to stay where I was. She told me to leave me phone on so we can stay in touch. But the cops are going to take the fucking thing off me, aren't they? She says she'll call up instead. They probably won't let her see me, but it might be something to let them know that she's keeping an eye. The Queen of Finglas is watching you. That's something, isn't it?

Ma brings me to the front door, peeks out, then nods that it's OK for me to go. She's a bit teary, I can tell, but she doesn't like to get upset, or to have me telling her what a great job she's doing with Holly. Fuck's sake – what a great job she did with me, taking me back all them times, despite everything I done. I want to tell her I love her. But she knows that.

I want to tell her that I never killed that girl; that I heard a crash and walked into her flat to see what was going on. But there's no point going on about that now. I'll tell the cops and see what happens. I give her a hug and say, 'This is a nice street, Ma. I'd forgotten that.'

'I suppose so,' she says, a bit puzzled.

I could tell her about me force field and that, but she'd think I was fucking mad. So instead I kiss her on the cheek and march off, quickly, before I change me mind or start blubbing. And I feel all right. I do. It's a lovely sunny day – so bright I have to put me hand over me eyes. As I walk into the light in front of me, I can list off in me head most of the people living on Pleasant Lane. I've been in their houses, said how's it going, got shouted at the odd time. Kicked footballs in their gardens. Washed their windows. Did messages to the shops. I was part of the place.

Holly is going to do the same, and that makes me feel like everything is going to be all right, no matter what happens to me now. At least I've done one decent fucking thing. For Holly. For me ma. But it's for me as well, you know? It's like the first time I've felt like a proper son; like a proper father. I feel like I've achieved something, just by walking out the door. Daft.

But like: people do this all the time, don't they? You know, they don't think about themselves so much but about their kids and that. They put them first, even if it means they go without. They sacrifice, yeah. Give up themselves for other people.

That's mad, isn't it? But it's brilliant too.

I feel different; I suppose that's what I mean. I suppose things will always be different now. It's the end of all that. Or the start of something else. I just don't know what yet.

But one decent thing. Yeah.

I'm still walking, can still see fuck all, though up ahead I can just make out some bloke getting out of a car. Oh fuck.

Ah, no. Don't be getting all paranoid now, Baz.

Just keep walking. Keep walking.

CHAPTER SEVENTY FOUR

Manda Ferguson

I hate this dress. Why would Conor ever think I like this dress? Why would he think I'd want to parade around in this symbol of patriarchal ownership? There they are, the nice virginal girls.

I put it on because I want to destroy it. I'd like to cut the hem, splatter on some paint, stick on some anarchist badges. I could turn up wearing my big boots. I can see his red and cranky face now. What the fuck, Manda? Do you know how much that dress cost?

Oh, I can't do it.

It would be mean. They'd be upset. I've tried to train myself to be single-minded, to drop all the petty emotions and focus on the higher truths. Sacrifice the ego and gain everything else. But I keep failing. I'm failing here. I stood on the landing all day yesterday – the front door is open now – but I didn't stop one person going in there. I've told them they are being used, that they are just another function of capitalism. The system needs you to be addicted, so you can be blamed, so the top few per cent can keep even more for themselves. But they just smile, bleary eyed. Yes love. Maybe you need a hit yourself.

The men in the flat glare at me. They want to do me damage.

I'm not afraid.

I switch on the television. Sky News. The group in Amsterdam would be disgusted with me now. Watching a Murdoch channel, sitting in my bourgeoisie dress. They were single-minded. They could sacrifice.

I feel alone.

Will Carol be at the wedding? I hadn't the courage to ask Conor. He would have gone silent anyway; pretended he didn't know what I meant.

I remember. I remember everything. But I'm probably the only one.

Was Jesus disciplined? Or was he a flawed man? He sacrificed himself, but he was scared: he asked for mercy. Would the group in Amsterdam disapprove of him too? There is no *you*; there is only the collective.

A man is knocking on the door of the flat opposite. *Hello*, I chime. He ignores me.

I get up to make peppermint tea, but then sit down. I can't settle, can't think. Already tried meditating, tried praying. No good.

Is it just the dress?

No, it's not just the dress.

Conor knows I'll never visit him in America. He knows I couldn't abide being in the seat of all that oppression, all that arrogance. Will he ever come back here? Why would he? He'll be gone. Mammy will be off to Spain. Carol is long gone. I'm here watching it all wither away. I'm helping. I'm going to the bridal sacrifice. I'm wearing the silly dress.

How can he leave? How can he pretend we're not connected, we are not *all* connected? My cells change and mutate each second. My thoughts and words pass in and out of me and into others. So where does *Me* end and *You* begin? There is no *Me*; not really. That's what the collective taught. That's what Jesus taught.

I watch the television.

The man's eyes are ablaze as he speaks; that's what strikes me first. But then I realise he is saying *exactly* what I have been thinking. *Exactly*. These people know what I know. Natural that they would. If we are connected, how could they not?

I go to the loo, and then examine myself in the mirror. I like my hair. I allow myself that vanity. You've never been brave enough, Manda. Not really. Never stuck with your beliefs until the end. Something always held you back.

Sacrifice. Can you learn to sacrifice?

Lipstick.

Oh, I disgust myself. I bought lipstick for the wedding. Silly vacuous girl, painting herself up for the boys. I take the lipstick and write on the mirror.

Lucifer's Hammer will bring us together?

No.

Still not brave enough, Manda. I rub out the question mark.

You know what you can do. Solve all the problems at once. And if you truly believe, well. Now's the time.

I look in the mirror again.

I giggle.

Padding back into the living room, I already feel out of myself; as if I'm floating above, wondering: will she? Will she really?

I look at the window. Should I open it or… No. Don't think. This is beyond thinking. Leap. Have faith.

I run.

As soon as I hit the window it gives way, frame and everything. I emerge into the twinkling sunlight like an Olympic diver: arms extended, body broom-straight. Once clear of the building, I feel myself rotate until I'm facing the sky, the trails of the shining dress curling around me. With legs and arms lightly waving, I descend into the skip, the pink satin spreading beneath. The toes of my left foot graze an election poster, which flutters after me like a faithful pet.

Am I frightened? I'm not sure. In these few seconds, I can pack in an ocean of thought. The friction of the air against my bare legs and feet is causing skin flakes to detach from my body and scatter across the street below like pollen. These morsels of me will fall upon the pavement, or onto cars or be inhaled by strangers. I'm worried that the impact will hurt, but I know it will be momentary. From there I will be released to the earth and the cyclical engine of creation: part of the mud, the flowers, the worms, the hedgehogs, the rain, the people.

What will happen to my thoughts? Will they dissolve? Will they float in the sky, like echoes? Can they exist without a Manda to think them?

I used to bore Conor and Carol with Bishop Berkeley's poser: if a tree falls in a forest and no one is around to hear it, does it make a sound?

Yes, of course it does. But if there is no one around to hear, why bother falling?

People will hear. I will soon be entering the thoughts of my family and old friends and almost everyone I have ever known: the same idea in dozens of minds. Suddenly all connected.

The impact is not as I imagined. I don't feel pain, but a galactic jolt to the senses: sight, hearing and touch all helplessly scrambled. There's a mash of noise, trembling, a light blue haze.

Then a presence. Breath on my face. Dark clothes.

There is mumbling, but I can only identify only one word.

God.

And I smile.